LOCKDOWN

By

Scott Black

Copyright © 2016 Scott Black
All rights reserved.
Print ISBN: 978-0-9963569-0-9
eBook ISBN: 978-0-9963569-1-6

For

Willard C. Wood, USN Retired,

who inspired me to join the Navy.

GLOSSARY OF NAVY TERMS

ADRIFT – Loose from moorings with no power and out of control.
AFT – Towards the stern (tail) of a ship.
ALL HANDS – The entire ship's company, both Officer and Enlisted.
ASROC – An Anti-Submarine Rocket.
ATHWARTSHIPS – being across the ship from side to side.
AYE, AYE – Response acknowledging the understanding of a command.
BELOW (BELOWDECKS) – Downstairs, the next deck below.
BLUEJACKET – an enlisted sailor in the Navy.
BOONDOCKERS – Heavy work shoe issued in boot camp.
BOW – The forward part of a ship or boat.
BROW – A railed platform between the ship and pier, used to walk on and off.
BUG JUICE – sugary drink such as Kool-Aid.
BULKHEAD – The wall.
BULLNOSE – An opening at the very tip of the bow.
BUNK – A bed. Also known as a RACK.
BUOY – An anchored float; for navigation or to mark a location of an object.
CARRY ON – An order to resume work or duties.
CAST OFF – To throw off, to let go, to unfurl.
CAPTAIN'S MAST – Disciplinary council from the ship's Captain.
CHAIN LOCKER – Compartment in which anchor chain is stowed.
CHOW HALL – (MESS DECK) A place to eat.
COMBAT INFORMATION CENTER (CIC) – The nerve center of the ship.
COLORS – Raising and lowering of the American flag.
CUP OF JOE – A cup of coffee.
DECK – The floor.
DEVILS CLAW – a two-pronged claw that fits over an anchor chain link.
DOG DOWN – "dog down a hatch"... close a watertight a door or hatch.
DOGS – One big lever or separate clasps around a door or hatch perimeter.
DUNGAREES – Blue, bell-bottomed, close weave, light denim pants.
ENLISTED – The general work force of the Navy and Navy Reserve –
generally requires a high school diploma (or GED) as a minimum educational
requirement, completion of Recruit Training and training in an occupational
specialty area.
FATHOM – A unit of length (6 feet) used for measuring the depth of water.
FORECASTLE – The upper deck forward of the bridge.
GALLEY – The kitchen.
GANGWAY – An opening in the bulwark or lifeline.
GEAR LOCKER – A storage room.
GEEDUNK – Candy, gum or cafeteria, sometimes called pogey bait.
GENERAL QUARTERS – Battle Stations.
GITMO – Guantanamo bay, Cuba. Ship performance certification trials.
HATCH – A door or access closure.
HEAD – The restroom.

JACK BOX – Access box to sound-powered phone circuitry.
KHAKIS – Standard tan (khaki color) uniform worn by Chiefs and Officers.
LADDER – A device to move from one level to another. Stairs.
LEAVE – Authorized absence, like vacation.
LIBERTY – Permission to leave the base, usually for not more than 48 hours.
LIFELINE – Wire ropes that keep personnel from falling overboard.
MESS DECK – The crew dining area.
MESS DUTY – A 90-day obligated kitchen duty. (aka MESS-CRANK'N)
MID-RATS – midnight shift food rations. Usually sandwiches.
MID-WATCH – The midnight duty; the most dreaded watch for losing sleep.
NAVY RESERVE – Reserve component of the U.S. Navy in which part-time
Sailors and Officers are called into Active Duty, or mobilized, as needed.
OFFICER – The leadership and management team of the Navy and Navy
Reserve – generally requires a degree from a four-year college or university
and completion of an Officer Training program.
OVERHEAD – The ceiling.
PASSAGEWAY – A hallway.
PORT – A place on a waterway with facilities for loading and unloading ships.
PORT SIDE – The left side of a nautical vessel.
QUARTERDECK – aft end of main deck where the BROW spans to shore.
QUARTERS – Assemble all hands for muster... refers to home or residence.
QUARTERMASTER – Petty Officer responsible for steering and navigation
RACK – A bed. . Also known as a BUNK.
RANK – System of hierarchical relationships.
RATING – A job specialty title.
REVEILLE – A signal signifying the start of a workday.
SCULLERY – A place to wash dishes.
SCUTTLEBUTT – A water fountain, rumors, and rumor control.
SECURE – To stop or quit work. To lash down an object.
SICK BAY – Medical facility located in a hospital, aid station or on board ship.
SNIPE – Nickname for anyone in the Engineering department.
SOUNDING AND SECURITY – roving patrol for detecting floods and fires
STARBOARD – The right side of a nautical vessel.
STERN – The aft part (rear) of a ship or boat.
SWEEPERS – Cleaning ritual that involves sweeping assigned areas.
SWAB – A mop.
TAPS – Lights out, time for sleep.
TOPSIDE – the upper decks, above the waterline, aka the WEATHERDECKS.
TURN TO – Begin work.
TWIDGET – Nickname for anyone in the Operations or Weapons
departments.
WEEKEND WARRIOR – term used to describe naval reservist.
WHEELHOUSE – bridge or location of ships helm.

FAST-FRIGATE PERSONNEL

THE OFFICER RANKS

Ensign (ENS, O1)

Lieutenant, Junior Grade (LTJG, O2)

Lieutenant (LT, O3)

Lieutenant Commander (LCDR, O4)

Commander (CDR, O5)

*****

THE ENLISTED RANKS

Fireman Apprentice – FA, Seaman Apprentice – SA, (E-2)

Fireman – FN, Seaman – SN, (E-3)

Petty Officer Third Class (E-4)

Petty Officer Second Class (E-5)

Petty Officer First Class (E-6)

Chief Petty Officer (E-7)

Senior Chief Petty Officer (E-8)

Master Chief Petty Officer (E-9)

OFFICER ORGANIZATION CHART

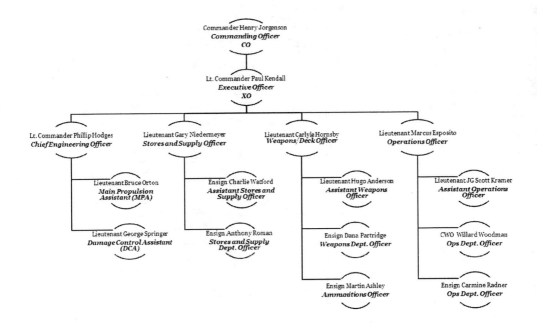

Commander Henry Jorgenson
Commanding Officer
CO

Lt. Commander Paul Kendall
Executive Officer
XO

Lt. Commander Phillip Hodges
Chief Engineering Officer

Lieutenant Gary Niedermeyer
Stores and Supply Officer

Lieutenant Carlyle Hornsby
Weapons/Deck Officer

Lieutenant Marcus Esposito
Operations Officer

Lieutenant Bruce Orton
Main Propulsion Assistant (MPA)

Ensign Charlie Watford
Assistant Stores and Supply Officer

Lieutenant Hugo Anderson
Assistant Weapons Officer

Lieutenant JG Scott Kramer
Assistant Operations Officer

Lieutenant George Springer
Damage Control Assistant (DCA)

Ensign Anthony Roman
Stores and Supply Dept. Officer

Ensign Dana Partridge
Weapons Dept. Officer

CWO Willard Woodman
Ops Dept. Officer

Ensign Martin Ashley
Ammunitions Officer

Ensign Carmine Radner
Ops Dept. Officer

R-DIVISION ORGANIZATION CHART

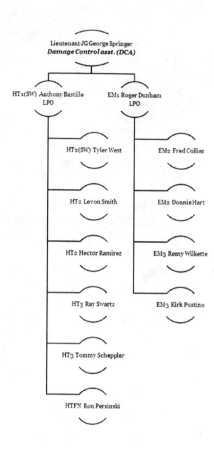

Lieutenant JG George Springer
Damage Control asst. (DCA)

HT1(SW) Anthony Bastille
LPO

EM1 Roger Dunham
LPO

HT2(SW) Tyler West

EM2 Fred Collier

HT2 Levon Smith

EM2 Donnie Hart

HT2 Hector Ramirez

EM3 Remy Wilkette

HT3 Ray Swartz

EM3 Kirk Postino

HT3 Tommy Scheppler

HTFN Ron Persinski

UCMJ

UNIFORM CODE OF MILITARY JUSTICE
SUBCHAPTER II. APPREHENSION AND RESTRAINT
809. ART. 9. IMPOSITION OF RESTRAINT

(a) Arrest is the restraint of a person by an order, not imposed as a punishment for an offense, directing him to remain within certain specified limits. Confinement is the physical restraint of a person.

(b) An enlisted member may be ordered into arrest or confinement by any commissioned officer by an order, oral or written, delivered in person or through other persons subject to this chapter. A commanding officer may authorize warrant officers, petty officers, or noncommissioned officers to order enlisted members of his command or subject to his authority into arrest or confinement.

(c) A commissioned officer, a warrant officer, or a civilian subject to this chapter or to trial thereunder may be ordered into arrest or confinement only by a commanding officer to whose authority he is subject, by an order, oral or written, delivered in person or by another commissioned officer. The authority to order such persons into arrest or confinement may not be delegated.

(d) No person may be ordered into arrest or confinement except for probable cause.

(e) Nothing in this article limits the authority of persons authorized to apprehend offenders to secure the custody of an alleged offender until proper authority may be notified.

PROLOGUE

Tyler West knew finding the blood soaked coveralls would change everything for him and the crew. He gripped the braided wire lifelines as the ship climbed a massive bluish-green hill of water. He held on for life; there would be little chance of survival if he toppled into the treacherous ocean. His stomach quailed against the downward force once the ship cleared the crest of one swell and crashed bow-first into another oncoming surge. His ride, a U.S. Navy fast frigate, cut an endless turquoise trench through the vast Caribbean Sea. Just beyond the edges of a hurricane, the speeding vessel bobbed and weaved to free itself of the storm's fading grip.

Despite his perilous circumstance, Tyler remained calm and steady; after all, it was his decision to come all the way out to the bullnose. Tyler stood on the bow, at the forward point of the ship; a place most of his shipmates would not dare visit in rough seas. No doubt, superiors on the bridge were observing his careless antics with trepidation, but he did not care. To claim a few minutes of mind clearing privacy, Tyler ignored the danger.

Around him, and within him, everything felt crazy, like there was a staggering maelstrom targeting Tyler specifically.

Finally some air, he thought.

His blue eyes, twins to his faded dungaree uniform, glistened from sun and brine and wind and, mostly, distress. Nevertheless, he fought to keep his emotions in check. Before him, the ocean erupted into a mosaic. The chaos and beauty hit him all at once; a kaleidoscope of colors and sounds. Violent whitecaps burst into backlit rainbows that danced in spasmodic beams of sunlight. The coiling and colliding swells produced a relentless energy that attempted to topple a four-hundred-thirty foot warship.

The bow crested again and Tyler could see the horizon against the fierce blue sky in the distance. There was a small chance they could avoid the worst of the storm, and the hope of reaching calmer waters provided a brief distraction from the foul and stressful thoughts that had been plaguing him.

The USS Miller was his ship; at least he thought of her as such; had thought of her that way. He once held an untouched and unchallenged sense of ego in claiming her; in recent days that pride had whittled itself away. Tyler's devotion to his first duty station was a mere shadow play of memories now, and his ability to distinguish the good ones from the bad had all but disappeared.

Cumulus clouds moved with swift abandonment as the puffs outpaced the vessel. In them, he sensed a turbulent urgency. Even the sky raced to get as far away from the ship as possible. *Why not?* Why anything in nature would want to be near him or the ship went beyond his knowledge. The fitful ocean world raged against the vehicle of foul cargo, chaos, and disorder, on which he stood.

Another wave hit and Tyler held strong. The ship was a bull and he rode her hard. *Maybe that's why we call it a bullnose?* Yes. This bullnose was sanctuary. No one would dare risk coming out to ride the bull in this weather to interrupt his introspection. He took in a deep contemplative breath, enjoying the music of the wind and the water, but the distraction was not enough. A nagging question just kept knocking at his brain. *If we find bloody coveralls, what other clues will they need?* Tyler had been thinking hard on this for several hours during the fruitless search. The Chief had said, "Other clues", along with the green bloody coveralls.

"Bloody coveralls!" he shouted at the ocean.

Bloody fucking coveralls. He silently mouthed each syllable with a jerk of the steel braided guywires.

Tyler reared a glance over his shoulder in time with a rising wave. He knew Smitty wasn't far off. The other sailor, Levon Smithe, was not as suicidal as Tyler, but his friend was also still topside and near the most dangerous part of the main-deck during a storm. He stood fifty feet aft gripping the starboard lifeline with one hand and cupping a Marlboro to his lips with the other. Tyler smirked; Smithe made the act of standing on deck in rough-weather look easy; his two seaworthy legs acted like shock absorbers against the violent movements of the deck.

Smithe took advantage of the eye contact and wagged a thumb for Tyler to join him closer to the safety of the area aft of the big gun and rocket launcher. That was Smithe, always worried about Tyler.

The best friends had met in training school where they'd received instruction for Hull Maintenance Technician duties. The advanced technical school for ship-fitting, plumbing, welding, and damage control was on Treasure Island in San Francisco; the place where Hull Techs are born. That was years ago, and now they were both 2nd Class Petty Officers; the HT2's were sent on a mission earlier and now, hours later, they were both exhausted and stressed.

Tyler did not want to move from his place of solitude. His friend was a reminder of the conversation from earlier in the day.

"Smithe, West," Chief Petty Officer Langston had said, "If you find 'em it'll give us clues to whoever did this." The Chief had displayed extreme confidence in Tyler's ability to solve the mystery. Langston had looked him in the eye, "go find those coveralls West," his grip tightening on Tyler's shoulder, "maybe you'll find other clues while you're at it."

Did the Chief truly expect an easy recovery of bloody coveralls, a most incriminating item, so that the higher ups would have the answer to *who done it*? Seemed too simple a thing to expect, but checking for implicating evidence, like clothing, was at least a reasonable first step. The U.S. Navy required all clothing be marked with a sailor's name, rank, and social security number. Tyler recalled his days back in boot camp; that regulation had seemed to be stupid. He remembered the ridiculousness of scribbling letters on a pair of boxers.

"Now it ain't so stupid!" He shouted aloud. His partner, too far away, had no chance at understanding the little rant over the noise of crashing water and whipping wind.

"Ty! Let's go...!" or something to that effect came the words from HT2 Smithe.

A vertical wall of water bent with the wind and hit the horizontal point of the main deck. Even knowing that Smithe was worried about a friend—who was stubbornly clinging to the bullnose for dear life—Tyler resented the attempted coddling. Still, he decided to move, they did not need another casualty this day. At last, Tyler pirouetted to face the rear of the ship. He prepared his mind for the return to safety. He breathed in and tried to visualize his next few actions, still clinging as the ship propelled on.

An obstacle course lay in front of him. Navigating his way to safer ground required precise accuracy, perfect timing, and of course, caution. Trying to predict the ship's motions would be fruitless with the erratic rolling. The grey deck glistened with seawater. *What would be less brutal*, he wondered; getting tossed in the ocean without a life jacket, slipping and cracking his skull, or just being on this ship today?

The morbid thoughts left him as an opportune ride of the ship's forward end provided just the proper angle to make a move. He acted. As fast as possible, without losing his footing on the wet deck, he launched himself. The anchor windless. A devils claw. Two fathoms of anchor chain lashed to the deck. Tyler traversed each impediment with easy sidestepping and cat-like reflexes; he reached the five-inch fifty-four caliber turret and grabbed a stair rail before the rising forecastle crested. The ship reached a pinnacle then crashed downwards with sadistic fervor, as if in protest to his triumph. His grip kept him secure against the ocean's rage.

"Fuck yeah!" He willed the frenzied ocean to take note of his superhuman accomplishment. His body trembled with adrenaline. Endorphins gushed. His blood rushed. He shivered, holding on to the front of the big gun. *I beat you!*

The ship rolled again violently; the sea mocked his brief triumph. Poseidon did not appear to agree that Tyler was Superman. *You have not won*, the sea spat back in defiant smugness.

Tyler lurched a few more steps and parked himself on the starboard side of the ASROC launcher near Smithe.

"They're gonna bitch you out for going to the bullnose," Smithe said, pointing up at the bridge windows above their heads.

"Screw them," Tyler said looking up, "I'm the one searching for bloody fucking coveralls." *If they want to write me up for getting some fresh air, I'll take the extra duty.*

Smithe shrugged.

"Smitty, what are we doing?"

With one thumb hooked into the pocket of his trousers, Smithe stood there as if the ship was welded to a pier—the rolling and rising not affecting his balance as he sucked on another Marlboro. He slowly drew in a deep breath of cigarette smoke, let it smolder in his lungs, after an elongated pause, leaked silvery vapors from his nostrils, and pursed lips. The willowy smoke-streams paused for a split-second before whisking away in the wind. He cupped a curved palm to his lips, making sure Tyler heard him.

"The khaki's don't know who did it, dude—that's why we're looking. They have no clue."

"So we're really searching for clues!"

"Yes!"

"Green coveralls!"

"Yes!"

Out-loud shouting of the obvious solved nothing but he could not help it, and he observed Smitty's uncertainty in their plan as well. They had been told to 'find bloody coveralls and other possible clues'.

If they know the guy wore green coveralls, then who it is should be relatively easy to identify—his name will be on them. Tyler argued this point with himself. In addition, green coveralls are too... *exclusive*. Only so many of the snipes have been issued a pair. And what other clues do they think will be found?

"What are they not telling us?" He eyed his friend. Smithe wagged his ball cap covered head.

"You're doing it again." Smithe said.

"Doin' what?"

"You're thinking too much."

"'am not."

"What makes you think they know something more than they're telling us?"

Tyler had no answers—and—he had all the answers. *Dammit!* So much about this day made no sense.

Their mutual exhaustion swelled; Smithe's hound dog features were unmistakable in the spotty sunlight as his droopy eyelids dangled at half-mast. He always has some amount of beard stubble, which grew at an alarming rate, but the fullness of his shadow had gone way beyond five-o'clock. His was a face Tyler had learned to trust over the years, and Smithe looked helpless.

Tyler was beyond frustrated and Smitty knew it.

"Why the hell would they put us out here?" Smithe asked, dodging a blanket of water crashing at his feet. The tributary washed away, Smithe attempted to close the door on their tête-à-tête with, "Get your head out of your ass, numb nuts."

Tyler contemplated the logic of sending men around the ship in search of evidence with no real leads. He glanced up to where the captain and others would be waiting for the results of their search; he could not see the bridge windows, but he knew they would be up there; the grey vertical wall behind Smithe rose straight up at least thirty feet. The men raised high above their heads, would be relying on those below to decide what their next move would be. Tyler had not missed the irony of their situation.

Smithe found another dry spot against the superstructure and dragged in more nicotine. *Whatever this is,* Tyler concluded Smitty was right, *there's way too much risk to be out roaming the ship in this weather looking for... well, who knows exactly?* The ship's leaders would not risk involving a search party, if they didn't have a good reason. Tyler and Smitty must find the coveralls and... whatever else... and that's that.

Just then, the starboard watertight hatch swung wide and out popped the head of DK1 Bryan Hendriks, summoning the two men.

"You finished with your cancer sticks?" the lanky first-class said before ducking back into the passage to avoid the crashing wave. Hendriks reappeared on the next roll to say, "We need to start down the port side."

What a tool, thought Tyler.

Smithe gave Hendriks an unpleasant frown and lowered his lips for a last drag. He flicked the almost finished cigarette in the disbursement clerk's direction. The wind instead caught the butt and carried the trash into the vast sea. They had been searching for six hours and their armed escort was beginning to get on both their nerves.

"At least the jackass hasn't puked," Smithe said and a smile crept across Tyler's face; the first in the many hours since the incident.

He snorted and sighed.

"Yeah Smitty. Now let's go find them bloody fucking coveralls."

SCOTT BLACK

TWO DAYS EARLIER

CHAPTER 1

A light breeze of scented tropical air swept across the bridge. The aroma was comforting; the ship had been to this port many times. Now, at fourteen hundred, the ship maneuvered slowly through the reef-lined waterway as the afternoon sun danced off the Caribbean's turquoise waters. It was Sea and Anchor Detail; their trip out of port would be a short tugboat assisted journey through the Annex channel followed by three hours of slow steaming out of the remaining shallows to the open sea.

The USS Miller glided through the tranquility of the Bermuda Annex seaway. The boatswain's whistle had signaled the message— *underway shift colors*—thirty minutes earlier, and a comfortable ease settled over the ship. On the bridge, the captain eyed several smiling and content faces. The three-day liberty in Hamilton and Saint George, highlighted by a ship's barbeque and an officer versus enlisted softball game at the Annex Naval Base, had been wildly enjoyable. The competitive team made up of enlisted men called on their base championship skills to crush the officers' team fourteen to two, which resulted in the officers having to dunk themselves in the Annex inlet while still wearing full uniforms. The frivolous games, food, and drinks completed a perfect respite for the tired men. The only regret for the ship's captain was not joining the officer's team for that swim in the inlet.

Commander Henry Jorgenson sat in the captain's seat reading the reserve crew manifest and jotting down notes in a green logbook. His wire-framed reading glasses perched on the tip of a pointed nose he'd inherited from his mother. The bad eyes? A gift from his father. His face was almond-brown and carried an almost rosy glow from *too much* sun. The sunburn did not hurt, but he felt stiffness around his eyes. He reached up, pressed a finger to his cheek, and felt the tight skin.

As a child, his family would tease him about the lightness of his brown skin. It would always darken in the summer months after he had spent days running around bareback on the outskirts of Louisville. Both his mother and father had much darker skin, and his roots could be traced pretty accurately to a couple of freed slaves, whom his mother often said were, "definitely of the black persuasion." Jorgenson chuckled at the memory of his mother's theory that "apparently some white woman got her blood mixed" in with the Jorgenson family tree. She complained to anyone who would listen to her explanation as to "why Hank looked so pale."

In Bermuda, Jorgenson had worn his ball cap while out in the sunshine and now he had a prominent horizontal tan-line that ran across his forehead from temple to temple and disappeared into his black, curly sideburns. Maybe he should have taken it off a few times. The ball cap, with its captain's yellow scrambled eggs on the bill, sat atop his head now. On the face of the standard shipboard cap was an insignia patch: the words USS Miller rested above an embroidered gray ship, and below the ship depiction was the Miller's identifier FF-1091; the FF for fast frigate.

Jorgenson cherished being back at sea, but this unusual deployment style would take some getting used to. The mission schedule was different from the typical six-month long Mediterranean cruises he had experienced on his previous tours of duty. Jorgenson regarded the new system with cautious optimism. The ship's mission, part of a new Naval Reserve Force Anti-Submarine Warfare Frigate Plan, was to patrol international waters off the eastern seaboard from Cuba to Nova Scotia; however, this ship would carry out its mission with only a skeleton crew of sailors assigned to her full time.

On the Miller assignment, Jorgenson found himself hopscotching the ship from Newport to Bermuda, from Puerto Rico to Mayport, picking up and dropping off weekend warriors for their required two-week training tour. This cruise, like all future deployments, would last no more than those few weeks. Reservists would fill the supplemental crew required to run the ship. This constant changing over of crew left the ship's new captain overseeing a vessel in which half the crew were unfamiliar and often inexperienced sailors.

At the helm, BM2 Perez, one of the Miller's full-time enlisted bluejackets, guided the vessel with precision as the Officer of the Deck, Lieutenant Hugo Anderson, gave steering orders to him. Two tugboats were towing them, and Anderson's job was to keep the ship steered down the center of the channel and midway between the assisting vessels.

"Perez, come to port two degrees," said Anderson.

"Aye, port two degrees," Perez answered.

With both hands engaged while turning the wheel, Perez focused his eyes on the gyrocompass dial and brought the ship to port.

Jorgenson completed his notes and stowed the logbook. Along the shoreline on both sides of the channel, several pastel colored houses glided past, and the captain stood and stretched.

"Mr. Anderson, I'll be on the fly bridge."

"Aye, sir."

Jorgenson stepped into the sunshine and let the warmth wash over his face. Two boatswain's mates operating towlines on the forecastle spotted the captain on the fly bridge and sent up a few salutes. He gladly returned a wave. Jorgenson had not made much progress in familiarizing himself with the regular crew during his first two months aboard. The ship's barbeque and softball game had been many of the crew's first opportunity to meet or even see the ship's new captain. With preparations for GITMO ongoing, two rotations of reservists coming and going, he had been too busy and primarily felt it was necessary to spend as much quality time with his young officer corps as possible. They were, many of them, green officers on their first command.

Jorgenson believed the last few days in Bermuda Annex and the barbecue had been excellent quality time spent with the enlisted crew. He wanted them to believe he was not avoiding them; Jorgenson was the new commanding officer of the USS Miller and with that title came a heavy responsibility to all his crew. The pressure to keep the pride of Newport working and operating at top standards was already weighing on him.

Nothing can go wrong, Jorgenson often thought, *not ever*. He repeated this mantra like a private battle cry that he shared with no one but the ghost of naval hero Dorie Miller. Jorgenson liked to think Miller would be proud of him. He imagined his fellow African American and naval brother in arms silently cheering him on from beyond the grave. As the first black captain in the history of the USS Miller, Jorgenson knew that he needed to be flawless.

Bermuda Annex harbor entry, as in many ports, operated using support tugboats for mooring vessels pier side. With that process, a civilian pilot had come aboard to direct the Sea and Anchor maneuvering. An old leathery faced man, the pilot, stood next to Lieutenant Anderson, staring through a set of weatherworn binoculars at the two tugboats hauling the Miller along the narrow channel-way. The tugs would work for another thirty minutes before reaching the edge of the channel where the Miller's power would take-over. For now, the ship's engines were keeping the screw slowly turning in the forward direction—allowing the tugs to do most of the work. The rules of piloting ships into and out of waterways were standard operating procedures. As an experienced captain, Jorgenson possessed a keen awareness of potential piloting problems. Off in the distance something caught his eye.

From inside the bridge, a prickly sounding walkie-talkie blurted to life. Radio chatter coming from inside the wheelhouse sounded wrong; Jorgenson stiffened.

When an order is given in any seafaring situation, the protocol is to repeat the command with an, 'aye', as confirmation that the recipient of the command had understood and will carry out the order, just as BM2 Perez had repeated Lieutenant Anderson's command to go port two degrees several minutes ago.

An unsettled anxiety snuck up on Jorgenson; he clearly understood the leather-faced tugboat pilot's order to, "Bring up slack," to the forward port tug, but there was no return 'aye' or 'aye-aye.' Two tugboats worked the detail. Both faced forward; one tug positioned at port and the other at starboard. No confirmation of the order came from the port tug. The ship drifted slightly towards port at a steady pace, and, the forward port tugboat started to curve to the channel edge, as if making a left turn.

Nothing can go wrong, not ever. Jorgenson thought with a frown as he scanned the channel again. The Miller was on a collision course with a stationary freighter that was ahead. The tugboat still had not responded. A single tug might not have the stopping power needed to arrest the ships momentum. The freighter ahead drifted, idle, dead center in the Millers path.

Jorgenson turned to the doorway and decided that if the pilot's eyes told any story other than *this situation is entirely under control*, he was going to take over. Thirty seconds went by and a repeat of the command from the pilot to the port tug did not come back after a second try. The tugboat pilot started to speak into the radio but hesitated and snuck a distressed glance at Jorgenson. The newest captain of the USS Miller knew, as did everyone else on the bridge, that the ship was moving too fast towards the cargo vessel. Evasive maneuvers were necessary. The Miller OOD, Lieutenant Anderson, hopelessly wagged his head side to side as if there was a tennis match going between the pilot and the idle freighter.

"Pilot," Jorgenson spoke up, "have your tugs prepare for full reverse. Mister Anderson, full reverse."

"Aye, full reverse," came simultaneous replies from Anderson and Leather-Face.

The tugboat pilot radioed his instructions to the two tug captains.

Jorgenson did not hesitate, "Helmsman, maintain this heading."

"Aye sir, two four seven, steady."

Anderson took two steps towards the helm and clamped a fist around the ships engine order telegraph, and pulled it back and down to its lowest position to the full reverse marker. At the same time he lifted a golden tube cover and barked, "Full reverse," into a brass pipe. A ringing clatter chimed, signifying the Engine Room understood the order. Leather-Face received confirmation that the working tugboat was aware of the necessity to reverse. Jorgenson could see the port vessel's lines going slack; it was clear that she had lost power as the towline drooped into the water and the boat only drifted.

The ship vibrated as the engine screw backed down its momentum. Although the abrupt change of direction was subtle, Jorgenson said aloud, "Hold on." When the forward motion finally halted, Jorgenson had expected more of a jerk; that did not happen; instead, the ship calmly idled to a slow drift. She then reared back as the reversing propeller cavitated, creating a heaving vortex, Jorgenson said, "Mister Anderson, full stop."

"Aye, full stop."

Anderson repeated the order into the sounding tube while lifting the telegraph to the vertical position to stop the bell. The return bell from Main Control in the Engine Room rang out again. The ship stopped all forward motion. The stationary cargo freighter floated, off course and adrift, only one hundred yards away. Without Jorgenson's quick action, the Miller would have rammed the freighter.

"That could have been bad," came a voice from the rear of the bridge. The quartermaster stood with his hands on his hips and appeared almost entertained by the ordeal.

Jorgenson managed a wry smirk and then broke the silence, "Could have been." His eyes darted towards Anderson, who had not helped the situation—after the first or second fail response from the port tug, he should have taken evasive action. Hesitation by the Officer of the Deck was unacceptable. The entire room seemed to be waiting for their new captain to reprimand Anderson.

Hating to disappoint, Jorgenson said, "Mister Anderson, a word, please." He stepped through the starboard fly bridge door first and Anderson followed his captain like a pup who knew he's about to get beat by a newspaper.

CHAPTER 2

Tyler West, a Hull Maintenance Technician, second class Petty Officer and certified Enlisted Surface Warfare Specialist, made his way aft from R-Division berthing to the Helo-Hangar for a quick early morning workout before chow and muster. He enjoyed the familiar walk along the starboard second deck passage while the ship slept. He took the starboard side journey, as always, which allowed him to pass the main space entryways and Repair Five—the engineering spaces damage control locker, located at mid-ships. With the exception of people at various duty stations in the engineering holes, bridge, roving Sounding and Security patrol, and several other operations and tactical locations topside above the second deck, the remaining crew would be either snoozing in their racks or just rising. He estimated there'd be another ninety minutes of quiet before morning reveille; plenty of time to pump some iron, hurry to the shower before the stalls get too crowded, and still be early for the chow line.

Down on the second deck, no one roamed about; not this early. He appreciated being alone. Over three and a half years prior, as a new third class Petty Officer, he had achieved ESWS: Enlisted Surface Warfare Specialist. The distinction was not lost on his shipmates. Most first and second class Petty Officers without certification had been pretty dammed pissed off.

The Miller senior enlisted organization had seen the new sailor's abnormal potential and purposely pushed Tyler to get trained in the first place; to humiliate the others. He had not known at the time that having a new third class go through training and actually successfully earn certification would become quite a motivating event for the ship's slackers. As a dubious honor for his effort Tyler was unceremoniously scheduled to the engineering hole watch rotations. This meant Machinist Mate and Boiler Technician departments had an extra hand to stand watch stations. *What a bitch.* An HT's job takes him to all parts of the ship; anywhere something needs repair; so, helping with the machinery and boiler responsibilities meant Tyler gained more knowledge. He ended up learning more than any other enlisted guy. His ESWS training also gave him an opportunity to work with all tactical, navigations, and operations personnel; this included full access to all the officer corps as well. He knew every procedure, every system, every space, and everything about the whole ship. His coworkers in R-Division would say he knew more about a damn fast-frigate than any other crewmember.

However, that was all behind him. He was scheduled to leave this duty station soon and in the recent months, he had convinced the Chief to keep him off the hole stations; there was usually always enough trained reservists to fill the gaps anyway. He would only be used if they were short personnel. These days he found himself doing shortened four hour Sounding and Security patrols, and spending his remaining days doing as little as possible. Tyler counted the days until he would leave the Miller. He accepted the title of short-timer; he rotated in less than a month, and although shore duty might be in his future, he accepted the odds of a last minute change to another ship being possible. Either way, getting off this ship meant liberation. He'd had enough. Enough of the work, which at times was easy, but mostly he wanted to get away from the people. He had seen many of his friends leave—either get discharged or stationed elsewhere. Most of the current crew were fresh; even the captain was a new guy.

Past the point of caring, Tyler only wanted to get this cruise over with and move on. He would go on leave for two weeks and relax—take a road trip, or go back to New York City. For sure he would be with his girlfriend, whom he had immaculate plans for, plans that, if he could get over his own nervous thoughts, would involve a ring. *Better late than never,* she would say. In the coming weeks, life would be wonderful; the Miller would be behind him.

As he passed through the mess decks, the smells of early morning preparations wafted from the galley behind the chow line partition. He was almost to the aft bulkhead when footsteps rattled the ladder leading down from the ships stores, breaking the privacy of his thoughts. On the ladder ahead, through the stair treads, he could see legs covered in dungarees; an enlisted man—RC3 Ephraim Aroche stepped off the last rung. The radioman carried a coffee pot in need of filling.

"Morning, West." Aroche asked, holding back a yawn; he was obviously in need of a second cup.

"Morning," said Tyler.

"You're headed to the hangar?" Tyler's morning workouts were no secret aboard the Miller.

"Yup."

"Better get your workout in, then stow the weights for bad weather. We're heading straight for a hurricane," Aroche said over his shoulder while filling his pot from the large, stainless coffee urn near the aft bulkhead. Tyler examined the urn's sight-glass for movement up and down, but the visible coffee in the tube remained steady.

"Are we?" Tyler was surprised, there were no previous forecasts for bad weather during this last leg of the cruise, "when?"

"About fourteen hundred," said the radioman as he ascended the ladder, back presumably to the radio shack.

This meant he did not have much time before mid-afternoon. He decided to hurry while the ride was smooth like glass.

He opened the hangar door and took in the sunlit emerald ocean view off the aft facing flight deck. If Aroche's information were accurate, the ship would be making its way into the kind of weather that creates havoc for Hull Technicians. Things did not get broken as much as when the seas were calm. As an HT, his world was all about what is broken. If there was something in need of fixing, the Hull Technician got tasked with the job. He liked to say to the other HT's in his best New York City vernacular, "if it ain't broke, we ain't gotta fix it."

He strolled to the forward bulkhead of the Helo-Hangar where a stereo component was half-melted to a stationary table. He laughed, now realizing why Smithe had *borrowed* some welding equipment while in Bermuda. Tyler had spotted the new tig torch, a grounding clamp, and a box of filler rods stashed away in Smithe's locker, and decided not to ask. Tyler popped in his personal cassette tape not knowing if the deformed tape deck would still work and pressed play. Smithe had run two fillet welds along each side of the Technics M205. It looked as if the he didn't have the welder heat setting just right until he'd finished half of one side; the left wall of the deck severely drooped. To Tyler's surprise, and delight, the sounds of Van Halen triumphantly filled the hangar. The screaming of Eddie's Ibanez careened into Tyler's ears; he was relieved to learn Smithe's handiwork had not ruined the tape deck. *Smitty's a genius,* Tyler thought, *now the stereo won't fly off the table in rough seas anymore.*

Tyler had managed to maintain this routine for the last few years on most days out at sea. The rigorous morning schedule kept him sharp and helped preserve his sanity. When not on watch himself, much to the annoyance of some shipmates, he would get up early to workout. Their beef with Tyler was not the working out; it was the damned getting-up-before-you-had-to part. Waking up early did not sit well with some of his comrades. In the military, sleep was often the most prized possession you could have. Why cut into sleep time, when you could exercise during work hours? Most guys claimed exercising as their Uncle Sam given right, and the activity must be completed on company time. Tyler's morning ritual defied this point-of-view.

However, this never became an issue for Tyler due to his having organized an official intramural workout team that broke for an hour during the workday every Monday, Wednesday, and Friday. As the ship's athletic Petty Officer, Tyler led the workout team himself. The Master Chief of the Command, BMCM MacCleary couldn't believe the request when Tyler approached him with the idea with an argument that the lunch-time workouts would be a de-stressor for the crew while underway, MacCleary had laughed his ass off, but still approved the request. Of the many things people appreciated Tyler for, getting the mid-day workout approved earned him an almost iconic status among his shipmates—well, perhaps not legendary, but something they all appreciated.

Despite the workout times during lunches, Tyler still preferred the quiet of mornings and the early AM energy boost. He relished being alone on the flight deck on days when there was no helo detachment assigned to the Miller—this gave him the run of the hangar. Somehow, the morning sessions helped balance the stress of his existence on a warship out to sea.

The ship often drove him mad. Sometimes all he wanted or craved would be a hint of peace, but there was no place to run. To be alone, to sit in a quiet place, vegetate, and listen to music.

He had developed this pacifying process as a teenager. Whenever he was angry, usually after being slapped around by his mother, he would run out of the apartment to St. Nicholas Park on the eastside of Harlem. The Walkman and headphones had been a gift from one of his mother's old flings. Many hours spent on a bench listening to whatever sounds filled his headphones would quell his ire and allow him to go back home, sane again.

Tyler had to give his mother credit; she always dated nice guys—after the old man was out of the picture. His father was a topic of discussion his mother never wanted to have. Tyler yearned for a relationship, but she never supported his attempts to find out the truth about dear old Dad. She continually tried to replace Tyler's father with a revolving door of lovers, but after a few months, each had always wised up and moved on.

His father—what a freak he turned out to be. He did finally get to meet the old man and he did what he could to maintain a relationship. Tyler often recalled those years and tried to block out the craziness of them. He had accepted the fact that he came from a severely dysfunctional upbringing, but his father was a complete mental case.

Light bounced off the glistening horizon. They would be steaming somewhere west of Bermuda, heading south south west by his reckoning. Judging by the sun, they were still heading the same direction as when they secured from Sea and Anchor detail out of Bermuda Annex late yesterday. He prided himself on knowing these details.

Tyler breathed hard as he placed the bar back in place. Another set complete. He stood up to add more weights. One last set made for a total of four, and the weight progressively increased. *Atomic Punk* by Van Halen screamed as Tyler pushed the two hundred and five pound barbell up from his chest then down again for six more repetitions.

He didn't over-strain, and without a spotter he wouldn't risk dropping the heavy barbell on his throat. *There are better ways to die.* After the good chest workout, he reset the bar and plates in the makeshift squat-rack he and Smitty had welded up; two hundred fifty pounds for three sets of six reps, and then finally three hundred pound dead lifts for three sets of eight reps. Finished, he stretched and bobbed his head to the beat of another song. As he lashed the last of the twenty-five pound plates to the a-frame barbell stand, he sang along with the voice of David Lee Roth.

The ship began to creep side to side, as they got closer to the storm. He knew the tossing and turning would become violent. He needed to get a move on; there were preparations necessary, especially now that the ship's course would have them headed into a storm. Tyler sang along to the end of the chorus, and then removed his tape from the misshapen stereo before leaving the flight deck.

CHAPTER 3

A gift, a premonition arrives, strengthening my resolve. A decision is justified and has now been made easier with a simple bit of information; a simple gift; a sea cyclone is in our path, and it is too large to circumnavigate. No turning back. I will not allow an unchecked abuse of position go on any longer.

Through narrow passages, I maneuver, avoiding human contact when possible. My inner monologue is loud, the clarity of my design vivid in my mind's eye. With careful and precise detail, I lay out the steps to rid the ship of a festering boil.

Since his first days on board, he has remained aloof and snobbish. In fact, all those who wear tan colored uniforms rub their self-righteousness in the faces of the enlisted underlings: the nonentities. Those men in khakis are defiant. Their insolent game is one of class warfare, using the military chain of command and self-appointment system of hierarchy. They come to the Navy with silver spoons in their mouths and resist interacting with the collective society of enlisted men. Theirs is an experience of superiority, and they stay hidden in lofty staterooms and dining halls.

My father had tried to explain the unruly military hierarchy to me. I was too angry to listen. Leaders must *represent the will of the people they represent,* he would say. I was too naïve and joined the Navy anyway. I falsely believed the military system would be a collective society that rebuffs those who abuse their power. I was wrong. This ship has accelerated the ascension of defiant abusers at the cost of others. My father's actions to rid society of an ardent abuser showed the world how to deal with insolent selfish leaders and their failures. The only way to make change is to overthrow those in power, not negotiate. And, the only way to deal with individual abusers of power is to rid the world of their existence. I've finally learned through my own experience on this ship exactly what my father meant.

I will rid this ship of its biggest abuser of power. He has risen to the top of my list of abusers and must be stopped.

There is an approaching crewmember.

Remain focused, my inner superior voice declares.

Proximity results in unclear thoughts and distractions.

You must focus.

I agree.

We are one, my inner voice and I. I cannot trust my outward corruptible self. He, that outer face of reason and rationality, is too weak and unresolved in matters of carrying forward my destiny: my father's will. There can be no speculation on my behavior; therefore I balance the competing voices through an internal switch between in-and-out. There is also my music. I have been hearing my music for some time. I have mastered the in-and-out switch technique for more than a year and am becoming an expert at diminishing all outward signs or frivolous outward behaviors that might draw attention to my purposes; yet, music, which entered into my mind and ears, has added to my processing as well. I cannot remember for how long the music has played. I only know that the sounds have replaced the ringing, which was constant before. I cannot tell when exactly; it may have started when the inner voice began, but to be specific, I cannot recall which came to my ears first, the voice or the music. No matter—I appreciate both equally.

Along with crescendo echoes, he reminds me of our purpose, *the defiant in society must be stopped!*

I am resolved in this intention.

The approaching crewmember pauses to talk, "What's the status of

27

that job?" asks the intruder.

Switch; "I'll be finished in less than an hour," instructs my outer-persona. My smile is bright, not brooding. The Petty Officer walks away satisfied in my progress. My music trumpets his walking away. I have so well mastered my cloaking techniques, that my shipmates, both nonentities and abusers, have no idea about my true self. I have also re-crafted my outer-persona into a better sailor despite the hardships of the abusers, or the Defiant One. There is no longer any focus on me. I am just another member of the crew, except for him, the Defiant One, who still offends people.

He is pathetic; the abuser—the Defiant One—he takes advantage of my outer-persona's weakness. Not after tonight; he will meet my true self, and I will rid this ship of the Defiant One.

My preparations are finished, and despite the rush of euphoria, I remain calm. It is best to focus on the plan. The salt air is cool topside on deck, even in the beginning ocean-swells. I am free of distractions. I walk through my plan. Here will be the dumping place, near a main deck exterior exit. Through this hatch is the escape path. And there is music, *oh my music*. Calming and rousing sounds at the same time. Cascades of notes begin filling my ears with melodies and songs. As I review the locations that will be used to aid in my progressive act, Mozart's *Piano Sonata No. 11: Rondo Alla Turca* buzzes in my ears. I hum along with the triplets of the second movement. I am so adept at recognizing the pieces, since the start of my mind's music; I have taken to naming the piece, its composer, and often the year of its recording. These are songs that I have copies of and know well. The Turkish March leads me... I close my eyes in bliss.

Ah, yes. My inner voice croons in satisfaction.

Here will be the hiding place...

The Defiant One prefers his predictable course.

28

This hiding place will service me well—a container exact in its necessity. A truer canvas of destruction there cannot be.

I continue movement through the ship, busying myself with obligatory tasks, knowing only hours stand between my goal and me. Stealth is in order, but most of all, the tempo of my composition must be on time. This night will serve notice to others. They will have no idea what happened to the Defiant One!

I, a worthy assassin, stalk the area. Switch. I pretend to be my outer-persona, doing busy cleanup work for the benefit of every passersby—my vocation is familiar to all. Glimpsing familiar faces, I whisper "nonentity," to the blue clad and "abuser" to the tan clad all while hearing music and my lecturing inner-voice—my teacher and mentor. With emotionless aptitude, I greet each of the inferior bodies who come my way, my inner being staying hidden.

Most nod or return insincere greetings to me not knowing my truth. Poor souls they; no comprehension of the important work I undertake. One nonentity momentarily pauses and asks, "Still working on that?"

He has no idea what I am working on; I breathe in and lift my chin with eyes still on my task.

Switch.

"Yup. I'll get this finished before chow," I say calmly. I urge the prying body away. He is gone. Switch.

My head is filled with sound—music and voices. A new tune, perhaps? I cannot always control the selection. My mind often wanders to new sounds and songs; even so, I do not enjoy the more modern tunes that sometimes play. The cacophony of loud beats and noisy instruments; all the wailing creates too much tension. I feel pressure, stress, and discord when modern music dominates my mind. I prefer the calming chords of my classical choices. There are a few; however, that do provide purpose. Songs that float and fuel my desires are acceptable; some have lyrics that meet my moods.

This place is too crowded. The inner-voice mocks me. *You should be able to appreciate new things. New songs. Otherwise, how do you adapt? A new tune would be good for you.*

Dancing in the Sheets by Shalamar begins to play, released a year ago. The beat starts thumping and the lyrics come in.

No—stop—not now—let me return to my classics.

Tchaikovsky, 1812 Overture, first recorded in 1916. This composition is not a slight thing. It grows into something magnificent. A building climax will allow me to finish my preparation work with a bang... perfect. I hum along to the masterpiece, not missing a measure, my memory for this music is extensive, even without my headphones I hear each instrument with resonating clarity.

Yes, this is the soundtrack of my expedition. So fulfilling has my journey been, from finding my purpose in life, to now, to this moment. My body quakes, but I will not allow nerves or fear, or even him, that outer-shell, with his weaknesses always competing for my mind, to persuade me from my goal—I switch him off when I do not want to hear his nagging. For months I have planned this, and the madness of two minds, the discord of music, all of this chaos, only serves to sharpen my senses.

A last pass through and all is ready.

Set in motion, my plan: an execution for the execution. I visualize every step carefully down the main dancing hall. Casual observers walk by, oblivious; each nonentity increases my resolve. I look up, inhale deeply, and, wait...

There is a notable person coming.

I gather my tools. He has pried a little recently, so I must not give him any cause for alarm—he requires textbook cheerfulness.

Tchaikovsky rings, the orchestral chaos building and building. I must sustain the outward persona and retain the rapport. He is not the enemy, yet he could foil my design, his service is important – he is unknowingly part of the plot.

Switch. A nod and a welcoming smile is the entire ruse needed; our familiar conversation easily sways my gullible shipmate.

He is your friend?

He thinks he is.

There is no tension present in his posture. No suspicion. Good.

Your dexterity is profound—the switch is perfect.

From above I am circling, measuring my own performance; the ability to hide temper and fury is perfect—fooling all, including my friend. I am prepared. The final sounds of cannons and bells and brass horns erupt within my mind, the climax of the composition propels my march alongside my naïve shipmate.

SCOTT BLACK

DAY ONE

CHAPTER 4

Tyler managed somehow to keep moving. His body quivered with fatigue from the long day of preparing the ship for foul weather and from the last four hours of patrol. The ship had tossed and turned since dinner; it was nearing midnight, and he hadn't had a break all day. As he had assumed, their options for circumnavigating the storm's surge were not in the quartermaster's plans tonight. His assignment had taken him from forecastle to stern and back—roaming every cycle through passages, above decks and below, taking gage readings, checking empty voids and in-use tanks for liquid levels, and reporting his findings.

"No floods, no fires, the ship is secure, sir," he had stated every top of the hour to the officer on the bridge and then again to the Engineering Officer of the Watch in Main Control.

Sounding and Security patrol was the only job that allowed the watch stander to move around the ship. Other duty or ship manned workstations are stationary. For this reason, Tyler and a few of his fellow Hull Technicians believed theirs to be one of the best positions to have on the ship. When on patrol, Tyler tended to spend as much of his time as possible topside, preferring the open space and fresh air to the fluorescent illumination of internal spaces, but not this night— never on nights with the ship tossing around like a cork in a bathtub.

Tyler stepped into the airtight vestibule outside the Engine Room. He allowed the spring-loaded door to collapse and equalize the air pressure. The ventilation surge pushed against his back. He did not want to be launched down through the open hatch, so he waited at the top of the ladder before descending. After a half-minute, Tyler stepped over the knife-edge and began to climb down. Exhaustion made his entire body shaky and despite being cautious, he lost his footing on the fourth step from the bottom. A sudden dip of the ship caused his right heel to slip. He landed with an awkward flop. Both knees slammed into the diamond deck unmercifully.

"Damn it!" An intense pain shot up and down his right side. He quickly got to his feet and rubbed his knees and right hip in vain.

The USS Miller was not a particularly big Navy ship, but its large open main spaces, the engineering holes, spanned the entire width of the ship—forty-six feet. The forward to aft length was just as enormous and from bilge to maximum overhead were at least three levels tall. When Tyler started working down in the main spaces, he was told not to get lost in there, because the search for you might take a day or two.

The holes were home to snipes—the engineering personnel; Machinist Mates and Boiler Technicians. MM's and BT's worked in main spaces. Fresh-air snipes, HT's like Tyler, and the Electricians, worked outside of the main engineering compartments. The Engine Room, the aft-most main space contained many of the shipboard systems, pumps, and equipment; fire-water, potable-water, steam shut-offs, electrical transfers, and heating ventilation and air conditioning duct work. There are three main spaces on the Miller; the Engine Room, Fire Room, and Aux-One. Main Control was the below-decks control center and was a part of the Engine Room. In Main Control, personnel carried out all propulsion orders from the bridge. The enclosed command hub and its large windows lay perched above the upper level—the windows overlooking two main engines. To enter Main Control one must go down one ladder and up another. Tyler got down the first ladder the hard way; now he needed to ascend a second. He limped across the upper level platform and flexed, trying to work out the tightening calf and thigh muscles in his right leg.

"Nice landing," MM1 Tom Harrison, said. The upper level duty man had apparently enjoyed watching Tyler's tumble. He sat smiling on a ragged swivel chair under an air duct.

"Shut the hell up," Tyler coughed. Even in the relatively open space, the air circulation and the profuse stench of lube oil choked him. His aching kneecaps did nothing to lessen his temperamental mood either.

"Want to play some cards tonight?"

"I want to sleep," Tyler said dismissively, stepping up the ladder for Main Control.

He entered the air-conditioned room and immediately felt better as cool air washed over his sweat-covered face. The climb up the second ladder had helped stretch his legs; the throbbing ache decreased. The control room buzzed with men rotating duty stations—men coming on duty and men going off. Two Engineering Officers of the Watch were finishing their EOOW turnover, two machinist-mates talked about the MMOW—Machinist Mate of the Watch station, and a short fellow from R-Division stood waiting to take Tyler's place.

The on-coming Engineering Officer of the Watch, Lieutenant Bruce Orton, stared at Tyler with a ludicrous grin plastered on his face. Orton was a tall man with a thin build and acne-scarred pale skin. His large crooked nose slanted to the left as if it had been broken. Or, as Tyler always said to Smitty, his nose looked as if it got bent from being up his superior's ass. He seemed to have the secret power of catching normally diligent and hard-working enlisted men just when they were failing to perform their duties.

What the hell is he smiling about? The man's attempts to antagonize normally were not that successful on him, but just a few moments ago, Tyler had seriously thought about dropkicking the somewhat harmless Harrison in front of the potable water units—just to let off steam. Now Tyler had to deal with *Orton the ass?* The officer often used his rank to take advantage of people, especially in situations involving groups of enlisted men. Tyler wanted desperately to relax and now this guy was trying to wind him up. *He is staring like a deranged lunatic.* Tyler closed his eyes briefly and concentrated on breathing in Main Control's fresher air in a meditative attempt to clear his head and ignore the annoying prick.

A few years earlier, the officer and the HT had gotten off to a rough start shortly after Orton arrived to the Miller. Orton had taken over as Damage Control Assistant—the department head over R-Division. Tyler interacted with him every single day. Orton was the division's boss. Tyler recalled having unpleasant thoughts about the man even before finding out he was a colossal-ass. *Now I got to listen to this gabby git.* Orton hadn't appreciated finding out that everyone in R-Division respected Tyler more than their new DCA. Luckily, for Tyler, Orton ended up reassigned when a new set of officers joined the active duty crew, and R-Division now reported to a different DCA. Things were better for Tyler after Orton moved to become Main Propulsion Assistant, the MPA for M&B-Division. He only had to deal with him on infrequent occasions.

Sounding and Security patrol turnover, like all other duty station hand-offs, follows a set protocol of information transfer and instructions that Tyler had partaken in a countless number of times. *Let's make this quick*, he thought. Once finished he would go back to the General Workshop berthing area and crawl into his little cubby. He very much relished the idea of getting away from all the bullshit the storm was bringing on; including Orton's provocations. He doubted punching an officer in the mouth would be the best strategy for getting to his berthing compartment peacefully. Out of the corner of his eye, Tyler could see Orton was now fuming as opposed to the obnoxious smile he had been wearing moments ago. Orton, as always, seemed to be at the end of his patience, and Tyler apparently emerged as an ideal punching bag tonight.

"What's going on with your leg, West?" Orton laughed as if he already knew the answer. Tyler frowned. If Orton had seen him fall, probably everyone in Main Control had seen his clumsiness through the windows. Tyler bit his bottom lip.

"Slipped."

"Slipped? Slipped on what?" Orton let out a soft snort.

Is he serious right now? Tyler finally gave in and shot Orton a look. The Lieutenant's protruding brow overhung black orbs in two deep sockets with eyes that were ready to pop out of his head. His slicked back hair seemed especially greasy tonight. "Ladder," Tyler said.

Orton laughed. "Clumsy goof-off. You lost a fight with a ladder?"

Tyler gritted his teeth. His leg hurt, he was tired, and wanted to go to sleep. Orton had found the limit of Tyler's patience at last.

I wonder how much trouble I'll get into for trying to straighten out this particular officer's twisted nose.

CHAPTER 5

With eyes locked on each other, the stare down between Tyler and Orton intensified. *Surely,* Tyler thought, *everyone else see's this potentially getting ugly.* The unusually quiet room suggested as much. No one moved despite the ship's jolting motion from side to side. The other men, Tyler assumed, were waiting for one of them to speak, to act—to do something. Even the previous EOOW, Chief Langston, delayed his departure from the control room to witness the standoff.

As Orton wore the uniform of an officer, Tyler would not make the first move. He tested what self-control he had left waiting for Orton to say something insulting or petty. Verbal abuse was Orton's usual approach when dealing with enlisted men. Orton the aggressor needed to say something out of line to give Tyler a chance to jump down his throat. He continued ogling without making a peep—maybe he was having second thoughts about getting into yet another argument with an enlisted guy.

Too bad, Tyler mused. He turned his attention to his relief, HT3 Scheppler.

Then Orton spoke.

"You are such a typical short-timer, West."

Here we go. As far as insults are concerned, that was not much of one, so Tyler ignored the jab and addressed Scheppler.

"It's going to be a rough one tonight, Tommy," he said before rapidly spitting out instructions. His voice droned in an almost monotone fashion. Most of the information was habitual so he performed his task swiftly—indifference was evident in his manner.

"Did you hear me, West?" Orton spat out in a slimy tone.

Before Scheppler had a chance to respond to Tyler's quick, almost unintelligible words, Tyler turned around to face Orton.

"A typical short-timer? What do you mean by that, sir?" Tyler hoped Orton discerned the disrespectful tone in his voice.

"Lazy arrogant shit," Orton said, "you best remember that you're my man now..."

Tyler said, "I ain't your man, dude."

Orton did not slow down, "... HT2, I won't let you space out just because..."

Scheppler spoke up, "I am ready to relieve you!"

He spoke the standard patrol turnover dialogue with extra emphasis and volume; someone on the other side of the room snorted at the outburst. Scheppler didn't have a problem with confrontation; he was always picking fights—he enjoyed causing trouble like a playground bully—but around officers, he usually snapped into his 'good sailor' mode. Scheppler was always anxious around khakis, and he maintained his stare straight at Tyler not wanting to face the berating officer. Tyler frowned; Scheppler's entertaining attempt to intercede only increased the tension between Orton and Tyler.

"Because what?" Tyler ignored Scheppler's tries to defuse the tension and continued the watch-station's formal exchange. He wished Orton would say the perfectly wrong thing that would allow him to...

"Easy, West," Langston said. The Chief, along with the two MM's were obviously content with watching a verbal argument without interrupting—but Langston was not going to allow an all-out fistfight. Langston moved a little towards Tyler like a referee ready to give the standing eight count. Tyler sent the Chief a reassuring nod of the head. He knew better than to do more than talk. Orton ignored the warning and poked out his chest.

"What are you, a month out now? So you think you can get away with doing everything half-assed." The officer's scowling face glowed,

"You've been slacking on everything lately, West."

Suddenly the temperature in the room felt too warm for Tyler.

"Slacking?" said Tyler, "Slacking? You think I've been *slacking*!"

"That's right." Orton fired back.

Tyler calculated the consequences. *He's not worth it*—he reminded himself. With that decision made, he waved a dismissive palm in Orton's direction. "I've done more for this ship than half the crew combined, and you know it, you overbearing fucker!" The room went silent again for several heartbeats—Scheppler looked flabbergasted. He had never seen Scheppler so shocked; Tyler almost laughed out loud.

"Like hell! And don't you dare speak to me like that, HT2!"

"You're right. I'm sorry; I know I should never address an officer that way..." Tyler shook his head apologetically. "You overbearing fucker, sir." Tyler added a half-salute before he turned back to Scheppler. The younger man's cheeks were red, and his eyes were open wide. It was obvious that the poor kid was restraining himself. Was he trying not to laugh? Or was he keeping himself from speaking up?

Tyler began removing and handing over the Sounding and Security patrol equipment to Scheppler. There wasn't going to be an actual fight now that Chief Langston stood between the two men acting out a series of mimed hand gestures meant to calm everyone—mainly Orton—down. His efforts failed.

"You've given me hell since day one!" Orton screeched. Tyler took offense to that and turned back around.

"I've given *you* hell? You've done everything you can to piss me off since you joined the crew." Tyler slapped a brass-clasped key ring into Scheppler's upstretched palm.

"Sir. You've tried pulling a lot a shit. And you've succeeded in getting good men—enlisted men—in trouble." Tyler passed Scheppler the green canvass double pin waste belt. "You remember that crap with

Ramirez? You claimed he hadn't finished his rounds. And what about Smithe in Mayport last year? You wrote him up for not shaving on a Saturday. Then there was Wilkette." He handed over the flashlight. "You wrote him up for bullshit." Tyler pulled a sounding tape with plumb bob out of his back pants pocket.

Orton interrupted, "Ramirez missed a high temp reading on the shaft bearing, and I reprimanded Wilkette because of repeated offenses."

"That's a lie. You did it to piss me off so I wouldn't have him for our playoff run. He's one of *my* best players." Tyler transferred the metal document case containing records of sounding levels and gauge readings to Scheppler.

"I don't have to answer to you; think I give a shit about some football game?"

Tyler spat a final barrage at the furious Orton. "Don't call me lazy. You're the epitome of lazy; you never worked a day in your life! Just go to hell." He completed the equipment turnover by taking a pen from between the two top buttons of his shirt placket, giving the plunger a few clicks and placing the writing instrument in Scheppler's breast pocket.

Tyler had hoped his last comment would shut him up, but Orton kept up the volley.

"Disrespectful, defiant, lazy and arrogant. That's you, West. Remember who you are; a nobody. Ship's athletic Petty Officer, my ass!" Orton's normally pale face had gone red, and the smirk he had been wearing when Tyler arrived, was completely gone. A few greasy clumps of hair were now in desperate need of a comb-over. Orton revealed his true feelings for Tyler. For the longest time Orton had tried to get the position of athletic PO eliminated. He believed military men, enlisted pukes especially, should work more and play less.

42

"Between Wilkette and *this* fucking moron," Orton aimed his pointer finger right in Scheppler's face, only an inch or so away from his pointed nose, all while looking Tyler in the eye, "there's no way in hell you'll ever make it anywhere in the Navy when you can't even handle whipping these miscarriages into shape. You're just a glorified babysitter helping them make up their racks."

"West is a ..." Scheppler tried to jump into the argument, but Tyler put a calming hand on the younger HT's shoulder. Orton turned his wicked attention to Scheppler, but before dragging the third-wheel into the argument, Tyler shouted the last of his part of the ceremonial dialogue, "I am properly relieved by HT3 Scheppler!" Tyler turned back to Orton and took a deliberate step towards the officer: their chests were only a few inches apart.

"You mark my words, asshole. You keep talking shit, and there's gonna be murder on the Miller. I swear! And no one'll be able to help you. If they try? I'm going to get an AK-47 to take you and all the other assholes out."

"I have assumed the duties of Sounding and Security patrol." Scheppler managed to spit out the final piece of the turnover.

"Get to your rack, HT2!" Orton said, his fists clenched at his side and two veins bulging in his neck. "I'll deal with you tomorrow."

Tyler made a dramatic about-face and stepped to the door. As he pulled the door open, the rush of Engine Room air, smelling of lube-oil, wafted in.

"With pleasure, sir! Goodnight to you!" He left. The drop-slide down the ladder-rails happened so fast that his boots cracked a loud echo upon hitting the diamond-deck. MM1 Harrison rolled out of his chair the moment the spring-action door shut behind Tyler.

"You got all that, did you?" Tyler couldn't help himself; he managed a soft chuckle.

"Only the end." Harrison shook his head, "Hey, you're not the only one who wishes that ass would disappear, but damn, West! No one talks to the khaki's like that. If you think Orton is just gonna let that go, then you'll be real disappointed when he brings you to Captain's Mast."

Yeah, I'm gonna get written up for that shit. Tyler wasn't worried about being punished for their verbal altercation. His only regret? Not attempting to align that fucking nose. That was just too bad. He envisioned beating Orton's skull into the control room floor. A momentary grin passed over his face imagining blood from Orton's re-busted nose dripping and staining the officer's normally pristine uniform.

Shouting came from the control room. Orton was laying into the Chief, or Scheppler, no doubt. *Poor Scheppler*, Tyler felt a little guilty for getting him involved, *but the kid should've just kept his mouth shut and let me deal with Orton.* Tyler glanced up and imagined Chief Langston trying to smooth things out with Orton.

The ship shook, almost sending Tyler tumbling past Harrison; the handrail gave him an anchor to grab. Tyler groaned, frustrated, aching from his fall, and feeling tension from the Orton altercation. "I'm about to pass out. Gonna try to make it up to R-Division in one piece." He started towards the ladder that led out of the entry room.

"Don't fall on your ass again," Harrison said.

Tyler rolled his eyes and headed up the ladder.

CHAPTER 6

The ship swayed heavily to starboard again. The tempest rolled the large vessel with ease—severe rocking followed by a few seconds of calm and then extreme rolling. Captain Jorgenson widened his stance as the Miller vaulted atop converging crests. He almost lost his footing, but managed to keep upright by holding onto the forward beam handrail. The normally cool brass piping radiated warmth beneath his clamped palms. He fought to recall how long he had been in the standing position. For the better part of an hour?

The helmsman glanced up and grinned at Jorgenson for a moment before returning his attention to his tillers. Jorgenson tried but failed to avoid eye contact with the boatswain's mate. The man was watching. Everyone was watching. He sighed; the wheelhouse crew waited to see what would happen first; the captain falling over from exhaustion, or the ship escaping the bucking big waves. They all had a good idea of how long the ship would be affected by the storm. Only the new captain's endurance was unknown. Most of them had to be pondering, *when will the old man leave the bridge?* Even Jorgenson had to admit that, he was acting like a greenhorn midshipman in command of his first skip.

The quartermaster turned away and shook his head as he attended to their navigation, assuring everyone what they already understood; their intended heading will lead them straight through one hell of a hurricane. Similar to an upside down pendulum careening right to left and left to right, the bubble incline monometer tipped out at thirty-five degrees to both port and starboard at least a dozen times.

The Officer of the Deck, Lieutenant Carlyle Hornsby, stood nearby the captain. With each upheaval of an obliging wave, the men on the bridge staggered like a pack of punch-drunk boxers. Jorgenson seemed to be having the most difficulty. Hornsby turned to him as each pitch threatened to topple the senior officer. "You should sleep," Hornsby finally said, "It's just a storm. We can handle this; it's not like we haven't been through worse." The Lieutenant managed to raise Jorgenson's confidence a bit. "Sir, you've been up here all evening."

Jorgenson glanced around the bridge. He recognized the men to be capable of handling themselves, but the screw up during Sea and Anchor the day before did increase his concern about leaving anyone unattended. *Nothing can go wrong, not ever,* he repeated for the hundredth time. The ensuing storm couldn't be avoided. Their route would take them straight through the eye of the tempest. *Stupid*, he thought, *I can't babysit every man on this bridge.*

He let his eyes close for a moment and at once felt the past several hours pulling at him. Jorgenson's body quaked. Unable to deny his exhaustion, he gave in. His desperate desire to oversee the operation of the ship's course must wait, he finally admitted. He decided to retire to bed; it was close to midnight on day two of a mini-cruise that would have them returning to Bermuda only seven days after departing. Besides, he wouldn't be of much use if he couldn't keep his eyes open. The sounds of sharp metal creaking filled the bridge as the ship tossed; by all accounts, this was the most severe weather Jorgenson recalled having been in—especially on a tin can; fast-frigates were not the steadiest ships in rough seas. His last duty station was a practically welded to the pier sub-tender that rarely got underway.

It's just a storm, eh Hornsby?—I will hold you to your words, Lieutenant. He decided he would sleep through the brunt of the storm. Once he confirmed the standing orders with the OOD, the quartermaster, and the helmsman, Jorgenson encouraged the bridge crew to be diligent as they neared the danger zone. Before leaving the bridge, the captain re-reminded Lieutenant Hornsby to instruct all Sounding and Security watches to stay inside and away from the topside main deck. The forward and aft lookouts had already been secured until further notice. The roving patrols could be made less dangerous if the men navigated through the bowels of the vessel without going out to the weather decks.

As he entered his private quarters, Jorgenson glanced at the six portraits mounted along the right paneled bulkhead, each one of a previous captain of the USS Miller. His picture would hang there soon enough. The six white men, each about in their mid-thirties and of average build gazed back at Jorgenson as he made himself comfortable. On the opposite wall, a small shrine to Dorie Miller, the man for whom the ship was named, adorned the bulkhead midpoint. The center black and white photograph depicted Miller, a serious faced black cook standing proud with a Navy Cross on his left breast. A second print showed the fleet admiral of the United States Navy, Chester W. Nimitz, pinning the chivalrous cross pattée on Petty Officer Miller. Several Navy Cross replicas, a folded American flag, and a colorful recruiting poster from the forties featuring Miller which read, "Above and beyond the call of duty", were attached along with the old black and white photos. The entire shadowbox backing of navy-blue velvet held itself together by means of a stained wooden frame.

Jorgenson quickly shaved, showered, and got into a fresh pair of skivvies and t-shirt. The stateroom temperature hovered on the cool side; socks would be more comfortable and he donned a pair. Sitting on the edge of his bed, he gauged the roughness of the sea and decided the storm remained about same as when he had departed the bridge. Heavy eyes yearned for closure after a refreshing shower. At the head of the bed hung a small drawing scrawled by his niece; he had taped the picture to the paneling after receiving a care package from his wife,

Emma. The parcel contained the artwork, a dozen homemade sticky-buns, a box of herbal tea, and a book entitled, "A Star to Steer By", by Hugh Mulzac.

Mulzac had captained the SS Booker T. Washington and had become the first black man to earn the title of *Captain* in the Navy. A popular subject for Emma and a topic of discussion for her and the history class she taught; examining naval history for her had the added bonus of being able to borrow artifacts from Jorgenson. She said the props gave her students a more realistic understanding of the topics. Jorgenson loved finding new and interesting objects to bring home.

Mulzac's book sat in his desk drawer; he intended to finish the last half on this cruise, but tonight he decided to skip reading and instead slipped immediately between the sheets. Jorgenson was thankful for men like Mulzac and Miller, otherwise where would he be today? Not in the captain's quarters. Even after all this time, he believed he still owed these men his gratitude for the opportunity to achieve the honorable position of captain.

He glanced back at the hand-drawn Crayola-filled portrait created by his little niece; in the sketch, he wore a white navy uniform, although for some reason she had drawn his hat with a purple crayon. He laid his head on his pillow staring up at the sailor with the purple hat. At once, the captain slept.

CHAPTER 7

I lean against the cool steel bulkhead in the port main deck. The Captain's Gig passageway. My trip here was stealthy and undetected. This night is perfect. The hurricane is in full throttle, and the ship is now at the ocean's mercy. All bystanders or busy bodies will be in their racks or possibly puking up their guts and will never notice my absence. Those feeble complaints coming from my outer-persona are all subsided.

There will be no detection.

Of course not. Tonight I will dispatch my task, my waltz, with precision and accuracy. This plan will go without a hitch and the leaders will not discover anyone missing until many hours after morning muster. The truth will remain a mystery. Perhaps people will assume the Defiant One fell overboard during the night. There will be hours of hand wringing and fruitless search and rescue. Hours from now the chances of recovering a lifeless corpse in this weather will be zero. Not unlike any other simple job, I have a plan of action, and there is work to be done. Wrap, thrust, twist: the three beats for the first box step. Pull, drag, drop: the beats for the second. I must keep tempo.

So simple.

I am sure.

Salty spray cools my forehead and face as I cling to the topside structure. A light throbbing in my temples marches to a drum of three beats per bar, two simple measures in three-fourths time. Strict and staccato, the repeating tempo gives structure to the words I continuously mouth silently.

Wrap, thrust, twist...

Pull, drag, drop...

With my wrist near my face, I push a button; there is a glowing illumination from a clock face.

It is time.

Slowly, as practiced, I lift the quick-acting watertight door handlebar. Unafraid of noise, for I had prepared the door for silence earlier; I wait for an accommodating ship's pitch, making the heavy door swing smooth and silent. My strength keeps the door from slamming, and I hold the metal access soundless. Catlike, moving through the opening, closing and only slightly lowering the handle; I'll need a quick return through this door in a few moments. A red glowing fixture lights the aft boat-deck passage; I disable it with swift proficiency; my preparation assured it so. Over the knife-edge to the inner passage that separates the boat-deck from officer's staterooms, I disconnect, again with an expert's knowledge, the two bulkhead lights. All is simple child's play.

Now the passage is pitch black. There will be sufficient time for my eyes to adjust, but the Defiant One, my prey, will be blind as he steps into the passage. How fitting, I cherish my momentary delight—the blind one will be blind. Half smiling, without sound, my lips form six words.

Wrap, thrust, twist...

Pull, drag, drop...

Forward of the officer's country joiner door, I step into the killing zone and take the few strides forward to the hidden vestibule and crouch into the crook of the wall; my breathing slows just as I had trained. My eyes are already adjusted to the dark, but I use the light of the wristwatch to again check; the time is zero three fifty. I bend at the waist reaching to my feet, lifting the leg of my coveralls and I clasp the steely weapon strapped to the skin of my right calf. The handle is moist. With my sleeve, I lovingly wipe the handle and shiny ten-inch metal. With the blade clutched tightly, awaiting in attack position, I push back into the corner of my hiding place.

In this moment, there are no worried thoughts. I am not afraid; my outer-persona is losing strength daily. He made a feeble attempt earlier today. His last ditch effort, to convince me not to go through with the deed, was unsuccessful. My determination is for him to be forever subservient. Even as abusers mar his reputation, publically announce and display his failures, send him for extra duty, and write him up for failure, he continues to be their obedient slave. He acquiesces to their programming.

He is learning.

He is frail. I will teach him.

An overwhelming sense of confidence and assurance washes over me. My greatest concern is not that I am about to take a man's life. No. My greatest concern is what song should be the accompanying melody to the Defiant One's downfall. Perhaps in this moment my personal soundtrack will be accommodating with a selection. A few track options play through my head, I decide on a tune, and my inner DJ agrees. The melody fills me. I listen to the vivid tones of a record player turntable in my ear. I smile.

CHAPTER 8

The ship heaves and rolls, crashing waves grip the forty-storied vessel and tosses her around effortlessly. Inside the port main deck passage, in the darkness, the violent bursting of water against steel is stifled to nothing. It is enough, though, to quell the pulsing blood in my temple. The passageway, the killing zone, is a perfect contained coffin tube, muffling the outside world to silence. The tempest cannot interrupt but in fact adds to the atmosphere I have created. The more the exterior roars, the quieter the interior settles. A just purpose promotes calm within the storm both in resolve and in the physical world lashing about the ship and me. All is calm within, and an airy coolness reigns in the killing zone, which is perfect and ready for doing the deed that must be done. I am sure there will only be a few more moments of waiting.

Then. Sounds of grinding lubricated metal burst the tranquility. A spinning screw gear and linkage pins rub against each the other. The sound reminds me of the scratch heard when starting a vinyl record. I hear the music now. Engelbert Humperdinck's *The Last Waltz* plays in my mind much like a record player. The Last Waltz; I hear the notes so clearly.

I wonder should I go or should I stay, sings Humperdinck

I stiffen.

The time is now. A quick acting scuttle is opening and voices broadcast from below in the Engine Room Control Room. I listen as the Defiant One, who is leaving his watch, barks foul comments at the remaining men in the hole. I grit my teeth in anticipation.

The band had only one more song to play.

The Engine Room is one deck below the killing zone. He, the

Defiant One, my prey, normally uses the vertical escape ladder and scuttle to return to the Officer's country and the Wardroom rather than the normal route of all other officers. No change tonight.

Other less abusive members of the officer corps exit Main Control through the main door to the Engine Room, down the ladder that lands on the evaporator level, crossing the platform and proceeding again up through the main space entrance to the second deck. My outer-persona has taken that path many times. This port side escape scuttle is the sole route of the Defiant One at the completion of his four-hour duty shift. This route distributes its ascender onto the main deck and nearer to the safe haven of the khaki-brass living-quarters and staterooms. He, the Defiant One, my prey, uses this passage to avoid the enlisted crew.

I will use it as a killing field.

The ship surges to port, lingers before returning upright, and then with a slight roll to starboard, rights again. Good, I foresaw the storm to be an ally, and so it shall be.

The Defiant One steps out of the round scuttle, lowers the lid, and tightens the locking handle. He steps past the hiding area. I can see well in the dark. His uniform is a beacon in blackness.

And then I saw you out the corner of my eyes... a little girl alone and so shy...

The record player is loud; surely, he hears? Stooped low and reaching for support, Lieutenant Bruce Orton presents himself for slaughter.

I wish for Orton to wonder why he is surrounded by darkness, and I hope his concentration is on seeing, for a last time, this bleak enclosure with its cold steel bulkhead and rough textured deck. I watch as Orton breathes. The last time his lungs will inhale dank air from the killing zone, for soon the cruel sea will accept another sacrifice. Drowning, such cruel cold suffocation is all I wish. I wish with all my will that Orton lives long enough to understand that he is drowning in a mixture of seawater and his own blood. For the remainder of Orton's life there will be no sun... no smiles... only pain and blood and wind and waves closing in around his water-choked, dying carcass. I feel satisfied that the Defiant One will only live long enough to comprehend that he is dead. There is no other end.

I had the last waltz with you. Two lonely people together.

I revel in the all-encompassing melody of Humperdinck's serenade. *I fell in love with you. The last waltz should last forever.* Now I repeat two measures of the approaching waltz. One, two, three... one, two, three!

Wrap, thrust, twist...

Pull, drag, drop...

The first box step will be swift: three beats only taking mere moments, yet every action plays out in a surreal slow motion medley of musical beats. A dance of death. Murderous rapture. I advance from the hiding place, ready to greet my dancing partner. His back faces me; I wait for an accommodating roll of the ship. A short walk, only feet to the officer's country joiner door and safety. I step over the vestibule edge into the main area of the passage. I time my move.

Wrap.

Three seconds elapsed.

With my knifeless hand I roundhouse an arm over Orton's left shoulder. My bicep and forearm hinge, compressing his throat and chin. I clamp four fingers over the opposite shoulder, brushing against his protruding clavicle bone. With ease, the lieutenant is immobilized. We both are swaying to starboard.

Thrust.

Six seconds elapsed.

The ten-inch blade of polished steel glints even in pitch-blackness.

54

With three of the thirteen saw-teeth under thumb, I cock the blade and plunge in with a swift two-step motion. On target. Below the ribcage, around or above the left kidney. The officer's standard issue khaki shirt, cotton t-shirt, and fleshy back tissue offer little resistance to the piercing metal. Warm liquid spews over my thumb and knuckles. Orton reaches up at the strangling appendage with wild hands, gripping my forearm,

Twist.

Nine seconds elapsed.

A meager yelp from the Defiant One breathily escapes his compacted windpipe. Like revving a motorcycle, I twist the hilt deep blade counterclockwise cutting a horizontal gash, left to right. The work here offers some tendon and bone supplied resistance; however, my ally the storm, steps in to aid in the maneuver; a severe roll provides enough leverage to complete the slice. The two of us are twirling dancers, held together in an awkward linchpin embrace. The Defiant One is erratically reaching out and clawing at my face, which I curl into the crook under his right ear. The first box step is complete.

But the love we had was goin' strong. Through the good and bad we'd get along.

"Why are you... cho... king... me?" the victim coughs; he is barely audible over the music. The glorious music.

Nine seconds in and this fool is three beats behind me; it is already time to pull and he thinks we have only just begun the wrap step—my quickness on display. Suddenly, unexpectedly, the words I had listened to for months emerge from my throat. "I am your man; I am your friend."

My voice echoes off metal bulkheads. I smile. I had not planned to say anything, but the words steep from my lips in unison with the music and the killing dance. My timing has been perfect to this point, so a brief improvised interlude will not skew the melody. The ship rights for a brief instant, but in this blissful moment it feels like the boat is frozen, steady and level, perfectly still.

As the blade passes through the mid-point of Orton's back, I feel my dissected specimen's weight fall and hang from my left arm and shoulder. I have severed his spine perfectly.

And the flame of love died in your eye.

He collapses. The Defiant One no longer needs legs.

My heart was broke in two when you said goodbye.

The chorus is about to pick up; it's time to begin the second box step.

Fifteen seconds elapsed.

Pull.

Hot fluid erupts and fills the space between our two bodies at the waist. The Defiant One claws more aggressively now. He is hanging on to my arm. He realizes his legs are no longer functioning. As the knife exits, the teeth saw bone and flesh. Pulling out the knife proves to be more difficult than pushing it in; good information to remember for the future. A rehearsal for future endeavors perhaps. I hadn't realized how easy this was going to be.

I lean back. As flowing blood runs over my abdomen and down the front of my legs. I twirl, pulling his body around with me, and reconfirm my grip on the muttering, almost dead, once defiant, now defenseless man. Only two more beats and my opus will be *fine`*, and the Defiant One, the one who deserves this deed, will be *con sordino.*

I pause for a moment and sway to my favorite part of the song playing in my head.

I had the last waltz with you. Two lonely people together.

I begin to sing the song quietly as I start the last part of our dance, "I... fell... in love... with you.... The last waltz... should last... forever."

The Defiant One reaches a shaking hand up to my face, which I dismissively slap away.

Drag.

Twenty-one seconds elapsed.

In precise military rotation, he, the carried, and I, the carrier, turn and begin moving aft. The listless Boon-Docker covered feet drag along the nonskid-coated deck plates. Heel scraping sounds along with "umphs" and "ughhs" leaking from the mouth of the Defiant One competes with the melody in my head. I smile. Not the Defiant One, but the Dying One. The cries continue along with a pitiful plea, "Please... help... " it takes every bit of his energy to work up his appeal. Beautiful sounds. Sweet rapture.

It's all over now. Nothing left to say. Just my tears and the orchestra playing.

The sounds of the Dying One disrupt the tranquility of the killing zone as well as my melody, so I lean low and whisper, "I am your man, and you are at your end."

La la la la la la la la la la. La la la la la la la la la la.

Then another sound intrudes. My record player screeches to a halt. The peaking storm outside roars, not the serenading sounds of Engelbert Humperdinck's angelic voice. What dares to interrupt my track?

A creak out of synch with the killing zone din alerts me to the unexpected.

Twenty-seven seconds and counting.

From several feet aft, this noise interrupts our dance! I freeze as much as one can freeze while hugging a flailing, legless klutz. With the knife out front, I wedge my wet metallic-smelling wrist across the crying man's mouth—only partially stifling the grunts.

Everything speeds up.

You fool, decries my inner voice.

The ship's motion seems to be working against me now.

Are you going to be a failure?

No—shut up—the body is heavier than before.

Finish the dance!

I must run. Thirty seconds elapsed!

Drag and drop! Only one step left; drop the klutz overboard—the final box step is nearly done.

Yes. I must... what is the next step... I am confused. Switch. There is an alarming signal—a door has opened, and there is white light filtering into the killing zone. Switch.

One more step!

Switch. The fantail passage knife-edge stands between the boat-deck and us. I quickly calculate the time and distance. Only seconds, three measures of three-fourth meter, nine quarter notes, that is what I need. Warmth rushes and swirls through my skin. My head flushed and hot begins to burst. My inner-voice and outer-persona fight for control over my mind. Switch—switch. Clashing pieces of modern rock music start amplifying. I feel my sweat-soaked body; is it sweat? My skin is hot; the lukewarm fluid I felt earlier is now boiling against my thighs.

The sound of the distant doorway seems to have roused the dying Orton. He is clamoring so loudly to break free of my grasp; his fingers scratch and claw at my wrists and forearms in frantic spasms; I consider cutting his throat to stop his tantrum. A fist hits my shoulder, but Orton is too weak to impart any real damage. I prefer his attempts to hit me with his weak arms to the blasted scratching.

One more step. Finish dragging and drop him over!

A hard starboard roll immediately makes completing the drag beat futile, the ship surges, almost willing me to go back and retrace my footsteps—I hold my ground but not without extreme effort. The ship returns for a port roll, and as I step my right foot over the edge passage opening my tranquil world in which to kill collapses. My dance is not complete as planned.

All is lost.

CHAPTER 9

Frantic knocking.

What can this be, only a few minutes of sleep?

He felt like he had just showered, shaved, and slipped into his inspection worthy rack. Jorgenson had been enjoying analyzing crayon strokes: an assortment of jagged and smooth lines. They were reminders of Picasso and Matisse, mirroring similarities to their avant-gardism; *an officer in purple hat*, an apt title, *exhibit di stateroo*m. The interruption, only minutes after his head hit the pillow, was unwelcomed.

Annoyed, he jerked, rolled over, and propped on to his left side— someone stood peering through his door into the darkness. His jaw clinched tight; an instinctive impulse, which relaxed muscles around the eyes and forehead, minimizing expressions of anger or irritation. The pretense of not being agitated did not diminish the annoying knocking and opening of his stateroom door, but the facial freeze disarmed those bearing the news or source of infuriation.

Captain Jorgenson did not hear the interloper speak, even so, his ire escalated in the instant. *Only just turned in and already the bridge needs me?* He sat up—his body heavy against the ship's perpetual-motion forces—the effort tweaked a nerve in his back above the shoulders as he twisted his torso. *This better be God damned good,* he thought. *The ship had better be falling apart... the message from that shadow in the...* his inner monologue halted; his eyes closed and intermittent fading pictures of windblown trees appeared. An unrecognizable face and thoroughbred horses were gliding towards the backstretch at a familiar track. The racetracks; the place where he first met Emma. These were memories. Had he been dreaming of her? If so the interruption of sleep would be all the more irritating. He reached back in his mind to grasp and hold on to the dream, trying to recall through a haze of fading thoughts. A gentle kiss, a walk in the park, and the husky scents of fall... the visions of sleep seemed to blend.

Jorgenson was certain that dreams of such vivid complexity would not be the product of a short nap. Perhaps his sleep had lingered longer. In an attempt to wipe clear his blurred vision, he strained his eyes to focus, glancing from the doorway shadow to his pillow and then to the brass clock mounted on the aft bulkhead. Darkness concealed the hand positions, but the room inclined in a different motion pattern, which signified to him a passing of time. An un-granted wish to sleep through the storm instead, aroused at the height of her raging outcries. The figure in the doorway respected his momentary delirium, patient for an acknowledgement to deliver the message. *The stateroom temperature is cooler than earlier*, he thought.

"What time is it?" Jorgenson said. He coughed nasally; his voice coarse and distorted.

The visitor stood swaying, hands on knob and frame casing to keep himself from tumbling over in the flopping side-to-side motion. The silhouette created an opening and closing bellows in synch with the rocking ship.

"Sir, it's Lieutenant Orton; there's been an accident," the shadow said. His panicked demeanor and fraught announcement disturbed Jorgenson at once; the quaking messenger, his identity revealed, Chief Engineering Officer Lieutenant Commander Phillip Hodges stepped in while closing the door behind as he entered the captain's stateroom.

In the dark, gripping the top of the enclosure, Captain Jorgenson swung his legs over the edge of his rack and tossed aside his blanket. "Tell me," he said as his sleep induced hesitation disappeared. A commanding strength returned to his voice. He reached to depress the bulkhead lamp brass plunger and the room illuminated. A glossy distance in Hodges' eyes told Jorgenson to expect calamitous news. Was the man shaking?

Fearing the worst, the weary captain visualized his clumsy Main Propulsion Assistant, Orton, crumpled in a heap at the bottom of some ladder. Jorgenson tried not to cringe as the image of a man, sprawled out on a cold floor, neck broken and dead, formed in his head.

"What happened to him?" Jorgenson said, now completely awake and aware.

"Portside, boat-deck," was the officer's only reply. Hodges' pasty face fixed into a vomit-ready grimace—*was he seasick?* The pupils in his brown eyes were wide. His breathing remained unsteady. Jorgenson somehow knew the lieutenant's mind had just darted back to the scene of the incident.

"You should come; now," Hodges said. He hurried to the wardrobe and pulled out a handful of khakis, "We're not sure...how...or..." his voice trailed off, "or what happened." He sorted through the clothing. "Orton is in bad shape."

Hodges crossed the room with his commanding officer's uniform. The two staggered about like drunks, locking arms to keep from tumbling over. Jorgenson grabbed the clothing and struggled to pull on pants. Thunder cracked from somewhere outside.

The commanding officer, donning whatever his helper provided, noted the position of the hands on the clock. The time was zero four twenty.

CHAPTER 10

Mind and body pulsates with a frantic beating heart; my coursing blood gushes through bulging veins as I advance passage to passage. With the greatest possible speed, I avoid slamming into bulkheads, yet the ship, once my ally, works against me. Only a few glorious moments ago my potential climaxed. I am on a downward spiral. Now, since I ran from the scene, only music—the swelling music—so loud I cannot listen, or understand, or recognize the song, matters. It is all I hear. Switch! Covering my ears does not relieve the sheer agony. My waltz, the final act, ruined by some bastard invader to the killing zone.

Stop running and go back.

No.

Go back and dispatch the intruder!

There is no need.

You did not complete the waltz! You must return and kill the witness!

There is no witness; he only saw blackness.

He watched you run away.

There—in the dark—entered an intruder. A light had erupted in the midst of the dance when a faceless bastard opened the hatch.

It was dark; he saw nothing.

Orton will identify you.

I am sure Orton is dead.

You are careless—you should not have spoken to him.

He is dead.

You are weak—just like your outer-self.

No!

I want to scream but suppress the urge. Switch. On the main deck, I

63

will my equilibrium to stop countering the ship's motion; I suffer a rising panic and work to quell it. Breathe. I've retreated far from the killing zone as fast as I can. The passageways spin around me. The music is overbearing. I fear discoverer.

You have always been afraid.

The spinning ship, incessant ravings of that other voice, and these crashing melodies raise a panic in me.

You're out of control.

My out-of-control body careens back and forth against the passage bulkheads up on the Main Deck. I stop. Calm...I need to calm down. Kind, cold bulkhead, my flesh accepts your cooling gift—I hug the horizontal beams to my face. I catch my breath and shake away a small amount of confusion. Better. Here is a good place. The passage ahead and behind are deserted. I place the bloody steel as planned. Good. This will not to found by any other than me.

The ship careens, and I fly into a heap on the deck. Compositions like waves collide; percussions detonate in my head. A realization—I have neglected something. I go to retrieve the hidden knife but the ship fights me bobbing up and down. All I do is cover my ears in a desperate attempt to end the infernal noise. Forget the knife. Move. The admirable item is well hidden. I will return later to fix my error.

That was a mistake.

Damn the devil-composer who created the notorious melody in my mind. Is the tune only in my head? The sounds of guitars, drums, and synthesizers ring out. Switch. I run.

Down the ladder to the second deck.

I'm in the head undressing.

A quick shower; the noise of the spray does nothing to outplay the wicked sounds ringing in my ears. My breathing is out of control; a dog panting on a summer's day. Blood of the Defiant One mixes with water at my feet—the evidence disappears down the drain. The volume increases, then, lowers, then grows louder, over and over; I hunker down in the shower, my hands on my ears again. Then—a moment of clarity surfaces. I realize what is happening. I have a choice: let this chaos be my moment of despair and uncertainty or allow me to grasp my triumph.

The Defiant One is dead.

You are not certain—you must go back and dispatch the intruder!

No, it is too late.

He is not dead.

He soon will be.

You are a fool.

The thought of khaki clad creatures rushing to aid Orton while he chokes on his own blood sooths me. I imagine the panic. I imagine the fear. I smile. Switch. No—no need to switch, I am in control from now on. My work is done—the Defiant One is dead. Accept the music, accept the madness, and be pleased with your deed. I am in control.

Take a breath.

Yes. I can breathe again. The music is still intense but more pleasant.

My motion matches measures of descending octaves; violins portraying the outside rain, washing the bobbing ships superstructure. I know the piece; Vivaldi, the Four Seasons: Winter, first recorded in 1942. My father brought this one to my attention many years ago—he made me a mix tape of this and several other 18th Century composers. He had developed a love for the classics while stationed in Germany during his military years. Later, as a disc jockey, he would become the aficionado who influenced and passed on his expertise, enlisting me in a continual game of *name that tune*.

Never do anything half way—if you appreciate something, learn all you can about the subject.

Vivaldi is a favorite. Initially the pizzicato notes frightened me; now the plucky staccatos construct a sense of awaited relief. The shower water is warm against my skin. Calm slowly returns. I reassure myself now. Yes, the deed did not go exactly as planned—but no matter now. Inhale. The friends of the Defiant One will not suspect me; they will never find me. Exhale. The weapon hidden; time to hide the coveralls now that my mind is clear.

You have failed.

I ignore him and exit the shower, dry off, and change into the clothes previously stashed. The time has been seven to eight minutes since the first box step and thrust of my knife. His blood flowed; he cannot survive—not ten minutes or longer when loosing so much blood. I'm convinced he is dead even if my inner voice disagrees, or my outer-self is frightened. No need to switch—I am in control.

I leave the shower room and scan the area around my safe hiding spot. I hum to the tune of Vivaldi's beautifully composed violins. To prove my regained composure, I decide to retrace my steps—dare I get closer to where Orton's body still lies? I wipe clean the ladder I had crawled down before my shower. I ditch the coveralls just as I had done with the knife, being more precise this time with the placement.

Walking with a purpose, I arrive at the next ladder meant to take me below to the third deck, my berthing compartment. Two stories above there is no doubt chaos, but here all is quiet apart from the quaking ship and my lovely mind melody. Calm. So easily, I calmed myself. Past fantasies of the moment pale in comparison to the actual deed; I had daydreamed of destroying my prey for months, and I am giddy with the result. The act complete joy engorges me.

Into my berthing compartment, I slip without a sound—my comrades are asleep, unaware of the deed. To my rack and I crawl into bed. Slumber will not easily come, but I'm confident in my adlibbed final movements, so I will try to sleep.

You've failed—they will revive him.

No. Maybe.

He will talk.

Can it be? Ten minutes have elapsed. Too much blood to revive.

You are a failure ...

NO!

I silently rebuke my inner voice while lying in my rack. Father, you are wrong. I have succeeded.

CHAPTER 11

A mix of cinnamon and vanilla scents filled the air. Small rays of light shine in from the bedroom window. Tyler's body grows warm when he spots Alexandra lying asleep in the middle of the queen-sized bed. The white satin sheets juxtaposed with her creamy Spanish skin and lacy black undergarments, shimmered. The lingerie is new: a baby doll dress, transparent at the breasts, draped over her stomach and ended just above her waist with a delicate finish. Her bottoms are a simple pair of lacy black panties with tiny red ribbons on either hip. Her legs gently crossed at her ankles, and her right arm tucked under her head. Alexandra had painted her lips a luscious red—something she rarely did.

Slowly, nervously, Tyler closed the door of the small room and crossed to the bed. He smelled of whisky and beer, but if he'd known her plans for his last night home involved elaborately sexy undies and lipstick, he would have never met the boys at the pub. She had to be furious. How long had she waited in bed? He spotted new candles on the nightstand with the wax mostly melted. She had waited several hours at least. Tyler undressed down to his boxers, being careful not to wake her. As he climbed onto the bed there were rose pedals spread across the duvet, which lay beneath her feet.

He reached a hand out and touched the curve of her left side. Her eyes blinked open, and she rolled over. "Screw you," she said, but she was smiling.

"I'm sorry," he grinned back and climbed on top of her while pulling the sheets over them both. She followed him to the head of the bed. They both laid their heads down on the same pillow with noses only inches away from one another. Tyler caressed her cheek; she placed her hand on his chest; each silently implored the other towards an embrace. Soon their bodies pressed against one another, and they wrapped themselves in white sheets, legs intertwined. Her strawberry flavored lips captivated him—his contentment fulfilled in her kisses.

She rolled onto her back, and he moved atop her. A soft rush of her new favorite perfume filled his nose. Alexandra played with the hair on the back of his neck; his skin tingled against her honeyed silkiness, and he cupped a hand in the small of her back pulling their thighs into one another. Alexandra moaned, greatly raising his enthusiasm. Tyler greeted the intense pleasure; he kissed her neck with breathy lips, making her giggle like a young girl. She was ticklish—her ears, neck, and behind her knees; he kissed everywhere and their mutual desires surpassed each other. He ran fingers through her long, black hair and swam in her green eyes, "God, I love you."

She smiled and went to return the sweet words—words they had exchanged before, but tonight they felt more real, "HMC Macon report to... officer's... country eh-sap..."

Tyler jolted. He found himself back in his rack, staring up at the cold metal bottom of the bed above. "Fuck no." he muttered.

"Chief Macon report to..."

Someone was telling Tyler to "double time" something. Then several silence intruding clicks from the 1MC speakers erupted then faded away. The R-Division common area became quiet again. Something askew arose in the night; even in his half-asleep state, Tyler detected the berthing compartment slumber ending. Semi-conscious, still infuriated by the disturbance and subsequent awakening away from his most pleasant sex dream, he could not be certain of the exact words spewing from the bridge boatswain's mate. It sounded as if a corpsman needed to go somewhere, or somebody required a medic or some sort of urgent attention. To the Wardroom—maybe? Tyler desperately summoned his dream back, and he floated between the warm embrace of Alexandra's arms and the cold rectangle of his rack.

"¡Oh Dios!" he could hear her voice again, "Tyler..."

Her entire body shuddered. Each moment intensified with each passing second. She nibbled on his ear. *Thank God*, he was just awake enough to realize the dream and thankful to be returning to the delightful memory that replayed in his subconscious. *If someone wakes me up again, I'll beat them senseless*. His eyes met hers. He inhaled the fragrance of cinnamon and vanilla candles.

CHAPTER 12

Quiet and deserted, the sprint to the boat-deck passage took the two officers down one ladder, aft through officer's country and then out to the port main deck. When passing each stateroom, Jorgenson held his breath for fear of someone popping their head out and asking questions he himself needed answers to. He tried to envision the upcoming sight based on Hodges' rushed description—only dreadful images came to mind. A collapsed individual on the deck would be the just relieved EOOW, Orton, wearing working khakis no doubt, the uniform of the day for standing hole watches.

From Hodges' nervous details, Jorgenson did not manage to conclude much about the sequence of events leading up to the discovery of the body—only that the likelihood of Orton's injuries being an accident was nil. "No way," Hodges had said. Jorgenson was worried they might have a crewmember on a rampage. He needed to get the officers and crew together for a head count as soon as possible.

As they approached the aft end of the portside boat-deck passage, beams of light flashed chaotically around a group of khaki-clad men hovered over a listless figure. The spotlight holders were obviously having difficulty keeping the makeshift working area lit for the medical team's efforts.

"Mister Partridge is getting us some lights on in here," someone announced.

Jorgenson squeezed in between the bulkhead and a work-light bearer and knelt down. Orton lay face down; HMC Macon and Lieutenant JG Scott Kramer were maneuvering him, wrapping gauze around the middle of Orton's back. Suddenly the area ignited with light, and everyone could fully see the bloody scene. A retch and moan came from the few men present. The captain barely flinched.

"Quickly Chief, what can I do?" Jorgenson said while repositioning himself near Orton's head.

"Not much, Skipper," Macon, replied.

As a Vietnam War veteran, Macon had seen things the captain could only imagine; he'd seen men blown to pieces that still survived. Surely, Orton was not that bad off.

"Can we save him?" Jorgenson asked.

"He's bleeding out." The older man shook his head a bit, and drops of sweat flew off his bulbous cherry nose and razor stubble covered chin.

Macon's discouraging comment spelled out his expectations for Orton's survival. He worked with deliberate firmness, yet Jorgenson wanted more of a sense of urgency.

"How long has he been here?" Jorgenson asked Hodges. He wanted a quick calculation of the life expectancy of his MPA.

Hodges blinked and looked around at the others; Kramer spoke up first. "Watford found him about ten minutes ago."

Jorgenson was immediately discouraged seeing all the blood sloshing around the deck plates. "Chief, we're gonna do whatever we can, you understand?"

Without lifting his eyes from his handiwork, Chief Macon said, "Captain, *I am* trying to save this man—I will answer your questions later."

Jorgenson nodded. Whatever the outcome, the Chief was Lieutenant Orton's only hope.

Orton gasped and fought to breathe, maybe even to talk; his throaty growls reverberated into the deck plates. The captain reached down and gently lifted Orton's face from scraping the rough non-skid flooring.

"Give me your shirt," he said to one of the youngest officers. Lieutenant JG Kramer, kneeling beside the body, immediately began to unfasten buttons.

As Jorgenson lay Orton's face on the makeshift padding, he scanned the ghastly scene surrounding them. Blood puddled around the body and began to soak into Jorgenson's pants. He sensed the general somberness of those in the room; it felt like they were already attending a funeral. Perhaps the Chief spoke true. There wasn't much that anyone could do to save him.

Familiar to the heat of battle, men got hurt, men died; but this? This was something different. Lieutenant Orton hadn't been struck down by some heinous enemy of the United States; he's been attacked by a fellow Navy man—a shipmate.

The ship remained in constant motion, making the corpsman's efforts to perform first aid next to impossible.

Only one of his young officers, the now tee shirt sporting Kramer, did anything but ogle the spectacle. Jorgenson and Kramer followed the orders barked at them by Macon, damming blood from the open gaping gash, steadying the clamped surgical cinches, helping to turn Orton when needed, and piling up the blood soaked gauze.

The others, Lieutenant Commander Philip Hodges, Ensign Dana Partridge, and the ship's Executive Officer, Lieutenant Commander Paul Kendall all stood staring in helpless horror. Jorgenson felt especially bad for Hodges; Orton and Hodges were close.

The blood against Orton's khaki uniform made for a perturbing juxtaposition. Rust colored fingerprints marked Orton's ashen face below the left cheekbone: a foreboding contrast of life and death. Had the poor man reached up to touch his own face, or were the prints evidence left by the attacker?

His guttural cries had faded to whimpers and tortured gurgles.

"Uhh," breathe, "ohh," breathe, he kept repeating.

Had the racket not been coming from the throat of the hacked up man lying in front of him, Jorgenson would have bet money that the sounds, a baritone bleat followed by a whoosh of sucking turbulent air, came from a trapped and tortured animal trying to escape a hunter's snare.

"Uhh," breathe, "ohh," breathe.

Nothing can go wrong, not ever. However, this scene was so wrong. His Main Propulsion Assistant sounded like he was dying right in front of them.

An accumulation of dark reddish liquid rolled over the deck and formed a glistening puddle at the Chief's knees. With each roll of the ship, cascading blood-rivers formed and surged along crevices, damming up against fillet welds where the deck met the bulkhead. The Chief's wrists and forearms were streaked in crimson as he worked to close up the gaping wound. Orton's clothes were once the khaki-tan color of the standard officer uniform; now the blood-wicked fabric appeared magenta.

The triage team worked against all odds to save the man despite the flowing blood and the raging storm. An abrupt incline caused everyone to lose his balance. Hodges stumbled and almost fell on top of his friend lying prone on the ground.

"Is there any heading we can take to minimize this God damn rolling?" Jorgenson blurted the comment to anyone who would listen.

"Uhh," breathe, "ohh," breathe, answered Orton.

Jorgenson's exasperation with the unrelenting storm intensified, and he willed Mother Nature, or God, or whoever was in charge of the damn storm, to stop the onslaught. But, why would the storm subside for him? How could he be an effective captain here in this chamber of death? He was not in charge. He could do nothing but gently cradle the dying Officer Bruce Orton, Main Propulsion Assistant for the USS Miller, in another man's bloody shirt. His private battle cry *nothing can go wrong, not ever* shattered to the sounds of Orton's painful moaning.

Jorgenson sensed the wandering eyes of the men encircling the scene—each fixated on the event that was sure to stain memories for years to come.

"The rolling," Jorgenson said, lifting his eyes to Partridge. Ensign Partridge trembled. His white pale face, blonde hair, and petrified gaze made him look childish. Where he tightly gripped a horizontal beam, his knuckles were bursting through the skin.

"Call the bridge and see if they can minimize the rolling."

Jorgenson doubted the bridge could do anything to relieve the tumult, but at least Ensign Partridge would have something to do; it would be a blessing to have one's mind distracted from this tragic event. *Run off on an errand Mister Partridge*, Jorgenson thought; *better to run than pity your dying shipmate.*

The Chief, teetering precariously above his handiwork and continuing to fight against the undulating compartment, lost balance for the third time, and reached up to brace himself with one scarlet hand while the other clamped down on the arterial spinal artery. The smooth bulkhead offered no friction against his wet palm. The ship lurched again and the Chief flopped over his patient.

The limp body offered nothing more than another, "uhh," breathe, "ohh," breathe.

"Shit!" Kramer reacted quickly, as did Jorgenson. Kramer grabbed the corpsman's belt from behind and the captain, whose hands were occupied from cupping the dying man's face, timed a head-butt to Macon's shoulder. Both actions up-righted the blood-soaked corpsman. The Chief now had that sense of urgency about him that

Jorgenson had wanted to see earlier. He leaned back over Orton.

"Thank you," Macon said gruffly. He shook his head as he examined the damage and gave instructions for Kramer to, "replace that packing," pointing to an oversaturated wad that was leaking. Macon sounded defeated. They had installed four scissor clamps onto what appeared to be fleshy tubes protruding out of a pack of raw meat. With brown greasy fingers, Kramer peeled the blood-blotched gauze away and crammed a fresh wad into the space. He retched but managed to maintain composure. Using what seemed like all of his weight, the Chief forced the cloth into the gaping hole as a desperate last-ditch effort to stop the bleeding. Kramer then placed a second wad over the wider opening and held down on the packed laceration while Macon began wrapping an elastic cloth into a midriff tourniquet.

Jorgenson's heart ached. This was pointless. Orton had lost too much blood. This was the finalization of a useless procedure—meaningless last steps.

His gaze wandered to the bulkhead where an erratic illustration appeared. Smeared bloody handprints. The ruby palm strokes across a white background resembled a finger-painting Jorgenson had in his stateroom. The artwork had arrived while in Bermuda—the pictures were accompanied by photos of his sister's kids; Louis, ten, and Josephine, seven; the artists of both the painting and the crayon drawing above his bunk.

HMC Macon wiped his hands on a clean patch of his shirt and shook his head.

"There's nothing else I can do, sir.... He needs a surgeon."

Jorgenson nodded; subconsciously he had reached that conclusion several minutes earlier.

The Chief added, "We need to turn him over..."

"To check the status on his vitals, right?"

"Yes."

The captain bent low to speak to the listless head in his hands. "Bruce, we're going to turn you onto your back."

Ensign Partridge reappeared in the doorway to report on the ship's course. Jorgenson noted that Partridge returned looking better than earlier; not quite as green. *Perhaps the errand did do him some good.*

"Partridge, give us an update." Jorgenson ordered before saying to Kramer, Macon, and Hodges, "Let's turn him."

Lieutenant JG Kramer and Jorgensen shifted their positions. Lieutenant Commander Hodges manned Orton's feet. As Jorgenson, Macon, Kramer, and Hodges positioned themselves for the body flip; the Ensign relayed the ship's course and the heading correction activities the OOD and helmsman were making to minimize the ships rocking. The men gently flipped Orton over. The panic in Orton's breathing was gone now. He moved his lips. Jorgenson leaned in closer. He distinctly heard the dying man say something other than "uhh," breathe, "ohh," breathe.

"He...pa... ph..." a breath. "Whisp...per..." breathe.

"He's trying to tell us something," Jorgenson said impatiently. Macon frowned. "He can't breathe without help. Kramer, take this."

Macon stifled Orton's mumbling with an aspirator and gave Kramer instructions for squeezing the bulb. The Chief corpsman started checking vitals.

Jorgenson inhaled deeply and glanced around; the place smelled rusty. Thick air hung around them—thick enough to leave what the captain believed to be a metallic taste on his tongue.

Jorgenson placed his ear next to Orton's face and reluctantly moved the breathing cup covering the nose and mouth. His shallow, breathless voice cut through his fading inhales and exhales. "He...was...m-my man..., Captain."

"Who did this, Bruce?"

"He...was... my...ma-an..."

"Talk to me, Bruce."

"He...was...my...man...the...last...w-wal-ltz..."

Orton said no more.

"Bruce?" Jorgenson beckoned as Orton's blank eyes glistened.

"Bruce!" *This can't be happening.*

A far off voice said, "No pulse." *The last waltz?* There were other shouts, but these quieted in his mind. *What could Orton mean by the last waltz?* The corpsman compressed up and down on Orton's chest. Kramer had replaced the mouthpiece and he squeezed and released the aspirator bulb.

Nothing can go wrong.

"Damn it, Bruce!" Hodges let out a faint cry. From the corner of his eye, Jorgenson saw Hodges plop down on the floor, lean against the bulkhead of the ship, while shaking violently. It seemed that Hodges' spirit had left with Orton's, leaving behind nothing more than a shell of a man in that dark passageway.

Not ever.

CHAPTER 13

A disturbance drew his attention away from her eyes. Loud sounds blasted in his ears, ending the sweet dream. An alert, accompanied by bright light, filtered through the royal blue curtains that divided his bed from the outside world. Tyler's rack, a rectangular box bordered by the ship's hull on one side and a wall of blue cotton on the other, was a sanctuary and he refused to open his eyes. He would not let go of this dream for a second time. Tyler turned his back to the opening. He slung his left arm over a warm lagging-covered pipe, which was part of a nest of pipes that ran parallel to his rack. An anchor for rough seas, the steam supply to the forward part of the vessel kept him from catapulting into the walkway.

The 1MC announcement was unrelenting. Tyler flipped over. His body got wedged between his bed and the rack above. He winced as a pain shot through his shoulders.

Jolted awake, he managed to shift around onto his belly and slide back the curtain, letting a flood of white light fill his eyes. He could see chaotic disorder at the aft, open end of the compartment.

Sleeping in the R-Division berthing compartment was a challenge with the normal clatter of those coming and going. Although his bed resided only two racks and a set of standup lockers distance from the open area, he usually avoided being startled awake by staying in the extreme forward part of the compartment. His rack was a prime piece of real estate because it was much quieter tucked in the corner away from Electrical Central and the General Workshop. The upheaval of the waking sailors was puzzling; what is this?

The ships rolling and surging seemed heightened as sailors careened like pinballs between the tight-spaced racks. HT1 Bastille walked towards him, pulled rack curtains open and shook men by the shoulders while yelling, "Wake up—let's go—its Reveille—get up."

Tyler, his head sticking out, made eye contact. The HT1 pointed at him and said, "Get up." Something in Bastille's voice was alarming; the tone was off and he barked each of his words.

Fireman Persinski climbed down from the top rails; Tyler only avoided a kick in the skull by retracting his head underneath the protective middle bunk. *The dangers of bottom rack dwellers.* Berthing compartments layouts maximize the usable space in the ship. In R-Division, the rack layout accommodated twenty-one: six on the starboard bulkhead, three on the port, and two rows of six back to back in the center along with two walkways between the bulkhead and center group. The row against the port side was shorter because it butted against Electrical Central's entrance.

The 1MC speaker screamed, "Reveille! Reveille! Reveille! All hands heave out and trice up!"

Across the aisle, a shipmate popped his face out of his cubicle curtain. He squinted and ran a hand over his dark face, looking just as annoyed as Tyler felt.

"What's going on?" Tyler asked his bunkmate EM3 Remy Wilkette who rubbed sleep from his eyes.

"Huh?"

"What's going on?" Tyler inquired again, louder; the movement of men increased the general din of the room.

"I don't know," Wilkette said.

Tyler whipped his curtains all the way open and Wilkette rolled onto his back, allowing Tyler to swing out first. All sailors that share close quarters together performed this dance. A person in one of the two face-to-face racks would let the other guy out first. There was not enough room for both to stand in the limited space. While Wilkette waited, Tyler swung out, grabbed the shirt and pants from the foot of his rack, lifted the locker lid to pull out a clean pair of socks, dropped the cover without bothering to engage the lock, reached for his black Boon-Dockers, and stepped aside so that his bunkmate could rise up.

Tyler and Wilkette both hurried to get dressed, although the rocking of the ship made not bumping each other impossible while doing so. "This better be good," Wilkette huffed, still half asleep.

"Wake up, asshole," Tyler said, "You're leaning on me."

"Huh?"

Tyler put a hand on the EM3's shoulder and pushed an arms distance between them. "It's not me; it's the ship," Wilkette said defending his staggering.

Once they were both dressed they walked the twenty feet to the gathering area. The ship made loud creaking noises as they entered the large room that made up the General Workshop, passing by the entryway to Electrical Central where a few other men were gathered. Once inside, Wilkette and Tyler went their separate ways; Tyler found HT2 Smithe while Wilkette disappeared amongst the small crowd of R-Division boys. Tyler spotted HT2 Ramirez awkwardly standing off in a corner. *What the hell is he doing here*? Ramirez was supposed to be on watch, but for whatever reason he stood in the General Workshop. *Who is on Sounding and Security patrol then?*

Smithe's eyes drooped, "It's hard enough to get sleep with the ship rocking like this—what'd they get us up for?"

"I think I heard something over the 1MC speaker earlier: a call for HMC Macon," Tyler said releasing a yawn; he had been trying to hold in.

"Damn," Smithe said, "you think someone's hurt?"

"Don't know... could be, in this weather." Tyler scanned the room in hopes of catching wind of anything unusual.

Tyler whispered to Smithe, "What's Hector doing down here? He should be on patrol."

Smithe only shrugged.

They were all told to gather in the General Workshop so the LPO's could take muster. Tyler tried to piece together what was happening. HT1 Bastille and EM1 Dunham took roll call as if they were expecting someone to be missing. From Tyler's quick scan of the room, all R-Division personnel seemed to be present. Tyler leaned into Smithe and said, "Why are they counting heads?" A storage rack, filled with scrap metal, rattled loudly against the bulkhead, and Bastille about jumped out of his skin. Dunham seemed equally unsettled.

"You think someone fell overboard?" Smithe suggested. Tyler doubted it; the distinct 'man overboard' alert would have sounded. The alarmed faces of the R-Division Leading Petty Officers Bastille and Dunham accompanied by their unusual behaviors suggested something much more ominous.

Both Petty Officers presumably retreated to Electrical Central to report that all R-Division personnel were present. Soon the two LPO's were back ordering everyone to remain within the General Workshop, R-Division berthing, and Electrical Central until further notice. Everyone was confused.

"I gotta go piss," said EM3 Postino. Dunham shook his head, unyielding, and announced to the entire group, "Sit tight. No one leaves this space."

A sinking feeling settled in the pit of Tyler's stomach as he and the others impatiently awaited news. After three minutes of unbearable silence, Tyler eyed Smithe. They were both thinking the same thing. "Squawk box?" He seemed to be asking Tyler for permission.

Tyler nodded in agreement, "Squawk box."

CHAPTER 14

Bruce Orton was dead.

Jorgenson laid a bloodstained washcloth on the counter by the sink in his stateroom head. His anxiety was building. The officers were gathering in the Wardroom. He needed another clean towel to finish wiping away the last of Orton's blood. His stomach churned, not out of disgust, but out of pure fury. He felt a sense of defeat and hated it. His tainted clothes lay in a corner on the floor as he wiped the last of the drying blood from his arms and face.

Behind him, the door to his stateroom opened and Lieutenant Commander Paul Kendall, the Executive Officer, approached.

"The departments are starting to report in; we should have a count in the next few minutes."

They had given the order for reveille, and a muster by berthing compartment and watch station. As far as he could tell, in the immediate minutes after they had tried and failed to save Orton, all of the officers were accounted for, and none of them were suspected of being anywhere near the port deck passage. On Jorgenson's orders, Kendall had personally went to each officer, either in their stateroom or at their watch-station, to call them to the Wardroom.

"Thanks, Paul."

Now for the enlisted. They needed to determine who was not in their rack or not at their watch station, ASAP.

"I'll let you know when all of the staff are present." Kendall turned and left the captain's stateroom.

In the wardrobe, he found clean uniform pants and a shirt pressed and ready. After dressing, he drifted over to the shrine of Dorie Miller. He surveyed the former naval hero in the old black and white photographs on the bulkhead; each of the photos was of the naval cook in one pose or another. Eventually his eyes fixed on the one of Admiral Nimitz pinning the Navy Cross on Miller's white uniform. That event took place on the USS Enterprise. Jorgenson had studied these pictures many times before; he practically heard the words issuing from Nimitz's mouth:

For distinguished devotion to duty, extraordinary courage and disregard for his own personal safety during the attack on the Fleet in Pearl Harbor, Territory of Hawaii, by Japanese forces on December 7, 1941. While at the side of his Captain on the bridge, Miller, despite enemy strafing and bombing and in the face of a serious fire, assisted in moving his Captain, who had been mortally wounded, to a place of greater safety, and later manned and operated a machine gun directed at enemy Japanese attacking aircraft until ordered to leave the bridge.

Nimitz's brief speech faded away in Jorgenson's mind. He recalled a quote by Nimitz that Emma had read him shortly after learning he would be commanding the USS Miller, "this marks the first time in this conflict that such high tribute has been made in the Pacific Fleet to a member of his race, and I'm sure that the future will see others similarly honored for brave acts." Jorgenson understood the history; his ship, the USS Miller, a vessel named in honor of this war hero.

This war hero, thought Jorgenson, who up until the Pearl Harbor attacks had never been allowed to touch a damn gun because of the color of his skin—but when push came to shove—Miller's white navy brothers didn't give a shit. The aircrafts were firing down on them so skin color did not matter so long as he fired that gun he was not allowed by law to touch. So long as he was strong enough to carry their dying captain. So long as he acted like the hero that he was, his white brothers *didn't give a shit* that a black man was firing the gun.

Jorgenson turned away from the photographs. He had worked damn hard to get to his current rank, but he knew men like Miller made it possible for Jorgenson to be standing where he was today. Now something had gone wrong, terribly wrong, and Jorgenson felt as if he had let Miller down. *We're trained to fight enemies we know are out there—not mad men hiding among us.* Who had murdered one of his own? *Nothing can go wrong. Not ever.*

"All officers are awake and waiting in the Wardroom, sir," The XO poked his head into the room and volunteered the update. Jorgenson simply nodded. Kendall disappeared behind the doorway.

Jorgenson replayed the dead man's last minutes in his head. The image of Orton during his final moments remained transfixed in his mind's eye, much like the gruesome memories he had of an assignment during the 83' barracks bombing in Lebanon.

Dispatched to the port of Beirut to evacuate wounded and dead to the carrier USS Nimitz, offshore, Jorgenson had spent twenty-four hours traveling with the dead. Wrapped in neat body blankets, those dead faces were zipped away from sight, not gripping at his arms, gasping and crying to live. Orton died in his arms; Jorgenson would now live with that fact forever, an indelible memory.

The captain put his hands to his head and face, massaging the eye sockets and temples and started out of his stateroom.

Moments later, Jorgenson found himself in the Wardroom at last, standing before his fourteen surviving staff officers, all with extremely anxious expressions on their young faces.

"Lieutenant Bruce Orton is dead." As he delivered the information, he observed their reactions. It was news to no one. A few may have been skeptical of the rumors they'd been told, but now that the captain was confirming the tragic news, their faces showed their collective acceptance of it as fact. The corpsman had worked fast to pack Orton's body in a bag and cart it off with the help of two boatswains mates, so he was certain no one glimpsed the corpse. The triage team went to clean up and some of them shared staterooms with others.

Lieutenant JG Kramer sat at the table with his head down. He picked at the tablecloth. He had cleaned up and donned a fresh khaki top. *Kramer showed real initiative helping with the triage,* Jorgenson thought and a brief warmth rushed through his chest. He made a mental note to thank the young JG. Like Jorgenson, Kramer was a rarity. There was a shortage of African American officers in the Navy.

"It wasn't an accident. He was attacked by one of the crew."

The still dazed Lieutenant Commander Hodges wedged himself into the corner of a black sofa against the aft bulkhead.

"We don't know who's responsible."

Jorgenson made an effort to continue but held his voice back; a void of air filled his chest and a sudden quiver arose that made his throat and jaw tremble. An opaque Bruce Orton peered up at him, desperately trying to breathe. He beheld the perplexed faces through this vision. They wanted answers that he did not have the ability to deliver now.

Lieutenant Commander Kendall stepped to the edge of the table and said, "The attacker is somewhere on this ship."

Jorgenson got hold of his voice again and said, "Yes. The XO is correct. We think he may be hiding somewhere, or he could be in his berthing compartment or somewhere at a watch station."

As if the ship herself decided to add more suspense to the dreadful news, a sudden shake threatened to topple the room. Jorgenson gripped the table edge to keep an upright posture and everyone swayed left to right.

"Sir," said Lieutenant Gary Niedermeyer, "What is the plan to apprehend him?" Niedermeyer was the most senior of the staff officers—yet he only had little more than three years' experience out of the Naval Academy. They were all so young. So very green.

Jorgenson said, "We do not know who did this Mister Niedermeyer. We are having the leading Petty Officers take muster."

"But, I thought Mister Watford saw somebody." Niedermeyer turned to face Watford who sat quietly with his head slung low at the end of the table. "Didn't you, Charlie?"

"I ah…" Watford started to speak until Jorgenson cut him off.

"What Mister Watford saw is for my ears only and no one else's… this information must be kept in strict confidence and delivered to the NIS."

The room shuffled. Jorgenson did not want anyone privy to what may possibly be vital information. Niedermeyer was Watford's department head; he must have pried some information out of his young ensign while the group had been gathering in the Wardroom.

"I want to be absolutely clear… and this goes especially for the department heads." Jorgenson began as Niedermeyer squirmed—his baldhead turned rosy. "This is not a drill. We're not playing war games here. We have a crew member—one of our shipmates who, for whatever the reason, attacked and killed a fellow shipmate."

Niedermeyer, along with several others, let out an audible sigh that caught Jorgenson by surprise. "Do you have something to say Mister Niedermeyer?"

Niedermeyer held his tongue, but folded his arms in protest and donned a disgusted face; however, Lieutenant Esposito seemed obliged to declare what their reactions stemmed from. "Captain, you just said one of the crew killed a fellow shipmate. The enlisted do not think of us officers as fellow shipmates."

"What do you mean?"

"We are, the officers, are not liked by this crew of enlisted."

Lieutenant JG George Springer stood up from the same sofa where Hodges sat. "Mister Esposito is right, sir. There have been several incidents with enlisted men treating officers badly." Springer's thick glasses magnified a set of horror filled bulging orbs.

The XO cutoff Springer and said, "You're being paranoid, George."

"Paranoid? Orton was stabbed to death!" shouted Niedermeyer.

This set off a barrage of comments, mostly disagreeing with the XO. Several sidebar discussions erupted, and the room all of a sudden was a clamor of raised voices and arguing points of view. Jorgensen listened to the points being made and commented on a few; but he quickly realized that allowing the chaos of hearsay and innuendo against the enlisted cadre did not serve them well.

"That's enough!" Jorgenson raised his voice to get back control of the conversation, "That's enough! We are not going to turn this into an officer versus enlisted crusade. We have no idea what really happened, but as far as all of you are concerned, the enlisted crew are our enemies?"

"They are the enemy!" shouted Esposito.

This angered Jorgenson.

"That comment is out of line! Mister Esposito, where were you when Lieutenant Orton was attacked?"

Esposito stammered. "Wha... what... do you mean?

"I'm asking where you were at the time of the attack."

"I... was in CIC ... on watch."

"Did you leave CIC at any time?"

Esposito was not certain how to answer; he looked around to his fellow officers for help. No one had anything to add, each was busy internalizing and formulating hi own response to the obvious question. "I ah... no... I didn't leave."

"No?" spat the angry captain. "You didn't leave to take a piss, or get a cup of coffee, or anything? Were there witnesses who can confirm you were there for the entire watch? How do I know it wasn't you?"

Jorgenson had not shared that he and Kendall believed none of the officers were to blame based on Watford's information, but he wanted to make a point. The whole room squirmed. The two men on either side of Esposito avoided eye contact with the now shaking Operations Department Head. Several others fought to keep their composure and breathed through stifled sobs.

"Captain Jorgenson?" Hodges eerie translucent tone cut through the room. Heads turned towards the shaky man.

"Yes, Mister Hodges?"

In a stuttered voice that shook along with his hands, he said, "Captain... the man who did this... do you think... I mean... am I a target because I wear khakis?"

"No," came the voice of Paul Kendall, "Someone just lost it."

"You don't know that," Niedermeyer argued back at the XO.

"We are in this together," Jorgenson said in a stern voice. "Everyone; this officer staff and all of the enlisted men, who are not to blame. Now, I don't believe it was anyone in this room." He looked around at the relief creeping onto some of their faces, "But that doesn't mean we are not all suspects—the NIS will ask us all the same questions I just did to Esposito. Whatever you think of the enlisted men, there are one-hundred and sixty-two men on this ship... a hundred sixty-one of them are not a murderer. Remember that."

Damn whoever did this!

"I have already spoken to Surf-Lant Command. There will be a follow up communication with the Naval Investigative Service as soon as possible. In the meantime..."

"What about the enlisted, Sir?" Lieutenant JG Kramer said, wide eyed and distressed.

"What about them, Mister Kramer?"

"Some of them, I mean those who may be in the same compartment with the killer, will be in danger."

"I agree with the XO," Jorgenson lied, "I don't believe anyone is in immediate danger." Although Jorgenson was not as sure as Kendall was, about someone *just losing it*, the likelihood of a maniac on a killing spree was slim. *Right?*

"We've not gotten reports from other locations around the ship about any other incidents," Jorgenson turned to Kendall to confirm, and the XO nodded.

"Not yet," blurted Niedermeyer.

Jorgenson could not disagree with him, so only added, "Be careful." He did not want to give anyone a false sense of security just in case. "This looks to be an isolated event; however, for the time being, no one is to be roaming this ship alone."

He turned to the Executive Officer, "Provided all crew are accounted for, which I expect, all men, unless on watch, stays where they are right now. No one leaves his berthing compartment. I will make an announcement over the 1MC system to notify the rest of the crew about what has happened."

"What if all the men are accounted for, sir?"

Jorgenson shook his head. The moment became instantly and absolutely surreal; nothing had prepared him... for this. Jorgenson drew in a deep breath and said, "We are on lockdown."

CHAPTER 15

Tyler glanced around the General Workshop, trying to get a sense of what measly activities each of the R-Division guys were doing in attempts to self-entertain while they awaited news. At the end of the workbench, EM1 Roger Dunham gripped the metal edge for support. He and HT1 Anthony Bastille, the division's leading Petty Officers, had gotten everyone out of their racks, but had not yet told anyone why— *just get up, that's an order from the bridge.* Several rumors were circulating through the workshop; Bastille and Dunham, keeping quiet, refused to deny or confirm any of the wild ideas spreading about— including the possibility of a real confrontation with enemy submarines versus the war games, they had been engaged in for the better part of a year.

"Hector," Tyler said, "who told you to come down here?"

Ramirez, the current Sounding and Security patrol, was the only man fully dressed, ball cap and all. He held the clipboard and the watch belt wrapped securely around his thin waist. He never handled rough seas well; tonight was no exception. "I was on the bridge and the OOD told me to go to my berthing compartment." The ship tossed and continued the violent bursts as sounds of rattling steal filled the room. "That's all I know." Ramirez sank into a seated position in front of the storage shelves.

Several guys slumped beside bulkheads and bench cabinets as the surging and receding ship pushed them forward and aft like swaying wheat grass—most tried keeping their eyes from clamping shut while waiting for the LPO's to say something noteworthy. A few chatted away the minutes in desperate efforts to keep awake; HT3 Ray Swartz and EM2 Donnie Hart hid nearby the berthing open area; they were told to "stay out of your racks" for some reason. Those two had been the most agitated that their personal space was off limits since the reveille announcement.

Tyler settled into the workshop next to the joiner door eager to listen in on the squawk box communications from Electrical Central. EM3 Kirk Postino and HT3 Tommy Scheppler were the messengers, playing tag with the squawk box, or as Tyler called it, the *gossip box,* as home base. Many revelations of embarrassing stories had passed over the gossip box. The system can easily be misused and sensitive information will sometimes escape. Tyler recalled a day several months earlier when whispers of a scheme to douse MM2 "Thumper" O'Brien had been unintentionally divulged. The guys in Main Control were going to drench the moron with a sound tube full of water. Thumper was a slacker whom everyone detested—even with the rumor outed, O'Brien never caught wind and the plan went without a hitch—he got drenched with gallons of water on the lower level of the Engine Room. Tyler yawned and smiled at the memory of the fuming idiot storming up the ladder into Main Control dripping wet.

EM3 Remy Wilkette sat leaning alongside the corner of a desk and bulkhead, eyes shut with sleep or meditation; Tyler could not discern which. Wilkette rubbed his temples every other roll as though his head ached—stormy seas aside, waking up from precious sleep time on a Navy ship was a cause for severe irritation; everyone's head felt like it was exploding by now. Close by Tyler lounged HT2 Levon Smithe.

Smithe and Tyler were inseparable. Smithe was from Billings, Montana. At six foot, Smithe stood two inches taller than Tyler did. In Tyler's world, Smithe was a man's man, an elk hunter. Tyler grew up in the city—his idea of open space was a parking lot. Smithe was the perfect sidekick; he didn't say much and always wore a smile, but when you needed backup, his size and broad shoulders provided all the needed detraction against any troublemakers.

HTFA Persinski stood opposite with eyes teetering between half and all the way closed; against the bulkhead with his head down, gripping the horizontal I-beam that ran the length of the wall, his body listed forward with every pitch of the room. Persinski had gotten himself a bad sunburn in Bermuda and was carefully keeping his back and shoulders from touching the bulkhead. His bright pink arms and painful-looking round red face contrasted against his thin orange-red hair. He was exposed for a only a few hours; the others all had received a nice shading of tan. Even the black guys, Hart and Wilkette; and Ramirez, the only Hispanic guy—but he looked African American—had all receive some nice sun. Hart had told the group that his natural tanned skin received a darkening each time the Miller crew had liberty in Bermuda. Tyler silently laughed at Persinski who winced with each tilt of the room.

The LPO's kept glancing at each other as if waiting for something to happen. Bastille moved to the garbage pail. He pulled the aluminum container—as far as a chain attached to the workbench leg would allow—to almost the center of the space and placed a length of cardboard as a makeshift table atop the can. Tyler caught Bastille's nod to Dunham for the other LPO to join an impromptu card game.

"How 'bout a game of hearts? Huh? Anyone?" Dunham said nervously tracing an outline of his mustache with a thumb and forefinger.

Tyler had no urge to play games. Based on the less than enthusiastic reactions from the rest of the men lounging around, neither did anyone else.

As the two secret keepers cut cards and held the makeshift table from toppling over, Tyler wondered if they would break their silence soon. Bastille jostled the deck, pretending to shuffle; his lack of concentration revealed itself as a smattering of spades and diamonds dropped to the floor on a deep roll to starboard. Bastille bent over nonchalantly, and the LPO's hands were clearly trembling.

Postino and Scheppler displayed the most amount of energy in R-Division, walking back and forth between Electrical Central and the General Workshop an uncountable number of times. The lack of any real news drove Postino to join Bastille and Dunham, and they managed to awaken Wilkette to make four. A game of hearts ensued.

Beside the door, Tyler re-tucked himself into a crook against the bulkhead, hoping to nod off. Postino and Scheppler's last update had been almost ten minutes earlier, before the game of hearts had begun in earnest. Scheppler continued the vigil, and reported some brief dialog from Aux 1, which turned out to be nothing new—the *stay in your berthing spaces* order came again across the receiver.

Then another static filled garble sounded from the squawk box in the adjacent compartment.

Tyler tensed; at last, Scheppler sprang out of Electrical Central and turned right into the General workshop doorway, "someone's dead," he said. Tyler caught Bastille and Dunham's reactions; they each made efforts to focus on their cards. When Dunham said, "I bid five." Tyler took that comment as confirmation of the LPO's knowledge of Scheppler's claim.

The entire General Workshop woke up. Hart and Swartz bolted in from the rack area behind Scheppler. "What do you mean someone's dead? What happened?"

"That's all I got... someone's dead."

Postino jumped out of his chair and slammed his hand of cards to the corrugated table, "I quit." He and Scheppler disappeared back into Electrical Central; neither Bastille nor Dunham tried to deter them from continuing their quest for information.

Faint shouting came through the electric static, "Get off the squawk box, Scheppler! You too, Postino!"

The men ignored the half-hearted decree. They were not going to follow that order. Swartz joined the listening party.

"Ain't nobody dead," Persinski huffed.

Tyler spoke up, his voice loud enough for all to listen, "This storm has been pretty nasty. I about face-planted off a ladder."

"You think some fool broke his neck because of bad weather?" Hart asked.

"Maybe," Tyler said.

Swartz's head popped in, "An officer's been killed!" His southern twang made the comment sound like, "An off-sirs bin kilt."

"Holy shit," said Persinski.

"They said *killed*? Or *dead*?" Smithe wanted clarity.

Ramirez added, "Only officers awake are them ones coming on or off watch."

"But why count heads?" Tyler asked.

Bastille did not offer to answer any of the questions.

"Get off the squawk box!" a distant sizzle came from Electrical Central, "Or I'll come down there and make you get off!"

Everyone looked up at Swartz who returned from the other room. "Kilt."

Persinski let out a loud laugh. "You're full of shit, Swartz. You make it sound like a freakin' murder."

"Kilt," Swartz repeated, "That's all they said."

"Which officer?"

Swartz only shrugged and disappeared again, returning to the gossip box.

"Nobody's been murdered, man." Persinski insisted, "It's just gossip."

"Something ain't right, though," Smithe said.

A bewildered mood settled over the room as the external torrent continued shredding the ship. Tyler sat silent.

A few theories about the potential for an attack came up. Persinski seemed convinced that the rumors were nothing but *bullshit*. Tyler did not believe so; sounding reveille, his dream about HMC Macon double-timing it to officer's country—*was that a dream?*

Certain details began adding up in his mind.

Murder? No way, thought Tyler—killing anyone was just nutty. *Who would believe...?* Then Tyler recalled his last words during the Sounding and Security patrol turnover. *Fuck.*

Tyler sank back while the other men prattled on about whatever had them all awake in the General Workshop during their appointed time to sleep. A distant hissing rang from inside the other room once again as the men conversed.

"Damn it, Swartz! Get off the squawk box!"

CHAPTER 16

A popping crack and then buzzing leaked from the 1MC speaker. Everyone stopped talking and listened for the imminent announcement. Whoever flipped the 'on' switch was quite close to the microphone on the other end. After a few nasally breaths, a voice broke the eerie stillness that had set in over the General Workshop.

"Let me have your attention, please," the words came out in an uneven pitch and laced with sorrow. There was a long pause; did Commander Jorgenson know his breathing was audible through the speakers? The captain cleared his throat, "Let me have your attention. There has been a horrible incident on board this fine ship. The incident took place a little over an hour ago. Our shipmate and friend, Lieutenant Bruce Orton, is dead."

"Holy Shit!" squeaked Fireman Persinski. He glanced at Swartz, "I didn't believe you." Swartz and several others immediately began sycophantically voicing theories about Orton's demise. Jorgenson continued over the loudspeaker, but his words were inaudible because of the chatter in the room.

"Shut the fuck up," said Bastille. Dunham and Bastille took anchored positions in front of the doorway; both listened as the captain continued.

"...as soon as the engineering team can get the second boiler fired up. That will get us back to Newport as soon as possible."

"We're going home," someone to Tyler's right, whispered, but Tyler remained too focused to glance over and determine who was speaking to him.

The captain spoke for several minutes describing logistics for movement around the ship and realigning duty stations. Jorgenson did not say whether Orton was murdered as the rumors on the squawk box had suggested. "How the fuck did he die?" Scheppler said, asking the question everyone wanted to hear answered.

*****

His voice quivered; Jorgenson let the last of his dread slip away as the prepared words came; a stiff grip on the microphone button made his fingers ache at the knuckles.

"There is someone on this ship who needs to think very carefully about the next few hours." He inhaled a deep breath as the men on the bridge listened. Hodges, finally cleaned up, hugged the doorjamb. The man looked sick, hung-over, with one foot on the bridge and the other ready to make an escape to the head. If he needed to vomit, Jorgenson wished he would just do it. Even so, Jorgenson appreciated the moral support. Several others remained on the bridge as well; Kendall, Anderson, and Kramer were present as their captain delivered the devastating news to the enlisted crew.

"There is plenty of time for us all to calm down. Although the ship is steaming for home, we are in no rush."

The XO nodded, assuring Jorgenson his tone was just right. "For you," he continued, "the best thing to do is relax and know that we will be ready when you are." Jorgenson paused as several crazy thoughts screamed through his forehead. *This is a bad idea. We cannot be certain that the crew is safe.*

"I know you're angry, but your best option is to turn yourself in." Jorgenson paused hoping the sound of his voice reassured the assailant that his intentions were true. "Talk to your superior officer; it will be best for you and your shipmates."

*****

"Oh dang," HT3 Swartz said.

Persinski finished Swartz's sentence, "They don't know who did it."

This is a public revelation Tyler did not see coming. Why would the captain announce to the entire crew the fact that a killer is on the loose? Everyone in the workshop seemed to be holding their collective breaths, and eyes wondered from each to the other. Scheppler turned his gaze to Tyler. Tyler could read the message in Scheppler's eyes. *Shit*, Tyler immediately felt regret about his public verbal bashing of Orton the night before.

"Calm down. It's probably one of the M&B guys," said HT1 Bastille. The normally laid back Bastille wore a bright pink face—not from a sunburn—no, his blood pressure had peaked. His attempt to calm the group fell short—although Bastille's comment gave Tyler a sense of hope—at least Orton had other enemies besides him.

Orton the MPA was the officer in charge of all machinery and boiler departments; *they must believe the killer is one of Orton's own people—who else would take him out?* Those BT's and MM's hated Orton; *hell, they hate him more than I do.* This thought didn't help Tyler feel better. His stomach churned.

The captain had said, "Just turn yourself in." *Why would the killer do that?* Tyler wouldn't. Around the room, everyone listened as the 1MC squawked to life again.

"I would like to lead us all in the Lord's Prayer," said Jorgenson, "Our Father, who are in Heaven hallowed be thy name..."

Mouthing the familiar prose, Tyler's heart ached and a sudden regret surfaced from the prayer words. His hands trembled, shivers rolled up his back. *What is the killer doing right now, praying along with the Captain?* The eleven men in R-Division all had their heads down at least. What about the other divisions? Tyler glanced around the room, spying on those joining or ignoring the prayer. Smithe wrapped himself in a distant trance with his lips mouthing the words. HT1 Bastille, hands clamped behind his back with eyes conveniently hidden behind welder's shades, spoke loudly, as his bright rosy cheeks billowed. Postino and Wilkette were sitting in front of the workbench, knees and chins to their chests; they kept their eyes closed. Persinski and Scheppler awkwardly joined the prayer. The rest, Tyler supposed, were in their own way praying. Hart, Ramirez, Dunham, and Swartz all remained silent.

*****

On the bridge, the crew held onto the nearest solid surface to offset the undulating vessel as Jorgenson uttered the final words, "And deliver us from evil." He held, not letting off the microphone button an extended moment in time, and then he said, "Amen;" slowly, he released the switch.

Hard plastic clicked with finality. The silence, save the splashing wind slapping at bridge windows, was deafening. His eyes traced a path from one man to the next, soaking in their fear and confusion. Their frightened faces foretold a story and he comprehended their uncertainty. This day would test all their mettle, but his mostly. Anxiety sank in as several tired and sea-beaten men all examined him, their captain. The command of the ship and his leadership was unquestionably on trial. He returned the black microphone to its holding clasp. A steady deep roll to port and the helmsman held the wheel as tightly as he could. Officer of the Deck, Lieutenant Hornsby, leaned forward peering through the windows at the rising sunlight off the ships starboard bow. Quartermaster Moreno, who had stepped out of the chart house to join the prayer, saluted Jorgenson with tears streaming and said, "Thank you, sir."

The captain did not return Moreno's salute, but appreciated the gesture. He gazed through the water rivulets on the glass before him and formulated what to do next.

"Hornsby, are the Security Alert Teams ready?"

"Yes sir," came the reply.

"Paul," he turned to the XO, "I need you the do something, work with one of the division Chiefs—come with me to the Wardroom, I'll explain on the way. Ensign Watford is waiting." They both departed the bridge.

*****

Fools, all of them—especially him: the hypocrite captain who allowed the dead one's irresponsibility to reign. What do you think, oh commander on high? Do the nonentities think prayer will ease their hurt? This pain is your payment. Your prayer, oh great Captain ... means nothing. The sudden inspiration to look towards the speaker comes and goes.

No perfection in the deed, yet, however sloppy, my act is still a triumph.

Not safely done.

I understand.

The plan has changed.

However, my goals have not been derailed.

Reflecting on the act, it would have gone to plan if an invader had not shown up. I will need to discover who that was and dispatch him, this time without interruption. We will be in rough seas for a while. The time elapsed since my waltz is ninety-minutes. An hour and a half ago I rid this ship of its worst abuser. I will have more time to deal with other abusers if necessary. For the intruder on my dance, his eyes had not adjusted to the darkness enough to see who was in the killing zone with Orton. Otherwise, wouldn't they have me in chains by now?

They must know something.

They do not know me as a killer.

There is no rush to act; I remain concealed... for now. I will continue to count the elapsing time from when my dance occurred— the more time between then and now, the less I have to worry. If my concealment becomes exposed, I will act. I will deal with this provoker, this witless witness. He may be my biggest threat—the most defiant abuser alive, now. When we are able to roam the ship again, I will seek to know who this intruder is and deal with him.

You will only achieve our goals if you finalize the plan.

I must stay composed and ready.

Shout the words.

No... I will keep silent.

The compartment smells of nonentities all around. Their tears disgust me. The sycophant cowering across the room cry's for the Defiant One. This is good payment for you and the rest for not seeing the truth. I stay quiet, and my music fills my ears, calming me.

CHAPTER 17

The Hull Technicians and Electricians in R-Division were not going to take any chances; if some mad-killer approaching his next victim were to come near the workshop, they were prepared. In the moments following the prayer several guys hastily rummaged through the General Workshop searching for whatever items they could find that would suffice as a weapon. Tyler attempted to stay calm—at least on the outside—inside he was a wreck. Surely, the men who witnessed his verbal altercation with Orton the previous evening were assuming Tyler was the perpetrator. Chief Langston among them; he would be giving his report about the hotheaded HT2 Tyler West threatening to murder Lieutenant Orton to the brass first thing.

Once everyone was satisfied that they had whatever object necessary for protection, they all took positions around the room. Tyler had remained planted in the corner of the workbench and not moved for several minutes while his R-Division shipmates continued their yakking, each throwing around speculations and accusations—everyone seemed to have a theory, everyone except Scheppler.

Scheppler had found a short length steel pipe that he held onto with tight fists. He tried to avoid eye contact with Tyler, but as Tyler studied the younger HT3, he slowly allowed himself to be drawn into a few moments of silent interaction. *He suspects me—of course, he does.* Tyler wanted to say something to Scheppler, but all the talking ended when noises erupted just outside the workshop.

Metal clanking footsteps, not one, but several pairs of Boon-Dockers, rattled down the R-Division berthing ladder-way. *Are they here to take me down?* Tyler quickly turned to Ramirez who seemed as alarmed as he. Almost everyone stood in the berthing compartment now; the others stormed out of the General Workshop to meet with the rest of R-Division. Almost simultaneously, Tyler and Ramirez got to their feet. With hands ready in clinched-fist positions, for what he couldn't be certain—a fight perhaps? Chief Langston, followed by Lieutenant Commander Kendall and two armed Petty Officers stepped through the doorway. The Chief and his posse scanned the compartment. Ramirez gripped his blackjack firmly while Smithe, Scheppler, Hart, Wilkette, Persinski, and Postino all stood with makeshift pipe-weapons. For a split second, two gangs stood prepped for a tussle. The R-Division squad, *Sharks* of West Side Story armed with plumbing supplies... and the Jets, who'd arrived toting guns.

"What's with the pipes?" asked Chief Langston, noticing the excess number of guys sporting one.

"Just a little welding and brazing practice, Chief," Tyler said with a smile.

Tyler tried to break the tension and give the visitors a sense that he was *not nervous* by making a wisecrack. "What's up, Chief, Mister Kendall, you should never bring a gun to a knife... ah, I mean a pipe fight," he pointed at the security detail wearing holsters. Tyler's comments did not seem to resonate with any of their guests.

"West," the Chief said scanning the remainder of the berthing compartment and briefly peeking inside the General Workshop; he decided to let the comment slip away. "Where's Bastille?" Before Tyler answered, the HT1 creeped out of Electrical Central.

Bastille cleared his throat from behind the group and said, "Mister Kendall, Chief, we are ready for you." *What is Bastille ready for?* After a confusing momentary standoff, the HT1 brushed through the Sharks and said, "Okay, we're going to have our racks inspected."

"Great," said the Chief, "West, you're first."

Rack inspection? Tyler expected to be singled out—but not for a rack inspection. Tyler perceived the Chief's fear, *he believes I killed Orton,* of course, he is afraid. Tyler deliberately walked to his rack; Langston followed with Kendall, each maneuvered between the tightly spaced sleeping bunks. The two gunners held back near the exit. Mister Kendall asked permission to search which Tyler granted. Besides proving there would be nothing found, Tyler had little to lose—at least he hoped.

"What are you inspecting for Chief?" Tyler asked.

"We'll know if we find it, West."

The unlocked bunk laid flat on the deck—he had not thought to trice up earlier; Tyler simply lifted the piano-hinged lid. "I'll do the looking," said Langston and took the lid from Tyler's hold. The Chief closed the lid and ran his hands over and under the blanket and sheet; pulled the pillow from its case; and lifted and folded the mattress first at the foot, then the head. He lifted the rack to the trice position and the XO used a flashlight to scan under it. Once finished with the external, both Langston and Kendall spent several minutes rummaging through everything Tyler kept hidden in his rack. The process lasted longer than Tyler expected. When they finished Tyler's bunk, he wanted to communicate his innocence to the Chief, but the search continued. Tyler expected the Chief and XO to be relieved after searching Tyler's bunk and finding nothing. But, the inspectors checked HT1 Bastille's and Fireman Persinski's racks in turn, theirs being the two racks above Tyler's; it looked as if they planned on searching everybody. Persinski stood at the foot of the racks, Tyler at the head. Persinski didn't keep his rack locked either; his wasn't even closed. Bastille stayed at the head of the aisle. *Why are they continuing to go through everyone's stuff?* Tyler wasn't sure if the inspectors needed to continue beyond his rack, surely the only reason they came to R-Division was to confront him.

Half way through the top rack Tyler glanced at Smithe, whose rack was on the same row as theirs, just one stack of racks aft towards the compartment entrance. Smithe made wide motions with his eyes from Tyler to the place to be inspected next. *Shit. He has welding gear in there.* Tyler recalled seeing the new grounding clamp and tig torch that Smithe had *borrowed* back at the Annex. There had been a strict Navy policy of enforcement for supplies—dishonest sailors made extra cash by hording equipment, taking it off the ship and selling the gear. Smithe would be written up for having government property in his bunk.

"Wilkette, you're next." Langston said. Wilkette squeezed through the crowd as Tyler and he exchanged a quick glance. As Wilkette opened his lower rack, the Chief and XO bent low to perform the process on his stuff. The reverse facing searchers provided an opportunity to save Smithe from embarrassment. As the rummage began, Wilkette stuck his head next to Langston to see what they were doing, "you finding anything, Chief?"

Langston jumped and knocked the back of his head against the top of the rack lid. Between the sudden banging of his head and the abrupt bobbing movement of the ship, Langston lost his footing and, if Kendall didn't grab hold of his sleeve, would have fallen flat on his back. "Damn it, Wilkette. Back up!"

Smithe and Persinski shuffled their positions between the bunks at the same time as the Chief's mini-heart-attack; they effectively blocked the view of Smithe's rack from fore to aft. Smithe silently moved the illegal items from his rack to Tyler who placed them inside his own storage locker. "Sorry, Chief." Wilkette said.

With Langston and Kendall distracted, Tyler gave a subtle thumbs-up to Smithe, closed his rack lid, and said, "Chief, do you need to get back in here?"

"No." Langston snapped, "And you should lock your rack!"

"Will do." Tyler said, locking his rack, with Smithe's welding clamp, torch, and filler rods inside.

The Chief and XO continued to be overly deliberate going through people's things. The inspection continued down the back line of racks, searching even the empty bunks. The group of men spent almost two hours in the sleeping areas, but they didn't stop. They searched every inch of R-Division: the General Workshop and every nook and cranny of Electrical Central. They even checked around the ladder. The detail of searching and effort to leave no stone unturned gave Tyler an uneasy feeling—he wondered if they had searched M&B berthing this thoroughly.

When the inspection ended, Langston gave the order that no one leaves R-Division until further notice. At last the Jets left the General Workshop and gathered in the outside vestibule space leaving the men of R-Division in the workshop to discuss their numerous theories again.

Immediately the babbling about the inspections began. "Why are they wasting their time inspecting R-Division?" Swartz huffed, "we all know the guy was probably a psycho MM or BT."

"It could have been anyone."

"They must have suspects."

"Guarantee you they'll find whatever they're looking for over in M&B berthing."

"Hey, West," Tyler heard someone say from the group. It was Scheppler. Tyler waved for him to break away from the group to have a private discussion; Scheppler hesitated, and then cautiously joined Tyler.

Tyler said in a matter of fact tone, "What's going on? Seems like you've been staring at me all morning."

"No I haven't; you've been staring at me."

"I guess you're thinking about that little altercation with Orton last night in Main Control?"

Scheppler went to say something, but Tyler stopped him and said, "You don't have to worry Tommy—I didn't do anything wrong."

"Okay." Scheppler said. He started to pull away and turned for a last word, "I never said you did."

They gave each other an accepting nod, and Scheppler rejoined Wilkette, Persinski and Postino.

Tyler walked out to the berthing compartment, past the inspection team. He heard Bastille protesting to something. *What now?*

The Chief, XO, and R-Division LPO's, Bastille and Dunham, remained in the vestibule talking softly for several minutes; Tyler strained to listen, but only whispers crept through the din of the compartment. Smithe stepped out of the workshop and approached Tyler.

"Hey."

"Hey."

"What were you and Scheppler talking about?"

Smithe always got right to the point. It's what Tyler liked most about him, he never beat around the bush. Tyler let out a soft, nervous chuckle.

"Well," he said, ready to confide to his best friend, "You're not gonna believe this, but, I think I got myself into a little bind here."

"No, you? Never." Smithe said, laying on a thick layer of sarcasm to his words.

Tyler explained how he had blown up in Main Control the night before and what he'd said to Orton. Each statement relayed aloud made him cringe. Even though he had threatened the man, that didn't make him the killer, but for some reason, Tyler felt like he was confessing to something he didn't do. At least, after the rack inspection, he felt a little relief, but the uncertainty of what was to come next still hung over them.

"Did you kill him?" Smithe asked bluntly.

Tyler smiled, "What do you think?

Smithe made up his mind quickly and said, "Well you should have; he was an ass... especially to you. But, naw. I don't think you whacked him."

A noise came from Electrical Central. HT2 Ramirez popped his head out; he had been listening in on the squawk box. Ramirez's half-open mouth and bugged out eyes told Tyler something worth noting must have come from Main Control. He waved for Tyler to follow. Ramirez walked with Tyler in tow to the center of the group gathered in the shop, away from the vestibule and the inspection team and LPO huddle. "They have a witness."

A collective intake of air occurred. Ramirez continued, "He saw the guy who did it."

Everyone jolted; Tyler and several others were ready to learn which shipmate back in M&B berthing had committed the deed.

"Well?"

"What did the witness say?"

"Who did it?"

"He didn't see his face," Ramirez said, disappointing several.

"The guys in Main Control said the killer's got blonde hair."

While they were all certain the killer was probably one of those blondies in M&B, every head turned to Scheppler, Persinski, and Postino: the only fellows in R-Division with blonde hair. Persinski had a hint of orange on his blonde head; his light Albino-ish skin and thin wispy locks often were mistaken for strawberry-blonde, but the burned face and forehead gave his scalp a flushed orange glow. Postino's head color was more debatable; his having hints of red and brown; with his short military crop and freckled neck and face, the look made him more of a ginger; unlikely the witness would describe his hair as simply blonde, but Scheppler was another story. Scheppler's German-blonde hair was undeniable. His metal cool blue eyes peered out from deep-set sockets, as everyone looked straight at him. His blonde hair, cut short in a military style, always fluttered in air currents; he maintained ample tufts of golden locks that he combed from above his right ear to his left, and his light sandy colored eyebrows and blonde mustache characterized him specifically as a blonde.

Scheppler's long symmetrical face contorted into an angry sneer, and he barked at all of them, "Don't look at me." The men did not listen and only gaped more. The HT3 tried to raise a smile, but failed. "Fuck you guys!" His voice quivered. He turned and left the workshop to hide near his rack.

CHAPTER 18

Scheppler's outburst served to break up the gossip fest. Tyler made his way to the berthing area and crouched down at Smithe's rack. The other HT's and EM's dispersed—Tyler assumed each would be dealing with the similar thoughts floating through his head; blonde haired guy; murder; dead officer. Rack inspections complete and nothing found; *not surprising*, still convincing himself the killer to be a disgruntled machinist mate or boiler technician roaming about M&B berthing.

Chief Langston and XO Kendall, both of whom still stood huddled in the vestibule near the base of the ladder along with HT1 Bastille, continued their whisper fest. Tyler's eyes narrowed as he studied their faces; their suspicions led them to perform inspections of racks—*what does that mean?* Langston did most of the talking as his eyes jumped and darted from the XO to Bastille to the berthing space opening. From the hand gestures Kendall used, Tyler surmised the XO to be challenging the details on whatever Langston proposed—shaking his head a few times side to side in defiance. Bastille appeared crippled by the ordeal, swaying his torso with the rocking ship.

"What'd ya think they're talking about?" Smithe asked.

Tyler responded with a simple shrug as Bastille broke away from the other two. Langston and Kendall climbed out of R-Division, followed by only one of the armed security detail who had accompanied them; half the posse stayed behind. The ships disbursing clerk, DK1 Bryan Hendriks, loitered in the vestibule as if waiting for something or someone.

Tyler rose up as Bastille approached holding out the Sounding and Security clipboard and belt, which he had absconded from Ramirez.

"It's been hours since anyone's been on patrol," Bastille said, "we need to catch up; they want us all to pair up for the time being. You two get first watch."

"You're shitting me," Tyler groaned. Doubling up meant half the number of rotations, twice as much work and almost half the time off. The extra effort wasn't the main issue though. *Who killed Orton?* The psychopath might be anyone and the ship was in the middle of a hurricane. *Aren't they worried about that?*

"Langston and Kendall are waiting for you two, go." Bastille said and firmly added, "*Now.*"

The two men quickly grabbed a few articles from their racks to complete their uniforms; Tyler took his ball-cap and Smithe grabbed a belt. They walked towards the vestibule creeping past Hendriks who locked beady eyes with Tyler. They stepped up the ladder where Langston and Kendall were apparently waiting. When the HT's got to the top of the ladder and over the hatch knife edge, Tyler realized Hendriks was also making the ascent up the ladder behind Smithe. The plan, it appeared, was no armed guard down in the berthing area after all.

"Oh shit," Tyler said aloud.

"What?" said Smithe.

This is it. Tyler expected to have his wrists slapped in cuffs now that he stood outside the confines of R-Division, the memory of his threats towards Orton still vivid. Langston had been present during his outburst; he would lock Tyler in the brig just for the safety of the crew. Hendriks squeezed past Smithe and took up a spot forward a few steps away from the group. Then, no one approached Tyler with handcuffs.

Smithe stood waiting for an answer.

"Nothing," Tyler said.

"... there's also M&B," the XO called to the Chief as he joined the HT's. Langston sent the XO a thumbs-up. Whatever conversation the men had been having ended as Tyler and Smithe appeared.

"You haven't searched M&B berthing yet?" Tyler asked boldly as the ship lurched to starboard with a purpose. Orton's men were all in M&B; they hated Orton more than anyone else did. Tyler had hated working under Orton every day. The day Orton was transferred from DCA to MPA, Tyler was ecstatic. It was easily one of his best days on the Miller. There must be motive amongst M&B division.

As the Chief neared, Tyler spouted, "Chief, I didn't do it."

Langston shot a sideways glance at the XO and nodded his head in an apparent acceptance of Tyler's innocence. This was weird. *Why do they think I'm innocent?* Langston started moving his lips to speak, but no sound came. Something apparently clogged up the space between his vocal cords and tongue; he only managed a wispy cough. Slightly panicked, he tried for what seemed like a full minute to cough up the blockage in his windpipe. He finally managed a guttural "Ah-uhmph, ah-uhmph," as he cleared the blockage from his throat.

"We need your help," Langston said, disregarding the spittle. He spoke quickly and timidly, never breaking eye contact with Tyler, but this was obviously for Smithe's ears as well. The puffy-redness of his eyes told Tyler all he needed to know about how the past few hours had been for the Chief.

Langston had managed to get assigned Chief of both M&B division and R-Division due to the lack of E7's in the repair department. Langston worked for Orton and acted as surrogate Chief for the HT's, reporting to Lieutenant JG Springer as well. Despite the man's obvious anxiety, he still maintained a dignity in the way he spoke, even though the shakiness of his voice.

"There's a thousand hiding places on this ship. The bastard got him with a knife of some kind. We need you to find it."

"A knife?" Smithe said.

Langston's words put an end to the ridiculous rumors circling through the squawk box conversations about Orton having his face blown off by a pistol. Another rumor had his head bashed in by a spanner wrench. The Chief's eyes bounced from Tyler to Smithe for a moment, eventually returning his intense attention to Tyler, "the son of a bitch wore green coveralls, and they'll be covered in blood. I want you and Smithe to search the entire ship. You will have DK1 with you."

Tyler glanced over at DK1 Hendriks, who draped his right hand over the holster strapped to his thigh like a western gunslinger. "Why Hendriks?" If the Chief expected them to search quickly, Tyler only imagined Hendriks slowing them down. The administration department Petty Officer was not used to roaming the ship, especially in the current weather conditions. Even standing there, the older Hendriks battled to keep from tumbling over.

Tyler wanted to point out to the Chief that Hendriks was a useless dipshit who sat on his ass all day.

"You need an armed guard; Hendriks is certified, and we have issued him a sidearm."

The Navy often moved idiots up the chain of command—all you needed was an open billet spot, in your job specialty, ahead of you. Tyler and Smithe, the 2nd Class Petty Officers—E-5's—were smack dab in the middle of the food chain. There were as many ranks above them as there were below. Enlisted Navy ranks ascended through three stages of development—apprenticeship stage; E1, E2, E3; then Petty Officers—3rd class, 2nd class, 1st class; E4, E5, E6; then Chiefs—Chief, Senior-Chief, Master-Chief; E7, E8, E9. A Master-Chief was the highest rank Tyler could achieve, but reaching that pinnacle was, for him, a farfetched pipedream—especially when he considered all of the ass-kissing morons like Hendriks who were above him in rank. Now here he was standing beside them *holding a fucking gun.*

The Chief reached out and put his hand on Tyler's shoulder, "Go find those coveralls, West," his grip tightened, "and maybe you'll find some other clues while you're at it."

Tyler was certain Langston's confidence in him came from Tyler's reputation for knowing the ship better than most. He seemed to be insinuating that if anyone could find hidden coveralls, the best candidate would be Tyler. He agreed; Tyler knew every inch of the ship. *But, why doesn't he suspect me?*

Langston continued, "We are on lockdown, West. No one comes or goes without an escort from here on out. And it doesn't look like that will be changing anytime soon. You need to find the coveralls, and find them fast. Your crew-mates down there are in danger."

Tyler was suspicious. Langston added, "We *all* are... until we find out who did this."

Lockdown? Why put us on lockdown? Tyler silently questioned, *why not just round up anyone who owns green coveralls. Only so many pairs get issued to people...* Tyler glanced from the Chief to Mister Kendall to the other gunner's mate from the Jets who had taken a position at the port bulkhead, which allowed him to see all movement in three directions; forward, aft, and athrwartships, sideways through the Damage Control Central passageway from the port to starboard hull-stringers. The realization of a lockdown hit Tyler right between the eyes. Nobody could move without one of these guards seeing you.

Langston removed his hand from Tyler's shoulder. "We'll start our search in the main spaces," Tyler said, "Whoever killed Orton would..."

"No." Langston said, cutting Tyler short, "That's not necessary. Start aft and work your way up one side and down another."

The Chief said the guys in each main space were already given the same instructions and a recheck would not be needed. *Why would you ask a BT or MM?* Langston didn't show much conviction in what sounded like feeble excuses to skip the main spaces. Tyler started to disagree; he wanted to search where Orton worked. The Chief seemed exceptionally confident in his plan. Tyler decided not to argue.

"All right, Chief, whatever you say."

Langston eyed them both, "Smithe, West, if you find 'em it'll give us clues to whoever did this."

"We're on it, Chief."

Mister Kendall had positioned himself adjacent to the forward second deck security guard and was silently beckoning the Chief to follow him. Hendriks joined Smithe and Tyler; the three of them waited as the Chief and XO headed off towards M&B. Chief Langston suddenly spun on his heels to say, "Oh, and West, one more thing-"

Tyler stepped to the point of his little brigade, "Aye, Chief?"

"This is not a regular four hour Sounding and Security patrol. Find the bloody coveralls. No matter how long it takes. When you find 'em, you're finished. Understood?" Langston did not wait for Tyler to answer. He left with the impatient XO.

Once Kendall and Langston were out of sight, Tyler began moving aft toward the stern of the ship, followed by Smithe and Hendriks.

"Where to first?" Smithe asked.

"Mess decks," Tyler said beginning to move.

"Great, I'm starving."

"Not the chow line, Smitty, we're going to cold storage,"

"Wait, why?" Hendriks said, picking up the pace to walk beside the two faster HT's.

Tyler glanced over at the nervous clerk and answered simply, "To see Orton."

CHAPTER 19

Jorgenson poured two cups of freshly brewed herbal tea with steady hands. Emma had sent the tea leaves along with a note that read "for stress relief." He hated the bitterness of the tea but accepted her insistence of its medicinal powers; a cup of herbal always worked for him. In the wardroom, Ensign Charlie Watford—Assistant Stores and Supply Officer—sat on the leather sofa against the aft paneled bulkhead. The captain had left the young ensign here while he prepared the tea in the officer's galley. Watford had started shaking uncontrollably while he relived the nightmare he'd witnessed earlier. He remembered opening the door, hearing moaning and grunts... in the dark he wasn't even sure who the bloody man on the deck was.

Hodges was the first person he'd found and brought to the scene. Hodges told Watford to wait in the wardroom while the triage team attempted to save Orton—most likely the last rational command from Hodges' mouth. *Hodges,* Jorgenson grunted to himself. He pitied the man, but trying to figure out who would stand in, at what time, as Chief Engineer was a stressor Jorgenson did not need now. With Orton gone and Hodges losing his mind, that left only Springer and Langston to divide the engineering responsibilities.

Watford sat perfectly still, his head bowed and cupped in his hands. For a moment, Jorgenson thought the Ensign was seasick; everyone was fighting to keep his meals down in this storm. Jorgenson's mind slipped back to his initial conversation with the ensign. The culprit had run off in the dark. Watford did not see a face, but enough of a physical description to get them started on the manhunt. Jorgenson recalled the man's shaky hands and quivering lip. When Watford first arrived on the scene and fled for help, he had seemed calm, frightfully cold. *It's sunk in with him now*, Jorgenson thought as he laid a cup of the nasty tasting tea on the table in front of him.

The ensign glanced up. "Drink." Jorgenson told him and pushed the white porcelain cup closer. "It'll help."

With trembling hands, Watford grabbed the cup before the tea vaulted from the table by the vigorous rocking. "This isn't happening." He mumbled before taking a sip. His look of disgust let Jorgenson know he was not alone in his dislike of Emma's cure-all. Watford took a second sip despite his apparent disapproval of the taste.

"If there's anything else you can remember...?" Jorgenson asked quietly.

"No." Watford said. His tone was quick and harsh, "I already told you everything I saw."

"Easy, Charlie." Jorgenson said, "I'm not going to make you go through the story again," Jorgenson assured him, "but you'll need recall all the details for the NIS authorities. I can't have you falling apart too."

"Like Hodges. You're talking about Hodges."

Jorgenson nodded. The fact that Hodges was showing signs of a severe mental breakdown was no secret amongst the officers.

Watford swirled the tea in his cup, "How did you manage to brew tea in this storm without..."

"Shit." Jorgenson stood and maneuvered around the corner to the galley entrance. He'd forgotten the teapot sitting on the counter. As he suspected, on the floor were shattered glass and a plastic and metal frame. *Maybe Watford and Hodges aren't the only people losing it*, he thought to himself as he cleaned up the mess. "Why would you leave the damn pot with the ship rocking like this?" he scolded himself aloud.

In his hurry to clean up the mess, he didn't notice Lieutenant

Commander Hodges in the galley. Jorgenson sensed a presence and turned just in time to see Hodges make it to the bin and lose his stomach. Obviously, the swaying ship was only intensifying Hodges' sickness. "Lieutenant," Jorgenson started to speak, but was cut off by a second round of Hodges gagging into the trash bin. The captain stood by, waiting for his officer to regain some composure.

The Chief Engineer attempted to stand upright; Jorgenson put one hand on Hodges' back and gripped his arm with the other to keep him from falling to his knees. Hodges let out a snivel and looked up at Jorgenson with tears dripping from his sockets. "Phillip." Jorgenson commanded, "Stand up straight." Instead, Hodges allowed his weight to fall into the captain and his body swayed to the motion of the ship. He reeked of sick—his slumped shoulders, unshaved chin, and wrinkled uniform made the normally soulful man appear even more pathetic. Jorgenson needed his officers to be leaders, not quailing cadavers and not vulnerable flapping butterflies caught in a cyclone, and Hodges' behavior was beyond contemptible.

The pitiful display gave rise to an anger that caught even Jorgenson by surprise, and all at once the captain laid into his Chief Engineer, "God Dammit, Hodges. Get a fucking grip." Jorgenson pulled Hodges to his full height, "You are useless like this." Hodges could only muster breathy whimpers as his irises morphed into solid peas.

As quickly as the outburst peaked, the ship's commanding officer got his temper under control. He let Hodges free of his grip and the sniveling dolt fell back into a dying wet noodle slouch.

"Walk, damn it." He commanded, and Hodges blankly obeyed drooping alongside his captain back to the wardroom where Watford was waiting and sipping on tea.

In only a few minutes, the tea seemed to have helped calm Watford's nerves. Jorgenson forced Hodges down to sit and spoke to him like a dog, "Stay," he said. Jorgenson then made eye contact with the ensign, prompting a nervous, "Sir?"

"Watch him. Can you do that for me?"

"Aye, sir." Watford said.

"I mean it." Jorgenson said and glanced back at the deranged ghost that had been the former Lieutenant Commander Phillip Hodges. "Watch him... and try to get him to clean up."

"Yes, sir." Watford said.

Jorgenson hoping the assignment would give Watford something to focus on just as he had done for Partridge when they were trying to save Orton. *Is this what has become of my command?* Jorgenson sighed, *ordering men to babysit each other.* He shook away the disgraceful thoughts and left the wardroom.

Jorgenson headed back to the bridge where a handful of men, those still mentally put together, were waiting. He had excused himself to check on Watford and to see if the man had remembered something else. He replayed the earlier conversation with Watford.

"... I'm pretty sure they were green." Watford said.

"Pretty sure or positive?" Jorgenson did not want any uncertainty.

"They were green."

CHAPTER 20

Outside the passage near M&B berthing, Tyler spotted an armed guard stationed within view of the mess decks and all aft ladders leading to and ascending from the second deck. Anyone wanting access to the flight deck or rear fantail risked detection by the guard from where they stood. The lockdown plan became obvious to Tyler; keep all main engineering berthing compartments under control with three armed guards—this allowed the remaining security detail personnel to handle all other living quarters. The security guard straddling a stolen Chief's mess chair was OS2 Steve Larson.

"Steve." Tyler nodded as he, Smithe, and Hendriks made for the cold storage ladder way on the aft bulkhead of the mess decks.

"You can't go down there," Larson said.

"Official business, Steve," Tyler said with confidence. Larson looked puzzled, but Tyler kept moving, not giving the sentry any chance to ask questions.

Down below Hendriks asked, "How did you know he'd be down here?"

"Where else would they put a dead body?"

Tyler stood there staring at the body bag. A visit to cold storage had seemed to be a logical first step, but now Tyler had lost all nerve. Hendriks stood at the doorway white knuckling his weapon. Smithe waited back, not at all eager or curious to see the dead face of the former Lieutenant Bruce Orton, Main Propulsion Assistant of the USS Miller.

At last, Tyler reached up and started to open the bag. Hendriks's quiet "Don't", came too late. He unzipped down to just under the man's chin before jerking back.

Tyler regretted opening the bag, regretted seeing the dead body, and even regretted concocting the stupid plan to visit cold storage to begin with. The pale face of Bruce Orton would forever haunt him. Tyler's mind again went back to the confrontation with Orton. *I did not mean...* Except for a faded-reddish smear on his cheek, Orton's face was so white, so pale. Tyler stood there gawking until Smithe elbowed his friend out of the way and zipped the body bag closed.

"This isn't right, Ty." Smithe shook his hands a bit as though to throw off death from his fingers after touching the corpse container.

Tyler did not argue with Smithe's comment, but some morbid part of him needed to see for himself what everyone was telling him was true.

"Let's go," Tyler muttered and went for the door without making eye contact with either of them. He didn't speak to Larson either; he walked steadily though he felt as if Orton himself was breathing down his neck to chase him as far away from the cold storage as possible.

Smithe and Hendriks chased after him up two ladder-ways. "West, where are we going?" Hendriks called out.

"We'll work our way up the starboard side first," Tyler said once they reached the ship's store.

"Starboard?" Hendriks said gasping, "I told you, the kill happened on the port main deck. Let's start there."

Tyler paused and leaned against the passageway bulkhead to give Hendriks a breather after running up two flights of stairs. "I've been playing this out in my head, who do you think did it, Hendriks?"

Hendriks puffed out his chest in between deep inhales, "I'm not accusing anyone. I don't know anything."

"Not a specific person... come on; it's no secret Orton didn't have any fans in M&B. So let's think. What's the fastest way to M&B berthing from where Orton was found?"

Smithe nodded a bit, catching on quicker than the DK, "Go through the center of the ship and then back down starboard. I gotcha, West. Our guy would've dumped his bloody coveralls somewhere down the starboard route… and if he's M&B…"

"This is the way he would have gone." Tyler pointed down the steps they had ascended a moment ago and visualized the assailant lumbering down and stashing the coveralls before he got to where the three were standing.

"So…" Tyler mused as he turned his attention to Hendriks, "I'm not going to waste my time walking up and down the port side knowing our guy probably took this route. We're gonna search the starboard side first."

Hendriks snorted and rolled his eyes at them both, "You two think you're so smart."

Tyler patted Hendriks on the shoulder, "Try to keep up, would ya?"

Tyler started walking, but for good measure said, "I can't believe they gave a gun to a guy who counts money for a living."

Hendriks never ventured anywhere other than his offices on the second deck, and Tyler wondered whether or not he would be able to handle the swaying ship—going on a Sounding and Security patrol will out any pollywog right quick. So far, he seemed okay, but Tyler planned to harass the clerk as long as he was stuck with him.

*****

The first hours of going up and down ladders along the starboard side went by quick; they searched trashcans and cubbies, behind ladders and in between beams and stringers; anywhere Tyler or Smithe could figure the killer might possibly stash clothes or a knife.

"Hendriks, what type of knife was used?"

"Don't know."

Tyler imagined the potential weapon—some sort of cook's knife no doubt; M&B berthing is located very close to the galley, so obtaining a knife would be easy. As they crept into their second and third hour of constant ladder climbing and descending and worked their way up the starboard side of the ship on each level, the three men grew weather-beaten and frustrated.

Tyler dug through his umpteenth trash bin and out of sheer frustration violently kicked one, causing a deep dent and a loud boot-to-metal echo that bounced through the passageway of the second deck.

Out of pure frustration, Tyler bellowed a rant that included every obscene word he could think of. Hendriks leaned against the bulkhead for the thousandth time. He was a little green in the face, but had managed to keep his composure so far. Even the normally unflappable Smithe dragged along. They were all discouraged, tired, and fed up with futile searching.

"Who was on watch when the murder happened?" Smithe asked, apparently eager for conversation after spending the last thirty minutes of their search in almost complete silence.

"Sounding and Security?" Tyler ran through the watch-stander schedule in his head, visualizing the logbook in Main Control, "I guess either Scheppler or Ramirez. It happened right around rotation... so yeah that's right... Scheppler would have been getting off while Hector was coming on."

"What about the other duty stations? The guys from the hole watches?" Smithe asked.

"I don't know," Tyler, said, "Do you?" he asked Hendriks who was swaying a bit too close for comfort.

"How the fuck would I?" Hendriks said with both palms up.

"Then back the fuck up would ya?" Tyler gave the DK a little shove and searched behind another section of bulkhead lagging—they were on the second deck located aft of the forecastle—almost to the bow.

"I need fresh air," Tyler said.

"I could use a cigarette." Smithe added.

"You two don't need to go out in this weather."

"I'm headed out, are you coming?"

"No." Hendriks said jeering at Tyler's insolence. "But, I'm keeping an eye on you two."

"I am." Smithe followed alongside Tyler, leaving behind Hendriks to wait for them while they took a mental break from their search. "I'm keeping an eye on you two." Tyler heard Hendriks shout as Smithe closed the watertight door.

As they exited, white-light burned his eyes and Tyler blinked several times. Even in the midst of the storm, the sun shone; the brightness lit up the entire sky as wind and a salty spray coated their faces.

"I'm headed to the bullnose," Tyler said, although he doubted Smithe could hear him over the exterior sounds of wind, water, and waves crashing against the metal ship. He started his march away from his friend, eager for solace. They were not yet clear of the hurricane responsible for the recent undulating havoc.

He had been given a tremendous task of uncovering the most important evidence. The recovery of coveralls would give everyone a level of certainty about who the bad guy was. The confirmation would also create a sense of truth that not everything was awry. *The killer wore green coveralls.* This of all things seemed to be a fact. Nevertheless, how did they know? The Chief had not said. Even so, why put so much faith in Tyler to find them?

Who knows the ship better than West? He imagined the captain asking the XO and Chief. *They've put a lot of trust in me*, but ironically Orton wouldn't have. The man would have blamed Tyler for not finding any evidence by now. Tyler winced at the thought. He was a *fuck up and a slacker*—Orton had told him so.

Tyler had joined the Navy to get as far away from his past as he could. He had always doubted himself, and leaving his days of drugs, disappointments, and fistfights was a first step to overcoming those past transgressions. Never going back—the Navy gave him something his past civilian life couldn't—a place to excel and show he was more than just an orphan destined to be a statistic. The military allowed even him to become something from nothing.

The distressful day proved yet again something important to Tyler; his place, here amongst these men, was secure. They all respected him; he was asked to find the bloody coveralls—there were more than one-hundred-fifty other guys, yet Tyler was the one person asked to find proof of a murderer. Tyler could not imagine why they trusted him with this particular assignment. Even after he'd threatened Orton, they trusted him with finding evidence. *Too hard on yourself*, Tyler thought.

A few hours ago, the mission of finding coveralls had sounded easy, but after searching the entire starboard side of the ship, he was beginning to wonder if the khaki's actually chose the right guy. Tyler gripped onto the guy-lines where port meets starboard and gazed up at the fierce blue sky as the scent of salt water filled his nostrils.

CHAPTER 21

Jorgenson informed all the men present that the ship's progress through the hurricane would continue due to their course. Their position, at ninety-five miles southeast of Bermuda, gave them another five-hundred or so miles to navigate before making port. After lighting-off the second boiler about six hours ago, they had turned northward and were maintaining a current heading of one-hundred forty degrees. This course would take them directly to Newport. They would arrive at Narragansett Bay in approximately twenty-eight hours. "The storm is keeping us from maximizing our speed." He said. There was still more than three-hundred miles of storm in front of them. The ship could only manage twenty knots in the foul weather. In calm seas, the USS Miller could surpass thirty knots.

The navigation discussion was an attempt to get everyone's mind off their fears—the topic was not working well to distract though. Each time Jorgenson took a breath or paused, someone else would bring up the murder.

"What can we do?"

"Do you think it's safe to sleep?

"How many more people will die?"

"Gentlemen—keep your heads on straight!" Jorgenson said slamming a fist to the table. The constant questioning and creation of theories began to drive him crazy; the deluge of immaturity grated on his nerves. The room fell silent.

Jorgenson gazed at the faces of each of his charge. How many of these officers ever actually faced this type of adversity in their lives? This question lingered in his mind; the unfolding events would be firsts for many. Half of the staff were junior officers fresh out of Naval War

College. A few senior guys had been assigned to single training vessels their entire careers—the Miller being no exception. Jorgenson needed to remind himself that the Miller was a training vessel. Not many of the officers had seen war. *They're afraid; half of them think they'll be next to die.*

The Wardroom door opened and the Master Chief of the Command, BMCM Roy MacCleary, stepped in. The man reminded the captain of a walrus. He huffed, as was his usual demeanor. There was always something MacCleary wanted to, "get straight", about the enlisted crew. The walrus approached, and Jorgenson rose to his feet eager to depart his present company. "Master Chief, join me on the bridge, would you?" Jorgenson knew MacCleary had come to speak to him about the enlisted men and confinement.

Once alone, MacCleary did not hesitate to start his pitch, "How long do you intend to keep this up?"

"Master Chief, I'm certain you know what's at stake here?"

"Sir, keeping the men locked in their departments..." MacCleary's ruddy face showed years of alcohol abuse. The red dimples and purplish lines crept between his rosy nose and eyes. As the most senior enlisted crewmember, MacCleary showed great concern for the safety and well-being of the enlisted crew. "You're just asking for trouble. A man will go crazy being zipped up."

"We cannot risk men moving about the ship." Jorgenson said.

"Well then, how 'bout you just lock up the guy you think is responsible?"

"I can't do that, Master Chief." The two stumbled their way towards the bridge. "A partial description is not enough to lock one person up. We have our suspicions, sure, but what if we're wrong? You weren't there, MacCleary; that passage was pitch black. Watford let in a little light when he opened the door, but he's not one-hundred percent on what he saw. The killer took off running and Watford was distraught."

"But the men cannot..."

"The men, Master Chief," Jorgenson said with finality, "will be fine. A lockdown is the only way to control the situation."

"There's a damn good chance that our guy is feeling pressure... if he snaps..."

Jorgenson cut MacCleary off again, "If he snaps, the armed guards have their orders." The thought of an armed guard carrying out his orders to shoot an assailant point-blank made a cold shiver scuttle up Jorgenson's back. *Let's hope it doesn't come to that,* he quickly assured himself. The Master Chief did not respond, and Jorgenson felt him falling back a step as they reached the bridge entryway. Jorgenson turned and faced MacCleary.

"Have the lead Petty Officers hunker down, Master Chief, because the men are not going anywhere."

"Captain on the bridge!" Came the call from the boatswain's mate as Jorgenson and MacCleary entered.

MacCleary did not care for the answers given by his captain, but Jorgenson was finished arguing his point.

Something caught MacCleary's eye as he headed towards the front of the pilothouse and glanced out the forward window. "Damn it, West!" MacCleary grunted. "Fucking idiot thinks he's invincible." MacCleary reassigned his agitation toward whatever he was witnessing out the window.

Jorgenson stepped up to the forward rail to see for himself. Out the window, Jorgenson could see HT2 West hanging on to the lifelines at the bullnose of the ship. Twenty-foot walls of water raised and dropped the ships nose and there he stood, apparently enjoying the view. "What is he doing out there?" Jorgenson said. Following behind West was HT2 Smithe, beckoning his comrade.

"He and Smithe have been out there a while," came the voice of Ensign Radner, the officer of the deck, spying the scene through the water streaked windows. "We've been keeping an eye on them—he's okay." Radner said attempting to reassure the captain.

Just as MacCleary made a motion to leave the bridge and deal with West's recklessness, the HT turned to face the bridge. "Wait a minute," Jorgenson said. The ship mounted a cresting wave, and West began to move. He measured each step like a tightrope walker and made the journey to the side of the ASROC launcher without as much as a slip. Jorgenson thought the feat to be quite impressive for a snipe. After a few minutes, the surefooted West and his partner disappeared from sight below the bridge windows.

"I ought to write his ass up for that foolishness," MacCleary huffed, eager to take his frustration out on West.

Jorgenson had not been aboard the Miller long; even so, judging by the limited feedback he'd received, HT2 West and the Repair Five damage control team were cited as best-in-class. West had excelled during basic engineering drills. Jorgenson put a hand on MacCleary's shoulder, "West and Smithe are doing us a service by searching the ship. I understand they've been at it all day—let's give them a little latitude, okay?"

MacCleary retorted with what sounded like a very sarcastic, "Aye, Captain." And pulled his shoulder back to relieve himself of the captain's touch, reassuring Jorgenson that MacCleary still bore resentment towards his decision to keep the enlisted locked away in their departments.

These men, the two HT's, were some of the finest sailors aboard. West had received four consecutive citations for his leadership of Repair Five. His work resulted in the Miller achieving the gold damage control award the previous quarter—the only ship stationed in

130

Newport to do so. West knows the ship better than almost every other person on board, but he has a temper. Langston had described the argument between Lieutenant Orton and West and much to Langston's and Kendall's surprise, Captain Jorgenson had still decided the initial search team must be Smithe and West while the rest of the crew would remain on lockdown.

MacCleary was well intentioned, but the correct decision in the current situation was to continue with a lockdown and continue with the search for bloody evidence until the ship reached port. *What the hell would you have me do instead, MacCleary?* Jorgenson thought as the angered boatswains mate excused himself from the captain's presence.

CHAPTER 22

"Down to the windlass room," Smithe said to Hendriks. It was as if he was reading Tyler's mind. Both the HT's advanced ahead of the DK. The excessive motion had slightly subsided, and Tyler decided the receded waves would allow searching the windlass room, boatswain's locker, and the spaces forward of the gunner's magazine, to be a little easier.

This area has many hiding places. Tyler had reached the forward transverse bulkhead. The large compartment below the forecastle held secret keeps; a boatswain's locker, the forward magazine antechamber, and several hawser cubbyholes, accessed from the forecastle underbelly.

"We'll get to that space in a few minutes," Tyler said pointing to a small latched hatch on the inner structure aft of the first transverse bulkhead that would lead them to a deep trunk space. "Think our murderer had time to stash shit way down there?" Not many people have seen or visited the sonar voids.

Tyler let his mind speed up and run through the checklists of their previous hours. A renewed energy to solve the mystery right then and there washed over him. *Our murderer,* Tyler could not get over thinking of the responsible party as *our murderer.* The Miller's murderer for the rest of time: the Miller Murderer, the murderer on the Miller—*it has a ring to it.*

He made his way around the boatswain's locker. He searched for bloody coveralls while deep in thought. The notion of *who* kept eating at him. If he thought hard enough, then *who* should pop into his skull, right? Of course, he of all the crewmembers knew the Millers secrets, all the systems, the nooks, the crannies... and all the men.

Who, he wondered, *will be the infamous one to earn, forever, the title of the Miller Murderer? Who would receive that moniker?*

Smithe made quick work of un-dogging the entrance to the carbon-dioxide storage locker and slipped the safety pin into the gusset hole to brace the hatch.

"You or me, Ty?" asked Smithe, but before Tyler could respond, Smithe stepped down to the first rung and into the opening muttering "Fuck" and something else Tyler didn't quite make out. Hendriks waited at the doorway as usual—not helping in the search at all. He persisted in observing Tyler and Smithe, never letting either stray too far, but when they did get along from him, Hendriks was always somewhere near the way out, sort of blocking them in.

"Nothing here."

"Nothing here." Smithe sang his line following Tyler's verse; the chorus acted as their new search team catchphrase. The two had the energy to be silly. The break out on the bullnose had helped.

They searched all lockers, holds, and keeps under the forecastle; they found nothing. Tyler led the team to the vestibule access to the ships sonar. After making quick work of loosening the latch dogs around the perimeter of the square hatch, he glanced down the sonar vertical access trunk.

"Where does this lead?" asked Hendriks, peering down the shaft.

"Come on now, Bryan, haven't you been going to the ESWS discussions?" Tyler said grinning. The DK had skipped the last few weeks of Enlisted Surface Warfare Specialist training to play poker with him, Smithe, and several other shipmates in the laundry. Tyler recalled the DK losing a few hundred dollars; he took every opportunity to play cards trying to catch up before payday.

"Oh, go to hell, West." The DK1 said.

"It's all in here," Tyler said, tapping his own head as he stepped over and down to the ladder leading to the sonar void, "everything I need."

"It's all in there." Smithe said rapping his pointer finger on top of Tyler's noggin.

"Fuck off, Smithe. I don't see a shiny pin on your chest, numb nuts." Hendriks said. There was a running joke that DK1 Hendriks could not pass the exams to attain ESWS certification. Three tries at the preliminary test, the Chief's Mess Review, and three *not this time* results.

"I don't give a shit about that pin." Smithe laughed because he really didn't care. Hendriks was the one who kept trying, and failing, to pass the exams.

"You better study up." Tyler called up from three rungs below the knife edge, "And don't ask Smitty where this goes either; down here is a secret HT hiding place." Smithe laughed out loud and Hendriks shut up.

Smithe followed Tyler down the vertical ladder. The shaft sank three decks deep and landed on another smaller hatch to the sonar dome entrance. The Miller, an anti-submarine warfare vessel, carried a sonar dome attached to her forward hull. The voids they explored now contained most of the electronic cabling and electrical panels for the active pinging sonar system. The larger space aft of the bottom of the shaft also housed two sounding tubes, which were inspected once every hour while at sea. This is one of the hourly check locations for the Sounding and Security patrol. The two searchers were very familiar with these nooks and crannies. A steel ship will have many voids or hollow spaces providing buoyancy needed to float. The space also offered ample hiding spots for a murderous killer on a rampage to stash his dirty work. Both men swept the space with their eyes along hull stringer beams, around electrical panels, and hard to reach nooks behind piping and cable runs.

"Don't you think it's odd," Tyler said to Smithe, "the first berthing space checked was R-Division?" This was his first chance to speak to Smithe without screaming over a raging storm or having the DK1 breathing down their necks.

"No—especially after you told me about your shouting match with Orton," said Smithe.

"But Smitty, they know I didn't kill Orton."

Smithe turned and faced Tyler. "What makes you say that?"

"Because I'm standing here," Tyler said. "If they thought I did it, there's no way they would put me on this search party, besides a simple search of my rack would not prove my innocence, either. They knew before they came to R-Division that I didn't do it."

Smithe took in Tyler's explanation and went back to searching.

"If they had knowledge of my innocence, why come to R-Division before M&B?"

"You don't know—they might have searched M&B before they came to us." Smithe said without facing Tyler.

Tyler kept his friend in the corner of his eye while searching with the other. Just then, the ship pitched, and both grabbed a hull stringer to keep from flying forward.

"It took the Chief almost two hours to go through our twenty-one racks," Tyler said.

"Yeah?" Smithe sighed. He knew Tyler wouldn't shut up.

"Well there's at least fifty racks in M&B."

"Yeah, but they don't all have men assigned to them."

Tyler let Smithe continue denying the coincidences—an idea in his head about what the khakis were up to kept surfacing, but Tyler wasn't sure blurting out a conspiracy theory to Smithe would be the right thing to do. The thoughts coming to Tyler were jumbled splinters, they were barely formed ideas, and the fragments needed clarity.

Clues—we are looking for clues—that's all.

Tyler had been sent out to find clues. He worked hard to achieve his goal. For now, he would log the hints in his mind for later recall. Smithe would make a good sounding board, but not now. "Maybe there were two rack search teams?" Tyler suggested, yet he knew that wasn't the case.

"Some whacked out reservist went off the deep end, man. That's what happened." Smithe said.

Well if so, thought Tyler, *there's no need for us to be exploring down here for blood stained clothes*—half the regular crew didn't know this space existed let alone *some whacked out reservist.* "You're probably right." Tyler said only to steady his friend's clear reluctance to discuss it further. They returned up the ladder to the impatient Hendriks.

*****

It had been six hours since the start of the search, with the bulk of their time spent on the starboard side. Now the three men arrived at the scene of the crime. Tyler, Smithe, and Hendriks stood in the port boat-deck passage, staring at a calamity that had yet to be cleaned. *Blood.* Blood was everywhere. Coagulated puddles of dark red created a sick patchwork; in certain places, smudges of thick scarlet grease paint draped red curtains and ruddy accumulations along deck rivets. A bloody handprint fashioned itself on the bulkhead at an awkward angle. As they inspected closer, more handprints and blood smears decorated the white on both sides of the passage. Tyler stepped gingerly, not wanting to tread on dried blood, and the ships rolling meant he needed to stabilize himself against the non-bloody parts of the bulkheads. This was difficult with little white space available.

A gagging sound erupted from Hendriks's throat. If seeing Orton's pale face hadn't made a believer out of Tyler, this moment did. "Fucking hell," Tyler slurred his words, choking on the smell of rust and taste of copper coins. "Why the hell hasn't anyone cleaned this shit up yet?" Tyler's stomach dropped, and his heart raced. He needed to speak just to keep the room from being quiet. Silence welcomed spirits, and Tyler sure as hell didn't want Orton haunting him.

"I don't like this," Smithe said, "Let's get out, now."

"No, we've got to search here." Tyler said.

"Hell no." Hendriks gagged again, "The idiot didn't undress right here."

Tyler knew Hendriks was right, but said, "You don't know. Now help us."

"Fuck you." Hendriks said, letting out another gurgling sound from his throat, "I'm waiting outside." He left them and stepped forward onto the port boat-deck.

Tyler and Smithe stood in place for what seemed like several minutes. "Isn't he supposed to be keeping an eye on us?" Smithe said.

"He's about to lose it. You want to smell dried up blood *and* vomit?" Tyler said.

"Mmm," came Smithe's reply, and the two of them began to search every inch that wasn't doused in blood but found nothing.

Something kept touching the back of his neck; the eerie feeling in the passage would not escape him. "Let's just get out of here," Tyler finally said, and Smithe eagerly followed; the two of them joined Hendriks outside of the hatch.

The three men continued their search down the port side, eventually arriving at the fantail and went up to the flight deck towards the Helo-Hangar. Above the hangar was *an interesting place to hide something*, Tyler thought as he gazed up at the vertical boxed Helo-Hangar. The container top was a dangerous location to be in the midst of the storm, but they needed to search everywhere if they were going to find the coveralls and knife—Tyler opted to delay the vertical climb until necessary.

"Let's come back to there," Tyler said, pointing up to the roof of the Helo-Hangar.

The search team combed the flight deck and Helo-Hanger then moved around to the boat-decks. "I'm tired of being out on deck, guys." Hendriks latched onto a vertical pipeline for support as he spoke. Tyler and Smithe rummaged through the crash-crew locker, lifting equipment and bails of rags that were being temporarily stored in the hold. Tyler examined under the boat covers and climbed into the Whaler and Captain's Gig and then with Smithe's help re-lashed the tarps as he went. Working quickly to secure the area, Tyler stepped around the port side of the Hanger exterior bulkhead and started to scale the vertical ladder.

"Be careful!" Hendriks shouted.

"Hendriks, I got this." Tyler said, dangling off the aluminum treads. The ship steadily pitched making the climb a precarious one.

Smithe moved to follow Tyler up to the roof of the Helo-Hangar known as Steel Beach. The Flight Crash team often used the high platform to catch some sun during flight operations.

"You'd better wait here." Smithe grinned at DK1 Hendriks as he ascended.

Atop the Hanger, Tyler squatted to lower his center of gravity and off-set the rolling motion; there weren't any places to hold on to. Smithe mimicked Tyler's posture although he dropped to one knee for added stability; the ship's rocking remained steady. Both worked fast to scan the area; there were several hawser lines coiled in two heaps, and a faded orange life-vest had been lashed to a vent pipe—Tyler knew the hawsers and life vest were often used as pillows for sunbathers who frequented the beach on sunny days.

"Look over here," Smithe, grunted, "Scheppler's handiwork."

"What did you find?"

Smithe pointed to a half-finished welding job near the edge of the platform left unattended. The abandoned gear was Scheppler's, no doubt about it. Tyler recalled sending him to repair a conduit bracket—the burnt metal bracket drooped sideways with half welded beads running around its base. Scheppler obviously meant to come back and finish the job, but that was a week ago. Meantime, the copper leads, one with a ground clamped end, the other a connector end, were left coiled in the rain; the other ends of each cable hung off the side of Steel Beach—long rubber-coated wires dangling over the edge and down to the welder that was positioned at the rear of the Helo-Hangar.

"Shit's going to get ruined." Smithe said, "I swear I'm not picking up after that kid anymore."

"Then don't." Tyler said, already climbing over the side and off Steel Beach. "Let's go below."

Smithe followed close behind him.

Once in the Helo-Hangar, Tyler squeezed out his soaking wet sleeves. Since leaving the bloody passage, Tyler could not shake the strange feeling of a ghostly presence surrounding him. Around any corner Orton would be standing there, ready to get back at him for the verbal assault during watch rotation—ready to be that same ass that Tyler knew he could be. Guilt arose in Tyler for not liking Orton—before. He'd threatened to kill the man, and now the stupid bastard was gone forever.

"What now?" Smithe asked, intruding on Tyler's meditation.

Tyler shook his head and walked to the phone mounted on the

bulkhead, lifted the receiver, and dialed the bridge.

After a brief conversation, Tyler hung up and turned back to Smithe and Hendriks. Two sopping wet chumps; their faces carried a day's worth of beard; both were ready to fall to the floor in a heap— especially Hendriks.

"What do you think?" Tyler said to Hendricks.

"I think we're fucked," said the old-timer. Tyler couldn't disagree.

CHAPTER 23

"You're telling me you searched this entire ship and didn't find a god dammed thing?" Langston's demeanor shifted, from optimistic to frustrated, as soon as he understood that no evidence had been uncovered. Tyler conveyed his story of the search, listing every conceivable nook and cranny they'd visited, with several nods and "uh-huhs" from Smithe and Hendriks. The Chief had been the main interrogator while Kendall and Hodges only listened to the tale. Langston stood facing Tyler while Lieutenant Commander Kendall steadily paced. Off to the back of the hangar, listening in, was Lieutenant Hodges. All three men looked exhausted. Hodges especially, was pale and unkempt. *They're starting to resemble ghosts.*

"We searched everywhere."

"So, that's it." Kendall said with a finality that surprised Tyler. The disappointment they conveyed angered Tyler; he hated letting people down—the XO especially.

"Maybe we should search M&B again and the main spaces?" Tyler suggested.

"That's not necessary," Langston said.

Tyler sent daggers through the Chief Petty Officer's soul.

"Why isn't it necessary?"

Langston hesitated. Tyler's logical mind required an answer; the main spaces are perfect hiding places. All the engineers were familiar with every inch of those compartments. Tyler's frustration peaked.

"Fuckin forget it. Whatever information you're keeping secret is none of my concern."

"West there are reasons..." Langston sighed. "Just let me know if there are any places, other than main spaces, that you can think to search?"

Tyler's arms tensed up, and Kendall stepped in, "Everyone needs to relax. We're stressed out and this storm is doing nothing to help. We'll find the coveralls once the weather clears."

"We can't find the damn coveralls!" Tyler let his frustration out on the XO. "We didn't find a thing! Outside of the bloody passage, there's no trace of the murder. We found nothing. Nothing! Whoever did this obviously took the time to cover his tracks. He probably dumped his shit over the side!"

This stirred everyone; the notion of a killer throwing evidence overboard was apparently news to the search leadership crew. Tyler couldn't believe their collective response.

"So no one in khakis gave any thought to the possibility of the killer throwing shit over the side?" Tyler was dumbfounded as he examined their perplexed faces one by one.

"He obviously ran to the fantail, stripped off the coveralls and threw them overboard."

"He didn't run aft, West." Langston blurted out.

What the hell?

"You know this? How?"

The three men remained silent. *They do have a witness.* Tyler hadn't been convinced of the witness rumor. *So, then you know who it is.*

Tyler asked Langston again, "Do you know who did this, Chief?" *What aren't they telling us!*

"We don't know shit, West!" Langston barked, putting an end to Tyler's rant.

Hodges, whose shoulders were already slumped in defeat, buried his face into cupped hands. The brass had indeed been counting on Tyler to find the coveralls. The only one of them showing any degree of calm and self-discipline was the XO. Kendall turned his head from Langston to Tyler—his severe face and eyes, a source of continual discussion amongst the enlisted, studied Tyler. Tyler had always disagreed with most of his shipmate's assertions that *the XO is a real dick-head.* The XO conducted daily cleanliness inspections and helped train the other officers. Lieutenant Commander Kendall dealt with a bunch of children every day; anyone would appear pissed-off all the time. Tyler respected the executive officer, and Kendall knew it.

Several months earlier a dispute over which department owned the cleaning duties for a portion of the second deck outside Damage Control Central had come up and caused a major argument between the Operations and Repair divisions; the XO needed to step in and smooth out the arguing men. The O-Div-Twidgets had always been responsible for sweeping the area along the starboard DC deck forward of DC Central. On this occasion, the dirty and un-swabbed linoleum flooring failed inspection—again.

The operations slackers blamed R-Division for the excessive scuffmarks. They claimed that the HT's had trampled the area during a fire drill—and the feud began. Tyler stepped up and took ownership for the cleaning, which relieved the XO of needing to make the decision for them. The next few weeks, all remained calm until an inspection failed again. Many of the R-Division guys were angry with Kendall, but Tyler defended the XO; if Postino and Wilkette had done their jobs properly there wouldn't have been an issue. Apparently, word had gotten back to the XO and Kendall went out of his way to make a point of thanking Tyler for his leadership in the matter.

As the three super-sleuths mulled over their dilemma, Tyler decided the day had been long enough. Without giving them another chance to assign him another task, Tyler made a move to leave—but an idea popped into his head. He had been thinking on an important detail for most of the day. The information would give clarity to several thoughts swimming around Tyler's mind about Orton and the killer.

"Mister Kendall." Tyler said. The XO turned towards Tyler as Chief Langston and Lieutenant Hodges continued their mulling over the possibility that the killer might have ditched shit overboard. "Orton?" Tyler mustered the courage to ask, "Did he get it in the back or the chest?"

The place went silent. Kendall seemed momentarily rattled as Hodges took a step backwards; the Chief merely averted his eyes, as if looking at Tyler might summon an instantaneous disease. Hendriks whispered something barely audible that sounded like, "Jesus." Smithe stood stoic almost as if he'd been expecting the insufferable question. They had not previously discussed it, but Tyler was glad to see Smitty was, as usual, standing tall alongside him at the moment.

Kendall did not disappoint. His stern *dick-head* gaze was a familiar tactic whenever dealing with bluejackets. *You want to know*, he seemed to be signaling to Tyler. *Yes, I want to know*, Tyler signaled in response.

"It was in the back."

The news sank in; the XO did not waver—the finality struck hard at Tyler's chest. A strong, stinging sensation crested in his eyes. *It was in the back*; so much clarity from such a small statement. He wanted to say something—to acknowledge that he understood, but Kendall's fierce *dick-head* gaze remained, and no words were needed. The executive officer's statement was clear to Tyler and everyone else. Tyler's ears started to burn, and his eyes filled with hot liquid.

"Fuck it!" Tyler said, "I'm hitting my rack." He turned and walked aft towards the open hangar door and fantail. He needed to put as much distance between himself and the flight deck as possible. From behind, he could hear Kendall barking at Hendriks, "Go after him!"

Tyler did not turn back and got to the aft flight deck ladder before Hendriks had made the hangar doorway. The ship rocked causing Tyler to stumble-step on the last tread of the ladder to the main deck. He swung around to port and ambled forward like a teeter toy; Hendriks fell further behind his pursuit. The ship was moving faster now that the hurricane waves weren't as intense as they'd been a few hours earlier. Tyler stepped to the port lifeline. He estimated the ship's speed to be over twenty knots—they had both boilers screaming. The fresh air filled his lungs and dried his eyes. He kept moving knowing that Hendriks and probably Smithe were coming.

CHAPTER 24

Tyler suspected that he might drop from fatigue and stress at any second; however, he couldn't help but retrace his steps back to the hallway of death. The sea breeze had been cool and clean—a sharp contrast to the dank staleness that stopped him in his tracks as he stepped through the fantail door into the port passage. He retraced his previous path through the corridor and arrived back at the scene; alone this time. His legs were shaking.

"Shit." Tyler struggled with the notion of walking again through the kill zone. The alternative was to turn back or cut through the joiner door on his right and go down a deck through the galley. Hendriks would be upon him any second. He made a quick decision and advanced to the internal passage. Tyler pulled the hollow metal door wide as possible. At the top of the frame he reached up, turned the screw end of the pneumatic cylinder a few turns, and... let it go; the slow release caused the air cylinder to engage a gradual shutting door. He stepped around the corner to the exterior passage and waited as Hendriks came from the fantail. The deception worked. Hendriks, followed by Smithe, moved through the slow closing joiner door assuming that Tyler had taken the interior path to the mess decks.

Tyler drank in the details of the enclosure and saw it for what it was; a death trap. He let his eyes explore every inch as he maneuvered through the corridor avoiding splatters of dried blood. Not finding anything during the all-day search troubled him greatly. Tyler intended to scan the scene once again, this time picturing the struggle brought on by new information.

He had been stabbed in the back. And, the killer had run forward.

Tyler imagined Orton lying on the deck, bleeding to death. He carefully stepped over the place he figured the body had bled out at. A few more strides forward. A ghostly Orton lay in his vision surrounded by several men trying to stop blood from seeping out of his torn back.

The ghastly scene rewound further back in time. Tyler's mind's eye concocted the actual attack. The knife-wielding killer approached the unassuming officer's rear and violently hacked at the victim's spine.

Tyler stood with both feet apart and two arms spanned across the passage that spanned the bulkheads as best he could against the tilting space. Orton always exited Main Control through the quick-acting scuttle. A few more quick steps forward and he studied where the first signs of blood splattered onto the floor. He readjusted the sequence of events and played it over again envisioning the whole scene in full.

Did the killer make plans to kill Orton specifically? He was leaving his duty station just after zero four hundred; anyone in M&B would be familiar with Orton's routine. No other EOOW took this route, only Orton. Where had the killer stood, waiting for his prey to come up out of the hole?

Or, was the event exactly as Smitty described; *some random reservist,* who just happened to be walking through this space, knife ready, decided to slash someone to death, just when the unsuspecting Orton came upon him? Was Orton that unlucky? Or, was the whole plot planned out by a devious murderer?

Tyler reached the far end of the passageway. He needed time to sort out details and rethink questionable bits of his speculations. He also needed sleep. He gave the death chamber one last glance and headed forward up the port side.

The ship shook side to side. The way was desolate, and the atmosphere of death brought on an unexpected loneliness. Tyler suddenly wished he had waited for Hendriks and Smithe. Then—a loud thud erupted in the passage. For a split second, Tyler glanced around searching for a loosened fire nozzle bumping the bulkhead, but he remembered that there were no nozzle stations in this part of the ship.

There was something peculiar about how the noise echoed in a metal hitting metal way. Ahead something on the deck glistened. He suspected what the object was, but part of him hoped to be wrong. He sped up; as he got nearer and as the shining object came into clearer focus, he slowed his steps. His breathing intensified as the object rested near his feet.

The glimmering object had fallen out of the overhead piping; the one place Tyler and Smithe never thought about. There were many nooks and crannies to hide something amongst the cabling and piping suspended overhead. *Why hadn't I thought of that?*

The height to the overhead in this section of the passage was more than six feet. A person hiding something up in those recesses would need to be quite nimble, or they could have used a ladder. He inspected the bulkheads on either side for a step or riser; something to aid the reaching into cables above. Perhaps the coveralls were up there too.

"West!" he could hear Hendriks approaching.

There were no ladders or steps in sight. Tyler didn't turn or even acknowledge the DK1. *How do I get up there?*

"What are you doing, West?" Hendriks called out.

Tyler carefully knelt down to inspect the knife; his instincts said to keep away any disturbances. He edged closer, creating a body shield over the object as Hendriks persisted in his shouting. His heart raced, and his palms became clammy. The air went thick, and his lungs struggled to fill themselves. The long blade, coated in an opaque layer of dried blood, shimmered. *More of Orton's blood.* The severity and length of the hunting knife surprised Tyler. He imagined pain: the unbelievable pain this knife might inflict. The serrated teeth would easily rip flesh.

Tyler, lost in his visions of a bloody struggle between killer and victim, could hear Hendriks hovering over his shoulder.

"There was no reason to leave me behind..." Hendriks's rant stopped as Tyler leaned back to reveal the murder weapon.

"It's the knife," Tyler forced himself to say.

Hendriks nodded. "Where did you..."

Smithe came lumbering up behind Hendriks, and for a minute, the only sound was the washing of waves on the outside of the hull and Smitty's heavy breathing.

"It fell from the piping." Tyler pointed up.

After the long moment of morbid reverence, Hendriks spat out the first thing that apparently came to his mind. "You guys never searched the overhead."

"No shit, really? Go alert Kendall," Tyler commanded.

Hendriks nodded and ran out. After a few moments of inspecting the blade, Smithe walked to the forward transverse bulkhead, lit a cigarette, and squatted heavily on the doorway sill; he was muttering something about the overhead. Tyler stood and hovered over the bloody weapon like a hawk circling its prey. He tried not to think about the silvery steel slicing through flesh and muscle to no avail. Pictures flashed in his head: Orton's anguished dead face, a knife penetrating a khaki covered back, blood flowing out of a gash and pooling on the non-skid decking, and the splattering on the whitewashed walls.

Tyler had been convinced they would never see the weapon; he had convinced himself that the killer had effectively ditched the blade and coveralls over the side of the ship. Not so. The once elusive instrument of carnage lay before him. A layer of slick wetness formed on Tyler's forehead and on the back of his neck. His stomach churned.

The feeling of sick hopelessness faded after a few moments, and his anger swelled. The Miller murderer had sprinted through this passage, stopped in his tracks, and somehow stashed the blood-covered knife in the overhead cable runs. Tyler once again looked around seeking a way to climb up to the overhead cables. He stepped up onto a horizontal stringer beam and reached up to the cables. He pulled himself up to the accessible area—it took some effort, especially working against the forces of the moving ship. *How did he get it up there? Who is that nimble and strong?*

He wanted to identify this killer himself. The man hadn't simply killed Orton, he had taken away every other crew-member's sense of safety and unity.

In the foreseeable future, Tyler conceded, he would always dream of this moment; walking up the blasted passageway in desperate anger, the ringing noise of the blade hitting the deck, and coming upon the blood-stained weapon. Tyler did not want to believe he had found the knife.

CHAPTER 25

The lockdown was not going to be over anytime soon; Tyler had learned as much during his conversation with Dunham and Bastille. After alerting the chief and XO about the knife, he and Smithe returned to their berthing compartments where they now skulked away in the vestibule at the bottom of the ladder with the LPO's. Munching on stale ham and cheese sandwiches, they discussed the strategy for breaking up the watch patrols. Tyler did not care for the strategy outcome, which would put him back on watch in only six hours; he was exhausted. Six hours on, followed by twelve hours off was the plan thereafter. This meant he and Smithe would find themselves doing a Mid-Watch soon; it had been a long time since he'd worked through the night.

"We've been from the fantail to the bridge several times today. There's no reason to double up on patrol." Tyler wanted them to consider only one watch-stander and an armed security. "You don't need two guys to check the fucking shaft-bearing temperature." Tyler had trained every one of the HT's on Sounding and Security—the work was efficient and effective. "Me and Smithe only doubled up because they wanted us to search for..."

Bastille cut him off, "We got orders, West—shut your trap." He had reached his limit with Tyler's insubordination.

"This is bullshit," Tyler said in a hushed voice. "How much longer are they going to keep us locked down here?"

"Just sit tight." Dunham said.

Tyler glanced back at the opening to the General Workshop. His fellow R-Division boys traipsed in and out trying to get some half-assed boom box to function. "Nobody is sitting tight, numb-nuts."

In fact, the entire cadre of R-Division acted as if they were on a sugar rush. Once the tape deck got power, they all started debating on what music to play.

Still working on Dunham and Bastille, Tyler wanted to keep the conversation going. They had information, and Tyler wanted them to spill their beans. "They said a blonde guy was running from the scene, right?"

To this Dunham reared his head back like a quarter horse, "Jesus, not that again."

Tyler said, "Why not round up blonde guys who own green coveralls?"

Dunham continued his cantering, "West, are you for real? Just round everybody up?"

"Fuck-off, Roger." Tyler turned to Bastille, "Why not get all the green coverall guys together and start asking questions instead of... instead of this?" he pointed up indicating the armed guards stationed above within a feet of the R-Division hatch. The two operations guys, OS1 Corey Kingston and Chief Dempsey had been assigned the security detail to the forward second deck. When Tyler and Smithe returned to R-Division, Kingston did not let them out of their sight until they had reached the bottom of the ladder. "How do we know one of the guys holding a gun is not the killer?" They both ignored his pleading.

Since finding the knife, the ship had become unnerving; armed guards outside his bedroom increased the stress. Tyler had been given direct orders to not discuss his search; he concluded the delicateness of maintaining control over all the crew was going to be managed by maintaining tight-lips and keeping armed security details at berthing locations.

"The blonde guy thing is just a rumor," Bastille said, "I told you all to stay off the damn squawk box."

"So, there's no blonde guy, then?" Smithe asked.

Tyler fumed. "Well that's just great. Even still, there's only like, what, thirty guys with green coveralls? Why not round them up? See who's missing their coveralls? Why all the charades?" Tyler said, grunting each sentence at Bastille who put his hands out in a calming motion. Tyler quieted, but kept up the rant, "I mean, it's got to be a hole snipe, one of Orton's men—how many of those guys have been issued green coveralls?"

Dunham and Tyler had always found a way to be at odds on most discussions—this one was no different.

"West, enough. You two go get some rest. Like I said, for now, just sit tight." Dunham and Bastille both broke away from Tyler and Smithe.

"Fuck!" Tyler drove his fist into the side of an upright locker located underneath the ladder. Bastille hesitated and shook his head side to side, but didn't bother turning back. He walked past the workshop door towards Electrical Central behind EM1 Dunham.

A catalog of disturbing facts ran through Tyler's head: Orton's body in cold storage, his conversations with Langston, Kendall's confirmation of the stab in the back, and finding the weapon on the port side in the passage where the killer had run. He and Smithe had finally managed to inspect the entirety of overhead cabling in that passage and did not find coveralls—did this mean the killer only concealed the knife? Why the port side? Why was the knife so far away from M&B berthing? Where are the bloody coveralls?

Bastille and Dunham said there would be several days' worth of plans for Sounding and Security, which led Tyler to believe no one expected to find their assassin anytime soon. Anxious thoughts kept coursing through his head when an epiphany hit him.

"Damn..." he muttered.

"What?" Smithe asked. Tyler's brightening face caused Smithe to tap at his shoulder—eager for information.

"What, Ty?" Tyler made a move for Smithe to follow him to the berthing area; as they walked past the General Workshop, an argument about which music to play broke out.

"Turn that hillbilly shit off!"

"I like country."

"I don't give a shit what you like—put something else on!"

"Fuck you!"

"Fuck you!"

Then the sounds of classical Mozart echoed throughout R-Division. "Oh hell no!" came the response of yet another shipmate joining in on the ongoing argument. *You don't appreciate the classics.* For Tyler, he wouldn't mind listening to the calming instrumentals while trying to nap. Bastille and Dunham are only following orders, and the innocent argument could lead to bigger outbursts. If there was any truth to his theory, the time between now and the end of lockdown could be a while.

"I think I know what the brass are up to."

"What?" Smithe said.

"They're not rounding anyone up or putting anyone in the brig because they're trying to smoke the guy out." Saying it aloud made the notion seem even truer, "They don't want to accuse anybody if they're not sure." Tyler said nodding in full realization. "They want a confession."

"A confession?" Smithe almost laughed.

Tyler stepped through the events. "The Captain told the killer to talk to his superior officer." Keeping everyone on ice means the killer is locked down tight. "They want to keep the killer where he is. If he's able to roam the ship, he'll get to other possible hidden weapons or makeshift weapons."

Smithe added, "With weapons, he'll try to escape."

"Make him think he has no way out," said Tyler completing Smithe's thought.

Get him talking to his LPO; there's no need for a brig when berthing compartments and watch stations will suffice. "Getting a confession means interrogation and pressure," Tyler said, and then a thought popped into his head, "holy shit."

"What?"

"Smitty—this is bigger than just a confession."

"What do you mean?"

"A confession means the murderer has no options—if they let the guy talk to a lawyer before he confesses, there goes the murder charge."

"Wow. Okay—I've been with you up to this point, but just what the fuck are you talking about Sherlock Holmes?"

Tyler had to laugh. He was going through his thoughts so fast that Smithe wasn't keeping up.

"So, here's what I think. To claim temporary insanity as a defense, the act needs to be a spontaneous event—I think. So, Jorgenson and the brass probably believe that our killer must've planned and plotted his attack." Tyler began his explanation and Smithe squinted as if he didn't quite follow. Tyler continued, "Think about it, did you see that knife? That's no kitchen pairing blade. That thing had to have been secretly brought on board and stashed away until he was ready to use it. Also, Orton's path—he always goes out of the scuttle in Main Control. Plus, and I've been thinking about this, I don't think the killer just wanted to stab Orton."

"As if only stabbing wouldn't do the job?" Smithe wisecracked.

"No, I think he was trying to dump Orton's body overboard. I noticed boot-heel scrapes on the non-skid in the passage—they were leading to the exterior hatch."

Smithe looked to be in shock as if these revelations were somehow supernatural. "You know what?" Smithe said.

"What?"

"You got some imagination, guy."

Smithe smiled and started quietly laughing.

"Shut it, Smitty—you douche. I'm being serious here."

"No," Smithe said with a reassuring grab of Tyler's arm, "I believe you—I just can't figure out how you came to all these conclusions so fast. They have nothing, and the killer knows it. They won't get a confession."

Tyler thought for a second, "But, by the time we get to Newport, the guy is gonna be pretty rattled; he may want to confess to get off the ship."

Smithe was not convinced. He leaned in close and lowered his voice. "We're the only ones who know the knife's been found. Come on, if you were the guy, would you start blabbing about it? Hells no."

Tyler finished Smithe's thought, "As far as anyone on this ship knows, the Captain and the officers are clueless. That means the killer also thinks the officers are clueless."

"They won't get a confession like this." Smithe said.

"But I bet that's what they're hoping for."

"Well," Smithe finished as he crawled into his rack, "that dog don't hunt, son."

Tyler agreed with his friend. The strategy to keep the crew held-up in their compartments was a lousy plan in Tyler's opinion. The killer was supposed to accept being discovered. *Bullshit*. Tyler, and Smithe, didn't buy it. Besides, the plan put all men at risk, especially those in M&B berthing where the killer was certainly residing. Being cooped up in a tight space would cause anyone to go nuts. Everyone is anxious already. Why make Orton's killer extra jittery by waiting? This situation made for a ticking time bomb. Tyler made a mental note to tell Bastille and Dunham about his suspicions, for now he needed rest.

At last, he got to his bunk, crawled in, and closed the blue curtain. He shut his eyes, but only for a moment; he was too restless to sleep. For several minutes, or maybe an hour, he drifted in and out of a half-sleep daze. Images of the knife, the bloody passageway, and Orton's ghostly-corpse haunted him. Trying to turn off his brain before drifting to sleep, he rubbed at his temples; the nightmare felt like it would never end.

CHAPTER 26

Desperate for control, Jorgenson calculated his options. Over dinner with his officers, there had been no small talk or conversing on anything other than the sharing of worried thoughts. Now Jorgenson was alone with Kendall in the Wardroom. The discovery of the murder weapon brought everyone to a new level of edginess; Jorgenson had contacted NIS with the new information, and now the agents would meet the Miller via helicopter somewhere in the ocean before reaching port.

If we could somehow get a confession, Jorgenson thought. The idea seemed plausible—at least that's what the command leadership believed. The Surf-Lant Command had instructed the Miller's captain to *maintain the lockdown* and *not approach* the suspect. He sat at the end of the table holding a ceramic cup half-filled with black coffee. The lesser motion of the ship allowed for table service, and the after dinner drink offered a momentary reprieve from the situation.

The executive officer did not share Jorgenson's optimism about the coming agents. "I think bringing the NIS to the ship before we get to port is risky." The XO paced from one end of the wardroom table to the other. "Are they flying out here only to fingerprint the knife? Getting a chopper out to us in this weather?" Jorgenson agreed on the helicopter assertion, but engaging experts on criminal behavior to help get a confession was something he welcomed. He also disagreed with Kendall. "You're being stubborn. This is good news for us."

Kendall continued his nervous pacing. "We ought to get to the pier first. It gives us the flexibility to move the crew around easier."

Jorgenson was not certain, but the fact that the NIS are criminal investigators ought to ensure they would do plenty more than just lock the crew in their departments and send out a few armed sailors with no formal tactical training. Either way, relief was on the way, and Jorgenson kept an optimistic attitude about this newest twist.

Eager for a shift in the conversation, Jorgenson brought up a concept that had been swimming around his brain for several hours. He wanted to get Kendall's reaction. "How well do you know the enlisted?"

The question caught Kendall by surprise. He gathered an answer and said, "Fairly well, sir, why?"

"Well I don't." Jorgenson said, "I haven't been assigned to the Miller long at all. Perhaps it's time I spoke face-to-face to the crew."

"What are you saying?"

A surprising dread painted the XO's face.

"Paul, I've already made up my mind."

"Henry, we need you on the bridge,"

Jorgenson shook Kendall off with a chuckle, "To do what, keep the ship from crashing into freighters. No, I don't think you need me, Paul. Otherwise I'd be there now."

"Sir, we don't know what his intentions are—what if he attacks you?

Jorgenson stood, "I'm going to visit the enlisted berthing compartments. Those men have been cooped up for close to fifteen hours and are probably getting restless. It might do them some good to actually see the captain—let them judge whether I give a damn about their condition or not—or if he attacks me, at least we'll have a clear reason to lock him in the brig." He stood and moved to the joiner door, "I'm going to meet with the enlisted. I think it's time they met their Captain."

*****

Eighteen hours since my waltz.

They will go through the stages of confidence to fear to anger to helplessness.

Noise engulfs me.

Screw up your face with concern.

That's how I keep camouflaged; I must maintain a straight face for as long as possible. Be like everyone else. Choose someone to mimic.

You must show concern.

For what?

For anything—just look concerned.

My fellow shipmates... so nervous and fearful are the eyes of our department visitor. My vendetta is for your betterment, my comrades. Don't you know this? The music in my mind and the music from their stereos blend in a hideous fashion. Let them wail that irritation if it will soothe them—if that will make them comfortable. These fools are oblivious to my torment.

An intruder arrives in my berthing compartment. The captain. Switch. I maintain my composure. How many departments visited thus far, old man? Is this the first, second... third speech you've given? The captain puts on a false-face of sadness, but his dishonesty shows through—I can perceive where others are blind. This masquerade of concern—similar to mine. His eyes water as he speaks. Out of fear, no doubt. I swell with pride in the satisfaction of causing the solitary tear to fall. "Whoever this troubled individual is..." speaks the Captain.

Ha, ha.

You cannot know what trouble is within me.

Half-hearted plea to empathize with his assassin.

Switch. I look on with sad eyes, mimicking the body language of those around me.

Troubled? He thinks we are troubled. Ha, ha.

Disgusting. He speaks of the glorious moment in which I ended the life of the Defiant One so eloquently... does he suspect I'm here?

I have carried out my father's greatest challenge and succeeded—my father will delight in my accomplishment—what about you, Captain? Do you delight in my feat? Do you suspect there are others yet to come? You'll get your chance to find out. I will not accept this lockdown for much longer—I must escape this compartment.

Back to our music.

Entry of the Gladiators by Fucik, 1897. This march is good; it fills me with joy; I remember the song from my first visit to a circus when I was nine. My father erupted at the insolence in the circus's use of this piece. I cringe at the memory. Fucik did not intend for his music to become something used to introduce clowns into an arena. The suggestion infuriates me as it had my father—that great pillar. We were led away from the arena and instructed never to return.

My father. These are the rarest of men to whom we should uphold and adore. The ridiculous association of *Gladiators* to clowns fits well with Captain Jorgenson's speech, so I listen as this clown gives his performance. I am angered at his insistence of maintaining the lockdown and the white lights.

My father's teachings of music and composition and recordings—these are fond memories. My father taught me that all men must die, be they defiant or else—faint in essence the sound of heartbreak is loud within evil men—do not mistake my comfort for you are deemed defiant. Anarchy is a precious gift.

The clown prepares to exit the ring.

Beautiful speech Captain. O Captain! My Captain! Our fearful trip is done. O heart! Heart! Heart! O the bleeding drops of red, where on the deck my Captain lies, fallen cold and dead. It will come to pass, but from me it will not be met with mournful tread. You allowed the rein of the Defiant One to continue, and for that, surly you too should die.

The melody of the Defiant One's demise returns; this ditty is my favorite of all time. I will reach and destroy Captain Jorgenson. He was too insolent to visit me in my space; he has his eye on me.

You should attack while he is present.

The exquisiteness of my strategies are the stealth in which they are to be completed. A public attack would be fruitless. I curse this lockdown. He would be an easy target if I could break away from the rabble I am within this compartment confined. This captain devised the unexpected: an effective ploy meant to keep me at bay—the lockdown was unforeseen. My next design will overcome this turn of events.

You failed at your previous plan.

I completed the act.

You failed to complete the waltz.

I will not fail again.

He has angered me—yes, sir, you have driven me to this decision. I will use the time between now and when we reach Newport to plan a new scheme that will include the destruction of the captain. By any means necessary, I will escape this compartment and this ship. We will see how this cherished crew reacts when its most prominent abuser is destroyed.

*****

Jorgenson entered the General Workshop. He spoke to the LPO's first before the remaining enlisted started spilling in to see to what they owed the pleasure of his visit. He allowed his eyes to move from one crewmember to the other; he gazed at Smithe, West, and Wilkette, who were standing together. West, the captain believed, is someone to be depended on in the midst of this crisis.

As the last man entered, the captain stood up from the chair. *Careful what you say*, he reminded himself. While he and the other officers had their suspicions as to the identity of their perpetrator, letting the men catch on would become a crisis of its own. Plus, if the enlisted crew found out something, any hint of circumstances about a shipmate being out of line, the situation may become catastrophic; they would take matters into their own hands, going after crew members; he did not want to pit one department against any other.

Jorgenson addressed R-Division as a whole. "So how are you all?" The question was stupid, and he knew it the moment it left his lips.

"As you all know we are navigating to Newport—we should arrive sometime tomorrow evening." The thirteen men in the room shuffled their feet. "I know this has been, for all of you, a difficult time. I hope everyone here is getting enough sleep."

The men looked ragged—definitely not getting enough sleep by their weary grimaces. A few nodded, and most gave unpleasant glances. He discussed the escort procedures and the chow time rotations, as well as stressed the importance of following them.

"I want to reiterate the importance of maintaining the lockdown rules; no one is allowed anywhere without an armed escort."

EM1 Dunham spoke up, "Sir, can you discuss the importance of keeping the white lights on?" Jorgenson guessed that Dunham must be getting many complaints about the lights-on mandate.

"Sure," several men perked up a little; Jorgenson had not expected this rule to be such a bone of contention. "We have all of the white lights on, in the entire ship. The reason is," he selected his words carefully, "as you all know, the person responsible for Lieutenant Orton's death is confined to his quarters—just like the rest of us. I don't know what his intensions are." He had their undivided attention now. "I don't want anyone else to be in danger. With the compartment lights on, the leading Petty Officers and security details have clear visibility of everyone, so any movement in and around the berthing spaces will be seen. Everyone is being watched." The explanation was met with some agreeing nods and "Okays".

"Make sense?" All of the Repair Department gave him a approving "yes." Jorgenson then addressed the topic of rumors and told the crew all he wanted them to know about what had happened—the reactions were mixed to his careful words.

He went on, "Whoever did this, whoever this troubled individual is, I know, must be hurting. It is in his best interest to speak with his lead Petty Officer so that we can get him the help he needs. I can only imagine what he must be feeling—what he must be going through right now."

Jorgenson felt much better about his decision to visit the men; with this group, the talk was going well. "As for Orton, keep that man's family in your prayers. I don't believe word has reached them yet about this ordeal."

Towards the end, he'd offered simple answers to a few follow-up questions from the two LPO's about midnight rations and mess deck visits. When no one else said anything more, Jorgenson decided the meeting was over. He shifted in his chair. The young third class standing near Bastille fidgeted a bit, and Jorgenson took the opportunity to address him directly.

"Do you have a question...?" Jorgenson squinted at the faded stenciled surname on the young man's dungaree shirt.

"HT3 Scheppler, sir,"

Jorgenson nodded for him to continue.

"Sir. How are the guys in M&B berthing? We got word them MM's and BT's are really scared." His accent was mid-western.

"I grew up in Louisville, son, where are you from? I can hear your Hoosier twang."

"Bloomington, Indiana, sir."

"Right. See there? We're practically neighbors." To this no-one reacted—not even Scheppler; Jorgenson decided to cut the small talk short. "Well, I think everyone is a bit on edge. So the machinery and boiler techs are doing the same as everyone else."

"We think because Orton was the M&B boss, we thought some BT took a spanner wrench and..." another fella blurted out the words so fast; Jorgenson only caught a few of them.

Bastille jumped in. "Persinski, it's *Lieutenant* Orton, and be respectful when you speak to the Captain." Bastille then apologized to Jorgenson for the outburst.

"HT1 Bastille, I think we're all a bit nervous and Fireman... Perkins..." Jorgenson looked to Bastille for help.

"Persinski, sir," Persinski said before Bastille could speak up for him.

Jorgenson picked up from the young E3, "Fireman Persinski makes a good point. Lieutenant Orton was the Main Propulsion Assistant, and as the officer in charge of machinery and boilers the men in M&B berthing are of a concern." Jorgenson collected the words in his mind before speaking his next thought. "We believe all the crew is safe— including those in M&B berthing and including you all here in R-Division."

Had he chosen his words carefully? He suspected so. Scheppler and Persinski, as well as the others who'd not been brave enough to ask questions, carried semi-satisfied faces. His nerves were heightened— several twitches worked up his upper neck and back—he evidently tweaked muscles recently, although he couldn't recall when. Jorgenson wanted to visit other departments, but R-Division gave him the most anxiety—these were the men charged with roaming the ship. Any wrong moves by these guys and lives might be in danger—he wanted their nerves to be at ease. As he started to leave, something compelled him to turn towards HT2 West and the two comrades standing nearby. Jorgenson made sure to look at West first, his eyes drifted over to Wilkette and Smithe for a moment, but then returned to West. The captain wasn't sure what he wanted to say, but instead only held out his hand for a shake, which West returned. Full of nerves for the upcoming discussions, Jorgenson left R-Division.

*****

The occurrence is unusual, if not completely absurd, for the captain to be smack in the middle of the General Workshop shooting the shit with the guys. Yet, here he was, casually sitting backwards legs astride Bastille's chair; his arms were resting on the back support. An inspection would be the only reason someone this high up in the chain of command might normally find himself in this space. Tyler instinctively glanced around assessing the cleanliness of his workspace. The captain, however, was not here for an impromptu inspection. Not at all. That was without doubt. But, as to why the captain had decided a visit to the repair workshop was necessary seemed unclear, and as far as Tyler could ascertain everybody gathered in the semi-circle agreed.

Commander Jorgenson was gaunt and aged as if since their last encounter many years had elapsed. The captain's deep brown eyes moved from person to person, and upon reaching his, Tyler sensed a silent communication coming from his commanding officer.

Jorgenson leaned forward in his chair. "So, how are you all?" The question was unworthy of a verbal response. The men shrugged. *How*

166

are we? We're going crazy, leaving only to fulfill long, tiring watch stations, and having to be escorted by an armed guard to piss.

The captain went through the status of the ship and began running through guidelines regarding the lockdown, reminding each of them of the rules. As he spoke, the captain scanned the group, his eyes moving like fruit flies, casually landing on this guy or that one, "as for chow hall, we'll be breaking up chow-time into teams." Tyler did not catch what he said next; he started thinking about food. He was still hungry—the measly mid-rats they had been given were only semi-palatable. Chow-time would be extraordinarily pleasing in that moment. Smithe careened an elbow in time with a ship's roll into Tyler's shoulder, drawing attention away from his food-filled daydream and back to the meeting. Dunham then asked a question about keeping the lights on; Tyler knew why the lights were on; that's a no-brainer—keep the killer from strangling someone in the dark—*obviously.*

"I'm sure by now you've all heard all sorts of rumors circling about. Let's keep in mind they are merely rumors. All you need to know for now is that Lieutenant Bruce Orton is dead, and that is why we are on lockdown and headed home. Whoever did this," Jorgenson's voice grew quiet. He reached up, removed his ball cap, and rubbed his head. His forehead had a brown horizontal line across it making his face appear shorter than it was. Jorgenson continued, "Whoever this troubled individual is, I know, must be hurting. It is in his best interest to speak with his lead Petty Officer so that we can get him the help he needs. I can only imagine what he must be feeling—what he must be going through right now." Jorgenson's eyes fell on Tyler for a moment before continuing to peer about the room, "As for Orton, keep that man's family in your prayers. I don't believe word has reached them yet about this ordeal."

A knot appeared in Tyler's throat. *Why is Jorgenson in R-Division, and why doesn't he call this what it is? Cold-blooded murder!* The beating around the bush was driving Tyler mad—why not be aggressive towards this killer? Call him out. Their handling of this infuriated Tyler; if he had his way, anyone missing green coveralls would be in irons.

After a few questions and some talk about M&B berthing the captain was done speaking, and the men dispersed. Smithe and Wilkette stood beside Tyler as the captain approached him and put out his hand for a shake. *What do you know that I don't, Captain?*

Tyler shook Jorgenson's hand; the gesture was most likely some sort of thank-you for finding the murder weapon. But, in the brief moment of the interaction, Tyler had an idea—too absurd to believe—and he got lost for a minute in deep thought.

No way!

Several dots connected in his head.

No way!

Perhaps the realization crashing into Tyler's brain was physically manifesting itself in his eyes—because the captain paused while holding his hand. The nausea percolating in Tyler's gut manifested from a mixture of awe and disbelief in the awful epiphany he was now having.

No way.

He let go of the handshake.

Jorgenson left muttering something about visiting the other departments. Wilkette turned to Tyler, "What was that about?" obviously referring to the handshake. Tyler ignored him, still rationalizing his concept.

Smithe answered, "West found..." he trailed off. Not wanting to say anything about a weapon, Smithe quickly covered his tracks, "something. While we searched there was a few things... we reported everything to the bridge, and the officers said we did a good job."

"Really?" Wilkette said, "What did you find, West?"

"Stop being nosy, Remy" said Tyler as he stepped away from Smithe.

Other crewmembers were already scooting over to them, eager to get in on the gossip. Smithe wasn't good at whispering. Tyler's swimming thoughts kept him from covering for his friends loose lips. His head started spinning.

Tyler scanned his fellow R-Division shipmates who were now standing around Smithe, each wanting to know what the searchers had found. He decided to hold off on what his rational self was screaming at him—*it couldn't be*, he decided and pulled Smithe from the circle-jerk.

In the quiet back corner of the racks, Tyler confided in Smithe. "Why did the Captain speak so gently about Orton's killer?" Tyler asked and Smithe shrugged; he was not in the mood for more of Tyler's wild theories, so they both took a break from the monotonous exchanges.

The captain had said something about visiting other departments as he left. They searched R-Division racks first...the captain visits and speaks to R-Division first... The hair on the back of Tyler's neck stood up on end. *No. The guy is definitely a mentally deranged reservist with blonde hair and green coveralls, creepily hiding out in M&B berthing.* And, that's that.

Familiar faces all around and Tyler could only think of one thing; who from R-Division would kill Orton?

CHAPTER 27

Most of the men wandered out of the General Workshop back to the berthing compartment. They were eager to take up the captain's suggestion to get rest when not on duty. Jorgenson had just left, and already several had crawled into their racks while others found quiet places to sit. Tyler got up to get a drink of water from the scuttlebutt. A perturbed Ramirez caught his attention.

Ramirez crouched near his bunk with shoulders flat against the bulkhead, both knees pulled under his chin and an arm wrapped around his shins. His other hand trembled as he picked at his lips and the black bristles above his upper lip, which served as his version of a mustache. His brown skin was ashen and spotted with rosy pimples and blemishes. Ramirez had a habit of always whistling while he worked, so his full lips were always pursed in a pucker. Tyler swore Ramirez was whistling or mumbling, but the volume was so low that anything he was saying would be barely audible. Tyler slowly approached, making sure no one else was watching. Ramirez was definitely talking to himself. Mixed in with a few undecipherable Spanish words, Tyler heard Ramirez mumble, "I don't think so... Couldn't be... You dream too much."

Tyler peeked around to confirm if, in fact, a listener stood by, but no one else noticed Ramirez's state of delirium. His uncoupled dark brown eyes parked themselves on some unknown object in the surroundings; he sat zoned out but muttered audibly. Ramirez didn't even perceive a presence until Tyler seized his shaky wrist and said, "Hector."

Ramirez flicked away the daze on his face, "¿Qué?"

"What the hell is wrong with you?" Tyler spoke as quietly as possible to avoid the interest of anyone else in the room.

Ramirez's face contorted and then quickly adjusted to appear unfazed. He stood up on legs that seemed a bit shaky, refuting his outward calm. His attempt to hide distress from Tyler failed.

"I, ahh, had a dream." An ashen hue covered his normal dark skin. "The Captain's visit made me remember—the talk about white lights..."

"Okay?" Tyler waited for a better explanation. The probability of Ramirez having a nightmare remained high given the high level of fatigue in everyone.

Ramirez kept his voice low, so Tyler leaned in to make sure he would hear. "The night of the..." He couldn't get the word out.

"Murder?"

Ramirez bobbed his head up and down. "I forgot something," he said.

Tyler remembered Hector being on Sounding and Security during the incident. *He must have witnessed something.* "Talk, Hector. Quit screwing with me."

Ramirez looked around before he leaned in close. "I was lying in my rack, and I swear somebody was standing over there." He pulled his head towards the two racks next to the forward port bulkhead.

Tyler got confused. Why did Ramirez go to his bed during the murder? "Are you talking about last night?" He should not be skulking around the berthing compartments while on patrol—Tyler tried to think of reasons for Ramirez to be in R-Division the night of the murder.

"No. Not last night—this was many nights ago."

"Oh. When was this?"

"I couldn't tell—it was a while ago."

Tyler was not sure what direction Ramirez was trying to take this discussion, but being a friend, he put on a concerned listening face even though he could care less about some dream this guy might have had some time ago.

"My dream—I mean it had to be a dream." He implored Tyler to listen and agree. "You believe me it was a dream, right?"

"Sure." Tyler hoped the story would end soon.

"I saw a guy with a knife."

Tyler perked up. "A guy with a knife, in a dream?"

Ramirez nodded in an exaggerated motion. Tyler and Smithe had found the knife, and they had told no one besides the khaki's. Most of the enlisted men had no idea how Orton died. Why would Ramirez make up a story about a knife when the theories from the squawk box described Orton's head being bashed in with a spanner wrench?

"So this guy," he continued, "I see him there putting a knife up to his..." Ramirez pointed to the middle bunk—Dunham's rack.

"Dunham? What about Dunham?"

"Up to his neck."

Telling someone the disturbing information seemed to bring a bit of color back to his cheeks almost as if revealing his story to Tyler relieved some internal pressure valve. Ramirez sped up his cadence as the confessional flood gates opened. "Someone was standing over Dunham. He was like, holding this knife, to his throat. Dunham's throat while he sleep'd. I'm watching this whole thing. Then I blinked, and when my eyes adjust to the dark, the guy's gone."

"Why are you just now talking about this?"

"I didn't even remember 'til just now. I mean... it was a bad dream. He just disappeared. I went right back to sleep like it was nothing."

Tyler studied him and gauged his confidence in the story, "Yeah, it was a dream." Tyler allowed Ramirez's revelation to take root. He'd automatically agreed with his friend that the weird story must a dream. A man with a knife that suddenly disappeared seemed too outlandish to have happened in truth. But, something in the details of the recollection told them both perhaps more than they were willing to admit.

"Get some rest, Hector."

"West." Ramirez said gripping Tyler's arm. "What if he really was here? What if it's the guy who killed Orton—I could've stopped him? And I just went back to sleep like it was nothing? What if the guy decides to kill Dunham?"

"You were dreaming." Tyler said, more to reassure him, "You just need to rest, man. We're all tense right now."

"Right, right. You're prob-ly right."

Ramirez sank back down into a seated position next to his bunk.

Tyler lingered at the open area of the compartment. He leaned against the bulkhead and scanned the room. These are his fellow R-Division crewmates. Their nerves are on edge—the tension in the room continued to build with each passing hour. He had an unsettling suspicion that things were going to get a hell of a lot worse before they ever got better. A few had overheard them whispering. Some had ogled the two while they were talking in low voices, and men were already chattering. About what, Tyler didn't know—their insight about rumors offered few prospects of learning anything noteworthy. Should he tell his men more about what was going on? New information might quell the gossip, or at least lessen the chances of the scuttlebutt storming out of control.

Tyler shook his head, certain that if the others knew, Ramirez's dream would soon become an accepted fact amongst the crewmembers. *How long*, before the story of *a man holding a knife to Dunham's throat* gets released through the squawk box to other departments. Not long, friends of his did not bear enough restraint to keep their eavesdropping to themselves.

Several eyes spied Scheppler who had yet to escape their suspicions after the blonde-haired rumor. Scheppler hardly came out of his rack since the accusation that a blondie had killed Orton began to gain traction. The hasty judgmental friends who were acting like unwanted cellmates increased the nervousness of the youngest member of R-Division. Instead of ignoring the suspicions as ludicrous, Scheppler acted as though he was too afraid to say anything that might confirm suspicions. He'd refused to participate in card games, every bit of his Copenhagen had been dipped, and his anxieties kept him from lashing out like the temperamental teen he was normally. The pressure of being a suspect gave Scheppler a chance to show how not to act when being accused of murder by your co-workers; he did not handle things well. To cap off his distressing past few hours, his lack of nicotine, triggered a bout of the shakes.

As Tyler passed Scheppler's rack heading towards his own, he paused. Scheppler almost leapt six inches off his mattress as Tyler touched his shirtsleeve; his frightened eyes widened to the size of saucers. "No one really believes you did it, Tommy." Tyler said, glancing back towards the others—all of whom maintained a rabid gazed on the blonde man. "They're just fucking with you," Tyler said. "You don't have to keep hiding in your rack."

Tyler sensed his stab at reassurance fell short—Scheppler's paranoia intensified by a steady stream of dubious bystanders. Even Tyler couldn't be certain whether or not to trust in Scheppler's innocence. His earlier epiphany guaranteed he would hold at least some level of suspicion for Scheppler and perhaps others he hadn't even considered before. Tyler laid down in his rack and closed his eyes. *We'd better figure out who did this soon*, he thought, *everyone is about to lose their minds.*

SCOTT BLACK

176

DAY TWO

CHAPTER 28

Tyler's eyes blinked open; the quietly creaking metal of their windswept ship declared the journey through the storm had continued. He pulled open the dark blue curtain of his rack and slipped out. The early morning signaled an internal alarm in Tyler, and he guessed the time to be around five o'clock on day two of the lockdown. As always, Tyler woke early, despite only getting a few hours of insufficient sleep. He stretched. The disgusting stench of briny body odor surrounded him. Long duty-station rotations and getting repeatedly slapped by nasty sea water out on the bullnose had resulted in a sour stench and clothes-to-skin stickiness. *I need a shower.* Even with the lockdown rules of no showers and the fact that at least two guards posted themselves on either side of the damage control passageway outside of R-Division, Tyler brainstormed breaking a few rules to get cleaned up. For him, the idea of sneaking out came with no real cons... only pros. His need for a shower outweighed all the negatives of criminal behavior.

He contemplated leaving the berthing space the old fashion way: he would lumber up the ladder, making as much noise as possible, and when guards approach he would tell them a story of broken sewerage pipes and the need for an HT in the forward head. At least if the guard did not go for the story, he would escort Tyler to the head to investigate, and Tyler could make a dash for the shower. This plan had its merit, but so did trying to sneak by the one guard on this side of the passageway. The back and forth of options continued in his head in sync with each gentle roll of the ship. His indecision came to a head when a strong whiff of foul air finally convinced him that being hollered at to go back down the ladder would probably be the worst outcome of this adventure. The compartment was quiet and everyone was fast asleep. Tyler stripped naked, put on a fresh pair of coveralls, and grabbed a towel, casually threw it over his shoulder, dropped a small soap bar in his pocket, and then headed to the vestibule. Gently skipping the third rung, which was loose and screamed when stepped on, he stealthily climbed the steep stairway. He avoided the noisy handrails and held the ladder frame as the ship kept rocking. By now going back down to the berthing compartment was not an option; already frustrated with missing his morning workout, Tyler decided he would not skip trying to shower as well.

While slipping out of the hatch, he glanced around to see that the one guard he needed to worry about, GM2 Karl Deetman, was half asleep in a chair facing the administration offices along the damage control passage. Deetman's head was slumped, and his hat covered his eyes. Tyler held in a chuckle. He suspected that the guard was playing possum—*I'll bet that guy is only half asleep.* Tyler moved, fast and quiet, out of the hatch, and hurried in the opposite direction, bee lining it for the forward head. He was so thrilled to get past the guard that he forgot about the squeaky joiner door until he cautiously pushed it. Tyler froze when the eerie creak assaulted his ears. He paused, waiting for the guard to come running, but after ten tense seconds, Deetman didn't show up.

Tyler released a sigh of relief, and he slipped into the head. He threw his towel down on one of the stainless steel sinks, not wasting a moment before stripping, and stepped into the third of the seven stalls. The stalls were sheet metal, each granting privacy only with a plastic curtain. He preferred the third out of all the stalls because number three offered the best balance of pressure between hot and cold supply lines. The effect was a powerful stream of soothing water that erased what seemed to be a month's worth of fatigue. Tyler let the cool water wash over him. It quickly became warmer heated water mixed into the flow.

Tyler washed his hair twice just to make sure that the stench from not washing for days would not follow him. As he scrubbed down, a tremendous sense of relief manifested. His internal clock knew the maximum time allowed to shower was three minutes, but he was already breaking the rules by being there. An extra few seconds of purgation won't hurt anyone. He let the water flow.

Five minutes later, he cut off the bronze handled valves, stepped into the space between the countertop and showers, and toweled down. There were several mirrors mounted in a long row above the sinks. Multiple versions of a naked Tyler West stared back at him, and he was momentarily startled to see a man he hardly recognized. His once bright sapphire eyes looked dulled; his toned body showed signs of expansion around his shoulders and waist—not flabby—just aged. He had thought of himself as a kid, a young punk, but the adult reflected back in the mirror changed his mind; he appeared more mature than he remembered.

"Fuck you," he growled at the sad looking guy in the mirror.

After slipping into coveralls, Tyler left. Once again, he evaded the sleepy guard and slipped back down the ladder. The steep first step almost caused him to lose his footing, not used to walking around bare-footed, but he held on to the hatch knife-edge, dangled for a moment letting the ships motion swing him side to side, and then mastered the last six ladder rungs in three steps, his feet hitting the ground softly.

He grinned after crawling inside his rack. He was now wearing a fresh pair of skivvies and a clean t-shirt. He felt amazing and was immensely thankful that he had showered. Any other day, during this time, he would normally be in the Helo-Hangar lifting weights and listening to his mix tapes. Not this morning. He didn't dare try to workout while they were still on lockdown. His eyes grew heavy despite having slept, at least for a few hours, and one would think that the shower adventure would have awakened him. He dozed off for a moment and woke again, in what felt like only seconds later.

He just couldn't sleep. His body was used to doing something at this hour. He wished he could go back on patrol to escape the ongoing sense of nothingness. The idea of being stuck in the constant company of his R-Division shipmates made him crazy. With nothing else to do, Tyler allowed his mind to wander back to the chaotic thoughts of the murder. He sunk his head into his feather pillow, but sleep did not come—only flashing images of bloody passages and shiny razor-sharp knives.

CHAPTER 29

"Flight quarters! Flight quarters!" echoed the voice of BM2 Demaso Menendez from the 1MC speakers, "all hands, man your flight quarter stations!"

Tyler lurched within the confines of his rack, feeling confused and only faintly comprehending what was happening. Awoken from a half-sleep he'd lapsed into, he wondered if the ringing announcements were actual calls to the flight deck or if his lazy daydreams were being morphed into a simulated flight crash team drill. The noise grew louder as his brain kicked in. He leapt out of his enclosure and padded barefooted, in his skivvies, to the workshop.

In the workshop, several guys lounged and laid around on the floor and on benchtops. "Flight quarters?" he said, surprised. There were several similarly stunned faces huddled in corners and crevasses around the shop. Not one of the men rose up right away, but instead each reared his head, eyeballing the next guy for some sort of reassurance that the call to quarters must be some sort of mistake.

There could be no mistaking Menendez' voice as it continued to blast from the loud speaker, "Set condition one-alpha for flight operations. Set condition one-alpha for hoisting and lowering boats, port boat davit. The smoking lamp is out aft of frame one-two-niner. All personnel not involved in flight operations stay forward of frame one-two-niner. All personnel remove hats and ball caps, and refrain from throwing FOD material over the side. The following is a test of the helo crash alarm--disregard this alarm." A piercing high-pitched wee-wauhp reverberated against the workshop bulkheads and overhead, jarring everyone to take some notice to the announcement, "Test complete—regard all further alarms."

"Let's go, girls," said HT1 Bastille spewing with graveling delight as he passed Tyler through the joiner doorway, "get off your lazy fucking asses. There's a helo on the way; we gotta land it." There was no mistaking the call; they needed to assemble the crash team for flight quarters.

"It's about time we get something to do," said Smithe.

"In this shit?" Persinski said from underneath the desk, referring to the rocking motion. He had been lying with a pillow and blanket so quietly that Tyler jumped upon hearing Persinski's voice. *Too goddam jittery.* The ship jolted again; a defiant response to Persinski. The metal storage rack rattled, signaling an alarm for all to wake up and get on their feet.

Tyler agreed with Persinski, though. Landing a helo in this sort of weather is a disaster waiting to happen. *I just fucking showered... now I got to go out there and get covered in sea water again.* In rough seas, getting routine work completed could be impossible; assembling and organizing a flight crash crew would be a much more difficult endeavor.

Tyler thought of all the steps needed to land a helicopter: pull the hangar back on its sliders to allow for maximum space on the flight deck, lay out fire hoses along the port and starboard decks, and get the crash crew outfitted. These are just the preparations. What would happen when the ship flipped and flopped? Someone is liable to trip on a firehose. With no rails on the flight deck, there was nothing stopping men from taking a dive off the edge. Although catch nets hinged to the outer facing could save your life, with vicious seas currently racking the hull the odds of hitting the net on your way over and being able to hang on would be slim.

Tyler lingered as everyone else stumbled towards the door to the berthing space. *This is madness.* He recalled a helicopter trying to take off during a storm once. The Miller had been off the coast of North Carolina. The fuselage stored in the hangar was lashed down to anchor points imbedded around the deck. The helo needed to launch because of some emergency, for what specifically Tyler could not recall. Some sort of distress from a civilian fishing vessel. As the crew had gathered on the flight deck, there came shouting and commotion from inside the hangar. After unclipping lashes from the stay brackets, every side to side roll had tipped and shifted the aircraft. The aircrew was supporting the weight, and four guys were losing the battle. To keep the helo from rolling over, the crash team rushed to help. It had been a harrowing ten minutes with personnel in harm's way on both sides of the bird. Tyler had jammed himself right in the middle. If the helo had tipped over, he would surely have gone over as well; but, that was the job—and today another helicopter would challenge the fates of landing in rough seas again.

Tyler shook his head, erasing the memory from the forefront of his mind. Too many worries crammed in—what about the FOD walk? Foreign objects and debris can get sucked into the aircraft engines. They could become projectiles launched in blade wind. To ease his mind, Tyler convinced himself that the storm's wind and rain had busily washed clean the topside decks all this while.

Now at his rack and rushing to get dressed, Tyler slipped into a loose-fitting pair of engineering coveralls; a green pair. The same type of coveralls the killer wore when he sliced through Lieutenant Orton's back with a ten-inch hunting knife. The soft fabric with a fire-retardant coated surface resembled velvet: not brushed, but cool and smooth. Did the killer appreciate the suppleness and quality of this fabric? If a small amount of liquid—rain or water—ran over the material, beads would form and roll harmlessly atop the fine fibers, only soaking in when left to stand. *Did Orton's blood do this?* Drops of blood would roll off perhaps but not pints of it. The massive amounts of Orton's blood would have soaked deep through the material—definitely down to the wearer's underwear. *We should be looking for skivvies*; Tyler smiled to himself while the other crash crewmembers Smithe, Scheppler, Bastille, Swartz, Persinski, and Ramirez got dressed around him. On second thought, if the killer had prepared well, there be no reason to search for someone's blood soaked t-shirt and boxers; he'd have been naked under the coveralls to reduce evidence. Tyler tried not to chuckle as he justified this ludicrous reasoning.

Tyler reached to pull a pair of socks from a corner cubbyhole of his rack-locker and realized a small picture frame had smashed and broken glass spread all over his clothes. The frame must have broken either when he grabbed the underwear earlier during his shower mission, or sometime between then and now. He picked up a stack of t-shirts, shook them free of broken bits, and quickly checked for shards of shattered glass; he would not have time now to clean up the mess. "Get the fuck up here!" Bastille wailed. Tyler and Smithe were the last two missing from the crowd ascending the vestibule ladder.

"Okay this is how it's gonna work," said Chief Langston to the group, "we need to stay with BM2 Ballard as we make our way back to the flight deck. Ballard will lead the way. Bastille, you and I will bring up the rear."

"What the fuck, Chief?" moaned HT1 Bastille. "Is this a joke?"

"No," said the Chief sternly, staring down Bastille. "We will follow the rules established for the whole crew. We don't get any breaks, even though the killer is not in our department." Tyler and Smithe joined the assembly.

"How do you know that?" Scheppler said with a smirk. He glanced around eager to win back the trust from his division mates. Tyler nodded to Scheppler. The other guys didn't seem to be buying the jest—especially Ramirez—his bugged out eyes had not subsided and Tyler shifted his position to block the path between Ramirez and Scheppler just in case either got spooked by the other.

"Quiet, this is a goddamned muster to flight quarters," the Chief said, "Here's what we got..." He gave further instructions on what path to the flight deck the group would take.

Smithe gave Tyler a nudge to turn around at the scene behind them. BMCM MacCleary and the XO, Mister Kendall, were in an intense conversation over something to do with berthing compartments. Tyler picked up a few words; *sleeping quarters, escorts to chow.*

"That is what's going to happen Master Chief!" The last comment came out of the XO loud and intense. Mister Kendall spun and hopped up the ladder to the Main Deck. The Master Chief loitered behind the crash crew. His upper face and forehead contorted into a deep frown.

The team departed for the flight deck.

After a silent five-minute walk, Tyler and the crash crew prepped themselves on the flight deck by retrieving equipment from the lockers behind the Helo-Hangar. The team laid hoses out, and then moved the hangar to its forward position. All the men donned their gear. Even the moderate rocking would create a difficult landing pad, so the crash crew stood by ready for the worst. Tyler and Smithe wore their silver proximity suits and held their head-covers under their arms. The helicopter came into sight just as the crew finished the prep.

BM2 Sanchez acted as an airdale signalman and chopped two orange-coned flashlights up and down at the helicopter as it approached from off the fantail. Tyler trembled with adrenalin, but not because the helicopter landing would be a difficult one; he had been a part of worse weather landings—no, he had forgotten something. In their rush to prep for the arriving aircraft, Tyler had never asked why the helo was coming out to the Miller. They would be back in port in less than twenty-four hours.

What the fuck is this about? Once the helo landed and the team managed to anchor the aircraft securely in its hangar, Tyler assumed he would find out. His job was to pull the pilots out of the chopper in the event of a crash—if there is a crash. Control the fire; secure the ship, save any survivors. Tyler and the team had performed many mock-crash drills, and he and Smithe would usually go in and carry or escort the pilots to the hangar. Tyler hoped, for this landing, they would not be needed.

From somewhere forward, Lieutenant Hornsby, the Weapons Department Head, appeared on the boat-deck and started shouting something into Bastille's ear. Hornsby wore a khaki jacket. Underneath a visible gun belt clung to his waist; the sidearm slung on his right hip. The staff officers were taking no chances about running into the killer.

The helicopter, which had appeared in the distance, started downward, finally slowing its speed and hovering above the swaying deck. "Yo!" Bastille waved his arms for Tyler and Smithe to join him. He shouted over the swelling sounds of a helicopter propeller nearing the flight deck, "When the chopper lands, you and Smithe need to go help the people inside. Walk them to the hangar," Bastille yelled into his ear. "The chopper is going to take off right after!"

"Okay!" Tyler yelled.

He and Smithe moved around the port side of the hangar. They traded Ramirez their helmets for lashing straps as they relocated. The circling blades provided concussive thumps that reverberated off the deck, and the waves splashed upwards from the side of the ship. However, the sea was no match against airstreams that were beating them down. Through the helo cockpit window, Tyler could see the pilot wave to the landing squad as he began to sway the helicopter to synchronize itself up with the rolling motion of the Miller. For a few unbearable and nerve-wracking seconds, the ship and helo seemed to argue and move against each other before at last they were as close to parallel as the pilot believed was necessary to land. The helicopter dropped to the deck. A loud metal-clanking sound erupted over the chopper's swirling whooshes. The pilot took a few extra seconds to lower the propeller thrust and gave Tyler the thumbs up; he and Smithe went to work. Smithe ran his lashing strap from the deck to a d-ring midway up the bird on the port side, and Tyler mirrored the starboard. Once secured they opened the sliding door, and Tyler offered a hand to the three passengers attempting to crawl out of the helicopter.

"Thanks!" came a loud high-pitched cry from the third passenger, whose hand landed on Tyler's shoulder. Tyler blushed, spotting the woman's cherry-colored blouse peeking out from under her windbreaker jacket. After leading the three passengers away from the helicopter towards safety, the chopper prepared to take off, leaving its passengers behind. Tyler kept an eye on the proceedings from inside the Helo-Hangar. Sanchez went into action; he released the lashings and the helo erupted up off the deck.

The woman and one of the men wore matching navy colored jackets with a bold yellow NIS printed between their shoulders. The third, a man with thick glasses and prematurely graying hair, held onto a metallic brief case with a monstrous death grip. As the helicopter took off, the woman's hand landed on Tyler's shoulder for support again. His face grew warmer. He took hold of her elbow; she used him to balance on one leg while digging something out of her left heel. She stood upright, straightened her jacket, and then shook out her loosened hair. She let out a casual, "Thanks, again," without ever making eye contact with Tyler.

The three helo passengers went on their way with Lieutenant Hornsby. Tyler and the others returned the equipment to the lockers, happy that the landing had been a success. Still on lockdown, the crash crew was immediately sent back to their division—the armed Ballard leading the way.

"Did y'all see that broad rubbing all over West?" Swartz, the crash crew's number two nozzle man, joked as they reached the R-Division hatch and climbed down single file into the berthing compartment.

Several heads came popping out of the General Workshop at Swartz's comment.

"She was not," Tyler said.

EM2 Hart was leaning halfway out of his rack, "there's a girl on the ship?"

"Yup, they sent in the NIS. One of them is a chick." Swartz responded, "she was gettin all touchy-feely with West."

"Shut the hell up, Swartz," Tyler said although he was quick to realize that bringing a woman on board would provide a well-needed distraction for everyone. It would give them something to talk about other than the ways Orton had been murdered. The NIS agent wasn't exactly a model, but she certainly was attractive enough to get Swartz all wound up.

Tyler went back to his bunk, eager to doff of his damp clothes. He recalled the shattered picture frame he'd discovered earlier and went to clean up the mess. He lifted the frame, careful to protect the photo. The photo of R-Division, taken on the flight deck, was from a Sunday barbeque a year earlier. Seven out of the twelve R-Division guys in the photo had been wearing green coveralls that day. Tyler did not remember the number of green coverall owners in R-Division—the once insignificant detail leapt out at him.

He was not the only person in the repair department who owned green coveralls; this revelation was not news, but the significance of the fact was no longer coincidental. He himself owned more than a few pairs; he now forced his brain to remember when he received each. His first pair of coveralls came to him for achieving surface warfare specialist and stepping into the hole duty station rotation. New sets of green coveralls were a prized commodity. When Tyler received his qualification to stand as Upper Level Main Control, Lower Level Main Control, and Machinist Mate of the Watch he was rewarded with two pairs. Then when he got through all of the Boiler Room stations up to the Boiler Technician of the Watch, he had received another two. Chief Langston usually controlled and selected who would receive the special clothing

"West," Langston said; he had been on a roll one midnight shift in the Control Room and was barking mad at the BT's for some innocuous reason, "I never thought I'd have a shit-chaser become one of the best damned BTOW's we got, but you've made me proud these last few weeks." The Chief had acted genuinely impressed with Tyler that night. BT2 Billy Pigg was one of Langston's guys being chastised for not living up to Tyler's standard. Initially, Pigg, a hard charging BT from New Jersey wanted to kick Tyler's ass. But, after he learned Tyler was from New York and they both rooted for the same football team, the New York Giants, Billy Pigg and Tyler became good friends. He'd left the ship the following year, and Tyler made a mental note to look up his old friend soon. Langston always made a spectacle of giving out those dammed green coveralls.

Tyler would never forget the transitory ceremony and how the Chief had handed over the plastic wrapped parcels, "Put them on, HT," the Chief pressed, "here are chevron pins for the lapels."

With all that had happened since the murder, Tyler's head overflowed with theories again: the captain coming to R-Division,

Langston insisting they don't search the main spaces, the intricate rack inspections of R-Division, and the two guards posted outside of R-Division verses the one guarding M&B. Tyler's throat closed. *My God*, he thought, gripping hold of his locker to keep himself from tumbling over in shock; *the son of a bitch is definitely in R-Division.*

CHAPTER 30

Jorgenson, along with the Executive Officer, led the NIS team from the Helo-Hangar to the Wardroom and then to the scene of the crime. They said very little. The orders received from Surf-Lant had been simple: maintain the lockdown, keep Watford sequestered in the Wardroom, do not approach the suspect, and wait for the agents to arrive via helicopter.

Special Agent Johnson, the female, stood in one spot—a spot that was clear of blood—Jorgenson and Kendall crammed into the narrow passage behind her—both leaned in to hear if she had any questions. Jorgenson thought it would be better if she stepped further into the passage to give them all a little breathing room, but this was her show and he didn't want to infringe on her process. She stayed at a conspicuous location that gave her full visibility of the space. She observed and scanned the whole area. The other two agents moved further into the space and were unloading photographing equipment. They began snapping pictures and taking notes. The ship had finally outrun the worst of the storm, and there was less rolling. The NIS team worked in silence. They stood there for more than five minutes without speaking.

Jorgenson was not sure if he should stay or go. He was feeling a bit tense in the tight quarters. There didn't seem to be many questions; they had walked in silence, and now the agents were busy documenting the scene of the crime in silence. He did not want to linger in this passage. Images of the triage team kept flashing in his head and hearing Bruce Orton's last words repeating over and over was making him uncomfortable.

"Agent Johnson; is there anything you need from myself or

Commander Kendall right now—should we wait in the Wardroom?"

Without turning around she said, "Tell me, what you believe happened."

Finally eager for something to say, Jorgenson began the speech he had been preparing. "Ensign Watford entered the boat-deck passage around that corner over here," He pointed left, which was aft towards the rear where the passage change direction and angled out towards the Main Deck. "On the other side of this bulkhead is the boat-deck. We believe he was trying to dump the body overboard by going through the watertight hatch just aft of here."

Jorgenson turned his attention to the opposite direction. "Lieutenant Orton exited the Main Control Room scuttle over there," he switched his position and pointed to her right, he was a head taller than her and his arm hovered over her shoulders. "We think he was attacked somewhere around there," he pointed to the midway point in the passage between the Main Control scuttle and where they stood. "When Watford walked out into the aft passage, he... I mean the attacker, dropped the body and ran forward." Jorgenson pointed forward and envisioned a perpetrator running into the darkness.

Agent Johnson did not reply. She remained quiet for a few moments then said, "What do you believe happened?"

Jorgenson was confused; he had just described what they knew. He paused and considered her question, again. He did not want to insinuate anything, so he asked, "What do you mean?"

Again, without turning, she said, "Why Orton? Do you believe this was random?"

It was a good question and one he had been considering for almost twenty-four hours since the event. "I don't know," he said blankly.

Without hesitation and almost as if he had said something she wanted to hear, she said, "That will be all for now, Commander. We will finish sweeping this area. I want to speak to Ensign Watford and examine Lieutenant Orton's body. We will then look through Orton's stateroom to see if we can find anything that leads us to who might have wanted him dead. In the meantime, we will use the Wardroom and the Lieutenant's stateroom as our base of operations. I assume you'll be either on the bridge or in the Wardroom if I need you?" she didn't look back for a response, just moved and began speaking to the photographing agent.

Jorgenson wasn't sure if he should say anything more. He turned to Kendall who shrugged his shoulders, and they both turned and went to the Wardroom.

CHAPTER 31

Twenty-seven hours since my waltz.

The corruptors dine with the corrupted. This is laughable, the captain and his fellow abuser attempt to find a seat with the crew for chow. What's wrong, captain, is your luxurious Wardroom palace too morose after the death of your progeny abuser? Would you stoop low and meander through the bowels of festering nonentities? Is this your idea of mingling, Captain Jorgenson? He watches me.

This is your chance; confront him!

No, not in this crowd—the deed would not be successful.

I see his eyes wandering to others as Edward Elgar's *Pomp and Circumstance March No.1 in D—Land of Hope and Glory*—let me observe this scandal. My outer-persona is adept at hiding in crowds; switch, I will enjoy this spectacle.

The nervousness displayed on every machinist mate, boiler tech, and repairman, as well as the anxious faces of guards and officers is endearing. I see you, captain.

His presence is appalling.

Yes. Let him wander in slovenly grace. As soon as this lockdown is over and we reach the pier, I will countdown the second stanza.

You must accelerate the plan.

I have time.

What about the outsiders?

The arrival of the visitors is puzzling—their appearance, once at the pier, is justified, but why now? The news of NIS agents is spreading through the ship. If I were truly a suspect, I would be in the brig by now. But, why bring them via helicopter, why not wait until the ship is moored?

Perhaps they have evidence.

Nothing physical.

What did the HT's discover?

Rumors! Only rumors spreading.

I think back to the glorious night. Elgar's song leaves me, and the charming voice of Humperdinck returns—the theme of my most excellent kill. I try to think of what happened exactly afterwards.

You hid the knife first.

I was rushed and did not clean the blood.

You did not finish the box step.

The intruder had interrupted. I became momentarily panicked, but then I gained composure and hid the weapon of choice. After the shower, I was calmer. I hid the coveralls as well.

Did the intruder jeopardize everything?

No... he did not see a thing. If there were a witness to the crime, I would be in chains—I am not; he saw no one. They found no evidence. Their ploys are intended to coax a frightened attacker out of hiding. These fools know nothing of what Father taught me.

Hide in plain sight.

Yes, Father.

The abusers are self-righteous fools at best.

Yes, Father.

Enjoy your chow, captain. I will enjoy mine. The deed is done. You are all mere pawns in a game in which I hold the key to victory. You are all blind. You are all afraid. I am the only one on this ship who is without fear. As soon as we are pier side, you will once again know chaos.

*****

Captain Jorgenson walked alongside Lieutenant JG Springer. Earlier Jorgenson managed to convince Springer to join him down below for chow. "We need to be among the crew," Jorgenson had said, "let them see we actually give a damn." Springer did not seem to care one way or the other. The captain surveyed the room.

After the agents had finished examining Orton's body, they returned to the Wardroom and grilled Watford for more than an hour. The repeating of the same questions started driving Jorgenson batty and he made his hasty exit from the Wardroom, deciding to let them eat alone while he went to the mess decks. Springer had set up the meeting with the LPO's in advance. The NIS Agents had become increasingly rancorous in their short time aboard—especially Agent Johnson, who was brutal in her questioning of Watford. "He did not see a face." Jorgenson had interrupted only to receive a nasty sneer from the agent. One would think the NIS agents were the ones who'd been cooped up in berthing compartments for two days.

When they entered the mess decks, Jorgenson sensed a familiar nervousness as he clenched his food tray. He stood cemented to the deck scanning the high school cafeteria for his buddies, none of whom attended lunch at the same time as he did—there instead was a sea of semi-recognizable yet unfamiliar faces eating chow, chatting quietly, and stealing glimpses of the awkward appearing captain with no friends. *Where the hell are they?* He did not want to simply plop down beside someone and strike up a conversation. *This is embarrassing.* Springer said, "Over here," and started towards the prearranged table, and Jorgenson followed hoping his momentary new kid on the block anxiety went unnoticed.

The LPO's from R-Division, HT1 Bastille and EM1 Dunham, acted surprised at Jorgenson's and Springer's presence as the two men sat down. Springer, the R-Division boss, held a somewhat informal working relationship with the LPO's and was easily able to strike up a conversation. They started talking about how things were being handled and how their men were acting. After Jorgenson received the information and update he wanted for the two repair department leads, he soon found himself ousted from the exchange, not intentionally, but what more could they say to him. After their report— that the person under guard is calm and acting normal—their banter became obtuse—all Jorgenson wanted to know was did they have things under control—a point confirmed in the first two sentences.

Jorgenson picked at his food, too distracted to eat. As every man passed by with a plate of food, he smiled. They said, "Hello" or "skipper." They all scrutinized him though—some covertly with sideways glances, but many openly stared. For a moment, Jorgenson sent HT2 West an endorsing nod. He still refused to believe West's story about the knife merely falling from the overhead; he almost believed West was being modest.

Jorgenson felt a chill; the thought of searching the ship made him think back to that passageway that West and his comrades must have walked through. He had ordered the area swabbed of Orton's blood once the agents completed their survey; only after their careful examination could the gruesome scene be finally cleansed, but some of the blood had soaked in, he was sure. Jorgenson did not revisit the crime scene. He had managed to avoid walking through the space on his way to or from the Wardroom. Would the passage ever be clean again?

The captain forced down some food. The grub tasted okay, but the greasy lunch wasn't the normal first-rate Navy meal—the cooks were obviously suffering from cabin-fever like everyone else. West glanced over at him. There were others staring, but West seemed to be examining him more than others. *He's observant*, Jorgenson thought, taking note that West was not just observing his captain. Without making it obvious, Jorgenson attempted to deduce who West was studying. West made eye contact with an enlisted member of M-Division; they gave one another some sort of signal. West's eyes went from the machinist mate, to a small group of boiler techs, and then he fiercely studied his own group. *What are you thinking, West?* Jorgenson wondered, *what's going on in that head of yours?*

"Am I right, Captain?" Springer said, awakening Jorgenson from his daze.

"I'm sorry, what were you saying?"

"Hodges. The way he's been acting since this whole thing started." Springer stated again with a nervous smile.

"I hope you don't find anything about *Lieutenant* Hodges' behavior funny, do you?" Jorgenson said. "Your shipmate deserves sympathy, not your judgment." Springer should know better, "I believe he deserves the respect afforded an officer, and that is something you should be keeping to yourself, Lieutenant JG Springer."

Springer's demeanor buckled, and swallowing the mouthful of grub he had been chewing became much more difficult than it ought to have been. Bastille and Dunham both suddenly discovered their forks to be more interesting than the conversation. "Of course, Captain," Springer choked.

"Gentlemen, this will be over soon." Jorgenson assured them. "Whatever happens, do not let him out of your sight," he said, "If he tries anything, you know your orders."

The two enlisted men nodded their assurance of the command. From the corner of his eye, he spotted the machinist mate wandering to the table where West sat. With his food shuffled about his plate, like a child trying to hide the fact he had not been eating his greens, Jorgenson stood, eager to leave the mess decks.

*****

Tyler felt relieved as he and the rest of R-Division entered the mess decks. The large space had the capacity to seat thirty people or so. One, of the two, armed guards stationed at the forward berthing areas, escorted them. Already seated and eating were twenty others; more than half of them were from the aft engineering departments, M&B. As the HT's and EM's stepped through a galley line, Tyler eyed who from M-Division he would sit with. He had made more than enough machinist mate friends from standing hole watches in Main Control over the years. He hoped to discuss how they were handling the lockdown over in M&B as well as the theories about the murder. He wanted more than the latest squawk box rumors.

Upon filling their trays with what appeared to be some kind of beef, Tyler winked at Smithe to follow him over to the tables where a number of M&B boys were set up. Chief Langston appeared out of nowhere and blocked their path across the mess hall. Langston and MMC Musgrove, who had metered the HT's into the line one by one, stationed themselves at either entry to the mess decks and acted as maître d's. "Sit with your department," Langston said holding up his hands as though to corral and block them from leaving the group.

"You're joking," Tyler said, but Langston pointed off towards a table on the opposite end of the room. Smithe grabbed his friend's arm to stop any further confrontation.

"I'm getting sick of these guys, Smitty," Tyler said before he turned and drudged off to where the chief had pointed.

Tyler and Smithe joined the rest of the men from R-Division, finding seats near two electricians, Hart and Wilkette.

"Oh God, look at this," Wilkette said, nodding off towards Captain

Jorgenson and Lieutenant Junior Grade Springer. He and Hart enjoyed a laugh over the captain's presence..

Tyler had spotted both officers long before Wilkette; Tyler had not even settled into his seat when the captain and Springer entered the mess hall. Jorgenson's arrival proved more of an intrusion than a reassurance. The assembly of enlisted men straightened themselves up, lowered their voices, and acted all of a sudden as though they were at some sort of dinner party rather than servicemen shoveling down postponed grub.

After Jorgenson retrieved a tray and sat down with Springer, Bastille, and Dunham, Tyler found himself awkwardly staring; the captain nodded. A bit of childish pride swelled in Tyler's chest for a moment, but he pushed the self-important feeling back down.

Anger quickly replaced the momentary swagger. *What do they know—and why aren't they taking someone into custody?* Tyler considered the possibility for his inner debate to be the result of paranoia—he might be suffering the same delusional prophesies as he had imagined Ramirez and Scheppler to be having.

He got back his inner bearing and glanced across the room, managing to gather the attention of MM2 Barry Fillmore. The machinist mate casually flapped a hand at Tyler, who returned the gesture waving for Fillmore to join him; he mouthed the words *I need to speak to you.* Fillmore gave a nod.

The room was filling up with M&B guys. There were several he did not recognize as full-time Miller crew—possible reservist murderers according to Smithe's reasoning; in total, more than thirty guys bunked back in M&B berthing. Almost all the men lined the galley and mess hall. He wondered if they were struggling with their sanity as much as his fellow repairmen. *One of these guys is a killer... either that, or my paranoid delusions are kicking in.* Tyler tried, unsuccessfully to convince himself that the murderer was not in R-Division but... All the facts were lining up against someone in his own department. His eyes wandered from the M&B men to the two tables of R-Division guys; he wanted to ask the room out loud, *any of you commit murder recently?*

Tyler silently studied each of the men seated eating chow and made a two-column list in his head. He put everyone who did not or could not have done the deed on one column, titled 'no' – that was a short list. Then he listed all the guys who would be able to pull off such a dastardly act on the other list, named 'yes'. After scrutinizing the columns and making cross references in his head, he scraped the stainless steel food tray clean and decided all his monotonous debating and internal list making resolved nothing. The only thing he could be certain of was that other than himself and Smithe, five other guys in R-division owned green coveralls and probably had the physical strength to take down someone of Orton's stature. *Am I really trying to figure out which of my friends killed Orton? How do I know another officer didn't do it?* It would be easy to blame an enlisted man. His thoughts grew irrational. There was so much smoke-screening going on. And what about those NIS agents? *Let's wait and see if the NIS points towards R-Division too.*

While Tyler swam in his thoughts, MM2 Fillmore had managed to sneak past the self-elected chow hall security kingpin, Langston, who was distracted with an empty bug-juice dispenser. Fillmore hopped between Tyler and Smithe, pushing each in a playful manor. "How's it going?" he seemed so relaxed, obviously taking the lockdown well.

"How you boys holding up?" Tyler asked. Fillmore smelt of fresh deodorant and had recently shaved. Showers had yet to be awarded to R-Division—Tyler had presumed the large number of M&Ber's must have been stinking up the joint down below too.

Fillmore shrugged, "All right, I guess. Crazy what happened to

Orton, huh?"

Tyler was uneasy with how calm Fillmore acted. "Yeah, crazy."

"Why they got a guard taking you all to chow?"

"You all weren't?" Smithe said, "Hell, we got guards watching us piss."

"Seriously? Man, they got you boys locked up tight; they sure haven't been that strict over in M&B. Of course, we're right next to the Mess Decks... so?"

Tyler careened his head left to right. "Ponderous." He said hoping Fillmore's stress-free attitude hinged from some perverse, deep-rooted fear of a killer sleeping next to him.

Fillmore laughed and leaned into Tyler's shoulder to lower his voice, "I don't know what they have guards around for anyways. The guns they're wearing don't even got rounds in the clips."

"No bullets?" Tyler said as hopes of a phobia driven syndrome in Fillmore evaporated.

"Seems like it's all for show. You don't want one of them operations guys having a loaded forty-five anyway—imagine the damage a shot from one of those might do, down below decks."

Tyler knew something was seriously wrong. He had seen full clips on both guards outside R-Division; their guns were locked and loaded—ready to shoot.

Fillmore nodded at Langston who was looking their way and shaking his head. "They're wanting us to go back. I'll see you when I see you."

"Right," Tyler said. He wanted to ask more questions, to get more information, but instead dismissed his friend. The fresh smelling Fillmore and his comment about no bullets gave Tyler more information than he had expected.

"Oh, so when we get to port—if I'm not on watch, I'll meet you on the flight deck for when they take the guy away, okay?" He stood to leave and Tyler grabbed at his arm.

"Wait, what guy?"

"The blonde haired guy in the Wardroom—no one knows him; he's a twidget reservist. They caught him running away after beating Orton with a spanner wrench."

"Hold on," Tyler said, gripping Fillmore's shirtsleeve, but Chief Langston blurted out a command for "M&B team one get back to your berthing." Fillmore left giving Tyler and Smithe a thumbs up.

Tyler was floored. There wasn't anybody in the Wardroom—the M&B guys had been given a line of bullshit. Fillmore and the rest had been going about their days believing the killer was captured and being held until the ship arrived at port. Smithe forced a crooked smile onto his face. Tyler breathed out a heavy sigh and pulled the bill of his cap down while trying to hold in the scream that was about to burst from his throat. He could not deny the clues anymore; the unsettling decoy to the M&B department added certainty to his theory. The khaki's knew planting such an obvious red herring in R-Division would only incite the murderer; Tyler narrowed the field down and accepted a simple truth: one of the R-Division crew was a killer.

CHAPTER 32

A large console of sliding knobs filled the entire glass room. Soundproof panels would not allow any external noise to enter. I remember in that startling silence, my breathing and heartbeat sounding as loud as a locomotive pushing through my ears. Only a boy of five or six, the visits to my father's radio station studio became journeys to a fantasyland that still fills my dreams. A music expert who could easily *name that tune* in a few notes—always ahead of the TV show contestants—became enlightened while living in countries far away from his boyhood home in Mobile, Alabama. Those foreign cultures helped shape his thoughts about humanity and the oppression of man. He became well read and aspired to and aligned his thinking to some of history's most prominent social activists. He gained public notoriety because of his views on society and its lack of equality. After his military service, he worked as a disc jockey. That job gave way to becoming a well know talk radio personality. After many years of fighting a battle with only his voice, he took matters into his own hands. My father is the notorious murderer of Kinkaid Walton, former Senator from Mississippi—a once leading candidate and likely Democratic nominee for President. Two years before the 1972 election, Senator Walton reneged on a promise to vote against an important bill facing the Congress. For purely political reasons, his yes vote paved the way for sweeping dissent in an already desperate liberal agenda. Walton represented all that was corrupt in the American political system. My father made him pay with his life. In the election, a fraudulent Democratic Party propped the inept George McGovern up against the criminal incumbent; Richard Nixon easily won a second term.

In the prison's family-gathering room, my father wore an orange jumpsuit. He would passionately continue to impart his knowledge on me during weekend visits. I learned about his strong convictions: the rights of men, destructions of authority, and the necessity for revenge against those in power who do not respect the rights of others. My thoughtful comprehension of these ideologies have allowed me to formulate a pathway of purpose. Those visits remain fixed in my memory. With vivid clarity, I frequently recall his descriptions of why and how he gutted the senator in the man's own bed. My father's hair had gone gray, but his brown eyes still glowed with an inner light of knowledge and profound superiority.

During his teachings on slaughter, he would blare the phonograph to conceal our discussions from nosey bystanders. The music was glorious. Hundreds of compositions in the prison library offered record albums and composer collections of all music genres. Sometimes we would just listen, and other times we would talk while the music played in the background. He always recorded our sessions and would give the cassettes to me as presents at the end of each visit. His handwritten notes on the cassette cases included the title, composer, year, and for the classical pieces, the year first recorded. That was always important to him, but I don't know why; I need to ask him one day.

My favorites were the classics, but I also appreciated when he would make tapes that had modern artists that I might hear on the popular radio stations.

The inside of the cassette covers always had a secret lapsed-time-stamp written in—this was a message between him and me—a marker of where in the tape I could find our talks imbedded. Sometimes I yearned to hear the replay of what we had discussed so much that I would fast-forward the tape to the precise spot and play just the messages over and over.

"Listen to these cassettes and learn the music titles and composers," he had said. "And above all, listen to our discussions. Appreciation of a thing is only superficial if one will not immerse themselves in the endeavor."

At the age of twelve, I went to a birthday party for a kid in middle school. He had an enormous in-ground pool. It was so large that the boys—there had to be twenty of us—all jumped in thrashing around. The roughhousing got out of control, and I got myself pushed under and wedged between the ladder and the pool wall. I was under for what seemed like forever; it was no one's fault—we were just kids. When the mother, or the father, I can't remember which one, finally pulled me out, the water had filled my lungs... and windpipe... and throat... and nasal cavities... and eardrums. The doctor said I was lucky to be alive. He assured me that losing part of my hearing was a small sacrifice to pay for getting my life back. Thing is, since that event, I can't hear so well, and listening to my cassette tapes is a real struggle. I need to turn the volume to the maximum level, and then some of the talks we had are barely audible above the music that's always playing in the background of the recordings.

At least I'm not completely deaf; I got into the Navy. The service entry hearing tests said my audible range was borderline acceptable for Navy service. I almost wasn't allowed to join—not because of my hearing—but rather my inability to swim. I put down on my application that I couldn't swim—this was a lie, but I was afraid to go in the water. They said I didn't need to swim—just get across the length and climb out of an Olympic sized pool. I made it through boot camp by getting from the deep end of that pool to the end where I vaulted out so fast, I head-butted the instructor who was leaning over the edge screaming at me to, "Get your fucking scumbag recruit ass out of that water!" That was the first time back in a pool for me, but I will never go into water again.

I can't remember when I stopped needing the headphones to hear the music. It's better this way. The Navy has rules against wearing headphones during work or on duty—my recordings are fortified in my mind.

In my bed *Peter and the Wolf: The Story Begins*: there is an air of melancholy in Prokofiev's notes. The violin strings of Peter's *da-da-da-Da-da-da-da-Da* float in a space between my ears and brings back memories I've long since suppressed.

Thirty hours since my waltz.

How easily I evaded the resting guard earlier. How uncomplicated slipping through unnoticed was. The simplicity of that endeavor—sneaking to the head with a towel tossed over my shoulder. I had forgot the horrid squeaking of that bathroom door. Even still, I made it to the head and no guard came to stop me.

They do not suspect you.

If they did, the watch would have been more alert.

If they had the slightest clue, their guards would be down in the berthing space. They would have put me in the brig until finding proof, but they know nothing.

Nothing!

Even if I am caught and put in prison orange, like my father, they can never bring back the Defiant One!

In the shower earlier, I had hummed a sweet song.

How confident you are.

Yes!

Too much confidence will turn dangerous.

After toweling off and getting dressed, I hurried back to my department, quietly humming to myself. No one even noticed my absence. *da-da-da-Da-da-da-da-Da*. That was easy—maybe too easy—

now that I know slipping away is possible—when the ship is beside the pier, I will slip away and enact my second plot.

There is a sudden commotion. A security alert team returns to our berthing compartment. "Rack inspection!" Chief Langston announces.

Why a second inspection?

What have they discovered that leads them here again? I am nervous now. The music changes. Chords and progressions crash— loud screaming guitars!

Control it.

It is loud... a finger tapping on a fretboard blasts notes at me. Someone is speaking; ear-splitting sounds drown them out. I need to listen to hear what is going on.

Breathe.

They search racks before arriving to mine. I go through my belongings in the form of a checklist—is there anything in there that would be of interest now?

The messages in your tapes!

Langston and the female spend extra time at my rack, even bothering to look at my cassette tapes. She says, "You got quite a blend of music here."

Who do you think you are questioning my music? You know nothing. You are nothing to me. I want to scream and slide my knife into her belly. Slit her abdomen until guts fall to the floor like that senator's guts did. Instead I grin, switch, "Yeah, I guess so."

The NIS chick puts the cassettes back. I hate that she dared to touch my tapes. A new composer: violins and cellos, oboes and bassoons; 1867, *Night on Bald Mountain* by Mussorgsky. My heart races in sync with Mussorgsky's tempo. They move on, taking nothing with them. I am not relieved by this. I am nervous. For the first time since ridding my world of the Defiant One, I am afraid.

Stay the course.

My bunkmates are confused by the second inspection as well. They are nervous. Do they suspect me?

No—they know nothing—these inferior nonentities.

My mind wanders as the search paces through the department. The music is jumbled and getting louder. I place my hands over my ears and push, trying to stop my torment. I manage not to cry out. Do they hear? For the first time, I am afraid, and a fury rises in me that these inferiors cannot imagine.

CHAPTER 33

Agent Johnson was no doubt in charge of this group. She commandingly dictated orders to the second agent and to the other man, who, Jorgenson had learned, was there specifically for fingerprinting the evidence. Her information gathering process followed specific steps, it appeared; they mulled around the officer's sleeping quarters. They were in Orton's stateroom—a two-person space shared with Lieutenant JG Springer. Johnson had pulled her wet hair up in a bun after leaving the flight deck earlier that morning and before heading to the murder scene. Now her brown locks were dry and frizzy despite the tight bun. Every so often, she brushed a few escaped curls out of her round face while she worked. At one point, she pulled a small leather wallet from her briefcase, retrieved two bobby pins, and forced the agitating curl from sweeping over her cheek and nose all the while instructing her fellow agents to "collect copies of this" and "take photos of that" and never once allowed her green-hazel eyes to wander from the documents she was inspecting.

The relationship between her and the two younger men didn't appear unpleasant, but the two men conveyed a tacit respectfulness towards her.

The fingerprinting had been completed earlier and so the youngest of the men, the man with the thick glasses, rummaged through Orton's wardrobe under orders from Agent Johnson to not disturb anything. He must only survey the closet for out of place items. The thick glasses guy was also instructed to "stop everything and retrieve the fingerprint results when they come in from the lab."

Jorgenson took note of the way Agent Johnson dressed. She wore a pair of short heels, but in every other aspect, she tried covering up her femininity. The black dress pants did not highlight her obvious curves; instead, the made-for-men style hid most of her hips in an effective veil. While she showed off a little bit of color in a bright red blouse, there was no hint of cleavage. The points of the blouse came up high to her neckline, and most of the shirt lay concealed under her black blazer—the just bulky enough jacket covered any evidence of breasts. No make-up, no jewelry—no wedding ring. Agent Johnson hid her sexuality through her PhD's. Jorgenson figured she was aware time was catching up to her and she was frustrated. She took the loss of her youth out on the men who stood before her. She existed in the world of young guns while slipping ever so slowly into her late-thirties. In addition, she probably wonders why she is still alone. *What a cute little story, Henry,* he told himself, knowing he would not dare make the background story he had assumed about her known to anyone else. She was there to work.

"Is the fingerprinting done?" Jorgenson asked, speaking for the first time since entering the stateroom.

"Well, as your superiors already suggested, we are going to try to get a confession." Agent Johnson avoided answering his question. She spoke without ever looking up, preoccupied with some papers that had been stored in Orton's desk drawers. Jorgenson recognized the enlisted performance review forms. She leafed through the pile, making scratches in her spiral bound notebook.

"The fingerprints?"

"Are being analyzed Commander. We have things under control." She let her voice and body language get into lockstep as a way to establish a pecking order. "Once there's a match I will confirm your theories. Until then, we will finish going through the deceased personal items, and after that we'll start interviews."

"We aren't certain who the knife belongs to, but why not just go get him now? Why wait—do the prints need to confirm anything before you take him in? We do have a witness." Jorgenson said, repeating the cautionary aspect of the situation, "If the prints are from someone else, we'll let him go." Jorgenson believed this to be a logical approach. "What's the harm in taking him now?"

"The harm is," she turned full on to face Jorgenson—he hadn't noticed earlier but her agent-face was quite intimidating, "we have a process to go through here, Mister Jorgenson. A process, which includes bringing the primary suspect and his shipmates in one by one for questioning. There is reason to believe his behavior pattern will respond to this tactic. I met him during the rack inspection. I believe keeping him in his berthing compartment is an appropriate decision."

Jorgenson let his face muscles flex into disarming mode, "Agent Johnson, they've been locked up for a long time."

From the corner of the room, the thick glasses man decided to get into the conversation and said, "There were remnants of a circular thumb or index finger on the knife, but not enough for a confident match."

Jorgenson's hopes for a quick resolution instantly vanished. "God dammit," he said a little louder than he wanted to, "No fingerprints, then?"

"We don't know that yet; there was a partial print." She turned to thick-glasses guy as if to cue him into agreement that there was still a chance to use the knife as confirmation of who Watford had identified. He nodded.

She continued, "But this doesn't change our approach. We are moving forward under the assumption that our best lead is Ensign Watford's description. And..."

"What else?"

She frowned slightly, "all other possible suspects—anyone who fits the description—people with vendettas against Orton—will all need to be considered."

Jorgenson realized that meant an extended investigation. Orton was not the citizen of the year; he had many times been involved in disputes. Ensign Watford's guy has a vendetta—*isn't that good enough.* Jorgenson remembered his orders from his superiors, *unless you definitely know it is him, do not apprehend, do not panic the crew, do not falsely accuse.*

"I followed my orders."

Suddenly a list of names and faces began to load into his brain. He had been avoiding going through this suspect prioritization process— Watford named the guy, or at least, he thought it was someone who looked familiar.

"The opportunity to take him is past. He has been sitting tight for more than a day. We have no reason to believe he's going anywhere. I assure you we are on the same side." She let out an extended breath and continued scribbling in her little notebook. "If someone else is responsible, we need to be ready—I want to ensure, through interviews that no one else crops to the top of our list."

Her rationale extended a small amount of relief. She had it right though. With the suspect named by Watford, they could have acted— put him in the brig. However, if they were wrong? What if it wasn't him? Prints would have made this easy. Now they must consider alternatives. What if they were wrong altogether? False accusations in a politically correct society would be a nightmare in the aftermath. This was a new military. In the old days, in the days of Dorie Miller, they might have rounded up everyone from engineering and thumped a confession out of them. Not in today's Navy—not in today's military.

Agent Johnson continued, "I want to get as many interviews completed before we get to port. Once we are moored we will be in civilian jurisdiction, is there any way we can slow down?"

"Yes, I suppose we can."

"My goal is to get his confession before we are pier side; the less chance he'll try something stupid like escaping."

Jorgenson thought about this for a moment. "I have an idea; we can anchor in Narraganset Bay."

She had doubts, "I'm not convinced that is such a good idea; he could swim to shore under cover of darkness—at least if we are next to the pier, I can station lookouts near the obvious escape routes."

Jorgenson let out a quick snicker.

"What is it?"

"Our prime suspect, Agent Johnson, cannot swim."

She managed a subtle smile.

"Well now, it sounds like we have a plan... it amazes me the number of Navy boys who cannot swim."

"He's one of them." A few Miller sailors lacked that particular skill. Everyone on board was aware of who the non-swimmers were though, which is why that particular trait about their prime suspect needed to be kept under wraps, lest the information gets out and the crewmen decide to take matters into their own hands.

"I know everyone on my crew very well," it was a little white lie, but he was certain about this part of the situation. If they were correct in their assumptions of whom he and Watford suspected, anchoring out in Narragansett Bay would be as good as staying in the middle of the Atlantic. "This sailor is not skilled in that aspect in the least. He won't even try to jump unless he's gone suicidal on us."

Agent Johnson said, "Commander, really? You know your crew very well. I doubt that. Based on what I've learned so far, you know very little about your crew." With this, she turned away, allowing something in her notes to get her attention.

Jorgenson's anger peaked—*that* was uncalled for.

"Agent Johnson." After a moment of awkward silence, she finally raised her head. He wanted to sneer, but instead drew on his best authoritative face. "Aboard my ship, I will be addressed as *Captain*— this is your jurisdiction to investigate, but I am in command. Are we clear?"

Her face remained stiff as if she had been expecting the rebuke. Perhaps her green-hazel eyes accomplished the task, or the way the collar of the red blouse laid against her pronounced clavicles, but she immediately disarmed him with a sophisticated agent-in-charge gaze and the simplicity of crossing of her legs.

She closed her notebook for the first time. Jorgenson thought she may have just decided to like him.

"I'm going to get a confession out of this fucker," she said. Her soprano pitched voice disrupted the calm of the room. The two men working at Orton's wardrobe and locker raised their heads for only a moment, then went back to their tasks. Her language surprised him a bit, but he could see the raw determination in her eyes. She was motivated and he was glad to see anger there. Jorgenson now believed he might actually get along with this woman. Alas, the moment of brief comradery floated away as she ruined the pleasantries with, "Captain?" She made sure he recognized her use of the word *captain*. "Do me a favor, would you?" she said glancing around as if looking for something or someone.

"Of course, Agent Johnson."

"Get that idiot, what's his name, Hodges? To stay out of here. Send him back to his duty station and snap him out of whatever daze he's in." She spoke harshly, "Keep him from coming in this room; he keeps trying to get in here to lie down."

Jorgenson grimaced, not feeling confident at all about sending

Hodges to any sort of duty station. Yet, somehow, he found himself replying to her much like her young accomplices, "Yes, Agent Johnson, of course."

CHAPTER 34

"Almost end of watch," Smithe said; Tyler could hear the relief in his voice. The rotations were exhausting; he and Smithe had been tasked with that long search rotation which had lasted almost fifteen hours. When Persinski and Swartz handed him and Smithe the watch over six hours earlier, he was already exhausted, and they hadn't even started.

They garnered the privilege of having Hendriks as an escort yet again. Before him, for their first four hours, SK1 Gary Ziegler had been their armed companion. "This guy's a whacko." Smithe had said to Tyler more than once during the early parts of their shift. Tyler couldn't disagree: storekeepers were an odd bunch—either everybody's friend or everybody's enemy. Ziegler seemed to bounce between the two distinctions every other week. They were well into the second day of the lockdown, and Ziegler was so frazzled that Tyler had asked if he needed to go and lie down several times.

"Just keep moving—keep moving," was all the moron seemed to be able to mutter.

To be truthful, Tyler didn't mind having Hendriks back. He'd proven to be decent company and someone new to talk to other than Smithe—who wasn't much of a conversationalist lately. They found themselves regurgitating the same tired theories repeatedly while cooped up in the berthing compartment. Occasional conversations outside of those in R-Division were welcome. The last few hours before his patrol, Tyler had took to hiding from everyone by closing up his rack curtain.

"We're about to anchor," Hendriks said.

"What do you mean, anchor? We're not going to the pier?"

Hendriks shrugged, "I was told we were gonna drop anchor. The Chief Engineer needs the status report for anchorage."

Tyler made a move towards Main Control.

"Where you going?" Hendriks asked.

"To see Hodges—if we're dropping anchor, he'll be in Main Control," but then he remembered, Hodges hadn't been down to Main Control since the murder.

Hendriks pointed a finger over his shoulder opposite to Tyler's direction, "We gotta go to the bridge."

"Hodges is on the bridge?" Tyler asked, recalling Dunham and Bastille recounting the story they'd learned of Hodges' break-down from Lieutenant JG Springer during chow.

The DK explained, "I was told that Hodges has been ordered to stay on the bridge."

The squawk box rumors had recapped Hodges actions over the past several hours.

"He's gone bonkers since the murder", "he wants to sleep in Orton's rack", and "Hodges is not fit for the duties of Chief Engineer."

"According to Lieutenant Hornsby, Hodges is not a pretty sight," Hendriks said as the three of them headed towards the bridge to give the status update. "The Old Man has him working, though. Hornsby tells me it's because of that NIS chick. Sounds like she's giving everyone up there a hard time."

"Glad they have to deal with her and not us," Smithe said.

"Wishful thinking there, Smitty." Hendriks shook his head. "They started pulling people from R-Division for private interviews since you've been on patrol."

"Let me guess, they are starting by interviewing everyone in R-Division before moving on to M&B?"

"Yeah," Hendriks seemed amazed Tyler could be so insightful, "how did you know that?"

"Just a hunch."

As they walked, "Sounding and Security patrol report to the bridge" came over the 1MC. Two minutes later, the threesome entered the wheelhouse. Jorgenson stood with two officers. "Let's keep this quiet," Tyler heard the captain say, "Nobody needs to know." The captain nodded at the three of them as he passed. Tyler gave the CO a quick salute and the captain departed.

From his vantage point, the current panorama brought on new emotions; Tyler peered out through the forward windows at Newport. The weather was finally clear. The view was far different from the recent raging hurricane in the North Atlantic. The water glistened, and vistas of piers, shipyards, and the further north Middletown shoreline called to him. Two vessels were moored pier side: the USS Valdez and the USS Edson. The idea of being so close yet so far away from land sickened him. They had anchored well up in the bay inside the Newport Bridge in a deep channel east of Jamestown. Tyler could see that they were practically dead center between the two shores to port and starboard. The pier was only a short swimmable distance away.

"Any reason we're not pulling alongside the pier?" Tyler asked and no one answered.

Lieutenant Commander Kendall volunteered after ignoring Tyler's question for several passing moments, "For the time being, the pier is not ready for our return—the harbor master needs to rearrange the vessels." Something about Kendall's response gave rise to several quick glances between Kendall and Lieutenant Anderson, the Officer of the Deck. Lieutenant Hodges, although present, did not join the XO and OOD in their rubbernecking contest.

"What?" Tyler said, "You afraid of the guy jumping ship? You sure made for an easy escape being this close to shore."

LOCKDOWN

The XO and Anderson shook their heads; then Kendall said, "West, please give the status to Mister Hodges." Then to Anderson he said, "I'll be in the wardroom," and he left.

Tyler wondered if the officer's topic of conversation when he arrived had been about swimming to shore. He walked to Hodges, who sat in a bridge chair staring blankly out towards... well, Tyler wasn't sure what. His expression was benign and his facial muscles flaccid; his lips were moist. A slight bit of drool gathered in the corner of his mouth.

"I have the ship's status, sir?"

The Chief Engineer did not respond. Hodges' interest remain fixed on the bridge windows or the clear sky beyond. Anderson sighed aloud, turned to the boatswains mate, and said, "Status?"

The boatswain spoke the procedural anchorage conditions out, and Tyler realized they were waiting for Hodges to give the command for setting the ship's engineering systems for anchorage.

Anderson said to Hodges in a direct raised voice. "We're ready for shutting down engines and shifting systems, Lieutenant Commander Hodges."

"Uh...thank you, West," Hodges absently mumbled. His voice was weak, wispy. He looked and sounded drugged. Tyler waited as Hodges, the ship's Chief Engineer, searched his memory for the words to secure the ships power and systems. Tyler held back an urge to laugh despite the fact that this pathetic spectacle was extremely distressing and not at all funny. Hodges panted. His eyes darted around the room like a stage actor desperately trying to remember his next line.

Tyler stepped in with Anderson's silent shoulder-shrugging encouragement, "Uh...Lieutenant Commander Hodges, wouldn't you agree we need to get our engineering systems set for anchorage?"

"Yes, yes," Hodges agreed. "Thank you, West, of course."

221

Tyler waited for more to come out of Hodges' mouth, but again, all the man could manage was more panting.

"Maybe you should have one of the boilers shut down, and keep one on standby." Tyler said. "I would recommend keeping boiler number one lit," Tyler glanced over at Anderson.

"Mister Anderson, do we plan on getting back underway anytime soon?" Anderson shook his head side to side. "And I think you should have number two boiler put into shutdown, don't you think, sir?"

"Yes, yes."

"Get a steam blanket on two." Smithe suggested.

Tyler nodded at Smithe, "Right. We should also power up the aux-diesel."

"Oh, fuck it," Anderson snapped, "West, please walk me through this with Main Control."

"Whatever you need, Lieutenant."

Tyler and Smithe coached Anderson through the systems shutdown and standby procedures—although the two of them wound up doing most everything, including calling down to Main Control for some of the commands. Hodges sat in the captain's chair muttering, "I'm sorry, I'm sorry," every time Tyler made a call through the sounding tube. Anderson seemed humiliated by his fellow officer's behavior. While Tyler somewhat enjoyed playing officer, splitting the duty of Chief Engineer with Smithe, he was relieved when Anderson thanked them for their assistance and at last sent them on their way to Main Control for watch turnover.

Tyler pitied Hodges, but that was not what was bothering him. They had finally arrived home in Newport, Rhode Island, yet the ship remained floating in the bay, anchor down. They were close enough for him to go diving off the side of the ship and swim for shore—the ship was that close—but he wouldn't attempt it. Tyler could practically feel the soft ground beneath his feet and smell the familiar scents of the harbor. They were so close to shore, the killer could easily escape if he wanted. Just a short swim. *If we bothered coming this close, why not moor? Go pier side,* Tyler wondered, *why anchor out here?*

Smithe suddenly stopped and said, "Ah fuck!"

"What? What?" Tyler instinctively looked around, and Hendriks gripped the handle of the holster gun.

"We gotta go back on watch in twelve hours."

"Yeah," Tyler wasn't following.

"That's god-damn four-AM, guy... you know how I hate Mid-Watches dude." Smithe was incensed.

Tyler chucked, "Alright Smitty ... we'll get through it." As surprising as Smitty's sudden realization was, he was happy to see a little of his friend's usual-self coming back.

CHAPTER 35

Tyler was almost thankful to be called in for an interview with the NIS agents; he couldn't bare another moment of listening to Postino strumming his electric guitar. He played the same chord progressions over and over; the song was "Don't Look Back" by Boston. Postino nailed the opening riff on his Gibson Les Paul, but not well enough to listen to for the umpteenth time. More than half of the department had been dozing when Postino plugged into his mini-Marshall amp and failed to check the volume before starting the jam session. Tyler was not amused by the sudden wake-up call. He had been trying to rest; his next patrol would be in the middle of the night; he needed to get some sleep before the watch, and the prospect of having to talk to the interrogators loomed. It was almost eighteen hundred on the second day of lockdown. The entire department delayed going to chow to complete the interviews. He had also learned that the NIS team had actually started their interviews in M&B department, and that's why they were getting to R-Division so late; this differed from what Hendriks told them while on patrol.

Tyler entered the General Workshop. The joiner door was operational and Tyler closed it thinking he couldn't remember the last time that door had been shut—if ever. The NIS agents had set up two facing chairs next to the workbench. He blushed to see the woman from the flight deck would be the one interviewing him. She sat cross-legged, scribbling in a notebook. A second agent sat at Bastille's desk several feet behind her. He kept his face buried in a stack of papers. Neither person greeted Tyler when he entered the space. The man with the thick glasses and silver attaché must be up in the wardroom but his absence didn't seem to matter. The female agent pressed a red button on a silver tape recorder with her pen. She then leaned back in her seat. The tape cassette slowly turned, making a small squeaky noise like rubbing a damp cloth on clean glass.

"HT2 Tyler West?" she said.

"Yes."

"Sit down." The woman's eyes lowered to her notes.

Tyler sat and folded his hands across his lap.

"Special Agent Bryce Johnson, Naval Investigations." She introduced herself. She neglected to acknowledge the other man in the room.

"Let's get started. Tell me, where were you between midnight and zero four hundred—the night of the incident involving Lieutenant Orton?"

"In my rack. Asleep."

"Where were you when the Reveille announcement sounded?"

"My rack."

"Did anyone see you there?"

"Yes," Tyler said. She was obviously toying with him before getting to the tough questions about his fight with Orton.

"EM3 Wilkette saw me. When I opened my curtains, he was in his rack. I asked him what was going on."

"Fine." she said and then made a few scratches in her notebook. She pulled back the first page and scanned the paper.

"When you leave, can you ask HT2 Smythe to join me?" The agent mispronounced Smithe's name. She said it with an *eye* sound. Smithe hated when that happened and was forever correcting people.

"His name is *smith*... like how you would say black*smith*. That's the way he pronounces it." Tyler tried to correct her on his friend's behalf, but Agent Johnson seemed disinterested. She nodded her head for Tyler to leave.

Confused Tyler paused in his seat, searching for the right way to bring up what was on his mind. "Are you going to ask me anything else?"

She peered at him and said, "Like what?"

He figured blurting out his contemplation was the best approach under the circumstances.

"Why haven't you asked me about the incident in Main Control?" She must have gathered testimony about his outburst from the men on duty in Main Control. Several people had already been in for interviews; surely, Langston of all people must have mentioned the shouting match and threats that had come between Tyler and Orton. Agent Johnson acted dumb, shook her head, and shrugged her shoulders. Tyler questioned, "No one brought up my argument with Orton?"

"Why don't *you* tell me about it?" Johnson said and went back to scanning her journal. She seemed incredibly preoccupied with her notes.

Tyler remained silent. He wanted the woman to raise her head and acknowledge him. Prove that she was listening. A few beats went by until finally she met Tyler's eyes with a lazy disinterest. *Why doesn't she care about my threatening Orton?* He was suddenly fire-hot. His throbbing forehead felt like it would burst at any moment. Postino's A to D then E to D chords were still slightly audible either in his head or from the room on the other side of the bulkhead.

"What's the process here?" Tyler asked, exasperated at the sheer incompetence, "I've been down in this compartment for almost three days—waiting for somebody to interrogate me. I told Orton there was going to be a murder on the Miller, and he is killed a few hours later. Then you show up, and you couldn't give two flying fucks about it!" Tyler fumed. He almost apologized for his language but decided to

226

keep that apology to himself. She irritated him, and the agent at Bastille's desk just sat there as if barely alive.

Special Agent Johnson allowed Tyler to draw in a few calming breaths before she nonchalantly asked.

"Yes, well... Why did you tell Orton that?"

"Because I was pissed."

"Over what?"

"It was," he paused, trying to remember and then recalled almost face-planting off the ladder; it was dumb, and Orton was just being his typical asinine self—"Nothing," he said, "It was stupid. Orton had nothing to do with it, really...I was just blowing off steam and he got the brunt of it."

"Okay." she said, "You can go."

Tyler couldn't be more stunned; he glanced at the man at the desk for confirmation on this woman's decision to let him go, but the other guy's disinterest was beyond obvious. He bowed over his important paperwork acting as if his continued writing was what was keeping the earth from crashing into the sun.

That's it? She must want more. More about Orton, more about who he liked or disliked, and who hated him. There's a long list! The stupid NIS Agent only sat there waiting for Tyler to leave. *They're not interested in anything I might say. They don't want my information.* He'd searched the whole ship. He'd found the knife. He'd been involved in so many different aspects of this crazy situation, and she didn't want to talk to him? The notion was ridiculous.

"Why did you ask me to come in here?" Tyler stood to go, but couldn't contain his anger and frustration, "We've been locked up for days with a killer on the loose, and you're doing bullshit interviews for what?" He was so angry he became dizzy; he needed to breathe—to calm down.

"Do you know who killed Orton? You know, don't you? Why else would you not see me as a suspect?" Tyler plopped back in the chair and folded his arms. Johnson paused her note scribbling—at least she appeared to be a little bit more serious.

"Is it the blonde haired reservist?" He laughed.

She did not respond.

Tyler closed his eyes to relieve the spinning room. When he opened them again, she simply asked him, "Well? Did you?"

"Did I what?"

"Did you kill Orton?"

Tyler resisted the temptation to reach across with his fingers and violently flick the stupid lock of hair that was dangling in front of the woman's face. He wanted to scream at her *of course not, even if I did it's not like you would be able to find out,* but then a familiar scent tickled his nose. The aroma of creamy almond vanilla soothed his seething wits. "Poison." He said, and the half-asleep man at the desk jolted awake enough to let out a subtle gurgle.

Special Agent Bryce Johnson, Naval Investigations strained to keep a straight face, "Are you telling me you poisoned Orton?"

"No." He hesitated, "You're wearing perfume. You weren't wearing any yesterday on the flight deck. It's Hypnotic Poison."

She was perplexed.

"Am I right?"

"You were the one who helped me out of the chopper yesterday,"

Tyler nodded. He recalled the momentary embarrassment and fought against the blushing heat filling his cheeks.

She managed a subtle smile, "You know the name of my perfume?"

"I bought the same stuff for my girl earlier this year."

"You're very observant."

"Really. Huh?" Tyler tried not to be obvious about inhaling her perfume, it made him think of Alexandra.

She smiled at him, "Please ask...*Smithe* to join me," she made sure to say his name correctly this time as she clicked the recorder off and went back to her doodle pad.

Distracted with thoughts of Alexandra, Tyler walked to the door, yanked it open, yelled "Smitty!" and went straight to his rack.

CHAPTER 36

The outburst happened so suddenly that no one could be sure who started the brawl. Tyler had sprung from his rack and found himself smack dab in the middle of the mix. He assumed the responsibility of pulling Persinski off Scheppler by the scruff of his collar: that's when he caught a light fisted punch from Dunham, who had also leapt in to try and break up the fight. Almost everyone joined the scuffle. Tyler rubbed his chin where Dunham nailed him, mistaking him as the aggressor of the situation. "Sorry, West."

Persinski, it appeared had started the whole mess by going to town on Scheppler. Swartz sat on the floor next to Scheppler, battered. Had someone stepped on him? Wilkette had avoided getting any shots by dancing around the melee until he reached down and pulled the staggered Scheppler to his feet; then he got rammed by a body and flung back into the lockers. The two young boys seemed to have gotten the brunt of the verbal abuse from Persinski. Scheppler also had endured the worst of the assault in the between the racks fighting pit. At some point, Tyler's right shoulder slammed into Swartz as he tried escaping the uproar only to be trampled by several others when he hit the deck.

In all, Scheppler, Ramirez, Swartz, Smithe, Postino, Persinski, Wilkette and Dunham were fighting—the only bodies not involved were Bastille, who was God knows where, and Hart who Tyler recalled was sent to Aux-One to help with an electrical issue.

Tyler wanted at Persinski, "You better leave the kid alone, before I break that pretty nose of yours!" He shoved past Dunham to get closer. Everyone had been denigrating Scheppler after his special interview in the wardroom; the workshop interviews were over, but Scheppler had been asked afterward to go to the wardroom and he hadn't reappeared for more than an hour. Wilkette and Ramirez had also been asked to the wardroom, but they both returned after a short time, a much shorter period compared to Scheppler. The blonde haired killer rumor was still on everyone's mind.

"He swung at me first, West!" Persinski said, not appreciating the iron fists Tyler had thrown at him to get him to let go of Scheppler. "You know I got sunburn you fucker."

"Shut the hell up, you friggin ass!" said Ramirez, his Spanish-Boston accent coming through his words. He climbed to his feet from the floor. He'd been sitting by his rack after being knocked back.

"I saw you, you dick! You shoved him. And you two should be on watch now anyway," said Smithe pointing at Persinski and Swartz.

"We're on break, dude!" Persinski was fearful of Smithe.

Postino started laughing, "You HT's are pathetic."

"Shut it, Kirk! They put us on break 'cause the security alerts are shifting over," Swartz said.

The security alert guards were getting lazy; they couldn't handle the walking and dropping off of the watch, so they settled for a break mid-way through the rotations to give them a breather.

Smithe, the unofficial guardian of the younger enlisted men, marched towards Persinski.

Dunham jumped to block his way, standing between two bunks, and gripping hold of either side to create a barricade. Dunham looked ridiculous. He stood at least a foot shorter than Smithe, but he had balls to face-off with him. "Stand down, damn it." Dunham warned the taller Smithe.

Postino laughed even harder at Dunham, his LPO. Swartz and Wilkette chuckled.

Ramirez stated the obvious. "Really Roger, you think you can take

Smithe—I wanna see this."

"Everyone calm down!" Bastille shouted at last arriving on the scene. He had been in the General Workshop and missed the bulk of the chaos. "Back the fuck off, Smithe."

Smithe stepped into Dunham saying, "Tell this idiot to climb off the racks," then everything broke loose again, each guy paired off and grabbed someone else pushing and shoving.

Ramirez, Dunham, Bastille, and Tyler all began shouting for everyone to "stop", and "calm the fuck down!" They all just half-wrestled in their tracks for a few seconds when all of a sudden the vestibule erupted behind Tyler. Loud footsteps were clamoring down the ladder. The two passageway guards, OS1 Kingston and FTC Dempsey appeared with their M1911's drawn. Each gunner held his weapon low, but with chambered rounds, the guards were ready to use the guns. The realization hit everyone square in the face, and they all stopped shoving one another.

"Okay. It's okay," Bastille said as he turned to face the gunners holding his hands up in a surrender pose.

"What the hell, Bastille!" FTC Dempsey practically yelled. His face was a deep pink, and his ears were almost as red as his hair. Tyler could see the Chief doing a mental head-count of the group and aided him by saying, "We're all here Chief. The only missing guy is Hart, he's in Aux One." Tyler sensed the reactions of Chief Dempsey and HT1 Bastille; he nodded his head as if to say, *yeah, I know.*

Bastille turned his attention back to Dempsey. "We're good. Just a little rough housing... everything's fine." He stepped towards the guards and urged them to go back topside. The two reluctantly backed up and returned to the second deck as Bastille turned to the R-Division gang.

Dunham, still blocking Smithe from charging Persinski, perched absurdly between two racks; a dangling skinny wimp with straight-locked arms angled like gussets supported between the bed boxes. Smithe could snap Dunham like a chicken bone. Bastille chided his fellow LPO, "Get down, Dunham. Don't be an ass."

Everyone focused on the wrong thing really. Tyler wondered how many of them realized the guards had been armed and ready. The men had only been a trigger pull away from a shooting in the berthing compartment. He recalled Fillmore's description, and visualized the damage a forty-five caliber weapon could do.

Dunham huffed and jumped down, moving aside for Smithe to get out of the row of racks. When Smithe passed Persinski he bucked up at him, and Persinski bolted back to the last bunk on the row, causing Tyler to let out a loud enough chuckle for everyone to hear. Persinski bit his lip, embarrassed.

"Everyone go to the shop," Bastille said, "We all need to calm down." Bastille waited for everyone to move.

"Now fuckers! Get in the workshop!" Bastille turned to Tyler. He lifted his chin as if silently confirming that Tyler had understood the relevance of the situation. *Yes, Anthony, your little secret is out—I know the game you've been playing.* Tyler fought off the urge to disclose his suspicions out-loud. *Which of us have you been assigned to watch?*

The men of R-Division wandered into the General Workshop; everyone eventually found a place to sit. Tyler got to his usual spot against the forward bulkhead. He sat on a five-gallon bucket that once contained mint green enamel paint but now merely housed an assortment of pipe and spanner wrenches.

Bastille made a ceremony of walking the perimeter of the room, instructing the group on the uniform code of military justice and about how fighting was a capital offense that could result in write-ups, demotions, and restricted duty. Tyler rolled his eyes at the notion of disciplining the entire repair department.

After twenty minutes of awkward chastising and the resulting quiet glaring from everyone listening, the ladder outside the workshop rattled to life with footsteps.

"Jesus, please not another barrage of storm troopers," declared Smithe. In stepped MS1 Bennie Parker hugging a box full of sandwiches, followed by GM2 Garth Williams holding two twelve packs of coke, and EM2 Hart holding his electricians canvass bag. Hart must have finished the repairs needed in Aux-One, and was picked up by Williams on his way to the workshop.

"Thanks Bennie," Dunham said as he took the sandwiches and placed them on the workbench. Williams was apparently the mess cook's armed escort from the galley.

"Commander Kendall said this would be easier than trying to schedule escorts for you guys..." Parker hesitated as he scanned the room as if expecting to meet somebody other than the entire repair division, "I know it's late for dinner, but, I mean everyone... you know, going back and forth to the mess decks." His checkered trousers and white t-shirt carried the customary stains and burn marks for a Mess Specialist. *He looks so out of place.* Tyler doubted if the cook had ever been down to the General Workshop before.

Hart joined the R-Division meeting, and was the first to grab a sandwich; this open the floodgates, and everyone went for the food.

Parker's abnormal nervousness came across as perplexing; the loud and obnoxious cook always had something crass to say, but today he was speechless as he handed out the rations. Who wouldn't be edgy? This guy usually keeps to his kitchen, but now he had to make food deliveries to every berthing compartment on the ship—one of which housed a vicious cutthroat. Why wouldn't he look out of place when everything else was completely *fucked*? The captain coming to the general workshop and the mess decks, the ship anchored in the bay instead of pier side, and armed guards escorting people to the shitter—the whole damned ship was out of order.

Within half an hour, the men devoured the meager chow, and in the following minutes, they all sat around acting as though the scuffle had never happened.

"So," Postino spoke first, "What do you think is going to happen after they find out who did it? I mean, do you think they'll send us home for a couple weeks while we're in port?"

Smithe said. "I'm sure we'll get a chance to go on liberty. Hell, I need a drink. I'm heading straight for O'Brien's Pub."

"I'm with you," Hart chimed in.

"You got family out this way, Smithe?" Dunham asked, grabbing a seat nearby. Although Dunham's attempt to smooth things over with Smithe after their altercation between the bunks failed, Smithe decided to play along with the rest of the group.

"My sister is staying in Little Compton, but that's temporary."

"Your sister hot?" Postino said.

"Screw you." Smithe growled.

Tyler laughed, "His twin sister is off-limits. By the way, she'll kick your ass as well as Smitty could."

Postino laughed. "I'll bet—but she'll love me." Smithe wasn't amused. Postino was the ladies' man of their group. A cool cat from California—he always had an air of serenity that drove Tyler crazy on the flag-football field. As the team's quarterback, no matter what the game situation, Postino would always say, "don't worry coach, we got this." His easy smile hadn't shown on his face over the past two days, but he was smirking now.

Bastille joined in. "What about your girl, West?"

"Alexandra?" Ramirez laughed, "Quiero tener un Alexandra. Dama salvaje, *yummy*."

Hart laughed apparently understanding the wisecrack.

"Whatever you just said," Tyler said pointing a finger at Ramirez, "fuck you."

"Apuesto a que es una cosa salvaje," Ramirez said smiling.

Tyler wouldn't admit Ramirez was making him feel embarrassed. He did not want to dampen the mood. They had all been ready to knock each other silly a few minutes ago, and now they were sharing a meal and some normal conversations, that did not include theories about the Miller Murderer.

Smithe said, "Leave West alone, Hector. Alexandra ain't no fling. He's been ring shopping for that girl."

Tyler turned to Smithe with a dumbfounded smile. *Why?* He thought. Then the taunting began; and would undoubtedly continue until he got off the ship. "Do you really want to go there, Smitty?" Tyler asked, "I can start telling secrets too—about a certain dancer from Fall River."

Smithe held up his hands, as though to say, "I got nothing to hide." *Don't you?* Tyler thought.

"Dancer?" Persinski said raising a thumbs at Smithe—but Smithe wasn't buying Persinski's attempt to smooth over their little altercation from earlier.

Bastille wore a large fake smile on his face. Tyler threw his bread at the LPO's head and said, "What are you smirking about?" Bastille only smiled, barely catching the roll between his smallest finger and ring finger.

"Quiero conocer dama de Tyler," Ramirez said.

"All right, knock it off, Hector. You're from New Bedford; you didn't speak a word of Spanish until you turned eight years old. You're whiter than I am."

"Hey, man, screw you." Ramirez sat down; everyone started laughing at him now. Wanting to direct attention off himself, Ramirez said, "How did you meet this girl, anyways?" He waited for an answer, "Hey, I'm being real, man."

Tyler dropped his gaze to the floor searching for something to say; he wasn't much for giving up private information, but what else should they talk about?

"Not much to tell." Tyler said, "Met her at The Blue Pelican about three years ago."

"Three years?" Wilkette said, "You've been stringing her along for three years?"

Swartz turned to Persinski and said, "I once had a girl hang on me for four years, man."

"Shut the fuck up, Swartz. What girl would bang you?"

Swartz didn't find Persinski's comment as funny as everyone else did. It wasn't that the chubby Swartz was unattractive, but his perfectly round head made his face appear like a cherub, and he often received jibes about being baby-faced."

"Well, West," Bastille asked, "What's the deal, you getting married?"

"Smithe just told you I've been ring shopping... so, yeah, maybe." Tyler snapped back. "What about you, Bastille? Tell us something we don't know."

"Happily married. Five years."

"Married?" Scheppler's head popped up, "Did any of you guys know this fool was married?"

They all did, but Scheppler's comment got a few chuckles that seemed to relax him a little.

"How about you Scheppler?" Tyler said, chomping down on a

mouthful of his third sandwich. "You got a girl?"

"Nah," he said.

"Little Tommy's a mama's boy." Persinski gave Scheppler a friendly shove, wanting to make sure they were still on good terms after their tussle, "I hear you talk about her more than anyone else."

"Didn't you set your mama's house on fire or some shit like that?" Wilkette asked.

"Hey, it wasn't like that."

"Hold on," Smithe said, raising up a hand with a grin on his face, "I need to hear this."

"It wasn't my mom's house. It was my stepdads." The recollection of the incident didn't seem to be as much of an embarrassment to Scheppler. His metal blue eyes brightened at the memory of setting his stepfather's house on fire. He stood and walked to the trashcan, depositing the remints of chow and jutted his shoulders out. He reached into a rear pocket pulling out a fresh can of Copenhagen and expertly loaded a dip into his smiling lips. He had obviously obtained the dip during patrol.

"Ass-fuck that he was. He was always slapping her around. My real dad never did that," he said, "and she'd never do shit about it. So I did something."

"God damn, Scheppler—what the shit, man?" Postino said, "You just decided to burn his house?"

"Down to the ground." Scheppler wiped a dribble from his face with the back of his hand and went to spit. Everyone reacted simultaneously with half the guys shouting "in the garbage can." He and Persinski were notorious tobacco users. They would spit anywhere. Scheppler dipped tobacco—he preferred Copenhagen but would use Skoal if the ship's store was ever out of his favorite. Persinski had a nasty habit of chewing Red Man; he always had a chaw tucked deep in his jaw.

Between Persinski and Scheppler, the stench of tobacco was always present in the General Workshop. Tonight was no different. Scheppler also notoriously spit in places he shouldn't and had gotten more than his fair share of beat downs for spitting on someone's shoes.

"Fucking hell, Scheppler, finish your story." Persinski said.

"Well obviously I got in trouble with the law. Judge suggested...or more like told me, to join the military, or else go to jail. I dunno why though. No one got killed or nothing like that. My stepdad had to go to the hospital for smoke inhalation; the idiot kept running inside to save his stuff. Whatever, I got what I wanted—my mom finally left his ass. I guess I finally got my point across."

"That's better than the reason Dunham joined," Bastille said, earning himself a crude flip of the finger from his fellow LPO, "Rich kid trying to get back at daddy, right Dunham?"

Swartz made another offhand comment. "My Daddy's a drunk." No one reacted to the confession.

"Okay..." Bastille wasn't sure how to follow up on that comment, but said, "Anything else you want to share, Swartz?"

The cherub faced HT just looked blankly out and said with a twang, "Nope. That's all. My Daddy's a drunk."

"Whose dad ain't a drunk?" offered Hart.

"Damn right," came several agreeing comments.

"That's why I joined the Navy—needed to get away from my father," said Postino.

"Me too," said Persinski.

"Okay so we all got daddy issues and joined the Navy—what are we, a bunch of strippers?" Tyler's jibe cracked everyone up.

"I ain't a stripper." Swartz was serious and the whole room erupted in laughter again, although it looked as if Swartz was not in on the joke.

"What about you Wilkette? Why did you join the Navy?" asked

Dunham after the Swartz admission subsided.

Wilkette did not hesitate—he seemed eager to talk about his past. "Well, my mother was a great inspiration to me. She raised me alone and wanted me to join the Army." This announcement drew a round of boos from the Navy men. "She wants me to go into government one day—joining the Navy was an easy way to get to college because I didn't get great grades in school." Everyone chimed in about how they all had sucky grades.

Tyler thought about the nickname that he gave Wilkette and Scheppler when they both arrived within weeks of each other: *Ebony and Ivory*. Wilkette's dark umber skin tone set off stark against Scheppler's waspish whiteness. Wilkette was such a nerd compared to Scheppler though. Two prominent ears and broad nose supported a pair of Navy issue black plastic horn-rimmed style eyeglasses and a triangle shaped face.

All of them had their quirks and mannerisms. Smithe smoked continuously and hooked his thumbs into his pockets. Ramirez never wore a hat and whistled while he worked. Scheppler and Persinski spit all over the ship. The always nonchalant Postino played his guitar whenever there was a break. Hart always was eating and kept orange peels in his mouth, Swartz wore his ball cap backwards, and Wilkette buttoned his shirt up to the collar. Tyler leaned back and watched as Bastille, the conductor, orchestrated the ongoing conversations. The men picked at one another, made jokes here and there about their past foolishness, and occasional laughter followed. All the men tried hard to stay in the spirit of bringing back some sanity to the department. The casual conversing was necessary, but the reality of their situation remained way too serious for Tyler to relax. One of the guys sitting around chatting like kids at their first day of Sunday school was a cold blooded killer.

The truth would only take a little more time to reveal itself; Tyler pondered how the killer felt about that. Is he sitting here as cozy as a fly in horseshit believing he's concealed? *You're slick enough to stab a man in the back, hide the weapon, ditch your clothes, and slip back to your rack without anyone seeing you,* Tyler thought as each man took his turn in the barrel. *I'll bet you've planned your next move already.* How might this scenario play out?

The brass and NIS want a confession—they possessed the knife, presumably with fingerprints, but that wasn't enough. He had seen enough cop shows to realize that even with prints, getting a guaranteed murder-in-the-first conviction was difficult.

Shit! That's it!

They need a confession for murder one. Tyler smiled at his epiphany—this was why they were still smoking the suspect out. This was the reason the NIS met us out at sea and why we weren't mooring pier side. Once the ship goes pier side, the local jurisdiction would get involved and then Miranda rights kicks in. Once the assailant gets off the ship, he gets a lawyer, and he'll be told to not talk.

"Mother-Fucker." Tyler said aloud and almost everyone burst into laughter. Apparently, he had not heard the question; someone asked if Tyler ever had any childhood nicknames.

CHAPTER 37

Jorgenson sat facing the Dorie Miller shrine. They were no closer to apprehending the killer than before. Drinking so much of the calm inducing tea was making him sick, yet he continued sipping away as though the concoction was the most delicious thing in the world.

"What do you think?" Jorgenson asked, staring at the face of the former navy cook in the photo. "Why Orton? Why did he go after Orton?"

Of course, Miller did not offer up a response. Jorgenson took a large swig and gagged on the awful liquid. He forced himself to swallow and put the cup aside while still staring up at Dorie Miller, waiting for the photograph to respond, accepting the fact it never would. *There must be a reason*, Jorgenson thought, *there has to be a motive.*

"I know why," spoke a voice. Jorgenson recoiled in his seat, believing for a split-second that the photograph had actually responded; the ghost of Dorie Miller had joined him in the stateroom. He had forgotten Hodges was in the room with him. Hodges the church mouse had not uttered a voluntary word the past two hours. He had blended into the bulkhead managing to become invisible. Jorgenson spun in his chair. "Lieutenant Hodges."

Hodges cradled himself in a chair tucked in the forward corner of the captain's stateroom. His officer's khaki uniform was disheveled and clung to his body; he hadn't shaved and several scrawny hairs protruded from his weak chin and clammy pale cheeks. His color had not completely returned, but he looked somewhat restored—thanks to the Chief Corpsman and a dose of sedatives. *Still seems off his rocker*, Jorgenson thought, *but improved.*

"Why do you believe Orton was murdered?"

"Because Bruce was an officer," Hodges said in a low whisper.

Jorgenson knew this theory had been floating about since the very beginning. Despite there being only one victim, many of the staff believed somehow that all officers were now targets. A ridiculous notion, really. There was nothing to suggest it, but he had to admit that there was nothing to suggest otherwise. Jorgenson needed to consider all possibilities, so he'd mentioned the premise to Special Agent Johnson. After many interrogations, she reported that the enlisted crew, as well as the prime suspect, did not immediately show signs of any officer bigotry. However, she added, the first round of questioning usually didn't reveal deep set truths either. Even so, the possibility of an ongoing officer killing campaign seemed less likely than ever.

"You manned the EOOW position earlier today." Jorgenson said, "How was it?"

Hodges would not look him in the eye, "I could not go to Main Control... I stood watch from the bridge." He said staring into space. "Anderson already told you."

Jorgenson nodded, "You're going to be all right, Phillip. You can't shut down on me; I won't let you."

"I'm sorry." His raspy voice mixed itself with a syrupy self-loathing whine, "I let you down, sir. I see that. But, I can't get it out of my head."

As the Chief Engineer continued to whine and explain more of his pathetic behavior, his direct report, Lieutenant JG Springer appeared in the doorway. Springer came next in the rotation for *Hodges duty*. Each of the officers were taking turns babysitting the emotional engineering department leader. Jorgenson had toyed with the notion of sending him off to the hospital via tugboat, but a decision like that would impart real damage to his career. *He just needs time to get over this*, thought Jorgenson as he gave Springer a slight nod of the head indicating he should take over. "Take a walk, Lieutenant. Clear your head. Captain's orders."

"Aye, sir." Hodges got up to leave, and Springer stepped aside to let him pass. "You coming George?" Hodges said with a whimper.

"Be only a minute, Mister Hodges, can I meet you on the bridge?"

"I guess so."

Hodges' whimpering was worse than that of a grade-schooler with a skinned knee.

Springer let Hodges walk away before speaking, "Is he all right?"

"He will be." Jorgenson was determined to make it so.

"Are you all right?"

"I will be." Jorgenson stood. He wondered whether they were doing the right thing, keeping the men locked down with the prime suspect. "Agent Johnson has been at those interviews since dinner—is she driving anyone mad yet?"

"Not exactly the sweetest lady." Springer said, "But she'll get the job done. I hope she makes an arrest soon."

Springer's nerves, like all the other officers, were being stretched to the limits, "That doesn't make me feel much better. He should be in the brig. If he gets loose, he'll come after the rest of us. The officers, I mean."

"You still think this is about Officers?" Jorgenson said.

"Come on, Captain, let's be realistic," Springer said, "We realize who the killer is, or at least we think we do. What else could this be about? Orton was intended to be the first of many."

Jorgenson could not reason with them. Paranoia pursued the officers. Every Navy man knew the secrets concerning the class structure that divided officers and enlisted. The lofty attitudes of too many officers seemed to pester the enlisted men with low tolerances for authority. Witnessing some of the exchanges, sometimes even Jorgenson felt offended by the general attitude of the officer class in the military. The common view of many officers was that the bulk of enlisted men are hoodlums needing an out for one bad situation or another: bad breakups with girlfriends, no job to rely on, no education to fall back on, or a dead-end family life. There were ample sob stories about enlisted men enrolled in the military for the sole purpose of escaping hard times at home.

If you asked a group of officers, they might agree with the idea that the majority of enlisted men think of them as stuck-up pricks. Enlisted men rarely consider the work and dedication required to become an officer. Many enlisted men believed the men who wore khakis, both officers and senior enlisted men, abused the power they held over the enlisted. But, in many cases, the officers did abuse it.

Are they so wrong about us? Jorgenson questioned himself as he halfway listened to Springer speak about how the enlisted have it in for them. *At the end of the day*, Jorgenson thought, *aren't we all just men?*

"Hell," Springer said, drawing Jorgenson's attention back on whatever he had been saying. "I'll bet half the enlisted crew itches to throw down with an officer. Remember the flag football incident? HT2 West pounded on Ensign Roman—about knocked him out over a bad call. Every time I go to R-Division, none of those men show me any respect. Their damn LPO's, Bastille and Dunham, run the show."

"I've always liked football." Jorgenson said, throwing the conversation in another direction, "especially since I joined the Navy. I like football and basketball. Any sport, really."

"Sir?"

"There's something profound about a pick-up game," Jorgenson stood up, brushing himself off. "The uniforms come off for one afternoon. We're not officers. They're not enlisted. There's no blue or tan clothes to decide which class we belong to. We're just men; men playing football. The military structure is gone. The game is only temporary, but the liberation of the premise is removed."

Springer managed a smile, "Yes, sir."

"I want to change the rules about the softball tournaments we sponsor—the officers versus enlisted game—we need a less military approach to those contests."

Springer bobbed his head up and down. His glasses magnified two blank orbs. There was something enjoyable about tormenting the poor soul. Jorgenson managed a small smile.

"Springer, next time your men decide to put together a scrimmage game, call me. I may want in." Jorgenson said the last line in the most serious tone he could muster.

"Of course, sir."

"In the meantime, relax a little. I know we're all worried about what is going to happen. But, you're especially on edge. I think you're too tense. You fidget when you're tense—you know that? Is this why the HT's call you Lieutenant Spaz?"

Springer let out a nervous snicker, "I wasn't aware you knew about that nickname, sir."

Jorgenson patted him on the shoulder before leaving the room, "I know a lot Mister Springer—not everything—but much. Now, go take care of Lieutenant Hodges before he gets himself into some sort of mischief... like trying to nap in Lieutenant Orton's rack."

CHAPTER 38

HT3 Scheppler stood his ground. His elaborate arm waving argument with Postino persisted as Smithe and West entered the General Workshop. Tyler jumped up atop a workbench with his back against the upper cabinets close enough to jump in if necessary. After the earlier incident, the potential for another argument escalating into a fight intensified—*these guys are children.* They had only broken up their little round-table touchy-feely rap session a few minutes earlier when the security guard had returned to fetch Swartz and Persinski to finish their patrol. Tyler and Smithe should be trying to catch some shuteye before going back on watch in a few hours. Instead, here were two of the main protagonists getting back into an argument.

"I'm telling you that's what they said, dick-wad," Scheppler said, holding his palms up defensively as Postino backed him into the space between the desk and the welding rod oven.

"That don't make any sense, Tommy." Postino was smiling in his cool-as-a-cucumber way. He turned to the growing crowd in the room, "You're like, public enemy number one."

Postino is a big guy, but he's not so big that hot-head Scheppler won't try to rip his head off, Tyler thought. Smithe tightened up and stepped towards Scheppler, whose face turned red and his shoulders tensed in reaction to Postino's public enemy comment.

"Chill out, little man, you don't want to get into another roll right now," Smithe reached for his shoulder, but Scheppler yanked away and shrieked, "Go fuck yourself, Smitty, or I'll kick your fucking ass too!"

"No, you won't, sport." Smithe put his strength on display—the quickness and dexterity he revealed impressed all present. Smithe may be the un-appointed guardian of the young HT's, but that did not mean he was going to take any shit from them either. All Scheppler could manage in retaliation was a quick, "Ow-owww" as Smithe's quick jab to the gut brought him to the floor. Getting into his own kneeling position, Smithe addressed the younger man in a calming tone, "We're all going to just chill out now. We don't want any twidgets with guns rushing down here again." Just as Smithe finished his sentence, the compartment ladder rattled to life. "What the fuck," Smithe said wearily.

Persinski followed by Swartz came waltzing through the shop towards the far corner; Persinski reached down behind Bastille's desk and pulled out the Sounding and Security belt that must have falling off in between the desk and welding rod oven. "Here it is," said Persinski turning to Swartz when he noticed Smithe gripping Scheppler and everybody watching. "I thought you guys were going to bed."

Smithe gave Postino the evil eye. The electrician simply laughed, leaned up against the bulkhead, and dropped himself into to a squat.

"Look man, he's the one starting bullshit rumors about what those agents are asking people," said Postino, apparently fired up over Scheppler's second interrogation story.

Scheppler, along with Wilkette and Ramirez, had been summoned to the wardroom for follow up questioning after the initial General Workshop discussions. The questions being asked in the second round were a mystery and because Scheppler had been up there for over two hours, the content of those discussions were of interest to all. "Listen, we've already been through this, right Tommy?" Tyler said.

"Screw you, man." Scheppler said after standing up, "I didn't do it."

"No one said you did," Postino pressed, "You were up there for a few hours, and we never heard from you, why... and what they wanted to know?"

Scheppler paced from desk to welding rod oven and back again—Hart, Smithe, Ramirez, Swartz, and Wilkette were blocking his escape to the door.

Tyler got down from the workbench and directed traffic, sending the guys to various different positions around the perimeter of the room. "Give him some air guys."

"I ain't slept in days! I can't get any sleep because I'm afraid of all you idiots!" Scheppler moved around the room facing off on everyone. He clearly wanted to punch somebody. "Whether you say it or not, I know what you all keep thinking!" He came to Tyler and raised a pointed finger. "I swear I didn't do it! But what about you?"

"Calm down." Tyler said as Scheppler started bucking up at him. Minutes after being gut-punched by Smithe, the kid was ready to challenge someone else to yet another fight.

Tyler wanted to keep him calm so he wouldn't say or do something stupid. "I believe you, Tommy. I don't think you did it. Neither did I. They would have us locked up if they really thought we'd done it, right? Everyone's paranoid—that's all."

Scheppler took a breath before speaking again, "Ok. I'll tell you like I told this mo-fo," he said pointing to Postino. "They didn't seem interested in whether I killed Orton or not. I told them where I was, you know, when reveille sounded—and..." he paused looking around at everyone, "and that's about it. They took me to the Wardroom and made me sit in a chair at the officer's table." Nobody said a word, only listened to the far-fetched story he told. "They left me there for hours. They didn't even come talk to me again except to tell me that I could leave, and that they would be watching me."

When Scheppler finished Postino laughed. "You see why I started questioning the kid's story?" Postino turned his aggression to Wilkette, "What about you Remy? Ramirez told me they asked him a whole bunch of stuff because he was on watch at the time. So what about you?"

Wilkette, who had taken a seat next to Hart on the workbench down a few feet from Tyler, dangled his legs lazily against the lower cabinet doors and shrugged his shoulders. "They asked me where I was when reveille sounded and about some magazines in my locker," he finished rather matter-of-factly. "Then they let me go."

Swartz, who was apparently more interested in the girly magazines stashed in Wilkette's locker said, "You got the latest Penthouse, Remy?"

Postino could care less about porn; he wanted answers about the special interviews. "Ramirez?"

"I told you shit-head. I was on Sounding and Security."

"What about the watch did they ask?"

Ramirez wasn't ready to feed into Postino's argument, "Don't worry about it; they asked me about where I was and who I saw; that's it—now let it go."

"Don? What about you?"

"Hey go fuck yourself man—you think you're on a one-man brigade to find the killer," Hart blurted out through an orange peel layered behind his lips.

"Wait—you got asked to go up?" Tyler asked Hart.

Tyler had not heard this. Hart was someone Tyler had been thinking about earlier.

"What the fuck, man? It's nobody's business." Hart looked perturbed he had to take the orange peel out to speak, but with all of the men staring suspiciously at him he said, "They wanted to know about some things in my locker... and when was the last time the passage lights on the portside were PM'd."

"What'd they ask you that for?" Persinski and Swartz both said in unison.

"What are you two, freaking parrots—because I'm a God dammed electrician you idiots! Why don't you two go back on patrol?"

Hart was visibly annoyed at the Postino interrogations, but his explanation of the questions asked in the Wardroom seemed to throw a little more suspicion on Scheppler's account.

"You see?" Postino said barking at Scheppler, "You expect us to believe they let you sit around for hours without interrogating you? No one else has been brought up there and not asked any questions, why you?"

"Shut up, dickhead! I'm not the only person who's been called up! There could be guys in M&B being interviewed—stuck in a room up there like me—or longer for all you know."

"Exactly," Smithe said eyeing Postino, "You don't know. None of us do. They may have the guy already cuffed and locked away somewhere, and they're just trying to find more witnesses to testify."

Postino did not agree, "I really doubt that. If there's a guy already identified, we wouldn't still be on lockdown."

All R-division personnel were present except for Dunham and Bastille who were sitting at their spots in Electrical Central. The nine repair HT's and EM's stood around; seven of them owned green engineering coveralls. *This is an opportunity,* Tyler thought.

"It's making us all crazy," Tyler said and then pointed a finger at Postino, "and paranoid." Tyler circled the room.

"I'm not so sure they'll be asking anyone to go back up for more questions—I think they're focused on M&B right now," Tyler lied. He enhanced the invention with dramatic effect by catching the eyes of each man intently listening.

"Everyone here has nothing to worry about." It was a calculated risk, but the killer was most likely in this room. The critical moment was ripe to say, "I heard the NIS is on to the killer... a reservist from M&B. I don't know who. What Smithe and I found during our search gave the NIS evidence needed to implicate someone—that's why I can say this: R-Division is in the clear."

Tyler let that statement float out as he peered at each face, looking for something. A response. If the killer showed any chinks in his armor, Tyler might perceive something in the eyes of one of his friends gathered in the workshop.

"Let's forget this little argument between Tommy and Kirk ever happened and move on, all right?"

Silence followed, and the room dispersed. Persinski and Swartz left to join their escort at the top of the stairs. No one said much. Tyler grinded his teeth; there was an unsettling acknowledgement that the killer was cool, calm, and collected. The less than noteworthy reactions from everyone was ominous. He had hoped for something unusual. A nervousness or shuffling of feet, someone smiling too much, an over-exaggerated sigh or twitch, but there was nothing. Only shock, at first, then a few general signs of relief on the faces of his comrades. Tyler looked over at his best friend. Smithe smirked.

As for Scheppler, the interrogators had some sort of interest in him. *Could punky Tommy Scheppler take an Orton size guy down?* Doubtful, but Tyler didn't rule out the possibility: Scheppler owned green coveralls. His temper was incomparable to those around them, but he was a wiry strong kid and Orton was tall in comparison; *hell if Scheppler was dumb enough* to jump Orton, there'd probably be a different body in cold storage. Orton would have beaten the life out of him.

Orton used to be the DCA for R-Division before his transfer to M&B. Who else was here back then? Tyler remembered having the unpleasant duty of dealing with Orton for a couple of months. So had

252

Smithe, Scheppler, Ramirez, and Bastille. There were the electricians who'd been here when Orton was in charge: Dunham, Hart, Wilkette, and Postino. All of them experienced unpleasant interactions with Orton during that time. *Could someone really be harboring that much hatred over a few less-than-pleasant encounters from that long ago? Who among them were capable of killing a man? Come on Orton,* Tyler thought, *you got to at least try to help me out here. Who did this to you?*

CHAPTER 39

The end is near, Jorgenson thought. He'd held onto this hope for the last few hours, but his inner confidence was starting to waver. No matter. As captain, he had to show an outward appearance of command and control. Dark thoughts kept showing up, undermining his goal of safely making it to port with the killer in custody, but if the Miller murderer did not break from interrogation soon, there would be no telling how the next day would unfold.

Jorgenson gazed at the face of Dorie Miller in the Captain's cabin; he had slipped away from the Wardroom, eager to escape the condescending presence that was Special Agent Johnson. He had left during the throes of what seemed to be her version of a tantrum over the fingerprint debacle. The thick spectacled man had been trying to explain the probabilities of re-sweeping the passageway for a fingerprint, as Jorgenson excused himself. Apparently, there had been no prints found on the knife. Now a confession was a top priority.

"Everything is going wrong," Jorgenson said to the Dorie Miller shrine, "and I'm running out of options." The photographs offered no solution.

News of the irretrievable prints had spread quickly amongst the anxious officers. Over the last hour, several had come to him personally wanting a confirmation. Jorgenson felt like he was letting everyone down, but what more could he do. *There must be something.*

The orders from Surf-Lant Command were clear; they wanted to punish this man to the full extent of the law, and a confession would be the only way to pursue this outcome. The brass insisted on this waiting tactic, but Jorgenson was worried. *Why would he confess? He thinks he's gotten away with murder! He knows we have nothing!* Jorgenson clenched his fists. *That son of a bitch is laughing at us! He's laughing at Orton!*

Jorgenson grabbed the first thing he could get his hands on: a small glass anchor he'd used as a paperweight, and flung it across the room. The projectile had been a Secret Santa gift from his deadbeat uncle who always gave cute nautical knickknacks to add to his ongoing collection of unnecessary décor. The trinket crashed into the bulkhead and made a loud thud upon impact, yet the supposedly delicate looking item landed on the deck intact. The gift giver had insisted that the item was a hand-crafted piece of art. *I knew that fucking anchor wasn't real glass.*

"I'll be sure to knock next time." Lieutenant Commander Kendall stood in the doorway, only inches from where the paperweight had crashed into the paneling.

"You left a dent." He said, looking at the damage, "Glad that wasn't my face."

Jorgenson hadn't noticed Kendall enter, and he now felt embarrassed by the outburst. "No one was supposed to see that."

"Of course, sir." Kendall replied while bending down to pick up the anchor. The executive officer rolled the glass object around in his hand, examining it for breakage. "Looks like the bulkhead took the worst of it." He handed the anchor back.

Jorgenson fidgeted with the anchor as he spoke to the XO, "I'm sorry. That was uncalled for." Concern about prolonging the lockdown boiled to the forefront of his mind.

"I'm wondering what our killer is doing to manage his surges of anxiety?" He said, confiding in Kendall. There had been minor reports of scuffles but nothing more. "If you believe Special Agent Johnson, the killer is waiting and hoping to get lawyered up with the civilian authorities." Jorgenson said, giving away more information to Kendall than he had intended. "It's beyond frustrating."

"Captain, you have been holding up really well—better than any of us," Kendall said, forcing a smile, "It's nice to see that you're human." Jorgenson nodded, keeping a serious look on his face as he returned the trinket to his desk drawer. Kendall waited for him to respond, but Jorgenson didn't share the same level of conviction about his outburst. His lack of control suggested mediocrity.

"Miller didn't overthink his circumstances; he just reacted to them." Jorgenson stood and strode to the Dorie Miller shrine. "It wasn't hard. I just pulled the trigger and she worked fine. I had watched the others with these guns. I guess I fired her for about fifteen minutes." Jorgenson left the ambiguous words floating in the air for a moment. Then, he pointed a finger at the pictures, and let out a low-sounding chuckle, "That's what Dorie Miller said about fighting the Japanese attackers—he just pulled the trigger."

"You know, I thought this ship was going to be a perfect fit because of this man, right here. Me, the first black captain of a ship named after a black war hero. It seemed fitting, but now I–"

Kendall broke him off. "Sir, you are not being judged by history— especially not the history of Dorie Miller."

Jorgenson wasn't convinced; the air in the room suddenly seemed stale. He needed fresh air. He stepped towards the door, but Kendall reached for his arm.

"To be honest with you, sir," Kendall squeezed his elbow, "I did not even realize you're the first black captain of the Miller until now... because frankly, sir, if you don't mind me saying, no one gives a shit."

Jorgenson was not sure why, but he found himself laughing all of a sudden. Not a simple chuckle, but an honest-to-goodness nose-snorting cackle. Perhaps he was releasing some amount of pent up energy, like when he chucked the paper weight at the wall, or maybe the melodramatic tone in which Kendall had delivered his little adlib came out so funny that the absurdity of his last line—*no one gives a shit*—was just laugh-out-loud funny. The confused XO only made him laugh deeper. He gained control long enough to say, "Thank you," and wiped a tear from his eye.

A few seconds later, he was able to say, "Did you need something, Paul? You came in here for a reason?"

"Agent Johnson is requesting your presence," said the still stunned but smiling Kendall. He appeared relieved the captain wasn't throwing objects around his stateroom anymore.

Jorgenson continued his giggling and led Kendall out the door. "I need some air. Let's go find Special Agent Johnson."

$$\star\star\star\star\star$$

After the Postino and Scheppler altercation, Bastille issued a command for everyone in R-Division to go to his bunk—which was an order for a timeout. Bastille had shrieked at them, "Lay down in your racks and cool the fuck off!"

The group's collective patience had worn precariously thin, and Tyler's perseverance vanished. He was happy to be in his rack though, and he pulled the blue curtains closed—making sure to overlap the seams to minimize the open crevices. After much adjusting and securing of the pillow, he laid on his back and again began rummaging through his thoughts on the murder. The witness said the killer wore green coveralls, but gave no other physical characteristics other than the blonde hair—which might be a completely made up story by the squawk-box gang. What if the blonde hair rumor actually came from the Wardroom? *Why float a false rumor of blonde hair around?* For some reason, the khakis were dead sure the perpetrator was someone in R-Division. *All right, Orton, help me out here. Who in R-Division owns green coveralls again?*

He owned several pairs, yet—*unless I'm completely bat shit crazy*—he took himself off the list. HT2 Levon Smithe, Tyler's best friend, owned green coveralls. *No way*, Tyler scorned himself for even the split second thought of Smithe as the Miller Murderer; the idea of Smithe as the possible killer of an officer, or anyone for that matter, was an absurd notion. So, that makes him a definite possibility. *Jesus Christ this is insane.* But, if the khakis had a suspect in mind all along, why would they send Smithe out searching for the knife and coveralls? It made sense that he and Smithe should be off the list—unless the whole reason they had sent he and Smithe was to keep an eye on them both. *Fuck!* Now for the other R-Division coverall owners...

The names came quickly.

HT2 Hector Ramirez.

HT3 Tommy Scheppler.

HTFN Ron Persinski

EM2 Donnie Hart.

EM3 Kirk Postino.

Fuckin hell. Each of these guys owned green coveralls, and he could not envision any of them as a killer. Hart happened to be a softy, but he was big enough to take down Orton if he wanted to. Ramirez? Tyler's closest friend on the ship apart from Smithe. The thought seemed ludicrous, but Ramirez was equally suited to pull off the stunt as Hart. Motive? Who knows? That has been one of the biggest questions so far. Whoever the killer is, his motives would remain unknown until caught and confessed—in the meantime—everyone had motive—and everyone did not have motive. The fact that motivation played a role at all seemed so far removed from his first priorities; piecing together the reason for killing Orton was far more excruciating than believing the killer might actually be from R-Division. The easiest motive? Someone snapped—lost it—took his rage out on Orton. Tyler did not cross Hart or Ramirez off his list.

Scheppler, while a complete hothead was a smallish guy compared to Orton, but maybe Scheppler got lucky and surprised the officer with a stab in the back—Scheppler stayed on the list.

Persinski, now he's a wild-card—*wait a minute*. Persinski had lost a chevron. He was an HT3 and had been written up and lost his crow—Tyler couldn't remember which of the two, Orton or Springer, was the DCA at the time. He's getting into an argument at least once a day—he's pretty edgy. With his physical stature, he could have easily taken down Orton, so, Tyler determined he couldn't take Persinski off the list.

The normally passive Postino had been rather aggressive over the past few days—might he be harboring some extra nerves after killing Orton? Postino remained on Tyler's list.

Okay—so all coverall owners stay on the list.

He pushed at the bunk above as if trying to burst the compartment open. With each flex of his pectorals, a searing ache shot through his muscles. The contractions distracted him from deciphering facts, and after several thrusts, the lower metal buckled a bit. Satisfied in the damage inflicted on the bed frame, he stopped the physical but continued the mental calisthenics.

At any moment, might he open his curtain to see Postino staring back at him, holding another knife, ready to kill—or Ramirez smirking with a spanner wrench? Would he wake up the next morning to hear Smithe being escorted off the Miller after confessing to the crime? Hart taken away in cuffs? Scheppler admitting to the deed? None of them seemed to fit the bill for a crazed killer, but after narrowing down the list to six, Tyler did not come up with any primary suspect. Everyone with green coveralls was capable—*probably*; all were present in the photograph taken on the flight deck many months earlier.

Tyler faced the curtain. He wanted to be ready in case one of his friends decided to go on a rampage. His breathing grew heavy as he pictured his six suspect's faces. *I cannot believe this.* Who did the khakis suspect? No sleep came; his thoughts being too plagued with nightmarish images of friends with a knife. Hart jumping Orton. Scheppler hidden away somewhere to take him by surprise. Postino saluting with one hand while gripping onto the knife with the other. Persinski sprinting up the passage, knife out in front of him. Ramirez lunging in for the kill. Smithe ... a knife... and... his nightmares were only just beginning.

CHAPTER 40

Moonlight Sonata. Composed 1801 by Beethoven.

Forty hours since my waltz.

The underside of the bunk above offers no diversion from the damnable Bastille who rants for everyone to "go lay down." My curtains offer a mild respite from the world, or it would be, if he would just shut his mouth. The ship, now at anchor in the bay at Newport, rocks gently; the currents offer calm, but my tempest rages on. Music is loud in my ears—not so earsplitting that it drowns my ability to consider the options before me. For the first time in many hours, I can hear my thoughts and they are significant.

Inside my rack enclosure, a single line of light creeps across my chest—a small opening in the curtains allows the intrusion. The beam slices across my bulging eye. This sliver-of-light-trespasser threatens to carve my eyeball in two; however, in retrospect, the light is less an intruder and more so an escaping blackness. Stay away light, I want to croon. Darkness is my companion; I tug on the blue curtain, and blackness surrounds me. The demon-father visits again; he watches from outside my curtain. Not in my mind as usual—only hovering over, judging my speech, my responses to the interviewers, and my facial expressions. I know he doesn't agree with my responses to the questions of that bitch investigator—I had to continually switch to be more of my outer-self, and he offered me no alternative statements to make, so my switching ability was put on full display. I really don't need to switch anymore—I have mastered my cloaking with relying on a switch mechanism.

I am inside out and obscure. I tell my inner-voice we are safe—that outer-self, the one they know me by, is all but dispersed. My voice's face begins to vanish; it was once my father's, but it is no longer. I hope he does not abandon me when I reach the pinnacle of my plan. His face has started to morph with Orton's sneering countenance. He cannot be Orton—my greatest triumph—can he?

What of Orton?

Orton rests in Heaven or Hell, if there are such places. I'd prefer Heaven—not because I want him in paradise or that I believe he deserves such grace, but because I know wherever he is, I will not run into him there. My destiny—and the will to live—does not lead to some eternal cradle; only deeds matter, and only men who fight oppression matter. To say that corrupt means corrupt the ends is to believe in the immaculate conception of ends and principles. The real arena is corrupt and bloody.

Those are good words.

Who is this?

I am you, and you are me.

Father?

Someone more than he.

Someone they call the killer is identified and is being held, but how and why is this? Do the authorities truly hold a man from M&B in custody? Beethoven plays. I am melancholy. An underling may need to take the fall for my beautiful deed.

Are you sadder for the accused or for yourself?

I had so yearned to accept the title of Miller Murderer. Orton's killer. Not taking credit seems cowardly. Even in death, Orton mocks me.

All of the devil khakis deserve to perish for their abusive and imperialist rule.

Most of the enlisted deserve similar misfortune for having blind faith in the chain of command. Anarchy I crave. They will all realize soon enough that their system is flawed. It was built on the wearing of a certain uniform.

The music changes. Mozart's *Requiem Dies Irae* plays. The chorale stanza after the quiet opening bars burst into life. I cover my ears to quiet the noise from disturbing the other R-Division men; they might listen and become vulnerable to the booming discomfort.

The time is late—you must act soon.

Am I asleep, or am I awake?

Violins burn and the choral voices scream and then... wait! A jolt of realization jumps at me. Blood rushes to my temples. A magnificent orchestration pierces my soul. With thunderous instruments and voices comes clarity—I breathe in and exhale—yes—yes—I understand.

The NIS questions.

Too many visits.

The captain to the workshop.

A second rack inspection.

To the wardroom.

The revelation of an incarcerated suspect.

All so convenient.

The friends of the Defiant One know who the killer is—and he is me. My only problem is this lockdown; I cannot achieve my goal with the ship anchored; there is little chance at getting to the captain. I must accelerate the movement of the ship to the pier and isolate the commanding officer... I must create the need for an evacuation. The captain will remain until the end, and I will fulfil my destiny.

You must find a weapon.

I will mend my past mistakes. I am happy the end is near.

CHAPTER 41

A dream inspired by a beautiful memory flooded Tyler's mind. He found a perfect vision behind closed eyes as he lay in his rack, slowly drifting towards sleep. The memory of Alexandra brightened. Light lingered at the horizon as she and Tyler strolled on the waterfront area of lower Thames Street in Newport. It is winter, so absent from the streets were throngs of tourists crowding the wharf. Tyler as always had been talking about the future—their future. They were both afraid to say the word *marriage*, but the idea of tying the knot came and went from their conversations often.

Always driven to do better, Tyler yearned for more from life; his personal vendetta against complacency was constantly on display. He would not end up a damn statistic and fought against the typical clichés about children from broken homes. "He's a failure, what do you expect?" "He didn't have a chance." "His father was a loser; his mother lived as a whore."

In the dream moment, with Alexandra, life was incomplete—there were things to be done, but for Tyler things were never happening fast enough, and they were never perfect. The Navy was only a stepping-stone: a way to get going. He had hoped his military experience would've been more fulfilling—more rewarding, but Navy life let him down a bit. He simply thought of the U.S. Navy as employment: a job that didn't pay enough and asked too much of you. He and Alexandra got by, but living in Newport showed them a life that ought to be so much more.

She smelled like Hypnotic Poison, and her green eyes sparkled. They were gazing at each other.

"What do you want?" he asked. She raised her chin and let her nose crinkle with a crooked smile. She flopped two wrists on his shoulders, and they shared a soft kiss. He tried to clarify himself, "From this—our work, my work..." he stammered trying to put the words he had so often repeated into new sounding syllables.

"You and your ambition," she said; she recognized the conversation—they often ended a nearly perfect evening discussing the unknown future. She only smiled and kissed him deeply.

"Allie, I mean it," he wanted her approval to feel this way. This was their little game. "What's your dream? We always talk about my goals. What are yours?"

"I know you mean it," she said, letting a fake frown come to her mouth; the late afternoon breeze crept through wisps of her dark hair.

His emotions simmered as she pulled herself tighter into his arms and chest, "Tyler, my love." He held her as if someone worked to take her away. "I want *this*." She cradled his larger frame. "I have everything I want, but you always want more, Tyler, to be here with you: this is my dream." She breathed in and curved her fake frown into a smile.

Tyler smiled back—crestfallen. He wanted to argue, but doing so would be futile. She beamed, and he knew he'd better not screw with her essentials. Life with Alexandra was not perfect; she would disagree and say they were in a much better situation than any she had ever been in before. For Tyler, their less than perfect existence needed some overhauls, but then again he always thought too much...at least that's what Smitty always said.

Awakened all of a sudden, Tyler sighed and scowled at the dented bunk above. His inner clock indicated the time to be early and before his watch was about to begin. He had not slept long.

His dream inspired a thought; one that he would need to convey to her, someday. His life with Alexandra was a separate and almost secret existence—so far removed from what he really thought about life. She

265

would never really know what he had to deal with in his job, so any reservations about doing what he needed to do, regardless of the dangers involved, were his alone. He should not let what *she might think* get in his way. *I have everything I need.* All the information to solve this mystery—*I just need to pull it all together, logically.*

Forced back into the reality of the Miller and the dire situation, he brought back an idea he had stashed away in his mind when he was out on the forecastle during the first day of the lockdown. What if the one thing, the very thing the witness claimed to be certain of was wrong— the green coveralls. What if we've been looking for someone who owns green coveralls, and that's not right? Tyler's eyes widened and he almost banged his face on the metal bed frame. What if the killer wasn't wearing green coveralls at all? In the blackness of the passageway—the witness might have made a mistake. On the other hand, what if he was, but they weren't his. It wouldn't be hard to swipe someone's coveralls; no one keeps their damn racks locked.

Tyler's mind went back to the last conversation he had with Orton—the night of the murder. He recalled their argument. Tyler had covered for someone once and suddenly a face appeared to him. "Oh my God..."

He knew. He was decided. His Sounding and Security patrol started in a few minutes. During the watch, he would confront the killer and end this.

CHAPTER 42

Jorgenson and Kendall arrived at Orton's stateroom.

"You wanted to speak with me, Miss Johnson?" Jorgenson said as he entered, surprised to see Hodges asleep in Orton's bed.

"Sorry if I woke you," she said.

"No." In fact, he thought, he hadn't really slept in many hours or days. The hour was late, but he didn't feel tired either. A dim bulkhead lamp lit the room; the aroma of body odor and cologne made a sultry scent and gave a quasi-exotic atmosphere to the drab stateroom. Apparently Hodges' sleeping in Orton's rack did not raise Special Agent Johnson's ire any longer; they both were silent—Hodges in his dreams and Johnson in her thoughts. Jorgenson let the scene sink in. At zero four hundred, the morning of the third day in lockdown loomed. It had been almost exactly forty-six hours since Orton's last words, and he felt as if they were no closer to naming a killer as they had been just minutes afterwards.

At least Hodges had finally dozed off. "I think that's the first time he's slept in three days." Jorgenson moved to the far bulkhead and a chair set in the corner.

"Yes...he told me so." She slouched at Orton's desk, her head slightly bowed. Even in the low light, dark bags drooped under her eyes. Tangles of hair seemed to be bursting from under several bobby pins. By the look of her hair, she was frazzled, yet she seemed calm. For the first time since arriving, her notes were pushed aside.

"There's only so much time I'm willing to waste trying to chase lunatics."

Jorgenson tried not to smile at her, "You mean Hodges?" Had she given in to Hodges? Perhaps she felt sorry for him as she attempted to hide her empathy, but her hushed voice told Jorgenson she might actually care.

"You didn't call me in here to chase him out, did you?"

"No."

She swung her legs around and pawed at an evidence folder on the desktop. She noticed XO Kendall standing in the doorway and said, "Perhaps you and I should speak alone."

"No, Mister Kendall is staying." He needed someone by his side at this moment; the last conversation about Dorie Miller and his duty as captain gave him reason to acknowledge Paul Kendall as a number-one who might be someone to keep at your side in the coming hours.

"Very well. I know you and I did not exactly get off on the right foot, Captain."

"I wouldn't say the wrong foot."

"Then you're full of it." She smiled at him. "I'm sorry."

"As am I." He smiled back but only for a moment. He sensed she wanted to convey some information that he wouldn't enjoy listening to. "What do you need, Agent Johnson?"

"You know the lab results turned up with no match; the weapon had no prints." Jorgenson had learned this earlier; it wasn't the only thing troubling her.

"You didn't expect to find a print though. The last we spoke, you said there wasn't much chance."

"I had hoped." She held up her thumb, pointer, and middle fingers. "He's come in three times. Three times, I hit him with a lot of stuff. Broken family, Orton's treatment and aggressiveness, told him we have several witnesses who say he wasn't in his bunk. He's not breaking." Crows-feet tightened at the outer edges of her temples.

"There are no legible prints on the knife; he denies owning it—even after exaggerating a subterfuge that several crewmembers claimed he owns a hunting knife. You know what that son-of-a-bitch said?" Her eyes flared wide. "He says, in a very concerned voice, get this; *did poor Lieutenant Orton get stabbed with a knife?* Like he didn't know. You believe that shit? He was practically tearing up. His denials are composed and well-practiced. He is a cool cucumber, your man there. If he is the one."

Jorgenson grimaced, "He is not my man. These are the events; I got a dead man and a junior officer who said he saw a green coverall clothed somebody drop and run. Who was it? I asked. Watford looks me in the eye and says it was..."

"Hold on Captain. I'm not maneuvering for culpability here. Ensign Watford may be mistaken; I know that. And, there are no other more absolving suspects. Unless we press harder to rattle him loose—I'm running out of time. With good, circumstantial, the witness testimony is enough to make an arrest; however, let's not create any false illusions. He may not be the killer."

She allowed Jorgenson to catch his breath. Kendall leaned with his back against the door in silence.

"He claims he was in his rack, asleep—the guys sleeping in the same compartment say he was there when the lights came on. We all believe he's our killer, however, our substantiation for detainment is limited, and after interviews, he is not rattled enough to confess."

"I cannot keep the ship in lockdown. My men are on the brink. Your friends at the JAG office may be concerned about murder-in-the-first, but at this point, we are putting everyone in jeopardy on the hope he might confess. We simply cannot keep this up."

She finally concurred. At least her eyes told him so.

Agent Johnson drew in a resolute breath and said, "I agree; later this morning I will call him in for a last ditched effort to get him to come clean. If he doesn't break, well, I'll arrest him based on the testimony of Watford. We don't have much choice at this point, now, do we?"

Jorgenson glanced over at Kendall; the XO nodded his head in an agreeing motion and said, "That's our plan?"

Johnson nodded and appeared to be scouring her brain for additional information, and she came up with, "In the event he doesn't admit it—we'll take him in, but..." This was a big but—something Jorgenson had not given much thought to prior to her describing the possible next steps; "We will need to pull the ship pier side; the civilian jurisdiction will want to conduct their own inquiry. With no confession and a weak eyewitness—they will most likely expect us to keep everyone on board until they rule out any other possible suspects." The scope of this alternative weighed heavy and Jorgenson realized there wouldn't be any other way.

Jorgenson had been hounding Special Agent Johnson to go ahead and arrest their suspect for so long, but now that she was agreeing, Jorgenson felt disappointment. He wanted the bastard to confess. He wanted to believe Orton's killer would get what he deserved... not be in court a few months down the road, anxiously awaiting the verdict of a less than certain jury. A fury rose inside him. Images of Orton lying in that passageway trying to speak, trying desperately to cling onto life long enough to tell them who had hurt him filled Jorgenson's mind. The sound of Hodges' cry, *Damn it, Bruce!* Echoed as he recalled seeing Hodges completely collapse under the unforgiving truth of what had happened. Now there was Hodges, lying asleep in Orton's rack, his only sleep in three days.

The murderer, the man who had killed Orton, who had driven Hodges to madness, and caused the necessity of locking up of the entire Miller crew for three long grueling days could possibly finagle a good defense or perhaps get away on a technicality. Worse—be the wrong man. The thought enticed a level of rage in him.

"That's the plan." He offered one last show of support. "Agent Johnson, get a confession."

"One last try. One last try before we make an arrest." She rolled her head back, cracking her neck. "When would be the best time to bring him in?"

Kendall put in his two cents. "Right after the seven forty-five watch turn over."

"Why is that?"

"Because we'll have all our best men on station then. The primary security detail will be in place after seven forty-five; they'll be well rested. If anything goes wrong, our guys will be ready."

Johnson nodded in agreement.

Then a sound burst from the 1MC speaker just outside the stateroom in the passageway. The three stared at each other in disbelief of what they were hearing.

SCOTTBLACK

DAY THREE

CHAPTER 43

Tyler's nerves were on edge as he headed out of R-Division. He and Smithe stopped to have a brief conversation with the guard, SK1 Ziegler, who would be accompanying them on their patrol. Not surprisingly, Ziegler's typical passive aggressive personality was in gear. It was early—zero three thirty; they would grab a quick coffee and go to Main Control to take over the Sounding and Security detail from Swartz and Persinski. Tyler spotted one of the R-Division guards posted just outside the hatch half-asleep in his chair. Tyler grunted and was not afraid to kick the man's chair as they passed by. The guard jolted in his seat.

A part of Tyler wanted to shout, *don't you realize there's a killer on this ship!* He sighed and continued walking alongside Smithe, with Ziegler in tow. He wanted to speak privately with Smithe, whenever they could put some distance between themselves and their escort. Smithe was yawning as he spoke, "It's going to be a long morning."

You have no idea, Tyler thought. The anticipation of confronting the killer was nerve-racking.

*****

Forty-six hours since my waltz.

So much music all coming at me at once! I cannot make out what song is playing. Now is the time to act. Most of my bunkmates are asleep. Swartz and Persinski have just returned from watch relief.

Either freedom or death awaits me at the end of these trials.

This is your crucible!

My plan will take down this ship. When the captain is the last standing, I will take him as well.

Noise.

Top rack—Persinski, just climbed up. Swartz is already breathing heavy in his top rack on the other side row. They will both be asleep in minutes.

You must get a weapon.

The General Workshop... there had been many weapons fashioned in the first hours of lockdown. I will obtain a pipe. No one is prepared for what is coming. The captain will order an evacuation; he will wait for the last crew to disembark. I will destroy him then.

You may need to sacrifice others.

I am prepared.

I hear the heavy breathing of two new sleepers; they've joined the others in slumber—the entire berthing space is a dead zone.

Into the workshop, I spot a well-suited heavy carbon steel pipe lying in a five-gallon bucket. This will do. Up the ladder. No sound except the loud measures of woodwinds and strings.

Follow your strategic tactics—step one, the guards.

The first guard is drifting; his head bobs softly. I move quickly.

I am upon him before he realizes what is happening; I pull the pipe horizontal against his windpipe and with a swift yank, his throat collapses. A twist and I feel the snapping of a twig under my forearms.

This guard was an unknown twidget. His eyes are wide as I pull him out of sight of the other one who is across the beam of the second deck passage.

Footsteps!

"Andy, you all right?" a voice echoes from around the corner; his slow paced speeds up when his comrade does not respond.

I am prepared for when he turns the corner. His gun is drawn; with all of my strength, I swing down; his forearm shatters. The gun drops, and the one-armed-guard collapses to a knee. His combination cry-of-pain and shout-for-help is cutoff as I shatter his jaw. He only has use of one arm to fend me off as I lower the pipe across his throat and push down to the deck. My hands wrap around the ends of the pipe and I can feel my knuckles rubbing against the cool floor when he stops thrashing.

He is small, but puts up a good fight for thirty seconds. The light in his eyes fades to nothing and finally blankness.

Hide the bodies.

That was easy. I fireman-carry each one swiftly to the forward head and stash their bodies in a shitter stall.

Step two--the weapons.

I remove both of their guns and a holster belt and wrap the leather around my waist; two weapons and the full complement of clips from both will provide enough ammo to make quite a stand. An appalling soundtrack of radio tunes play: Pat Benatar, Michael Jackson, Kool and the Gang, Eurythmics, and Journey all fight for my attention. Overlapping chaos. Where are my soothing classics? I slap my temples.

Step three—the Fire Room.

Yes, Father.

I go to move but stop—the pipe was a great choice; I felt a similar euphoria with the pipe as I had with the knife: close proximity. I take the improvised killing tool and quickly start down the starboard passage. The main entry door to the Fire Room is only a few steps away. The ship is eerily quiet—not for long—soon the entire ship will be in chaos.

*****

"You're fucking insane—that's what you are." Smithe's surprisingly forceful words made Tyler flinch.

The two had just left Main Control and were walking through the Mess Decks to start a round of flood inspections in the sonar-cable locker under the fantail. Their escort, Ziegler, was steps behind—giving Tyler an opportunity to speak with Smithe about his plan.

Tyler had taken a few minutes down in the hole to bring Smithe up to speed on his intentions. The noise of the upper-level platform allowed him the opportunity to speak in private. Now out in the open space of the eating hall, Smithe fumed.

"I'm telling you, I'm certain." Tyler spoke softly, hoping Smithe would take the hint to keep his voice down. Not that any person was nearby—it was the Mid-Watch, but the worry that someone turning a corner might overhear Tyler's accusation was present on his mind. He wanted desperately to get Smithe on board, "It's him, Smitty. It couldn't be anyone else."

Smithe took the hint and said quietly, "He doesn't own green coveralls."

"Yes. I've been thinking about that. I..."

"Why have we been searching for three damn days for green coveralls?"

"The question is: was the killer wearing green coveralls at all?"

"But, Watford said the guy was wearing..."

"Watford made a fucking mistake."

Smithe stepped up to the sonar-locker access-hatch and started turning the dogs.

Tyler continued, "Hell, I'm not convinced anything we've been told are facts."

"What do you mean?"

"Well, here's what's bothering me. You know the whole blond-haired guy rumor?" Tyler spoke as he followed Smithe into the locker and mulled around pretending to look for flooding. Ziegler stayed back, outside the watertight door. "We heard about the blond-haired guy, when... like, less than an hour after the first rack inspection."

"Yeah, so? It's a rumor."

"Started by *who*?" Tyler asked.

Smithe didn't respond, but Tyler could tell his friend was becoming mildly interested in the conversation.

"Smitty, Smitty. Hear me out." Tyler stood toe-to-toe with Smithe. "What if the rumors and facts and all the other miscellaneous information... what if all these messages are being planted for the sole purpose of throwing the killer off? To make him think the investigation is focused on someone else?" Tyler let the notion of a conspiracy drill into Smithe.

"You're talking about a planned rumor mill?"

"What if Watford recognized the guy from the get go and knew exactly who he was?"

Smithe let out a nervous laugh, "What if Watford did, and he thought he saw blonde hair? The rumor ain't no rumor at all."

"Smitty," Tyler put a hand up to Smithe's chest, "if I'm right, and I think I'm a hundred percent on this, then the possibility that it was a blond-haired guy is absolutely absurd. You can't make that mistake—I don't give a fuck how dark the passage is."

Smithe stared at Tyler.

They left the aft end of the ship and moved to go up to the sounding voids in the forward areas.

By the time they arrived back at the Mess Decks, Smithe seemed to accept—at least for the moment—the hypothetical theory.

Accepting his role as a third wheel in a conversation he wanted no part of anyway, Ziegler said, "Dickheads. Wait up, I'm grabbing a coffee."

Smithe plopped into a seat at one of the tables.

"Okay, why did he kill Orton?" Smithe asked once Ziegler was out of range of their voices.

"Orton held back that promotion, Orton is... was ... a prick who constantly battered him..." Tyler paused. "That's all I got."

"You're nuts," Smithe said under his breath.

"This all makes so much sense now."

Smithe shook his head nervously. "I don't want to waltz right up to him and start chatting him up about how he may have stabbed Orton to death. We should just go tell the brass."

"Don't you get it?"

Tyler dropped into the opposite seat, which connected to a cantilevered support strut under the table, and Smithe rose up like a kid on the other side of lopsided seesaw.

"The brass already know who it is. Watford saw who it was. It's our guy. Orton dies. The brass convene—maybe call into Surf-Lant command—they come to R-Division, do a once through. Make sure he's not diving off the deep end. He plays it cool in front of the rack inspectors. Fucking hell, Smitty, if they were unsure from the first minute, I should have been put in the brig! I fucking told the guy I was going to kill him in front of a chief, and an hour after he's found dead, that same chief looks me in the eye and practically says, 'I know you didn't kill him'... I'm not nuts; this whole situation is fucking nuts!"

Tyler was fuming, and although he was working to keep his voice low, he knew the volume was getting louder.

He pointed a finger at Smithe, "They've known from the very beginning, and they've been keeping an eye on him ever since. God damn it. They want a confession, and they're gonna keep us locked up until he comes fucking clean!"

Smithe let Tyler pant out the rest of his vent. Then he said, "And you think you're going to get a confession."

"No. I'm just sick of being locked up."

"You need to calm down, man."

"Smitty, the NIS agents aren't getting anywhere with him. I think I can reason with him. I think I can convince him to turn himself in."

"I don't think you can." Smithe said in an angry tone and made for the exit. Tyler bolted out of his seat and grabbed his friend by the belt, pulling him back. Smithe swung around with his elbows wide boxing Tyler out of his personal space. Tyler needed him to get on board with his plan. He wasn't about to confront the killer on his own.

"Tyler," Smithe said in a seriously aggravated voice, "He's one of us, you understand?"

*****

Through the main entry door, down a ladder, and across to the control room with my pipe in hand. My gun belt holsters a standard issue model M1911 forty-five caliber pistol—the leather band fits nicely around my waist, keeping the second weapon nestled firmly behind the buckle. Inside the Fire Room, on the upper level, BTFN Quintin Drake is recording readings from the gauge board in the Control Room. "You can't be in here," he says as I enter through the spring-loaded door. I crash the pipe into his skull reshaping the side of his left temple. He falls in a heap.

His sacrifice is necessary.

Just as I had feared allowing either of two guards to live, I pounce with both feet on Quintin's face. His whole head now faces the wrong way. He won't be alerting anyone.

Out through the Control Room door to the ladder that leads to the lower level below, there is another.

I reach the bottom of the ladder and appear to BT2 Ryan Clayborn from around the starboard side of the boiler. He looks confused, "What are you doing?" he says. The gun feels heavy, but weekly trips to the naval base gun range have primed me for the M1911. I deftly chamber a round, raise the barrel, and fire. He falls. The shot is loud—even more so than the third act brass-section prelude in Wagner's *Ride of the Valkyries*, but the main space lower-level is so far removed from the upper entrances that no shots can be heard from outside the space. Smoke from the barrel floats listlessly in the stale air. The BT is trying to crawl away; such a useless effort.

"Where you going, Ryan?" I ask, shoving him onto his back with a thrusting boot under his shoulder. I speak softly—acknowledging that he is an acquaintance. The music contorts into a twisted duet of distorted guitars and rolling tympani's.

"Don't! Don't kill me," he pleads. I place the gun to the center of his forehead, leaning over so that I might look him in the eyes. I pause and listen to him cry out desperately. "Please, don't! Please!" This is Ryan, a fellow weight lifter; he is one of the rare ones I speak to outside of my own division.

Do it.

Another unsatisfying tune is rising above the others.

Why haven't you pulled the trigger yet?

Ryan is pleading with me, "Please, just put the gun down, please! Don't kill me." He sees my finger playing with the trigger, and he starts a prayer.

Kill him! Pull the trigger!

Ryan's head splits apart. A bedlam of arrangements crest, punishing my reluctance. I will not hesitate when the others arrive.

Now for the climax of our opera. At the front of the boilers, my plan is still in motion.

Step Five—expose the ship. Disable the in-space automatic fire system.

Done.

Use a spanner to crack the Teflon seal.

Done.

Open the valves.

Done.

Liquid floods the bilge, and a sweet aroma mixes with eye-stinging fumes—boiler fuel fills the space around me. A rainbow forms in the mist, spitting from the fissured Teflon socket. This should make for a glorious fire. There is a switch ready for me to light up the Fire Room. Fire is a beautiful thing. I depress the ignitor.

A large compressing boom echoes; an orange-yellow ball shoots from the flame thrower and careens from one boiler face to the other, sending liquefied fire in all directions; hot, incinerating streams spew at me. The compression had jolted me back more than expected; I hear a voice yelling at me to hide—am I on fire? I finally catch my breath and see that my dungaree shirt in burning—not engulfed but still charring my skin. I remove the shirt and toss it into the blazing front of boiler number two—my t-shirt is intact, although my arms, neck, and jaw are charred. I'm not dead, so my play continues.

Step Six—the waiting game!

To the escape trunk—I hide behind the spring-loaded door. Until the call for evacuation, I will hide in here.

*****

Tyler did not back down, and their standoff felt awkward. The two friends had never fought. Over the years, many arguments and disagreements, as happens between friends, had always ended with a beer-toast to agree that the other guy was a complete fucking idiot. Tyler couldn't recall ever having the urge to punch his best friend until now. He was *this close*. Their unspoken mutual respect always carried over into everything they did; now standing on the Mess Decks, they were an instant away from shattering a long friendship.

Tyler idled up in defiance to Smithe's posturing; he would not be able to drop Tyler to his knees in the way he had made Scheppler look so helpless down in the General Workshop yesterday.

Smithe's normally gentle, blue-grey eyes had turned to granite with a mix of anger and fear in them, "we'll talk about this later."

"This is later. We'll do it right now." Tyler said angrily.

They stood in silence for several beats, and then Smithe walked away shaking his head.

Going to the khaki's was not an option. Tyler had lost all confidence in the leadership after spending three days locked away with a murderer. He waved at Ziegler who'd been idly sipping a cup-of-joe watching the cock-fight; Tyler said, "Let's go douche-bag," and he followed after Smithe.

"Hey!" Tyler shouted after his friend.

Smithe had gotten a twenty-step lead up the starboard second deck passage.

"You're a fucking coward!"

Smithe kept walking and even sped up. He put fifty feet between them. Tyler vowed to punch him if given another chance and began shouting up the passage. "That's your problem Smitty—you expect others to handle everything for you."

"Fuck off!" Smithe finally shouted over his shoulder.

"It's time to stop hiding behind me like you always do."

Smithe suddenly halted. *Here we go.* If they were going to duke it out, this was the moment.

"You know what...?" Tyler started.

"Hold on!" Smithe cut him off shrilly.

Reaching a hand up, Smithe signaled Tyler to stop walking. There was something other than their argument suddenly on Smithe's mind—his demeanor shifted, Tyler noted; even with his temper flaring, there wasn't anyone more inclined to shutdown Tyler mid-sentence, mid-rant, or mid-step than Smithe. Tyler complied and stopped walking.

Smithe rounded like a pointer locating a fallen duck—something had grabbed his interest. He pulled the ball cap off his head and curved his neck as though he was looking for something. "You smell that?" Smithe asked.

Before Smithe's words reached his ears, Tyler caught a scent of sweet-sulfur and scorched paint. A pungent bitterness filled the air where they stood in the passage just outside Aux-One. Smithe's eyes went wide.

"Fire." They almost simultaneously said and both went into auto-IIT-damage-control mode.

"I'll check Aux-One." Smithe said.

"I got the Fire Room." Tyler turned, retraced his steps aft, and shouted to Ziegler who was at the other end of the passage. "Smells like a fire—standby!" Tyler reached the Fire Room door and pulled open the spring-loaded vestibule door.

A cloud of black smoke burst into Tyler's face and the passageway. He leapt back coughing and pushed on the door trying to make the spring-mechanism compress faster—smoke billowed out. Smithe had already gone into the other space to investigate.

Tyler sprinted back the way he and Smithe had just came, towards Ziegler, "Get Smitty out of Aux-One! I'll notify Main Control." Tyler and Ziegler pirouetted and passed each other. Tyler rounded the corner, flew through the Engine Room door, down the ladder, across the upper deck, up the ladder, and into Main Control. "We got a main space fire!" He shouted before anyone knew he had entered. MM1 Adam Murray, the EOOW almost fell off his chair.

"What? Where?"

"Fire Room –it's bad—class bravo; we need to isolate systems; get auxiliary equipment lit—light all fire pumps."

The other guy, an MM Tyler didn't recognize—no doubt a weekend warrior—was dumbfounded and said nothing as Murray didn't hesitate. "Got it," he said and reached for the communication phone to the bridge as Tyler retreated to Repair Five.

Before he reached the corner leading forward, the 1MC sounded. "General quarters! General quarters! All hands man your battle stations! Fire, fire, fire. Fire in main space number two—Fire Room."

Tyler felt a clump form in his chest. *What's going on?* The ship was perfectly still outside of the harbor. *Did a dipshit BT toss a lit cigarette into the bilge?* Thick black smoke meant this was fuel oil fire. *Who let loose a goddam fuel leak?*

CHAPTER 44

Thick black billows wafted through the overhead cables and pipes; the vestibule door was not keeping the fumes from escaping. In no time, the compartment along the starboard second deck filled halfway with smoke. Tyler reached Repair Five where Smithe was busy donning his firefighting equipment. Zeigler loitered in the passaged looking lost. When Tyler approached, Zeigler said, "Should I go to my station?" The security alert teams assigned to keep an eye on the R-Division guys had apparently not been given orders on what to do in case of General Quarters.

"That's up to you, Gary; we gotta fight this fire, and I don't want you anywhere near here." Tyler's message was clear, and Ziegler wasn't ready to argue. He looked around, and after trying to decide which way to go he left, choosing the path leading away from the gathering smoke.

Tyler squeezed past Smithe, reached into the locker, and grabbed a set of insulated gloves from a hook. A few steps to the Fire Room door later, Tyler sucked in a lung-filling gulp of clean air, jumped into the smoke filled vestibule, and went to work securing the main boiler room hatch. His eyes teared up from the thick burnt-fuel-oil-smog. With expert accuracy and speed, Tyler closed and sealed the six dogs locking down the hatch. More smoke leaked into the passage. There was no time to think—the Fire Room had to be sealed—there may be men down below fighting an inferno—their only chance would be to extinguish the fire or retreat up the escape trunk that led topside to the Main Deck.

In the passage, Tyler spotted a body coming his way; he shouted to MM2 Barry Fillmore, who'd just come into view from the mess decks at the far end of the long passage. "Set zebra!" Black smoke floated through the overhead cables.

MM2 Fillmore stepped through, turned, and secured all eight dog locks around the perimeter of the watertight door. The space between Tyler and the transverse bulkhead that created the aft boundary of the Fire Room began filling up with men. For the second time in a week, R-Division would be startled awake with a catastrophe. Smithe stepped out of the locker fully geared up, and the remaining main space fire team assembled and dressed out at Repair Locker Five.

"Let's go. Let's go." Tyler said, although he knew his team would have the necessary sense of urgency. All the men quickly and quietly prepared themselves. Before Tyler huddled a mass of people donning firefighting uniforms, personal protective equipment, and communication gear. No one spoke. Either because they were all still asleep, or because the smoky passage revealed the gravity of their situation.

Smithe stood nearby as Tyler, Ramirez, Persinski and Scheppler prepped for dressing out into firefighting gear; all buttons buttoned and pant legs tucked into socks. Persinski, still suffering from sunburn, gingerly snugged his shirt collar tight and tied the normally dangling laces of his Boon Dockers.

Tyler, the On Scene Leader, wore a fire jacket, oxygen breathing apparatus and helmet. Tyler's red with horizontal white striped helmet had the initials O.S.L. stenciled in white spray paint across the front. His breathing lungs also had a stencil that read *OSL OBA*. He stepped out to the passage and scratched several checkmarks and words on a message pad.

"We need to isolate the Fire Room," said Tyler with a commanding bark after he saw his investigators ready and standing by. "Investigators, confirm this is the only space entrance with smoke... report back ASAP."

Swartz, one of the two investigators, asked, "What about our OBA's."

"Start em up." Tyler knew this was an area of concern for Swartz, who had once experienced the misfortune of misaligning an OBA canister during a routine maintenance check and nearly suffocated from breathing his own carbon monoxide. Tyler gave him an encouraging thumb up signal and the HT3 engaged the canister and started breathing. The leather lungs of the apparatus expanded and contracted with each breath.

Someone said, "I think the only smoke is from the Fire Room." The investigators both departed to do a lap around the second deck from the forward front bulkhead of Aux-One to the rear bulkhead of the Engine Room. This would confirm for Tyler that all other main spaces were one-hundred percent clear of smoke and fire.

Tyler agreed about the location; he and Smithe would have discovered if the other spaces were involved in the fire. The likelihood was this is only a Fire Room fire. He was so confident that he wanted to get going on space systems isolation. He needed to cut off and re-route electricity, fire-mains, potable water, and ventilation. He shouted without looking around, "Electrician isolate electricity to the Fire Room; establish positive ventilation!"

There was no response to his command, and a silent pause settled over the group. Then someone spoke up.

"West," the team's messenger said, "we got no electrician."

It hit Tyler, *no electrician—where is he?* Tyler scanned the faces of his fire-team; someone was missing.

"That's you today. Messenger, assume the duty of the electrician, secure the Fire Room power, establish positive ventilation, report back." The messenger leapt into action and disappeared through the forward watertight door.

Where is he? Our killer-electrician is not here.

Tyler needed a backfill for the messenger. "Fillmore, for today you're the plug man AND the messenger, put on an OBA." Fillmore nodded and retrieved one of the spare OBA's from the locker; the same OBA his suspected killer should be wearing. Tyler couldn't concern himself right now with the whereabouts of the guy he was only a few minutes ago trying to convince Smithe to confront.

"As soon as the Chief gets the sound-powered phone connected to DC Central, pass this update on." Fillmore grabbed the note and waited. Chief Langston, the last of the fire team to arrive, connected and placed the sound-powered phone headset over his ball cap. The Chief looked as if he had finally gotten some sleep; he had fresh mattress-creases in the side of his face.

The nozzle-men, Smithe and Ramirez, and the hose-men, Scheppler and Persinski, began laying out the canvass covered firehoses—snaking them forward and aft along the available floor-space outside the Fire Room entry.

Tyler listened as Chief Langston read his note into the phone mouthpiece. "Repair Five On-Scene-Leader reports the following: main space number two main hatch is sealed. We have a bravo fire—black smoke. No flames or heat at upper level. Positive ventilation not established. Investigators are out. Over." Tyler's notes were shorthand descriptions, but the Chief added in the necessary filler-words in speaking the report to Lieutenant Springer, who would be on the other end of the sound-powered connection in Damage Control Central. The other Repair Party On-Scene Leaders: Bastille in Repair Two and Dunham in Repair Three would be listening in on the DC Central Reports of the fire-fighting progress.

Step one for fighting a main space fire was to attain positive ventilation. He had sent the messenger-appointed-electrician off to complete this task. Once established, Tyler would lead the fire team into the space.

They were all dressed in protective jackets, gloves, OBA's, and helmets. This was not a drill—although his team had fought two other fires in the past, Tyler realized this one was not routine. The black smoke, the ship being at anchor, the lockdown situation... this was no ordinary shit-can fire. And, one of their normal team members—the Repair Five electrician—was missing.

Tyler pulled at the vestibule door again, this time locking it in the open position. Most of the smoke had dissipated into the passageway ceiling. He reached down and put the back of his hand to the hatch. Not hot.

The investigators returned from their main space perimeter walk. Swartz shouted from behind his OBA mask, "Confirm fire isolated to Fire Room, condition zebra is set on second deck..." he added, "Fire Room is sealed." The words were muffled from behind the rubber OBA mask, but audible.

"Fire room is sealed, aye," Tyler said confirming his understanding of the report.

The new messenger-appointed-electrician was now jogging from the forward watertight door.

"Positive ventilation and Fire Room electricity is isolated," said EM3 Postino.

Tyler gave acknowledged his doing the job quickly, and said, "Positive ventilation, aye. Electricity, aye."

Tyler reached down, turned the quick-acting-scuttle wheel, lifted the round scuttle-hatch just enough to let air through the opening. He held a sheet of his messenger note-pad to the gap. Forced air rushed into the opening and the white paper fluttered; this told Tyler what he needed to know. Postino had remotely shut down the Fire Room ventilation and set the passageway air conditioning supply-feed flow and return ducting to positive. They had airflow going into the Fire Room—positive pressure outside, negative pressure inside. Tyler prided himself on keeping his backup fire-team positions properly trained and it just paid off with Postino flawlessly stepping into the role of repair-party-electrician.

"Positive, confirmed!" Tyler said.

Tyler shouted out the commands to activate the water hoses and for all to engage their OBA canisters.

To the investigators said, "Keep check on perimeter, keep me informed."

They shouted, "Maintain perimeter, aye!"

Tyler squeezed his head into the OBA rubber mask and lifted the lever inserting his own potassium superoxide canister into the rebreather. He gave the required deep breaths and felt the lungs fill and collapse as the group readied to enter the Fire Room. Smithe was the team's number one nozzle-man; close behind him was the number one hose-man, Scheppler. Ramirez was his number two nozzle-man, and behind him was the number two hose-man, Persinski.

Fillmore and Tyler un-dogged and lifted the main hatch. All traces of smoke sucked down into the open entryway and the air rushing into the opening pushed at their backs. Once the hatch was secure in the full open position, Tyler leaned over the edge. As far as he could see along the starboard entry platform, there were no flames—just smoke.

He turned back to Smithe and Ramirez; through the translucent eyelet, openings of their masks the three friends acknowledged their shared understanding of the task at hand. Everyone gave a thumbs up that their OBA's were functioning. The hose teams descended the ladder way.

On the upper deck black smoke filled open pockets in the overhead crevices. Through the perforated decking and equipment, they could see flames flickering from the platform one deck below them. The flames were at least two decks in height. The front boiler-facades and upper-deck piping lagging were burning. Tyler gripped Ramirez's right shoulder and Smithe's left, tapping and pointing for them to start the flow of water. "Beat the flames down," he shouted. Muffled "OK's" came from beneath facemasks—Ramirez lit up his umbrella nozzle, and Smithe lit his two and a half inch fire nozzle. The space lighting flickered, and Tyler wrote another note.

Halon OOC—EM reroute all main bus's—isolate FR.

Before Fillmore could deliver the note, Tyler grabbed his arm and shouted "stay back near this ladder; I will signal when I need you." Fillmore nodded and left.

Smithe doused the upper platform with salt-water. The fire sputtered through the perforated deck grating. Powerful surges arose from the front of boiler number two.

The hoses discharged a flood onto lagging covered pipes, structural beams and stringers, equipment, and service panels. To the team's right an electrical box burst; the bluish sparks cascaded brilliantly. The team was in the middle of a shit storm of flames, smoke, and arcing equipment. Smithe, Ramirez, and Tyler led the charge and they steadily pushed deeper into the pit of hell-fire. Their own lives and perhaps the lives of all their shipmates were dependent on their ability to contain this inferno.

Keep the flames to the front, Tyler kept thinking. If any fire came up under their feet, through the deck grating or from behind, they *would be fucked.*

After an extended period of water dousing, they had diminished much of the flames crawling up the boiler fronts. Smithe pulled the team to midway across the upper level and drew Tyler's attention for the need to go below. Tyler concurred and the four nozzle and hose men along with their On Scene Leader synchronized their motions to maneuver the hoses back around and down the ladder.

Flames and pluming smoke engulfed the lower level. This was by far the worst fire this team had ever encountered and Tyler praised the four hose-men with shouts of, "good job", and "stay focused. The water surged out of the two nozzles; Smithe fought the flames, Ramirez's nozzle kept the heat away from Smithe and the rest. They could do this; although the blast furnace spit white-hot from the inferno, Tyler knew the water was not their best option for this blaze. They needed Purple-K Powder and Aqueous Film-Forming Foam. The physical exertion and labored breathing in the OBA's would soon be limiting their stamina. This was a problem, and Tyler quickly gauged they would not last long enough to complete this job—not with only two water hoses. Their OBA canisters only carried forty-five minutes of breathing capacity, and they had been battling for at least twenty minutes. They needed to get to the PKP and AFF stations quick!

On the lower level, Smithe and Ramirez reacted to Tyler's command through the rubber mask to converge on the number two boiler, which appeared to be the origin or at least the majority of the surging combustion. The team curved like a snake and blasted the boiler front with gallons of salt-water. The bilge below the diamond deck was aflame. They needed a path to the PKP-AFF station tucked under the overhanging beams that supported the Control Room above. Only two yards from their feet, the station lay idle and undisturbed. If any BT had been down here when this fire started, they had not even tried to startup the Purple-K Powder—which was their first line of defense after the Halon system failed.

Tyler stepped back to the ladder and shouted up to the loitering Fillmore, giving him another message—one that he hoped the khaki leadership would understand was just a precaution; *fire almost OOC—prep 4 evac.* He underlined the word, 'almost'.

Tyler excelled in the commotion of damage control events. *The chaos of firefighting!* He had always laughed at that statement. There was nothing chaotic about putting a fire out or stopping a flood. Hull Technicians are aware that effective damage control, like surgery, required precision, knowledge, and skill to make quick decisions that are correct. Tyler made a quick decision. To their front, flames vacillated wildly attempting to beat away the dousing water-spray; behind them several flame-bursts climbed the lagging and face of boiler number one. If trapped in an uncontrolled class-bravo fire, Tyler would give the command to abandon the fight.

They had one shot; Tyler patted Scheppler on the shoulder and pointed to the PKP–AFF station. Scheppler's gaze magnified through the gas-mask eyelets. Tyler knew the eager Scheppler would not hesitate.

Scheppler gestured down to the hose he was wielding behind Smithe. Tyler assured him with a thumb, "I got it."

In a timed transfer of hose from hand to hand, Tyler climbed behind Smithe, and Scheppler released the canvass tube. Scheppler took several quick strides to the PKP station. In less than a minute, Scheppler had uncoiled several feet of hose, stripped off the necessary wire-seals and cotter pins, and punched the activation plunger. He stepped to the side of Smithe and held the PKP nozzle wide open. Streams of violet-purple potassium bicarbonate jetted from the nozzle. A curtain of powder laced the boiler fronts. Smithe subsided the water bath where the PKP was killing the flames.

In what amounted to only sixty-seconds, Scheppler had knocked down the vast majority of all the fire. Smitty cut the water nozzle off, letting Tyler take control of the number-one hose. He stepped around

Scheppler and grabbed the AFF-foam hose-gun. In the moments that followed, Smithe and Scheppler applied AFF-foam and PKP to the entire platform and up the port and starboard sides of both boilers where fire had crept around the corners.

Ramirez cut the umbrella spray. The heat came at them with an intense blast. The room temperature had risen to almost an unbearable level. Tyler signaled to keep the foam and PKP flowing. He and Ramirez re-opened the water nozzles slightly and set the brass-valves down to flow cooling rivers across the surface of the diamond deck below all of their boots. He wrote a note and dashed to the ladder for Fillmore.

A class Bravo fire, caused by flammable liquids, required them to contain the fuel or another flash might erupt before they even had a chance to take a breath. Tyler shouted for Smithe to, "Fill the bilge!" Ramirez found the valves and, although fuel was no longer flowing, shut them down.

After a while, the temperature in the space began to lower.

Fillmore, along with Postino and the investigators, Swartz and EM2 Hart, soon returned. They delivered a black leather-bound meter, and with a quick check, Tyler determined the oxygen levels to be okay for them to remove their masks. The monstrous fire was for the most part out.

The men removed their OBA masks.

An excited battle cry came from Scheppler. Smithe smiled and the entire team shared high-fives and smiles. Exhilaration overtook their exhaustion.

"West, we got a casualty over here!" Postino shouted from the port side of boiler number one.

"Damn." Tyler said under his breath, and all smiles quickly faded. He and the others gathered in a semi-circle around a charred body sprawled on the diamond deck.

"Tell DC Central the worst is over," Tyler handed Fillmore a message. "Give them this." Fillmore left. The others stood without speaking. Tyler broke the silence. "We still have work to do. Spread out; inspect for burners. Smitty, keep the AFF flowing. Swartz, Hart, we've contained the main fire, but let's scan the entire space. I want no chances of a re-flash. Postino, secure the lighting and re-route the exhaust to pull some of this smoke out."

The team went to work and Tyler's mind went back to the whereabouts of their missing comrade.

CHAPTER 45

The complexity of dealing with an on-board fire might be overwhelming—to some. Even though Jorgenson had the proper training and was familiar with the steps and procedures, he had never experienced a major shipboard fire.

The sounds that had exploded from the 1MC speaker in Orton's stateroom was the General Quarters announcement. The OOD, Lieutenant Hornsby had received a call from Main Control that the Sounding and Security patrol had discovered the fire in the Fire Room. In retrospect, Jorgenson wished he had been notified before sounding GQ, but the fact that there was a serious fire now burning in the main space gave them all little room for second-guessing. They needed to get this thing under control as soon as possible.

There was not much to see from the bridge. Tuffs of black smoke intermittently billowed from the middle section of the ship. He could only wait for news as reports came from the fire team's On-Scene-Leader, HT2 West. Jorgenson felt compelled to describe the process to Agent Johnson and her comrades.

"Messages arrive by way of a messenger who runs notes from the On Scene Leader to the repair locker phone operator. Lieutenant JG Springer, down in Damage Control Central, receives the messages from Chief Langston at the Repair Locker. Springer is our command and control for the DC teams below."

The NIS Team seemed to follow, but whether or not they did, was of no real concern for Jorgenson. He had bigger issues than Johnson, her agents, and their collective understanding of the convoluted shipboard procedure. The fire alarm sounded over thirty minutes ago, and from the content of the messages, it sounded as if West's crew were embroiled in one hell of a fight.

"Report." Jorgenson said again; the last update had come in too long ago for his liking—even though it was no more than a few minutes. The time between communications and the path through the line of participants was excruciating.

Anderson's ear collapsed under the pressure of the plastic cup, which served as the earpiece of the sound-powered phone. Anderson maintained a cool monotone, "Nothing," he said, repeating the same response given after the last two requests. Behind Anderson along with Jorgenson were Kendall, Hornsby, and Hodges.

Anderson suddenly jolted, signaling that an update was coming in. "The fire has not completely engulfed the Fire Room, sir, just the lower level—but West reported OOC is possible." Anderson listened to everything Springer was saying, then relayed the message as, "They may have to abandon the fight and try to suffocate the fire. DCA says maintain condition Zebra."

"What does that mean?" Agent Johnson asked nervously.

"It means evacuation," Jorgenson replied. "They may lose control of the fire." He turned to Kendall.

"Paul, organize rescue tugs."

"Aye, sir." Kendall said and stepped away, pulling Hodges along.

Jorgenson made eye contact with Agent Johnson. She kept her arms folded tight to her chest and pressed a knuckle to her jaw. As soon as news of a fire had reached her, she wasted no time in articulating her theories.

"HT2 West is one of our best, Agent Johnson. He and the team will handle this."

She lowered her hand, realizing she was giving off signs of anxiety that she did not care to share.

"I know." She said matter-of-factly. "However, this evacuation will derail our main priority Captain."

Jorgenson understood. She wanted to confront the prime suspect without civilian authorities involved.

She leaned closer to him and lowered her voice. "Captain, I hate repeating myself, but this fire seems a little too convenient. Evacuation? There could be an escape attempt. A security team needs to be organized immediately to locate the suspect and take him in."

"The main priority is to control this fire." Jorgenson frowned; he realized she had a good point though. "The suspect is with his fire team, and this will keep him occupied. Besides, I wanted to lock him up. You and the powers that be all disagreed with me and said that there was nothing overly dangerous about leaving him with the rest of my crew." He felt as if this was a long overdue lecture, "I let you take over this investigation, but I will not allow you to send a security team into an unstable environment so that they can distract men fighting an out of control fire. You will not put any more of my crew, along with this entire vessel, at risk."

Agent Johnson's eyes narrowed, but she said nothing in response.

Another minute passed and another update arrived from Damage Control Central.

"There's something Lieutenant Springer wants you to know, sir." Anderson tugged at the headset and held the receiver out to Jorgenson. For a moment, Jorgensen was confused, he instinctively grabbed the assembly, put a cup to his ear, and spoke into the mouthpiece. "Springer? What is it?"

Jorgenson did not immediately respond to the words Lieutenant Springer was transferring through the line. After a brief pause, he said, "Thanks," and handed the phone-set back to Anderson.

"West needed to replace the repair team electrician." Jorgenson said to no one in particular, but the words were for Agent Johnson.

"Why?"

"He is not at Repair Five."

"So, our guy is not with the fire team?" Agent Johnson's voice rose with each word.

"Springer says they don't know where he is—but he is definitely not wearing an OBA fighting the fire."

Agent Johnson almost collapsed and let out a "Fuck!" They had been counting on keeping him in one place, but the ship had gone to General Quarters. Her initial suspicions seemed to be more accurate than Jorgenson had believed.

Another message was coming in from DCC—"They are making progress on the fire." Anderson pulled the mouthpiece away and said to Jorgenson, "At this rate, they'll be getting this under control soon." Anderson's editorial was appreciated but not necessary.

No updates came. Fifteen excruciating minutes passed. Jorgenson was ready to explode. "Can we get a head count?" Jorgenson said; he turned to Anderson. "Have Springer get all Repair Lockers to provide a count of their men."

Anderson gave the command. He turned to Agent Johnson, "Benefit of the doubt. Maybe he got hung up and made it to another Repair Locker? Or there could be others not present?"

Three minutes went by before Anderson received the reply from Springer. "All are present and accounted for except for the Repair Five electrician."

Agent Johnson started pacing; her head slowly shook from left to right. "Jesus Christ—what if he set the fire?"

"But we have no reason to believe he did. All the men were accounted for in their compartments." Jorgenson said but then realized the comment sounded feeble—the last head count had been at midnight. How could they be sure where anyone was when General

Quarters sounded?

Agent Johnson continued voicing her epiphany, "He's an electrician—he's trained in fires and knows that condition zebra would be required if a major fire starts... especially in that particular main space. But he needed to be..."

Lieutenant Anderson interrupted Johnson, "The fire is under control."

Jorgenson's heart pounded; he could feel the rush of blood through his ears in relief.

Agent Johnson wrapped herself in her own thoughts.

Kendall reappeared, followed by Lieutenant Hodges.

The thoughts in Jorgenson's head crashed and collided in a montage of conflicting theories and emotions. He bit the inside of his cheek, tasted blood, and snatched the phone from Anderson. "Springer..." he said in a nervous but commanding tone, "This is Jorgenson. Where the fuck is Wilkette?"

CHAPTER 46

They were all somewhat relaxed now; the fire had not gotten further out of control, and their inspections were revealing small breakouts, which they extinguished with CO_2 bottles. Tyler found himself on the upper level dousing patches of smoldering insulation with a hand held extinguisher. Around him, piping and lagging smoldered—although the fire was mostly out, intermittent flames continued to spark—sending whiffs of smoke upwards with each re-flash.

It would take a while to douse all the patches of flame. The Fire Room was immense; the room spanned the full beam of the ship, forty-six feet port to starboard, and the span from aft to forward bulkhead was even larger. Although the platforms around the upper level were narrow and difficult to maneuver while wearing an OBA carrying a forty-five pound CO_2 bottle, Tyler worked steadily.

From his high vantage point, the twin boilers stood tall and charred. The forward, number two boiler, had received most of the fire damage, and Tyler inspected each inch of its perimeter for burning ruins. Below, Tyler could hear the blast of CO_2 extinguishers as Swartz and Hart doused burners around the rear lower level fuel pumps. The rest of the team organized flood-evacuation hoses on the lowest level; they would need to pump the firewater out of the bilge soon.

The upper level was mostly secure apart from a few hot spots. The room had been practically engulfed, and Tyler's team had beaten the flames to the lower level. Tyler removed his OBA, laid the extinguisher down, and used it as a bench for a quick breather. He was proud of his team and disgusted at the same time. *How did this fire start—and where is Wilkette?*

From below Smithe shouted for Tyler to join the group on the lower level.

Smithe stood by a charred body of the BT that Postino had found. "Why didn't he go for the escape trunk?" Tyler tried not to picture him alive and gasping for air as the harsh black smoke filled his lungs.

Ramirez knelt down beside the body. "Holy shit...West... this guy's head is fucked up." He pointed, "Right here, see how his skull is cracked?"

The bone had a majority of the flesh burnt away. "It's Clayborn," Tyler said.

"How can you tell?"

Tyler touched the dead man's wrist, "he's got a tattoo right here." The words John 3:16 were just barely legible under the soot that had gathered. "Not sure how his head got caved in, but fire wouldn't do that to his skull."

Tyler wanted to be sure there were no others. "Postino, Swartz, Scheppler... check the bilge."

He turned to Hart and Persinski. "I need one of you guys to inspect the forward bulkhead in Aux-Onc. Hart, we had a lot of fire over against that wall, there could be a loss of integrity, check for cracked pipelines, and smoldering lagging." Hart nodded and left.

"Persinski," Tyler thought about his sunburn, "go topside and get that OBA off. Alert Langston; we got no chance at lighting off a main boiler. The auxiliary diesel is the ships only source of power now. We need to route the main-bus to the lighting only in the Fire Room—he'll know what to do." Tyler looked around, "Fillmore." The messenger came over as Tyler wrote a note. "Tell DC Central to keep the Fire Room isolated—no one in or out. I will call if I need you. We have things under control but it's still too hot in here. Re-flash fires are still likely. We'll start pumping out the bilged soon as well."

303

"Gotcha boss!" Persinski said. Fillmore only nodded, they both departed, "Barry," Tyler said soberly, and Fillmore turned. "We'll get him out of here ASAP—let the chief know to get the stretcher ready. I'll give the word when the corpsman can come down here." Tyler knew that Fillmore and Clayborn had been friends.

He suppressed a grimace—instead, keeping his face straight to aid in Fillmore's ability to manage the emotion of losing a friend. Once Fillmore and Persinski were up the two levels and out, Tyler made his way back up to the top level to retrieve his own OBA and extinguisher he had left up there. As he gathered the equipment, the guys on the lower level were attempting to pull up the large deck plate in front of the boiler.

*****

Forty-seven hours since my waltz, and I feel everything spiraling out of control.

You have failed again.

No. No—the fire should still be burning. Why is the ship not in peril? Why is the fire out?

You are incompetent.

"I'm not incompetent!" I shout. I don't care if my words are aloud. I must finish... I must fulfil my... my destiny is in jeopardy...

Music, loud and chaotic, blasts. I cannot think; the music... drums, synthesizers, blaring electric guitars, and shrill screaming voices all converge in my ears. There is no stopping it.

Damn these HT's. They arrived too soon; the fire did not have a chance to spread far enough.

You need to act.

The fire team is right outside this escape trunk. I cannot stay here;

it is only a matter of time before I am discovered. They already know I was missing from the fire team. They will be looking for me.

My plan. The evacuation. I was to wait in the escape trunk until the 'abandon ship' sounded and instructions for the crew to go to the tugboats. I was to sneak up and find the captain.

Your ineptitude.

I planned this well.

You did not set a good fire.

The fire team is to blame.

This plan is foiled.

I will draw the captain to me.

Demand to see the captain.

Yes.

You will need to sacrifice yourself.

Only if I fulfil my destiny and rid this world of another abuser.

You must.

I need another plan that will draw the captain to me. Not in this space though. I need higher ground. A place where I cannot be cornered.

In the open, you will be vulnerable.

Not everywhere in the open—there are places that are at the same time open and hidden—there is such a place. I know where to go.

You will need bargaining chips.

Yes. I know this. The HT's will suffice.

Do not fail a third time.

*****

Tyler maneuvered atop the upper level and contemplated how long it would take to finish putting out the rogue fires that were re-sparking everywhere. Below the other men were still working on the deck plates while keeping an eye out for bodies.

The escape trunk door suddenly slammed open as Remy Wilkette burst out with a gun. The echo of a single shot, which hit the underside of the upper decking, immediately got everyone's attention.

Tyler instinctively crouched behind a nest of vertical pipes that shielded his position but allowed him to watch the events below. Wilkette looked beyond crazed and exhibited behaviors Tyler had never seen in his friend before. He waved what appeared to Tyler to be a security weapon around—one of the standard issue M1911's—a forty-five caliber. He continuously slapped the side of his head with his free hand. He wore only a scorched on one side t-shirt and his dungarees.

I have to get that gun away from him. Tyler looked around for a weapon. *Will a CO2 container do?*

"Where's the rest of the team?" Wilkette looked around frantically. He then raised his voice to a screeching-yelp. "Everyone come out!" His normally low-pitched voice sounded strained. He pointed the gun at Ramirez and Smithe then waved it in the direction of the other three men frozen beside the boiler.

"What the hell is wrong with you, man?" Trust Ramirez to voice exactly what Tyler and everyone was thinking.

"This isn't everyone. Who is missing? No one is supposed to be missing! Where is West?"

Wilkette hadn't spotted his hiding place—which would be great if Tyler planned on staying up the ladder while the rest of his team was in danger below. He considered leaving for help. However, Wilkette might panic if he heard someone sneaking around on the upper level. Maybe Tyler should bang around on purpose as a distraction. It could allow Smithe a chance to jump Wilkette and get the gun. Tyler slowly moved towards the ladder, ready to be the distraction.

"West went up to DC Central." Smithe said and stepped into the open space halfway between the boiler and Wilkette.

Dammit Smitty! Now he couldn't risk making a noise. Wilkette was obviously unstable. Who knew what would happen if he thought Smithe lied to him?

"Ahh!" Wilkette cried yanking at his ear. His gun hand roamed. The gun's barrel focused its aim on Smithe, then on Ramirez, Scheppler, Postino, and Swartz—all in turn.

"Okay. Okay... then, everyone take off your fire gear." He looked over at Smithe and Ramirez. "Move in front of the boiler with everyone else. All of you need to take off your shit."

"This is fuckin crazy..." Swartz began. Postino shushed him. "Shut up man and take your fucking OBA off!"

"We got a fire here, Remy," Ramirez said pointing to a flame creeping up the lagged pipe only feet from Wilkette. "Nobody's stripping their gear for you."

"Give me the gun." Smithe moved closer.

"No."

The guys were keeping Wilkette distracted and talking. Tyler chanced slinking towards the ladder as silently as possible. It was more than thirty feet away.

"What's got you all worked up?" Smithe asked calmly. He took a few cautious steps towards Wilkette. Ramirez began to move towards the rest of the men.

"I'll kill you, Levon. I'll do it."

"No you won't, Remy." Scheppler interrupted Wilkette. "Come on, man, we're friends. What's going on?"

Wilkette curled his head around as if trying to escape a vice tightening in on his ears. "It's the music," he confessed, "all I want is to turn off the music!" He rubbed frantically at an ear. "It's so loud!" His voice cracked. "The music is so damn loud!"

"Easy, Remy..." Scheppler said soothingly, "There is no music."

Wilkette glared. "You don't hear? The music—you all act like it's not even there. There are messages beyond the songs."

Tyler made good progress, and in an opening between the equipment, he saw Smithe and Ramirez positioning themselves to take out an obviously insane man. Tyler was only a few feet away from the ladder now. *Maybe I can get downstairs without him hearing me. I can bash this CO_2 bottle into his head.*

"You need to put the gun down before someone gets hurt." Scheppler tried once again to reason with his friend.

"Must I?" Wilkette raised a dark eyebrow and peered through his glasses. "Hurting someone is the least of my worries."

"Why ya'll trying to reason with this dipshit?" Swartz yelled. "He's fucking crazy! Obviously he killed Orton."

"Yes. I killed Orton. For the greater good..." Wilkette pointed the barrel at Swartz.

"Sometimes sacrifices must be made."

The loud blast caught Tyler off guard, as did the sight of Swartz's head bursting open. Globs of bloody matter erupted from the cherub-faced HT's cranium. His body dropped, and blood gushed from the open space in the crown of his fragmented skull. Tyler stopped in his tracks, breathless. He gazed at Wilkette's fingers wrapped around that trigger and then back at the headless corpse. The gun was not a bluff.

"Fuck!" Postino cursed. Smithe brought both hands to the top of his head. Ramirez and the others stood silent and shocked. Postino was the closest person to Swartz in proximity; blood and brains splattered over his cloths.

"You son of a bitch." Came Ramirez's venom laced words.

"Now. Let's try this again. Everyone take off your fucking gear, or

308

he's next." Wilkette pointed the gun at Smithe's head. Smithe, however, stood his ground and did not move.

Ramirez and Postino began removing their helmets, fire-jackets, gloves and OBA's. Scheppler took off his helmet slowly and said, "You just fucking killed Ray, and you killed Orton... didn't you Remy? I can't believe this."

"It had to be done." Wilkette shook his head. "He thought he was better than all of us. He abused his power and needed to be punished."

Scheppler said, "I covered for you. All this time. I saw you come in after my shift was over, but I told them that you were in your rack the whole time." Scheppler looked at Postino. "That's why they had me up in the Wardroom so long. They were asking questions about Remy." He turned back to Wilkette. "But, I protected you man. I didn't say a damn thing, and now you're down here playing target practice with our friends?"

Tyler could tell this bothered Wilkette. He curled his head around in several circles as if trying to dislodge a parasite that was clinging to his scalp. Tyler took several more steps towards the ladder and managed to get a foot on the first rung when he heard Smithe say in a raised voice. "Wait!"

Wilkette had pointed the barrel of the gun towards Scheppler. He did not heed Smithe's plea to wait and said, "You're a good friend, Tommy, but you make me weak." Wilkette fired. Scheppler fell back against the handrail. The gunshot blasted a staccato-echo of metal on metal.

Scheppler was neither dead—nor even shot—the bullet must have lodged in his OBA canister. It did not go through. The instant smile of relief on Scheppler's face disappeared when Wilkette squeezed the trigger twice.

"No!" Smithe yelled and lunged at Wilkette. Tyler could see that both shots hit Scheppler—one in the face and another just below the OBA, maybe the groin, Tyler guessed. Scheppler pirouetted down to the deck plates. Ramirez and Postino also jumped towards Wilkette.

Tyler sped up. He leapt down the ladder. Smithe was yelling "Remy stop! Remy stop!" as another two shots and a loud cry from Postino pierced the Fire Room. Tyler got to the lower level and was just about to reveal himself at the edge of the boiler when he heard the scuffle had subsided and Wilkette started screaming, "Get back, get back!"

Tyler stopped and peeked around the boiler edge. Three new bodies lay on the deck plates—Swartz and two additions. One of them, Postino, writhed in pain. The third body, Smithe's, did not move; he still wore his firefighter's jacket and OBA.

Wilkette quickly and deftly unlashed the forty-five caliber M1911's clip and inserted a full magazine. He grinned triumphantly. "You are all defiant, but you cannot defeat me."

Tyler's anger swelled. His best friend was down. He wanted to rush Wilkette and tackle him into the bilge. Obviously, a frontal attack on a man with a gun wasn't the best tactic. Especially since, he had ample ammunition along with the willingness to shoot his closest friends. There were multiple clips on the gun-belt and several more protruding from his pockets. Tyler needed a weapon—something, anything that would take an assailant down with a single blow. Only charred and smoking bits of insulation surrounded him—no spanner wrenches—no plumbing supplies.

"Get up in the escape trunk." Wilkette said to Ramirez, the only man left standing.

"Where you gonna go, Remy?" came a voice.

Tyler was at once relieved. Smithe slowly rose up cradling his right arm. He had been shot.

"So, you're still alive?" Wilkette hissed.

Smithe took a step towards Wilkette and said, "Just got tired of trying to hear that music you keep talkin about."

Wilkette growled and rushed forward. "You gonna take that gear off now?" He pushed the pistol into Smithe's forehead. A small trace of smoke escaped between the gun and Smith's forehead as the hot barrel branded a circle in his skin. He didn't even wince.

"Get in the escape trunk, and go up the ladder! We're going to Steel Beach."

Ramirez helped Smithe removed his OBA and jacket, and the three men stepped across to the far side of the space near the exit. Ramirez was the first to go in. Wilkette placed the gun against the back of Smithe's head.

Tyler started breathing again after hearing Smithe speak. He quickly formed an idea to run and grab Wilkette from behind; there was about twenty-five feet separating him from the hostage taker, but just as he was about to pounce, Postino's whimpers from the floor made Tyler hesitate. Wilkette quickly corralled the two hostages into the escape trunk, and they ascended the vertical ladder. Once the escape trunk's airtight door settled closed, Tyler darted toward Postino.

Postino pushed into the side of his right hip, "He wanted to kill me... Smithe grabbed the barrel of the gun, and he got me in the leg." He pointed an unsteady bloody finger at the disfigured body on the deck. "He blew Swartz's fucking head off!"

Tyler picked up a discarded fireman's glove, folded it, and pressed the makeshift gauze into the wound at Postino's hip. "Keep pressure on it or you'll bleed out," Tyler said in a whisper.

"Well that's fucking great." Postino leaned his head back and gritted his teeth. He sat up a bit and said, "Scheppler?"

Tyler moved to Scheppler who was lying on his back, his eyes barely open. He was alive. He held his left hand to the side of his throat as blood seeped from between his fingers. The face shot had ripped through Scheppler's neck just below the jawbone. His dungarees were soaked with blood from the groin shot.

Tyler crouched low and said, "Tommy, can you hear me?" Scheppler's metal-blue eyes rolled back for a moment before focusing on Tyler.

"Listen, I'm going to go get help. You just hang in there."

He started to stand, but Scheppler reached out and gripped onto Tyler's wrist. He moved his face side to side as if to say, 'don't leave me'. He tried to talk, but only wispy gurgles came from his pale lips.

Tyler removed the OBA facemask and hoses from over Scheppler's neck and knelt down, "You need medical attention right now."

Tears filled Scheppler's sockets and overflowed down his soot-streaked face. He gripped Tyler's forearm and managed a guttural, "hurts."

Tyler pulled Scheppler into his arms, cradling him as if he was a young child as a few fires smoldered in the lagging insulation around them. Scheppler had gotten to the PKP station—he had put out the fire—he had done his job—his duty—wonderfully.

"I'm right here," Tyler said. Scheppler relaxed his head into Tyler's embrace.

A large puddle of blood formed in the diamond decking; some escaped into the seam between two plates. With one hand, Scheppler gripped Tyler as the other uselessly rested on the dwindling ebbs of red fluid seeping from his torn neck. Tyler peered into Scheppler's eyes as they faded and blinked shut; his head slowly fell back and his hand became limp.

Tyler squeezed the dead HT in his arms before gently lying him down. In the bilges, at the front of both boilers, small bursts of re-flashes began to erupt and flames climbed up the boiler fronts.

Postino said, "You gotta stop Wilkette."

Tyler nodded. Stop Wilkette. Easier said than done. *How am I going to stop him?* "Wilkette said they were going to Steel Beach, right?"

Postino nodded and suddenly footsteps clanged down the ladder behind them. Tyler jumped to his feet; it was Fillmore. "Hey, the Chief's been waiting for..." Fillmore's eyes widened, "What the hell, West?"

"Have DC Central alert the bridge. Wilkette is on a killing spree; he has a gun. There are two hostages, and he's headed topside. Let them know..." Tyler paused for a moment, "I'm going after them."

"West?"

"By the time they decide what to do; all my friends will be dead." Tyler pulled at the escape trunk door, "You have your report! Get someone down here to help Postino. The fire is re-flashing. Go!"

Fillmore ran off towards the main entry. Tyler took a quick peek up the ladder. The trunk was clear; they were likely up to the Main Deck by now. He took a last glance at Scheppler and nodded at Postino, before leaving.

CHAPTER 47

Tyler sprinted up the two story vertical ladder. *How can I take out Wilkette without a weapon?* As he reached the top rung, an idea popped into his head. Wilkette is going to Steel Beach. Tyler recalled the welding leads he and Smitty had found during their search on the day of the murder. Scheppler, you careless son of a bitch. Those electrical leads left on top of the Helo-Hangar were just what Tyler needed—at least an absurd notion in his head made them useful.

The exit of the escape trunk let out to the Main Deck port passage. Tyler slowly pushed open the spring-loaded door and peeked aft through a narrow slit. If Wilkette intended on getting to Steel Beach he would go back to the flight deck via the fantail of the ship. With everyone still at General Quarters this way would be deserted. There was no sign of anyone.

Tyler stepped out, and instead of going the same way as Wilkette and the hostages, he sprinted in the opposite direction. He had a crazy plan, and it involved getting something from the General Workshop. The smarter thing to do would be to go to the safety of DC Central and let the brass handle this situation, but they already had their chances to get this under control for too long as far as Tyler was concerned. *No.* Tyler figured Wilkette had this all planned, and he'd been allowed to lounge around the General Workshop refining his bloodbath for hours. "Fuck!" Tyler shouted in anger as he reached the ladder leading below. For almost three days, the brass had dragged their feet while Wilkette simmered on this plan. In just over an hour, Wilkette had snuck out of R-Division, set a fire, and decimated the Repair Five team and, God knows who else, without any resistance.

By now, Fillmore had delivered the message, and the bridge was probably all standing around with their thumbs up their asses trying to figure out what to do next. Tyler would not let the dithering officers and NIS take the lead on saving his comrades.

He leapt down the R-Division berthing compartment ladder and got to the rack area. He reached into his rack for the welding ground clamp that he, Smithe, and Persinski had hid during the first department inspections. He slipped the clamp into his back pocket. He then rushed to the far end of the workshop to fetch the same high frequency welder that Smithe had used to melt the Helo-Hangar stereo to the workbench. In one swift motion, he lifted the large machine onto his back, turned, and lumbered to and up the ladder out of R-Division.

Tyler rushed towards the area where Wilkette would be forcing his friends up to Steel Beach. He carried the heavy welder to the boat-deck where the lead ends lay tucked away outside the starboard hangar bulkhead and plugged it into a two-hundred-forty volt outlet near the doorway. He connected the cables to the unit lead inlets, power and ground, and switched on the unit. An orange light indicated the electricity was flowing. Then he turned the volt and amp knobs to full. The now live welding leads, which remained in the same spot where Scheppler had left them, were ready to flow high frequency electricity through them. If anyone up on the Helo-Hanger roof touches those cable ends—completing the circuit—they'll receive quite a shock.

"Hector, move over there!" Wilkette's high-pitched voice came from above his head. Tyler quickly leaned against the bulkhead superstructure to keep from view. He touched the clamp in his back pocket, pulled in a deep breath, moved to the vertical ladder that led to the top of Steel Beach, and started to climb. He did not want to surprise Wilkette, so he kicked at the ladder rungs with each step. Before he reached high enough to see over the edge of the platform, a startling thought came to him; what if he shoots me before I get to the top. *This may be the dumbest idea I've ever had.* Before he could decide to go back down the ladder, a hand gripped the back of his head and pulled him the rest of the way.

"You think you can sneak up on me, West?" Wilkette roared and pushed Tyler to his knees; he held the gun up to his face. Tyler ignored the gun and looked around. Ramirez kneeled with his hands clamped on top of his head. Smithe, also kneeling, held his injured arm tight to his side. Despite a bloody nose and the gunshot wound, Smitty looked ready to rumble. Good. Tyler felt a wave of relief; his best friends were still alive—two men as angry as Tyler.

"I wasn't trying to sneak up on you," Tyler said, "I'm just here to talk."

"Get with them!" Wilkette screamed, and Tyler was shimmied to a spot in line with the other two. Wilkette's eyes flared around as he waved the gun about, "Do you have a weapon?" Wilkette pulled at Tyler's clothes searching for a concealed anything.

"I have nothing, Remy. You took my fire team; now I'm here with them. That's all."

The hysterical Wilkette winced. "It's so damn loud! How can none of you hear the music?"

Wilkette walked closer to the trio and suddenly grabbed Smithe's injured arm causing Smithe to grit his teeth and groan. Tyler held back from lunging. Wilkette pressed the gun's muzzle firmly against Smithe's temple. He had proved several times over that he would not hesitate to put a bullet in another skull.

"Why did you come here, West, are you stupid?"

"Remy," Tyler held his hands up, showing Wilkette that he was surrendering to him, "I want to help you get out of this mess. Listen to me...please, I just want to talk."

Smithe barely breathed, not wanting to give his captor a reason to flinch, but Tyler could see the determination in his friend's eyes. All of them were willing to fight—maybe gain advantage and flip the bastard off the edge of Steel Beach. Tyler slowly shook his head to send Smithe the message not to resist. They needed to get Wilkette to calm down before trying to jump him.

The active welding leads lay atop a hawser rope right at Wilkette's feet. At one end—the lead closest to Ramirez—a ground clamp was attached. The other wire laid loose with a copper connector end exposed; the end Tyler would use if necessary. With the amount of electricity attempting to cycle through those wires, if Wilkette touched them, he would light up like a Christmas tree.

That was the plan, but Tyler did not want Wilkette to blow Smitty's head off in the process. He took a deep breath and asked one last time, "Remy, please! Listen to me, can we talk about this?"

CHAPTER 48

Two tugboats cruised toward the Miller. Jorgenson wanted the tugs ready for evacuation; they had never confirmed the main space fire being completely out. With the Repair Five team decimated, getting the other repair lockers mustered to re-sweep and secure any potential re-flashes was taking too long for comfort. Unlike the work West and his team had completed before being hijacked by Wilkette, the ship's security teams failed to get anything under control.

"We can't get a shot from here," the one agent said to Agent Johnson who was on the phone with her superiors. "What type of rifles do you have on board? Agent Willis here is a pretty good shot; we have to move fast."

That was only one of their problems; "Mister Hornsby, give Willis access to our magazine." Hornsby and Agent Willis left. The other man, the thick glasses guy, seemed out of place, and Jorgenson presumed the forensics technician was not used to being in the field, especially action that had him cornered on a burning ship with a gun-wielding madman firing at will.

That was the other problem, Wilkette kept shooting; at the security team; at the tugboats. Anywhere topside in range of the Helo-Hangar was dangerous; Wilkette seemed bent on firing at anything that moved.

"I want to get our squad in place to approach the hangar," Jorgenson insisted to Johnson.

"I agree; we are at least fifteen or twenty minutes away from positioning a sniper in a helicopter. If we can get Willis in place with a weapon, this is most likely our best tactic."

Kendall spoke up, "What about the evacuation?"

Moving the crew anywhere near mid-ship to aft, topside would be impossible. To get the crew off the boat meant dangling sailors off the forecastle—very risky. Wilkette has taken them all hostage.

"Take the crew forward, below decks. If necessary, we'll go off the forecastle with rope ladders." He turned to Johnson. "Let's have our security team set up a perimeter near every possible escape route below the Helo-Hangar. If he decides to run we'll have him cornered." She nodded in agreement. "Have the tugs stay a safe distance back, Paul, until we need them."

Lieutenant Hodges remained on the bridge and was surprisingly lucid. He hung over the edge of the starboard flying bridge trying to get a glimpse of something. Not much was visible from either the port or starboard flying bridges, only the very outside edges of Steel Beach. The major portion of the area above the Helo-Hangar was not viewable through the two-hundred feet of super-structure. Jorgenson's heart raced. The situation had unfolded so quickly and now the ship floated helplessly in the bay. Wilkette had positioned himself in a wide-open space with no way for anyone to sneak up on him. *Smart boy,* the captain couldn't help but think.

A painful weight rested on Jorgenson's shoulders. For what reason did Wilkette take hostages? Why kill his shipmates? He's been calm and collected for three days, and now he decides to go crazy. Jorgenson, the Miller leadership, the NIS, and Surf-Lant Command had thoroughly discussed Wilkette's possible motives for killing Orton, and although Jorgensen argued against the NIS theory of Orton somehow offending Wilkette by holding back a promotion, they all had agreed on the probability for killing others; their consensus was that it would be unlikely. Wilkette's only vendetta was against Orton—at least it had seemed so; the kid had displayed no destructive behavior attributes. He had snapped.

"I should have put him in the brig the moment we suspected him,"

Jorgenson said to Kendall, feeling the weight of guilt and regret, "those men were counting on us to keep them safe! And look at what we've done!"

"I'm not worried; this will be over soon." Lieutenant Hodges stood in the doorway to the flying bridge. His face contorted into an angled grin. "West is going to get him."

Hodges strolled along the forward bulkhead panel. He ran his fingers atop the surfaces and caressed the equipment. He reached the captain's chair and hopped up swinging his feet to rest on the window ledge.

Agent Johnson glanced at Jorgenson and shook her head. Jorgenson preserved more concern for the unexpectedly childlike behavior of the suddenly insightful Chief Engineering Officer.

"What makes you say that, Philip?" Jorgenson asked, hoping in that scattered brain, Hodges was privy to vital information, or some secret that would raise the confidence of the group.

"Springer's the DCA of R-Division, he'll tell you... he'll tell you about West—what kind of HT he is." Springer was still in Damage Control Central; Jorgenson wasn't going to phone him and ask what he thought about West. Hodges continued, "That West knows this ship, and he knows his guys. Whether Wilkette needs to be talked down or taken down... West will handle it."

Jorgenson wondered if Hodges was about to curl back up into a mindless shell, or turn into a raving lunatic. Was this a period of doubtful calm, or just another stage of lunacy? Not wanting to send him in reverse, Jorgenson decided to encourage the comments. "All right, until that sniper gets in place, let's just hope you're right. For now please coordinate with Mister Anderson and..." He looked over at Anderson, "between the two of you, work with Springer to get that fire back under control."

Anderson nodded. Hodges swung around, and jumped to the flying bridge platform. He leaned over the side structure and squinted his eyes. "Aye, Captain!"

"Jesus," Jorgenson mumbled quietly.

"The security team is ready." Agent Johnson stood near the port bridge exit chambering a Beretta M9, nine-millimeter handgun. Hornsby had returned, and held out a handgun for Jorgenson. He hesitated, and then said, "No, you hold it for me." Hornsby holstered the weapon, but kept his out and ready.

Jorgenson made the announcement to everyone. "I'm going to talk to Wilkette."

Johnson nodded.

The security team moved down the port ladders that led from the bridge to the superstructure platforms, and eventually into positions forward of the hangar. Another team was moving into a position aft, below the flight deck. As they came into and out of sight of the loft above the Helo-Hangar, gunshots from Wilkette scattered them for cover. The team remained hidden, mostly behind the main stack known as the Mack.

On her radio Johnson communicated with Willis, her agent turned sniper. He had gone with Hornsby to a position on the ladder, which went from the second deck above the main deck. There was not good visibility of Steel Beach, but if Wilkette showed himself towards the edge of the port side, Willis would have a clear shot.

The closer they moved towards the hanger, the less visible the rooftop became. Not once, had Wilkette shown himself as Jorgenson and his security moved down the port ladder to the starboard boat-deck. The Mack was at Jorgenson's left, and all he could do was hide from the line of fire.

CHAPTER 49

We must believe that it is the darkest before the dawn of a beautiful new world. We will see it when we believe it. There is a necessary sacrifice, but the lines between fantasy and reality have all blended—together, the sounds are too great. Many songs playing again and again, each tune trying to out sing the other.

Almost forty-eight hours since my waltz.

Who's watching...? "Are you listening to the same music as me? Don't you hear?" The faces of my shipmates tell me otherwise—is it fear or resentment? *I'm just... in the twilight?* The music grows louder with each step we take—they may be resentful of my enlightenment.

Silence, please, if only for a moment; I need silence so that I can think! Let me bathe in the glorious review of my days accomplishments.

Swartz was a delightful experience. The music was too loud to hear if he cried out. Why fear the inevitability of death? As the bits of brain and blood smattered the piping and deck, Ramirez backed-off.

I fired again at...

... and they all came at once. Too many to deal with? No. Too many hostages, perhaps. Postino is lucky because of Smithe. I missed my target—his chest—because Smithe grabbed my gun; silly move.

You must only fear God; act in the name of the righteousness—not justified anger.

These are father's words.

I am your father.

I know.

They serve as an apt reminder of my resolute task. They all know by now my intent is to clean up the scourge of corruption, yet letting

Postino live gives them hope.

More songs fill my ears... And now ... wait, what music is this...? "Ha." This music... this enrages me.

In an elevated position above the steel and cold ship, I am warm in the sun. The turquoise water ripples in a slight breeze, and the morning light peaks over the horizon. Suddenly I find myself standing atop Steel Beach, but I do not remember the journey. How did I get here? When did I get here? These thoughts? Are they in this moment or am I only recalling them? I cannot decide.

There is so much noise! "Do you hear it?" I grip a shirt collar in my free hand. The stupid prick is defiantly mute. He begins to tremble. I shake him, "Answer me! Do you hear it?"

"Hear what?" someone dares to ask—his voice is distant and dampened.

The question infuriates me! "Hear what? The music! How can you not hear the music?" So clearly does the sound of Beethoven fight with that of Michael Jackson now.

In a distant fog of sound something soft but staccato is sounding... "Remy... Remy..." The speaker is Smithe. His eyes are clear and soft—not judging—Smithe has always been a non-threating defender to those who needed him.

"Do you hear music, Remy?" Smithe asks in a calm voice. This cannot be so; I will not allow him in—this is unacceptable. Callousness, hatred, and denier of truths—he will pay. I will annihilate and perpetuate a cherished belief at and upon those that otherwise ignore my cause. I am just, and I will enact my destiny. Yet he continues to speak, "EM3 Wilkette, I think you need help," he says, "Let us help you."

I cannot deal with this pitiful playacting any longer. The butt of the gun will do; I swing at his face. He does not attempt to block the strike of his nose. His face is bloody now to go along with his damaged arm and branded forehead; his eyes widen. There!

There is his anger.

I use it like fuel.

Ring of Fire plays loudest now. Smithe and Ramirez are with me. What happened to Scheppler?

Oh, yes, that's right—I...

And Swartz? Where is he?

I cannot remember.

I see tugboats in the distance, and I see people maneuvering into position below.

Stay away from the edge. They can't see you, if you cannot see them.

The people below are either in my mind or in my reality, but time has merged, so I must preserve my position. My work will soon be over. I fire my weapon—a quick count of my ammunition—I have plenty of bullets. They flee and hide at the base of the Mack tower. If they dare move, I will kill them. My two captives—no longer friends—obey my orders.

"Hector, move over there." I wave the gun in Smithe's direction, reminding them what happened to the brain of Swartz. Oh, that's right, now I remember. *Killing me Softly with His Song* by Roberta Flack. Released in... what year was that?

What happened to Scheppler?

You don't remember?

From confidence to fear to anger to helplessness—just as father had described.

If only...?

Yes, I agree.

I regret not having put the Defiant One through more of these emotions before his demise—too bad. If only I had my knife...I would reenact that beautiful moment for myself right now and pierce one of them just as I had done with Bruce Orton. I want to relive that moment again. Where is my knife? I must retrieve it. What I am doing is beautiful! Anarchy—such a beautiful thing! Why can't anarchy be the norm?

Anarchy means change.

Yes, Father,

Change means movement. Movement means friction. Only in the frictionless vacuum of a nonexistent abstract world can movement or change or anarchy occur without that abrasive friction of conflict.

Just as the tapes had said. My music is loud, yet I hear another noise barely audible over the malicious melody.

The vertical port ladder!

I grab a handful of hair as the intruder joins the party. "You think you can sneak up on me, West?"

"I wasn't trying to sneak up on you," he says, "I'm just here to talk."

"Kneel with them!" I am so angry at West. Why did you come here? I had thought of you as smart—just unenlightened—the alpha rat running about the cage, seeking enlightenment. Someone who would eventually escape. Now you prove to be as stupid as the rest. Why can't they just listen to the music? The music will save their souls. I grab Smithe and press a thumb into the hole in his arm.

"Why did you come here, West, are you stupid?"

Search him.

He has no weapons. He is foolish.

"Remy," West holds his hands up, "I want to help you get out of this mess. Listen to me...please, I just want to talk." He dares to take a stand against me; the gun in his face does not seem to bother him much although he pulls back. I take aim at Smithe's head.

"Please," West pleads, "can we talk?"

Say nothing.

There is something about West. The way his eyes do not show me any emotion. The lack of fear and anger—his confidence. I see something new burning in his eyes. Not fear—something different.

"You killed Orton, right? I think I know why. Listen, Remy, things are not looking good for you. But, you can make this a lot easier. Keep your mouth shut and ask for a lawyer. Don't confess...simply turn yourself in."

What is he saying—is he trying to help me?

"No one else has to die today." West's eyes remain steady; is this a ploy by the Defiant One's companions to rid them of me?

West hated Orton.

So why would he...

"I know you, Remy. I know you. You don't want anyone else to die, do you?"

For a slight moment—there is blissful quiet—but then? No. The music! I cannot hear what West is saying.

"The Defiant One is dead! He has fallen, and soon so will his followers!"

Above there is a helicopter and I begin to laugh. I shoot my gun at the chopper. To West I say, "HT2 West—Tyler—my bunkmate—you almost had me—you almost tricked me, but you are one of them."

West is as disposable as the rest... but is he capable of being enlightened? Out of all the fools on this ship, he is the one who most deserves an explanation.

He will not get one.

He looks at me with eyes that are different from the others; his eyes tell me he wants to understand even if he cannot be trusted—at least he wants to know.

Tell him nothing.

"No, no, Remy..." West is saying something. His voice drowns in music—loud and clear. Down to one unmistakable tune. West's voice traces a line on the edge of reality and fantasy as the final song plays. A gentle melody. The Last Waltz by Engelbert Humperdinck: the original melody and soundtrack to my first noble slaughter. Something astonishing occurs to me; I've lost myself. The Defiant One took my sanity. This tune and all the others? I have no control now. This tune is Orton's revenge—*he* is the one playing the music. Trapped within a glorious and agonizingly beautiful symphony, I smile and sing.

"I wonder should I go or should I stay—The band had only one more song to play."

West and the others see me waltz with Orton on Steel Beach.

CHAPTER 50

"How long has that been flying around?" Jorgenson snapped at Agent Johnson when he spotted the news chopper flying overhead; a camera operator was hanging out of the side taking footage of the Miller and the unfolding events. They huddled behind the Mack with little left to hold onto—*can the damn news coverage at least wait until this plays out?* Jorgenson peered at the witless morons who wanted to videotape the death of sailors and wished that the Godforsaken helicopter circling the ship would crash and burn.

"We need to establish this as a no fly zone," he said at Johnson. "The last thing the Navy needs is for our sniper to take out a military man on live television." Jorgenson felt so close to losing everything; he'd lost control over his crew, the situation, and what little bit of dignity there was still left to grasp. The last thing he wanted was his shortcomings as captain publically displayed on the ten o'clock news.

"Don't worry," Agent Johnson said. She sounded too reassured— after all, the events of the past hour had not exactly boded well for her reputation either. They, Jorgensen and Agent Johnson, were both in the deepest vat of shit he could imagine.

"We're already on it. The chopper will be gone soon enough. But, it plays good cover for when *our* chopper arrives. Are you ready?" she asked Jorgensen.

He heaved in a deep breath and nodded. "Here goes."

Jorgenson stepped away from the edge of his hideout behind the Mack, cupped two hands around his mouth, and shouted. "Wilkette. Petty Officer Wilkette, I want to talk to you!"

CHAPTER 51

Wilkette seemed to be listening—for the moment; that was something at least.

"I'm telling you, Remy, you can get out of this." Tyler repeated, not sure if his desperate ploy was having any effect. "You can get out of this. No one else has to die, right?" From the corner of Tyler's eye, he could see Ramirez and Smithe. As Wilkette intermittently averted his attention away from their general vicinity, Tyler kept talking while making hand signals to Ramirez and Smithe. He wanted them to catch on that the welding leads were electrified. At one point, as Wilkette was preoccupied with the men below, Tyler reached around to his rear pocket and showed the clamp to the other two. Tyler hoped his silent communication got Smithe and Ramirez to spot the welding leads and figure out the general plan.

Good, Tyler thought, but if he could continue to calm Wilkette down the welder might only be a backup. He felt sure that if Wilkette continued to listen, he might surrender. Hope fueled a desire to reach his former friend somehow.

"I know you don't want anyone else to get hurt, Remy. Don't want friends to die, do you?"

Wilkette's half-burned face twisted into an expression that parodied deep contemplation, and for one blessed moment, the madness seemed to spill out of him. "No," he said at last. He then paused, distracted, listening to whatever that crazy noise in his head was.

"Listen to me then," Tyler said urgently, "There's going to be a defense team. You can tell them you were abused... that you lost your mind for a second when you hurt Orton. All right?"

"They're going to do everything they can to make sure I wind up on death row." Wilkette smiled at the thought. "So why not die here today with the rest of you?"

"We're not going to die. There is hope." Tyler shook his head. He had mixed feelings, there was a bond of allegiance building; the younger man could possibly be starting to believe they held a common understanding, but his comment about *dying with the rest of you* startled Tyler.

Wilkette was thriving right now on the madness of the situation; he wanted more blood; he wanted as bloody a day as possible, and he turned the gun to Tyler's face once more, "But I'm not finished yet, West."

From below, a voice rang out.

*****

Jorgenson waited for a response from the roof of the Helo-Hangar.

"If he shows himself, make sure your guy takes him out." Jorgenson said anxiously.

"Don't worry," Agent Johnson assured the captain from behind the Mack. "Willis is a good shot and the edge of the roof is in his scope."

Jorgenson and Johnson had given the command to take out Wilkette the moment the opportunity presented itself. Any second now, Wilkette would be dead, and hopefully he wouldn't be taking anyone else with him. The body count was already high enough. "Tell him not to hesitate," Jorgenson said in a low clear voice, and Johnson forwarded the command through her walkie.

Suddenly, the sound of gunshots rang out from atop the hangar. "Shit!" Jorgenson leapt to the Mack.

"The helo," Johnson said, "he's firing at the helicopter."

One of the security alert team members gave Jorgenson a nod in agreement with Johnson's assessment. "What's the deal on the sniper helicopter?" Jorgenson asked.

"They're in the air; ETA is five to ten minutes." Johnson said to the captain.

He contemplated putting himself out in the open again, "Should I wait?"

The question was mostly to himself, but Agent Johnson went to say something, and the words stuck in her throat. After a brief pause, she said, "Up to you."

Again, her radio crackled with Agent Willis's voice, "do not have a shot, repeat, no shot."

"Looks like it's you or our airborne sniper."

Jorgenson stepped out from behind the safety of cover again. "Petty Officer Wilkette, its Commander Jorgenson. I want to talk."

*****

Tyler heard the captain's voice. Wilkette suddenly became still. He crouched low and listened along with the three HT's. *What is he doing?* Tyler imagined the captain standing on the boat-deck within easy range of Wilkette's bullets.

Wilkette shifted his position and pushed the gun barrel to the backs of the three HT's, moving them closer to the platform edge facing forward, towards the boat-deck, the Mack, and the sound of the captain's voice. He and Ramirez still kept their hands interlocked across their heads, but as he moved, Tyler angled his torso slightly so that his back knee was further away from the edge. His posture was cattycornered and he had a good view of the boat-deck as well as Wilkette to his right. He was on the left, Smithe in the middle, and

331

Ramirez on the right; they all made a small barricade between the edge of Steel Beach and Wilkette to the rear. Wilkette remained back far enough to be out of the line of sight to those below. Wilkette then crouched to a knee and Tyler was certain this was the chance he'd been looking for.

Wilkette remained focused on the captain and he didn't catch the fact that the HT's were able to signal each other. At once, upon reaching the edge, Tyler shot a glance to the scene below. Captain Jorgenson stood with his hands up and out to his sides.

All of a sudden, Wilkette fired two shots. Tyler winced, almost believing the captain had been shot at, but the bullets were meant for a helicopter that had started hovering over their heads. Tyler could see the chopper bank and retreat; the fading thuds of the blades told Tyler that the helo had only moved to the forward end of the ship and out of sight.

After a minute the captain, who had ducked behind the Mack, shouted, "I want to talk!"

Wilkette said nothing, or at least he said nothing to the captain; he continued mumbling and ranting to himself. Tyler could not make out all of the words, but he kept repeating something like 'defiant' and 'abuser'. Tyler also heard him distinctly say, "... fair trade... nonentity for abuser... destiny for my father."

Then Wilkette screamed so loud that Tyler jolted, "I want to make a trade!"

Wilkette's unfamiliar high pitch and raging tone was unsettling; it sounded as if a ventriloquist was manipulating the once quiet and meek nerd who had always buttoned his shirts to the collar.

Immediately from below, the captain shouted, "okay, sounds good—let's work this out."

Wilkette shouted back, "One HT for one officer!"

*****

Agent Johnson's walkie buzzed to his left; he heard Willis report, "No clear shot... not in the scope."

He hesitated momentarily, but he knew what he needed to say. It most likely meant climbing to his own death, but to stand here and watch the crazed Wilkette gun down three more innocents was not something he was willing to chance.

"Okay. I'll come up." Jorgenson believed if he started up the port ladder Wilkette might expose himself.

"Captain, sniper-helo is one minute out," Agent Johnson said, "stall for a minute."

Jorgenson said out of the side of his mouth, "I'll get him to the port side; have Willis take the shot." He stepped further out into the opening aft of the Mack near the middle of the boat-deck.

*****

Forty-eight hours since our waltz.

Yes. Two Days.

The movement is immense. Brass, tympani, strings—all vying for the focus of the measures. With each bar comes another rousing cascade of triplets ascending and descending: first the horns and then the violas and violins. The agitating figures duel for volume over a chorus's voice. Tremendous complexity in its beauty. I see a helicopter above and fire my pistol. They shall not witness my accomplishment; their presence only adds to the tremendous loudness in my ears.

You need only remove the head of the serpent.

Yes. The captain is presenting himself for slaughter.

Captain. O Captain! My Captain! Our fearful trip is done.

He is defiant.

"He is defiant."

He is the abuser

"... the abuser."

Where on the deck my Captain lies, fallen cold and dead. It will come to pass, but from me it will not be met with mournful tread. You allowed the rein of the defiant; you must die.

"I want to make a trade!" This is best. I will trick them into believing my sincerity—agree to send HT's to safety. They will agree. I will draw the captain to the open deck below. I will have an open shot before he reaches the ladder.

What of the HT's.

"No one shall escape."

I agree. You may be sacrificed. The deed will be completed.

On this sacrificial platform, I will make my stand and fulfill our destiny.

*****

Another helicopter was approaching. Tyler could hear it in the distance. Wilkette remained back mumbling and Tyler heard him say, "no escape."

This is a ruse. Tyler feared the captain was walking into a trap that would have them all sacrificed. Wilkette was listening too intently to the noise in his head to catch on that the second helo was not a news chopper. Tyler made eye contact with Smithe and Ramirez who were both ready to pounce. This would be their only chance at survival. They all knew Wilkette was not backing down; he was ready to kill again.

A quick twisted knot formed in the pit of Tyler's stomach—a

diversion was needed—now. Tyler started a one, two, three countdown in his head, but before he got to three, Smithe acted out the part of the distractor.

Everything happened at once. Smithe jolted and spun to face Wilkette, Ramirez and Tyler both leapt up, and four quick blasts rang out followed by a painful stinging in his right arm. They were wrestling and then a body went airborne; Tyler twisted his head in time to see Smithe fall sideways. Wilkette broke free of their grasp and pulled the trigger for a fifth time, but the M1911 was fully recoiled and empty. For a split second Wilkette froze. Tyler realized he had the upper hand for the first time; he pounced on the welding cables. Wilkette popped out the magazine clip and reached for another. Ramirez dove at the welding lead with the connector end and jammed the clamp onto Wilkette's skin, pinching the bicep. "Ah!" Wilkette yelped before sinking a loaded magazine to the hilt. Tyler gripped the other cable by its rubber sheath and shoved the exposed copper at Wilkette's forearm. The instant contact with the moist flesh completed the electrical circuit, and Wilkette stiffened. At the same time, Tyler pulled the clamp out of his back pocket and locked the connector end to Wilkette's wrist. Tyler felt an intense electrical charge shoot through his body. His teeth clamped shut and he flew backwards. The electric shock stopped as quickly as it had started. He was dazed, but quickly regained his awareness.

Tyler watched as high-frequency voltage flowed through Wilkette. Every muscle in Wilkette's body tensed; his face muscles jerked and twitched in such a way that he appeared to be smiling at them all. After several more seconds, Tyler yanked at one of the leads and Wilkette collapsed on the ground. He convulsed a few times and then lay still. Tyler kicked the gun off the edge of steel beach; the pistol clanked down to the boat-deck.

Below, an army of people erupted from hiding places. Above, a second helicopter had arrived. The whooshing blades hovered low, only yards above the ship's highest point. Tyler breathed in deeply catching his breath.

"Is he dead?" Ramirez yelled above the helo din.

"I don't think so." Tyler looked over to the unconscious Wilkette.

"West, I wasn't asking about him."

Tyler turned. He saw Smithe lying flat on his back—blood seeping from his chest.

*****

"Don't know—they all pounced on the fucker." Spoke the voice on the other end of Agent Johnson's walkie-talkie. When the shots were fired, Jorgenson had scampered to cover. Security team leader FTC Dempsey along with Agent Johnson began shouting commands for the men to secure the rooftop and secure his weapons. Men scurried around, and Jorgenson wondered what had just happened. He had seen HT2 Smithe jump back, and then he lost sight of all three when the other HT's followed.

From above, through the roar of helicopter thuds, Jorgensen could hear West shouting in cries of agony.

*****

Tyler fell to Smithe's side and he grabbed his friend—urging him to respond.

"Smitty? Smitty!" Tyler pushed on a gushing chest wound. He quickly pressed fingers to this best friend's neck; he could not find the vein that should be expanding and contracting. Tyler shook him; yelled at him to wake up—to come to, to open his eyes, anything!

He lifted Smithe's arm, and it slipped out of Tyler's grasp with a thud to the deck. He held his hands on the chest wounds. He again reach to Smithe's neck.

"There's no pulse!" he yelled.

Tyler began frantically giving Smithe chest compressions in a desperate attempt to get his friends heart pumping. Ramirez tried to help—concern and fear in his eyes. Three separate bullet wounds had pierced Smithe: two in the chest and a third in the stomach. He had provided the needed distraction for Tyler and Ramirez to jump Wilkette with the welding leads. Once again, he'd had Tyler's back.

"Smitty, come on, stay with me..." Tyler pleaded, hardly noticing the pain in his own arm. He leaned down, listened for a heartbeat, and checked for a pulse at Smithe's aorta. When there wasn't one, he returned to doing chest compressions. "Hector, check his breathing— get him some air!" Tyler started a CPR count, "One, two, three, four, five, breathe," he said, and pulled open Smithe's mouth and blew a deep lung into it. He repeated this several times.

"Wake up... wake up, please..." Tyler begged; desperation rippled through his lips making the words garbled and wet. He was trembling and crying. He pounded at his friend's chest.

He was not sure how long this went on before he felt a hand touch his shoulder, "Tyler, let him be."

Tyler swung his arm back at Ramirez and went on attempting to revive Smithe.

"He's not dead! I'm not going to let go like this!" A knot in his throat choked him. He couldn't breathe; tears streamed from his eyes, and the pain in his upper arm burned. He could feel warm liquid running down his right arm. Smithe had jumped ahead of his count. He had called Smitty a coward earlier; he needed Smithe to know that he did not think was a coward.

Through blurred vision, Tyler could see Ramirez kneeling beside him while he continued pressing down on his friend's chest.

"Stop," Ramirez said to him in a calm voice, "Tyler, all you're doing is pumping the blood out."

Tyler angrily rose to his feet, "I'll kill him!" he started towards Wilkette, who was still unconscious. He kicked at the limp body of Wilkette.

FTC Dempsey cut him off. Dempsey had just climbed onto the platform and now tried to get Tyler to calm down.

Tyler swung at Dempsey, who willingly took the punch. Dempsey hugged Tyler close, but Tyler pushed away. Ramirez grabbed at him, and between Dempsey and Ramirez—they both worked to keep Tyler away from the comatose Wilkette.

Tyler roared, "Let go of me!" He yanked back so ferociously that Ramirez tumbled backwards towards the edge of the platform. Before falling over the side, Tyler grabbed him by the collar and pulled back. Ramirez fell to his hands and knees.

"That's enough!" Ramirez shouted at Tyler.

The helicopter, which had hovered over their heads while Smithe perished, slowly flew off.

*****

Executive Officer Kendall arrived to the boat-deck with Lieutenant Hodges, and Jorgenson quickly briefed them on what he knew. They observed several men going up and down the vertical ladder to the roof of the hangar.

"Captain," said Kendall, "Are you hurt?"

Jorgensen shook his head no, dismissing the XO's concern. From atop the platform, FTC Dempsey yelled to the crowd below, "We need a medic up here ASAP!"

"What about Wilkette?" Jorgenson shouted up.

Dempsey looked around and said, "It appears as if they electrocuted him."

"What do you mean electrocuted him?" Jorgenson questioned.

"I mean just that, sir; they zapped him with welding leads."

Jorgenson was in awe, "Is he dead?"

Dempsey wagged his head left to right, "No. He's alive. But, sir, Smithe is down."

The way Dempsey shook his head, Jorgenson knew they would be counting another casualty, and his heart stung.

Agent Johnson made a trip to the top of the hangar and back down. She gave Jorgenson, Kendall, and Hodges a description of what her take of the scene above was. "Looks like they electrocuted him alright."

Hodges laughed, "I told you! I told you that West would handle this. He took care of it the only way an HT would know how—he welded the son of a bitch to death!"

Jorgenson frowned. "Paul, get us to port—use the tugs—whatever it takes. Take us pier side."

"Aye, sir," came the reply, and the XO left.

Agent Johnson continued, "I put cuffs on him, but he's unconscious. Your medic is trying but the other guy, Smithe, he's gone."

Jorgenson looked away.

*****

Tyler's whole body shook. He fell to his knees and pulled himself into a sitting position a few inches from Smithe's face as HMC Macon tried but was unable to revive him.

When the chief corpsman left to organize a stretcher, the emotions of the past three days let loose; Tyler began violently sobbing. Ramirez put an arm around his head and pulled him close into a gentle headlock. Tyler squeezed Ramirez's elbow just to have something to hold onto. He felt as though he would never catch his breath. Unable to pry his eyes from Smithe's prone body, he heard Ramirez crying too. Two survivors wept for a dead friend who had saved their lives without hesitation.

CHAPTER 52

As two tugs pushed the ship to the pier, Jorgenson left Hodges and Agent Johnson below on the flight deck. He climbed onto the space called Steel Beach and paused atop the narrow platform. It offered so little maneuvering space. Jorgenson wondered how, through the whole ordeal and with all the struggling, no one had fallen off the side. He surveyed the two men who hovered over the lifeless body of HT2 Smithe.

How many comrades did these boys lose today? The captain moved forward but then thought twice about talking to them, and instead he just stood quietly. Eventually the two HT's were instructed to climb down to the flight deck so the bodies could be moved. HMC Macon and Agent Johnson's partner Willis were strapping Wilkette to a stiff stretcher.

Jorgenson aided in moving Smithe's body, allowing others to drag the semi-conscious and handcuffed Wilkette down.

Below, body after body arrived to the flight deck to join the procession. In addition to Steel Beach, corpses had been found in the forward head and in the **Fire Room**. Kendall and Agent Johnson preoccupied themselves with speaking to Ramirez. West had moved to the edge of the flight deck and was looking out over the bay. Jorgensen walked towards him, and West turned to face his captain. Jorgenson solemnly saluted the young enlisted man and then held out his hand.

Without West's actions, the likelihood of more deaths would have been certain. Wilkette had wanted the blood of the captain badly. Jorgenson knew that now. West had been insubordinate, had ignored protocol, and had put himself in danger, but in the course of his reckless actions, lives were saved.

341

West's grip was reluctant and on the weak side, but he didn't immediately drop the handshake.

"How long did you know it was Wilkette?" His voice quaked.

"What do you mean?"

West's grip tightened.

"No bull-shit, Captain. You knew the killer came from R-Division. You had to suspect it was one of us from the beginning." West shook his head. "Hell, I figured it out two days ago. So, how long, Captain? How long did you expect us to stay locked down there with a killer?" West flung his hand away forcefully.

Jorgenson was not immediately sure how to respond. No one had been debriefed, and all the information was kept between him and a small circle of people; how could West have known? After a moment of silence, in a calmer voice, West demanded, "When did you know? When did the NIS know?"

There would be no legitimate excuse for the decisions made by the NIS and by his superiors, but above all else, the Miller crew expected the decisions of its captain to keep them safe. He had clearly failed at doing so. West's simple question, directed at the people making the decisions over the past three days, held them responsible for the deaths of good men like Smithe. West deserved to know the truth.

"The night of Lieutenant Orton's murder Ensign Watford walked out to the passage. The assailant, who wore green engineering coveralls, dropped Orton and sprinted out of sight. The passage was dark, and Watford couldn't be sure, but he thought the person appeared to be a black shipmate—dark skin, dark hair. Watford thought it was EM3 Wilkette."

"Why didn't you lock him in the brig?"

"We didn't... think he was a danger."

Jorgenson felt West examining him, trying to determine if he should trust his word.

"We found a lot of tapes in Wilkette's rack, full of varied music." Jorgenson knew most wouldn't understand the significance of this; he alone had heard the final words of the dying man. Jorgenson decided to confide to West what he recalled of the final moments of Bruce Orton's life.

"Lieutenant Orton's last words to me were *the last waltz....*" The moment would forever remain vivid. "There was a cassette in Wilkette's locker with that song on it."

A question formed on West's face. "And the knife had no prints."

"Correct." Jorgenson continued his confession. "The NIS had no case with only a weak eyewitness and someone's music collection."

Jorgenson wanted West to know why they had left Wilkette in the berthing space with the rest of them. "We thought Orton would be his only victim. And... he got along with everyone in R-Division. No one believed he would attack again." He trailed off.

"Plus, he was being watched," West added.

"Yes."

A heavy weight pressed on Jorgenson's chest. The opportunity to defy his superiors' judgements was gone. His power to prevent the terrible incidents had been squandered. His restitution? He would forever second-guess and distrust his future decisions. Jorgenson suddenly felt old as West studied his face.

"You needed a confession from him." West said.

"Yes."

"Doesn't look like you're gonna need one now." His gaze moved from his dead friend's body, not even five feet away, back up to his commanding officer's guilt stricken expression. Jorgenson didn't say anything.

Jorgenson was certain that West was full of mixed emotions. Anger and frustration and sadness and disgust collided inside and wrestled for dominance. Jorgenson saw that he'd lost the young man's respect and trust—and rightly so. Jorgenson wanted to say something, anything, to mend the broken promises of respect that had grown between the officers and enlisted—the bond between him and West, but he couldn't think of another damned thing to say.

*****

The light cascading from the east lit the flight deck up bright. Smithe's face beamed; the loss of blood gave his dead features a translucent glow in the sunshine.

Tyler stood beside Jorgenson staring down the line of bodies laid in a neat row across the width of the flight deck. A team placed body bags beside each corpse and began to fill each.

Too many dead. Tyler thought. The captain began speaking again, and Tyler tuned him out. He could barely hear the man over the ringing in his head anyway. What would Jorgenson do if he silently walked away? Still, he couldn't help but remain and listen for something, anything, which would help explain away the incompetence.

"I'll never make up for these mistakes, but you have my word, I'm going to try to be a better captain in the future."

Tyler thought about saying all sorts of reassuring cliché comments but his kind heart had been broken on Steel Beach a little while ago, and all he wanted to do was leave so he could grieve alone.

"There is a black and white photograph that hangs on the bulkhead of my stateroom," Jorgenson said as he peered off into the distance.

Tyler struggled to envision the photos hanging on the bulkhead in the captain's stateroom, and then he remembered. "I know the photo, sir." Before Jorgenson had come aboard for the first time, R-Division had been assigned the task to refurbish the captain's stateroom. Tyler, Smithe, and Ramirez teamed up for the work to repair bath fixtures, install a new bed enclosure, and replace wall paneling. Tyler remembered he had hung a few photos and several shadow boxes of naval memorabilia.

"The one of Dorie Miller." Tyler said.

The captain turned. Tyler could see an acknowledging crinkle start to rise in the corner of Jorgenson's mouth. His brown eyes gleamed in the sunlight. The captain reached his arms behind his back and took in a full breath; he seemed to be searching for words—words Tyler believed were destined to be inspirational, but Tyler didn't want to listen to leadership sermons and began searching for an opportune moment to leave.

"Miller's story is meant to inspire all." Jorgenson said.

Tyler nodded.

"Not only people of my race."

Okay—go on. Tyler fidgeted.

Then Jorgensen said something Tyler didn't expect.

"I think it's all bullshit."

Jorgenson looked around.

"Inspirational? Miller never meant to be inspirational." he said, "Dorie Miller grabbed a gun, aimed it at the enemy and pulled the fucking trigger." The captain looked at Tyler, "that's what you did today."

The simple but daunting words were not exactly what he had expected. Below a bustle of boatswains' mates on the fantail worked to moor the ship. As the dock got nearer, deck hands tossed monkey-fist ended heaving lines to the pier.

"Since my first night aboard this ship, I've been staring at that photo wondering what I would do if I was given the chance to pull that trigger. Today, I found out." The captain studied his own haggard khakis with the dark macabre splatters. The blood was from helping carry Smithe's body. He then scanned Tyler's similarly disheveled and stained uniform. This blood, Smithe's blood linked their two uniforms: one blue, one tan, and Tyler accepted a faultless fact—they both shared the pain. In anguish and in blood, Tyler and the captain were equals.

The captain drew his gaze to the pier and the maneuvering of the mooring lines. "Why do we wear this uniform, West?"

Tyler had a reason—a good one—for wearing the uniform. He needed a way out, a route to escape his awful existence. Orton had his, so did Smithe, and they both were now dead partially due to the uniform they wore. Orton was the target of a maniac with a diabolical pact of retribution against authority—Orton had worn khakis and defied the wrong guy. Smithe, Scheppler, and the others—they became collateral damage in a warped game of smoke him out. Wilkette outplayed the brass at their game. His demented vision of squaring up the unbalanced perspective of things had ironically brought some form of equality.

A boatswain's mate leaned over the main deck, attaching a rat guard to the aft mooring line. Gathered in a large group, ready for the brow to span from ship to shore, were military police, emergency medical technicians with gurneys, and a bunch of civilian suits Tyler presumed to be NIS and FBI personnel. Further, up the pier there was a police barricade with a large throng of on-lookers.

Tyler made a half step back and raised his right arm in a respectful salute to his commanding officer. "I wear this uniform for the same reason you do, Captain."

Jorgenson returned the salute as the two men shared a quiet moment of mutual respect. Tyler did not enlist in the Navy to wear a uniform, but in his four years on the Miller, he had learned what it meant to wear one. Tyler turned and walked towards the Helo-Hangar; as soon as he could, he wanted to get his bullet wound stitched up, get changed out of the bloody mess of denim hanging about his body, and get into a fresh set of dungarees.

CHAPTER 53

Captain Jorgenson stood next to the brow on the quarterdeck as body after body transferred off the Miller. The two guards Wilkette had attacked were the first to go. Pangs of loss rattled inside his chest as each body received identification, was tagged, and signed over to the coroner. HT1 Bastille stood near performing the identification duties as the dead proceeded off on stretchers. Orton's body moved next, and then the two boiler technicians they had found in the Fire Room. Bastille remained strong as he fulfilled his obligation, but his distraught face seemed to age a little with each naming. The body bag holding HT3 Swartz was unzipped and Bastille tensed up, but HT3 Scheppler broke him—rivers of tears cascaded from the normally stalwart man's eyes. Finally, the body of HT2 Smithe arrived. Bastille could not speak.

Jorgenson said to the medical examiner, "This is HT2 Levon Smithe." The medics rolled and carried the fallen hero's gurney to a waiting ambulance.

Jorgenson said to Bastille, "Thank you for identifying them."

Bastille, who still had no words, nodded and quickly walked away.

EM3 Postino rolled up on a stretcher.

Jorgenson scanned the pier; Emma waved. He forced a smile and a thumb's up as if to say everything was *okay;* it was a lie—one he would have to manage in the coming years. Part of him wanted to run down the gangplank and hug and kiss her, but his duty kept him stationary on the quarterdeck as he oversaw the aftermath of the massacre.

He turned his gaze back to HT1 Bastille, who along with EM1 Dunham, EM2 Hart, HTFA Persinski, and HT2 Ramirez, circled Postino's stretcher. It appeared as though the surviving members of R-

Division had come out to say farewell to him before Postino went to the hospital. HT2 West was not present amongst the group of R-Division's survivors; West stood down on the pier with his head resting on the shoulder of a young woman. His arms wrapped tightly around her waist. The woman's tearful face showed the kind of anguish that only loved ones, who had waited days for the ordeal to end, would know. In West's body language Jorgenson could see that he was sobbing into her shoulder—very likely relaying the story of how his close friend had died today.

Jorgenson remained stoic on the fantail.

"And then the flame of love died in your eye. My heart was broke in two when you said goodbye..." Jorgenson heard singing, and it sent a frightful chill down his spine.

"I had the last waltz with you!" came a familiar high-pitched voice, "two lonely people together! I fell in love with you—the last waltz should last forever!"

Jorgenson felt a panic course through him. Awake and alive with his wrists and ankles strapped to a stretcher, Wilkette serenaded his captors as they rolled him to the gangplank. "It's all over now! Nothing left to say—just my tears and the orchestra playing."

"Hello, Captain!" his maddening eyes darted at Jorgenson, "I see you there. I hope you enjoyed the performance. La la la la la la la la la. La la la la la la la la la!"

The paramedics could not get Wilkette off the ship fast enough. Jorgenson turned away. *It's over—it's all over.*

349

CHAPTER 54

Tyler let the water run over him. It ran pink with the mixture of Scheppler's, Smithe's, and his own blood running down the drain. In the head alone, he was thankful for the moment of solace in the shower. He would see Alexandra again tomorrow, for tonight; he would remain on the ship. She had cried when he told her of Smithe's death. In the shower, Tyler had allowed a few final tears to escape, but now there was no more crying. His shoulder stung under the water pressure; the stitched-up bullet wound oozed.

Tyler thought about his job and about R-Division. He tried to imagine what the next few weeks would be like while they re-figured how to run things with half of R-Division dead, arrested, or in the hospital. *What is the Miller's mission now? Will she get back underway...the captain says we will...* Tyler heaved a sigh; the USS Miller—Honor, Courage, Commitment. *What a bunch of crap. The fucking shitters are gonna really get backed up now with no HT's left to run plumbers-snakes down the drains.*

He and Bastille and Ramirez will need to pick up the pieces and pull the department back together in the short time he had left, or at least until they get more HT's on board. He deliberated if they'd ask him to stay or keep him from rotating off. If they asked, he would most likely agree—*where the fuck would I go now?* Any new duty station is going to bombard him with questions about what happened here.

He turned the water nozzles and toweled off and groaned at the idea of returning to the berthing space—the place where Remy Wilkette had begun his deceitful game. *He had us all fooled.* The vision of the bunks of his dead friends weighed him down. He would probably request to move his bed as well; the idea of being so close to Wilkette's former rack made him sick.

Out of the head and walking towards R-Division, he felt anxious. Tyler gazed upwards as he walked, trying to clear his head, when he spotted something. Stuffed in the over-head piping and cables, a wadded up bundle of green fabric caught his eye. He stopped dead in his tracks. "Son of a bitch," he said aloud staring up at the bloody green coveralls.

A stomach-turning nausea crested in him; all the relentless searching they had done trying to find the bloody coveralls, only for Wilkette to have hastily stashed them within feet of the R-Division entrance. *So he had been wearing green*, Tyler thought, *Watford was right after all*. Wilkette had stolen some poor sap's coveralls. *That bastard had been trying to frame someone else*.

Tyler tried to imagine finding these at the onset of the search. The authorities might have wrongly accused the person whose name is stenciled on them—unless the unsuspecting fall guy could prove his innocence—but the bloody evidence would be extremely incriminating. Especially if there was any question about the identity of the person running from the scene.

In his towel, Tyler sprung up vertically and gripped a corner of the cloth. The coveralls were wedged through two cables. Tyler violently yanked the clump free from its perch. He un-crumbled the dried, blood-caked fabric.

His heart jumped as he studied the stenciled words on the breast patch. Painted in bold, white letters was the name, "TYLER WEST."

THE END

ACKNOWLEDGEMENTS

There are a good number of people I need to recognize for their support and inspiration in making this book possible.

I must thank my wife DeAnna who has been at my side always—in fair winds and foul—she is my constant muse.

Thanks to Victoria and Kate for being two wonderful inspirations in my life. IROTETAK, INC.

Thanks to my family and friends who have over the years heard me tell this story many times (with flamboyant discourse and melodrama, I'm sure). Your never-ending curiosity about the characters and events have built in me an understanding of this virtuous tale—I have always appreciated your listening.

Thanks to Willard Wood, my Uncle Bill—a lifetime serviceman and true hero. He enlisted in the United States Navy in 1966. During the Vietnam War, he was assigned to a (PBR) river boat and patrolled the Mekong River, inserting and extracted SEAL Teams and other Special Forces for River Division 533. Discharged in October of 1969, he reenlisted in the Naval Reserve in 1972 and eventually served in Saudi Arabia during Operation Desert Storm in 1991. He retired from the Navy after 28 years of service as a Senior Chief Petty Officer. As a civilian, Bill Wood is also a hero having served as a Delaware State Police Trooper from 1974 to 1995. He continues to be an advocate and spokesman for Veterans affairs. Upon hearing I was tinkering with a book idea about my time in the Navy and on the USS Miller, his immediate reaction was, "Get it done, son. I can't wait forever." Thank you, Brother.

To the men of the USS Miller—especially those shipmates who were there during the events of June 16, 1985—in particular the family of Lt. James K. Sterner Jr. [deceased]— my unending respect and loyalty to our true story outweighs all embellishments I've made in crafting this fictionalized version. The senseless killing of an innocent man and the events of those days and nights in lockdown provided much inspiration and detail for writing this novel—I am forever reverent and grateful.

I have always been inspired by the story of Dorie Miller—it was a blessing to have served on a vessel that received its name from one of America's most rousing heroes. I must acknowledge how much invention and creativity his memory and omnipresence produced as well as his courage and devotion.

I must also acknowledge the hard work and input from Stephanie Hornsby. Her words and ideas are the glue that holds this book together. I was lucky to have such a creative and insightful collaborator at my side during the construction of this book. Thank You.

THE TRUE EVENTS

In the summer of 1985, I had been assigned duty to serve aboard the USS Miller FF-1091. One terribly long night the ship was rocking and rolling in a Caribbean Sea hurricane. In the wee hours I, along with my Repair Division crewmates, was jarred awake by a call from the 1MC (ship loud-speaker system). We were told to wake up, get out of our racks, and muster in our work area—the ship's general workshop. In the minutes that followed, we learned that one of the crew had been stabbed, and within an hour, a second announcement told us that our shipmate was dead. This horrific news was startling enough, however, the scariest part of the entire ordeal was this: the killer was hidden among us.

I was instructed (along with two other shipmates) to roam the ship and look for bloody coveralls; this was just an hour or so after the murder. The seas were very rough that morning, and we had a hard time walking around the ship. When we reached the passage inboard of the boat deck—the place where the incident had occurred—there was blood everywhere on both the deck and bulkheads. My search party never found the bloody coveralls, but by the end of the eight hour shift, the entire ship had been put into lockdown.

With men confined to quarters when not on their watch stations, the ship raced to Newport, Rhode Island, our homeport, and upon arrival proceeded to anchor itself in the middle of the Narragansett Bay. The FBI and NIS came aboard to lead an investigation that would have us sequestered in our berthing spaces for three full days.

I will never forget the days and nights of fear and anger or the immense frustration that peaked as our quarantine conditions lingered. We did not know who the killer was, and in the hours that passed, our feelings of true helplessness in the acknowledgement that we knew nothing worsened. We were in lockdown with a killer.

In the end, on the afternoon of the third day, we found out who did the deed, and I could barely catch my breath as I learned the killer was my own bunk-mate—the man who slept in the rack next to mine. For three days we (me and several other R-Division men) had waited with him, confined to our quarters: three days that are seared into my memory.

SB

ABOUT THE AUTHOR

Scott Black was born in Long Branch, New Jersey in 1964. He attended Middletown North High School where he played football and started dating his life-long partner and wife DeAnna; they had actually been in the same Kindergarten class way back in 1970. Upon graduation Scott joined the United States Navy and served eight years. After military service, he worked his way through college, earning a Bachelor of Arts degree in Natural Sciences and Mathematics, and has held various engineering and management positions in several manufacturing companies. Corporate life has offered many opportunities to travel the world, and Scott has visited more than thirty countries. He and DeAnna have two daughters: Victoria and Kate.

In his spare time, Scott has always found creative ways to release his energies; a former singer, musician, and actor, his love of the arts drives a desire to continually engage in creative endeavors. He has walked the boards as a member of The Rhode Island Shakespeare Theatre and was once the lead singer / front man in two Jersey Shore rock bands. The love of arts and the lure of books has built a new passion in him: writing.

Scott enjoys spending time with his wife and two daughters and currently resides in the Greater Atlanta area. His next writing project is currently in the works.

Follow Scott Black
www.scottblackauthor.com